Chloe and the Spy

Chloe and the Spy

JUSTINE WITTICH

Five Star • Waterville, Maine

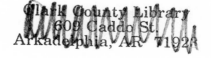

Five Star First Edition Romance Series.

Published in 2002 in conjunction with Justine Wittich.

Set in 11 pt. Plantin.

Printed in the United States on permanent paper.

Library of Congress Cataloging-in-Publication Data

Wittich, Justine.
    Chloe and the spy / Justine Wittich.
        p. cm.—(Five Star first edition romance series)
    ISBN 0-7862-3749-X (hc : alk. paper)
    1. England—Fiction.   I. Title.   II. Series.
PS3573.I925 C47 2002
813'.54—dc21   2001051239

For Judy Hershner, my critique partner for this book. And, as always, for Pete, who, with true grace, survives life with a writer.

Prologue

Brussels, 1882

"If it's all the same to you, I'd prefer not to die just yet."

"You bloody well don't have a choice. Either you expire voluntarily, or someone else will make the decision for you. I strongly recommend the first alternative."

Adrian, Viscount Harding, heir to an earldom and extensive land and business holdings, paused in his restless pacing and eyed the lean figure propped languidly against the waterstained wall of his squalid room. Rain beat against the single narrow window, blowing in around the warped frame and seeping into the ancient, rotting sill. The atmosphere was redolent of several hundred years of unwashed inhabitants and moldy walls. "I can take care of myself."

It was all very well for his companion to talk about Adrian's disappearing. Fitzhugh Kent could go back to England, take a hot bath prepared by his valet, and sit down to a warm, well-cooked meal in clean clothes . . . before going out to mingle with civilized people at one of his clubs.

Adrian inspected his own stained, greasy twill trousers and jacket, unable to visualize a future in which he was wearing anything cleaner. He nurtured a stubborn belief that the rough clothing would retain his shape when he stepped out of them; his personal hygiene of late defied contemplation. But no one knew better than he that Fitz Kent, spy master extraordinaire for Her Majesty Queen Victoria's govern-

7

ment, couldn't be bothered to worry about his agent's sartorial problems.

Interrupting Adrian's bout of self-pity, Kent continued, "Let me review. You overheard five Armenian nationalists plot a takeover of their country, a takeover that will doubtless trigger widespread massacres. I must say this all sounds rather farfetched, but your report is too detailed and the situation too delicate for me to discount it." He shrugged his elegant shoulders beneath the rough clothing of his own disguise and added cheerfully, "You've yet to bring back bogus goods."

"Believe me, they're serious. Fitz, the ordinary citizens they recruit will have no idea how ruthless and power hungry that little nucleus is . . . until it's too late." Adrian shivered. He remembered the cold eyes of each of the five men. The stone walls of the dank basement room had reflected flickering light from a lantern balanced on a squat keg. Adrian had inspected the keg earlier; the contents matched those of the haphazardly piled barrels he had hidden behind. *Gunpowder.*

Sweat beaded his forehead as he recalled his fevered prayers that no one would upset the lantern. He resumed his pacing.

"Have you any idea who tipped the rebels off to your identity?" Fitz asked.

"Not a clue." During every minute of his roundabout journey to Brussels, Adrian had reviewed the events leading up to his near capture. Somehow, someday, he would find the bastard responsible. He was alive, but his heart was filled with hatred for whoever had betrayed him.

"When I arrived for work at the railroad the day after the meeting, a chap I worked with pulled me aside to warn me a stranger had been inquiring about me, asking for Adrian Harding and describing me perfectly. Just then I saw one of the men from the night before, the rebel who was second in command, with my superior. He looked right at me, and I didn't stop to think. I just leaped on a train that was pulling out. That bastard was the most bloodthirsty of the lot."

" 'Bloodthirsty'?"

" 'The deaths of ten thousand serfs are as nothing,' I believe was his quaint way of putting it."

"Adrian, have you any idea what complicated diplomatic channels we'll have to swim through to get this information to what passes for government in Armenia? The Russians have the best contacts, but first we'll have to convince them the report's authentic. Even if they believe us, they won't necessarily help. The Turks will be even harder to bring 'round. The warning may not even get through in time."

Kent stepped away from the wall and brushed flaking paint from his stained and threadbare coat with the fastidious gesture most people reserved for cashmere. "In the meantime, you're a marked man, so you can't come back to England and live as Adrian, Viscount Harding. They'll find you no matter where you go. Whereas if you're reported dead . . ."

Adrian finished his friend's sentence in a voice filled with despair. "They'll stop looking." Halting in front of the single grimy window, he rested his forehead against the pane. Until now, Fitz's idea had seemed a bad joke. "My God! What about my parents?" His vision of the future was a bottomless void. "What about my life? There's a girl in London who has good reason to think I'll offer to marry her."

"You can resume your life when the crisis is past—once the threat is eliminated. And take my advice. If it's the Satterfield chit, you'll be better off dead," Fitz advised. Concern filled his voice as he continued, "Look, Adrian, I know how anonymous you can make yourself. Yet by your own account, during your journey to Brussels you were waylaid twice and attacked by bandits on yet another occasion. Do you think those were coincidences?"

Adrian let his arms fall to his sides. His shoulders slumped. "I wish to hell I'd never gotten into this."

Fitz shrugged. "Then you never should have been so clever with languages."

"Go to hell."

"Probably." Smiling wryly, Fitz returned to essentials. "However, you can't remain here. The rebels found you already. A distinctly sinister sod turned up in the alley behind this building just this morning. My men 'helped' him board a cargo ship headed for Greenland. Others will slither in, and we can continue disposing of them, but sooner or later one will slip through our net, and then Bob's your uncle." He smiled deprecatingly at his own wit. "Book passage on the *Beggar's Bride*. She sails at eight tomorrow morning. My agents will guard you until you're safe board.

"You'll die officially in a mid-channel explosion about noon tomorrow. Once you're back in England, find a job on the docks. The waterfront is riddled with anonymous bolt-holes, and you do have that interesting knack of invisibility."

Adrian rubbed his hands over his face. His eyes burned with unshed tears, tears he would never allow Fitz Kent to see. He felt seven years old and scared out of his skin. "If I survive this, remind me to shelve my linguistic gifts." He turned again to stare out the cracked window. The daylight was fading.

His hand on the rusted doorknob, Kent asked, "Do you need money?"

"I thought I was to get a job at the docks." Adrian kept his gaze fixed on a crocodile-like fissure in the bottom pane.

"Right. Well, if you run into a rough patch or if you should pick up anything useful, you might keep an eye out. Someone will come 'round now and then."

The situation suddenly struck Adrian as decidedly humorous. "How comforting, old chap. Now go back to England, and instruct some clerk at Whitehall to tell my family I'm dead. But be sure the obituary sings my praises."

As the door closed, Adrian was horrified to hear his own brittle laughter echoing in the dank air. Then silence filled the dingy room.

Chapter One

"Damn you, Lionel! If you kill me because of your bloody horses, I swear I'll haunt you forever," Lady Chloe Lockwood grumbled as she crawled across the velvet squabs of her father's swaying traveling coach toward the door.

Sounds of neighing horses, a shrill female voice, and shouting men—her twin brother, Lionel, the loudest of all—filtered in from the outside. Chloe decided it was time to act.

Hitching her cherry-colored silk broadcloth skirts above her half-boots beneath her, she released the door latch. It swung open, flapping with the movement of the coach, then back again as the well-sprung body lurched to its right. Like a pendulum, the vehicle settled once more to the left, and the door swung outward. Chloe leaped toward safety—which appeared from nowhere in the form of a lean, muscled body equipped with strong arms that closed tightly around her before collapsing beneath her on the gravel drive.

The mixed fragrances of hay, horse, and clean, healthy male filled her nostrils. Pressing her nose against a twill work shirt pulled tightly over the unfamiliar toughness of a male chest, she inhaled deeply, savoring the mixture as she luxuriated in the fascinating contours beneath her.

Perhaps she had been a trifle premature in her decision to remain single as had her aunt Heloise. This proximity to a man was more than pleasant; it was invigorating.

"Miss, are you all right?" The urgency in the soft tenor voice pierced her drifting thoughts.

"I'm going to turn you onto your back. Are you injured?" She felt his muscles bunch as if to rise, then, "Miss, you'll have to let go of me so I can move." His voice sounded strained.

She realized her fingers clutched his broad shoulders with a grip she could duplicate only if she were about to fall from a precipice. "Oh, dear. I'm frightfully sorry," she said without remorse. Reluctantly she released him and rolled to one side. "I'm fine. You . . . you saved my life."

As she spoke, she looked at his face for the first time. The deep blue gaze that met hers mirrored the startling awareness she herself felt. The man was a stranger, and undoubtedly a servant of some sort, but she felt . . . recognition. As if she had been waiting for this encounter all her life.

As she opened her mouth to tell him so, his gaze became blank. She had the odd feeling his soul had departed while she watched. His lean, aristocratic features were still clearly defined beneath tanned skin, but the life, along with any animation, had leeched from his face.

He rose lithely and extended his hands to assist her to her feet. She accepted the courtesy in a daze, feeling detached from the sounds around them.

"Thank heaven you're all right." Lady Heloise Lockwood's no-nonsense voice brought her back to earth. "That was well done, Drury. Would you be so kind as to give my nephew a hand? Those ill-trained horses he insists on dragging all over England are sure to damage one another if someone doesn't take charge."

The words broke the trance into which Chloe had fallen, and she threw herself into her aunt's arms, grateful for the familiar scents of lavender and laundry starch permeating her tucked white shirtwaist. "Oh, Aunt, wasn't my arrival exciting? I'm so very glad to see you."

Heloise released her and stepped back, her dark brown eyes inspecting her niece with their usual thoroughness. Chloe had no fear of such scrutiny, although she knew even her father sometimes quailed beneath the steely glint in his twin's eye. She met her favorite relative's gaze with a confident, hopeful smile. "Do I look like someone who's teetering on the brink of spinsterhood?"

"Indeed, you look like a passably attractive young woman who is wearing some sort of buckram garment instead of a corset."

Glancing over her shoulder, Chloe saw the servant named Drury leading Lionel's fractious stallion away from the other four horses, who appeared to have calmed somewhat. Could he have overheard her aunt's accusation? The mortifying realization warmed her all over.

"We shall discuss your lack of proper undergarments later, in more private surroundings," Heloise said. She strode toward her nephew, who stood, red-faced and furious, tugging on the lead line he had detached from the rear of the traveling coach. A high-spirited mare danced at the other end. "And what have you to say for yourself, Lionel? These horses should have been sent north by train. Instead, you've risked your sister's life the last three days dragging them behind the coach."

Lionel started, his customary nervousness in his aunt's presence communicating itself to the horse, who reared. Before Lionel could speak, Drury appeared from the direction of the stables and removed the tether from his hands. The mare quieted and followed the servant docilely. Lionel said hotly, "It was that bloody red-haired cow waving an apple! Damn it, Aunt, your maid put the wind up my horses before they'd even come to a stop! Don't she know how high-strung thoroughbreds are?"

"I doubt she does. She's farm bred," Heloise said without apology. "Even though you have not yet seen fit to greet me properly, it was kind of you to deliver your sister. I trust you will stay for a light luncheon."

A chastened Lionel leaned forward and kissed her cheek. "Good to see you again, Aunt Heloise. I'll be glad of something to eat. We left the inn at dawn this morning."

Heloise surveyed him dispassionately. "Have you ever considered that your sister might have become fatigued traveling at such a pace?"

"Chloe? You're on the wrong road there, Aunt. She's the one who wanted to hurry." Lionel gave his sister a grateful look. "She knew she'd arrive that much quicker if we pushed."

Chloe hoped her exhaustion didn't show. She loved her brother dearly, but the trip had been dreary. Single-mindedly intent on his own plans, Lionel had fretted the whole time about the inconvenience of delivering her. She had mendaciously assured him the rigors of traveling from dawn till dark would be an adventure. For propriety's sake, her mother had forbidden her to ride, so she had sat in the coach with only two carpetbags of books for company. The lithe, rangy figure of the servant Drury caught her attention as he led away the last two horses. "Aunt—"

Ignoring her, Heloise motioned to the sweating coachman, who was courageously holding his team steady. "Take the coach around to the back and unload Lady Chloe's trunks." That order given, she gestured imperiously toward her niece and turned to lead the way up the broad stone staircase to the door held open by a gray-clad butler.

Thwarted in her attempt to question her aunt about her

intriguing rescuer, Chloe grasped for an opportunity to follow him to his destination. "We can't go inside just yet. Come, I want to show you the present I've brought you." Before her aunt could reply, Chloe seized her by the hand and dragged her toward the brick walk that curved around the left wing of the house.

Aiming straight to the subject uppermost in her mind, Chloe demanded, "Aunt, is that groom new? I feel sure I don't remember him from my last visit." To her horrified delight, her body quivered at the recollection of the groom's protective embrace as they tumbled to the ground. Was this the physical attraction she'd read about in books? If so, her plans for the future required re-examination. Another little shiver struck her as she recalled the sense of awareness she'd seen in his eyes before he had banked that burst of flame.

"Of course you don't remember him. I hadn't set up my stable when you were here last. Drury came to me last fall. He was highly recommended by the vicar's wife, as I recall."

They walked toward the large oval of graveled drive beyond the service entrance. As they passed the door, a sturdy feminine figure topped by a cluster of improbable black curls burst out.

"Miss Chloe! Ye're 'ere!" Molly O'Day enveloped Chloe in an exuberant hug. Though the top of her head scarcely reached Chloe's chin, the woman's grip nearly lifted the girl from the ground. "I'm s'posed to act more dignified-like," she said, releasing her. "I'm 'ousekeeper fer yer aunt now. Did yer know?"

"I guessed from what you're wearing, Molly. Has anyone told you that black makes you look taller and thinner?" Chloe grinned. "And if you ever become too exalted to give me a welcoming hug, I shall have to lecture you."

As she finished speaking, the coach came around the curv-

16

ing drive and rolled to a stop. Harry Ikehorn, the coachman, removed his hat and wiped his brow. His weathered features wore a relieved expression.

Lionel appeared in the coach's wake, his face still suffused with anger. "You should sack that red-haired wench, Aunt. My horses could have been injured. And I don't know what m'father would have said if the coach had been damaged."

"I intend to speak with Gladys. Now go into the house with Molly. She'll serve you your luncheon," Heloise soothed.

Chloe had had enough. She stepped forward and leaned close, peering into her brother's eyes, a scant inch above her own. "Lionel, you're an ass. I was *in* the carriage, and *I'm* not after the poor girl's head. Leave off."

Over Lionel's shoulder she caught the fierce scowl that flitted across the face of the groom her aunt had called Drury. If she hadn't glanced in his direction at that particular moment, she would have seen only the bland expression of a well-trained servant, as once more the life faded from his features. Was his face made of India rubber?

"I want to supervise the footmen when they unload your gift, Aunt," Chloe told her, not moving her gaze from Drury and the coachman as they unhitched the matched grays.

The groom's sure, economical movements mesmerized her. Why were his twill shirt and trousers a size larger than necessary for the neatly constructed form her body recalled with embarrassing clarity? She could almost feel the heat of that muscular frame. She allowed her imagination to supply the play of muscles in the strong thighs beneath his baggy trousers as Drury strained to pull the reluctant lead horse from the traces.

She felt color rise in her cheeks as she pictured her mother's hysterics if she knew her gently raised daughter was entertaining such thoughts, but Chloe adamantly believed there was nothing improper about her interest in bodies. Even though her art teacher had insisted that insipid flowers and pleasant vistas were the only acceptable subjects for a young lady, she had ignored the stricture and continued her observations, frequently capturing the human body on paper.

Aunt Heloise's groom's loosely fitted clothing concealed something quite out of the ordinary, Chloe was positive. Why would he dress so strangely?

Heat suffused her body. "Dear heaven," she murmured. She realized she was staring at a groom, the gift she had brought her aunt the furthest thing from her mind. With that lowering discovery, she walked to the side of the coach, arriving just as Drury turned the last horse over to a stocky individual with curiously watchful eyes.

"Would you be so kind as to unload the roof of the coach first?" she asked, flashing a mischievous smile, aware of the charm of the misplaced dimple at the left of her lower lip.

Drury showed no curiosity, simply swinging himself to the top of the coach and removing the ropes holding the canvas in place. Under Chloe's watchful eye, he peeled back the cover, revealing the objects beneath. The muscles in his lean cheeks twitched, the corners of his mouth deepened into an appreciative grin, and his white teeth flashed in an outright smile.

"One is mine. The other is for my aunt. Do you think she'll be pleased?" Chloe called up to him.

The smile disappeared as if it had never been. "I'm sure she'll be surprised, miss," he answered woodenly.

Irritation swept Chloe. Naturally friendly and outgoing, she was accustomed to talking with servants as if no social barriers existed. Her aunt's groom, by his very detachment, fueled her determination to break through his reserve.

"What are you called?" she asked curiously, even though

18

she was aware of his name.

He knelt on top the coach and directed his gaze to a point somewhere beyond her left shoulder. "Drury, m'lady."

"Do you know how to ride a bicycle?"

"Yes, ma'am." The admission came grudgingly.

Delighted, she smiled up at him. "That's wonderful, Drury. You can help me teach Aunt Heloise how to ride."

His thoughts racing, Adrian handed the first vehicle down to Harry Ikehorn. Closer contact with the vivacious creature below him would be as dangerous as returning to Armenia. During her leap from the coach, Lady Chloe had lost her hat and most of the pins which held her dusky curls at the back of her head. The errant breeze lifted a lock from her shoulders, blowing the shining strands across her cheek. She pushed them back impatiently.

Adrian thought she was the most beautiful woman he'd ever seen.

"I'll hold this one upright while he lowers the other one," she instructed Ikehorn. "Then Drury will show me where they are to be stored." She took hold of the handlebar with one hand and the seat with the other.

As he lifted the second bicycle, Adrian cursed silently and comprehensively in six languages. The familiar exercise failed to alleviate his frustration.

Ever since his "death" he had purposely avoided even thinking of attractive women of his own class. Actually, he'd not allowed himself to consider *any* woman as other than a person with whom he exchanged a few words, completed whatever the encounter demanded, and promptly forgot.

During the year and a half he'd worked at the Bristol shipyards detachment had been simple. In a totally male environment he had become one with the rough fellows who frequented the docks. Only the books he hoarded in his squalid little room and vengeful thoughts of his betrayer had kept him sane. Such mental and social hibernation had shut down his physical urges. His survival depended on it. Now, unaccountably, his loins remembered the pleasures to be found within a woman's body and wasted no time reminding him.

If only he were back at the docks, away from temptation. But that was impossible. The beam that fell on his shoulder six months ago had ended his isolation. The doctor who dealt with shipyard emergencies had put him in the charity hospital, and it was there that his mother's niece, his cousin Bess Shadwell, had found him. Was it fate or the Machiavellian contrivance of Fitzhugh Kent that had brought Bess there that day on an information-gathering tour with a charity group? Her husband's church wasn't even located in Bristol. He was vicar to the congregation of Upper Whiddlesby.

Bess, Adrian's favorite cousin, had turned her back on society to marry her beloved Robert, a seminary student who, if the twelve relatives preceding him in the succession died of the plague, would be a marquess.

In Adrian's weakened condition, Bess's tears had nearly broken his composure.

"We were told you were dead," she whispered, her voice thick with emotion and her hands clutching his good arm as if she were afraid he would disappear. "I don't understand, Adrian."

His whispered, carefully edited version of the reasons for his disappearance triggered more tears.

"You can't go back there," Bess declared when he finished. "I know just the place for you to heal." She rose, retied the strings on her fetching bonnet, and reverted to the demeanor of an efficient vicar's wife. "I must talk with someone first. Look for me the day after tomorrow."

On her way to the door she turned and said in a hoarse stage whisper that reminded him of shared childhood secrets and deviltry, "You still like horses, don't you?"

Then, without waiting for an answer, she had disappeared. A week later he had found himself established in the comfortable groom's apartment above Lady Heloise Lockwood's stables, where he recovered rapidly under Molly O'Day's competent, if brusque, care. And Heloise Lockwood had promised anonymity.

Each time he thought of the growing circle of people who knew his secret, Adrian shuddered. Even after all this time, someone might still be hunting him. The small, organized faction had triggered rebellion and dissent in Armenia. The news reports of massacres had appeared in the press, and Adrian frequently spent tortured, sleepless nights raging at the uselessness of diplomatic channels.

What did the lives of thousand of peasants mean to the power-hungry men in the labyrinth of Whitehall? More and more often the answer to that question sickened him.

The presence of Lady Chloe Lockwood could prove to be a disaster. Tamped-down desires clawed at his insides. She was vibrant and heartbreakingly alive. It nearly hurt to look at her. And he was dead. He'd been dead for nearly two years.

She wasn't wearing a corset. Her haunting softness as she lay in his arms was still imprinted on the length of his body. As he climbed down from the top of the coach, Adrian felt himself harden. He inhaled, recalling the clean, sweet scent of primroses.

Oh, yes. Lady Chloe was going to be a problem.

Chapter Two

As the stocky groom and two footmen carried off the last of her trunks, Chloe realized Drury was halfway to the stables. "Don't go just yet. I want to see where we're going to store the bicycles," she called, hurrying to catch up with him.

His look of resignation dismayed her. The man clearly wished she were in China.

"Certainly, Lady Chloe." The man was so ostentatiously subservient she wondered if he was new to this type of employment. She'd never before considered that servants had ever been anything but servants. But then what else could Drury have been? As she followed her aunt's groom into the tidy brick building, Chloe surveyed him through the eyes of an artist.

Perhaps it was his hands. His long, neatly manicured fingers were particularly fascinating. They were the hands of a poet, a musician, a gentleman—of anything but a groom. She itched to sketch them. And his eyes. How did he manage to withdraw all light and expression from them that way? Her memory of the intelligence glowing in their blue depths when he'd held her in his arms outside the carriage was vivid. Even more memorable was the unreasonable sense of recognition she'd felt when she first encountered his piercing gaze. He had to have felt *something!* She refused to believe he hadn't shared that psychic connection.

"We'll keep them in this empty stall handy to the door, m'lady. Are you wanting to ride today?"

"I rather doubt it," she said, abruptly brought back to the

present. She lifted the trim skirt of her traveling dress a discreet inch above the ground and led the way to the door. "But I feel sure Aunt Heloise will not have any difficulty learning to ride an Olivier. The wheels are nearly the same size," she added optimistically.

As they crossed the graveled oval, she saw Heloise studying the bicycles propped against the coach. Chloe called out, "One is for you, Aunt. The other is mine. Aren't they wonderful? Think of all the lovely excursions we can take!"

"I find 'wonderful' an extraordinarily inaccurate description," her aunt observed dryly.

Chloe heard a choking sound from behind her, but when she looked over her shoulder, Drury's features were blank, and she continued brightly, "I felt sure you would want to keep up with the latest mode. The *Times* says these are extremely safe, and I've brought you a divided skirt. I nearly ordered bloomers for you, but I knew the dressmaker would tell Mama, who would simply expire."

This time the choking sound behind her was louder. Her aunt's lips twitched. Summoning her brightest smile, Chloe continued, "Well, actually I wanted the bloomers for myself, but you would still have had a divided skirt. It's truly attractive."

"I feel certain I shall find the skirt more acceptable. Although I harbor great admiration for Amelia Bloomer, those remarkable garments are somewhat extreme." Heloise's eyes twinkled, and she inspected one of the bicycles more closely. "Are you positive I shall be able to master this vehicle?"

"Drury has promised to help teach you. We'll have such fun!" Chloe smiled engagingly at the groom. "Would you take a turn in front of the stable to show my aunt how easy it is, Drury?"

★ ★ ★ ★ ★

Chloe's free and easy manner with her aunt fascinated Adrian. Since his arrival he had noticed that the local gentry and the villagers treated her with respect bordering on reverence. Her niece addressed Lady Heloise Lockwood the same way she did him, which was as if they were the best of friends. She was irresistible. And she terrified him more every minute. Drawing a deep breath, he replied, "Certainly, m'lady."

He pedaled around the oval and then out the carriage drive, wobbling slightly until his body recalled the skill. Adrian thought of Oxford, where he and his friends had spent many sunny Sundays exploring the countryside. It was with regret that he returned to the two women, even though his practical side told him nothing could be gained by feeling sorry for himself. "You should have no difficulty learning, ma'am," he said as he braked in front of them.

"See, Aunt? I told you so. And, Drury, please call me Miss Chloe. Lady sounds as if I were in London, and I shall have to put up with enough of that when Mother drags me there." Her full lower lip pouted prettily.

Adrian's stomach tightened. Speaking her name aloud seemed like an incredible intimacy, but he had no choice. In past months he'd discovered how few options were available to those of the servant class. "As you wish."

"Come in to luncheon, Chloe. After you've eaten, you must supervise Gladys while she unpacks for you. She is unaccustomed to the work, but she is willing. Perhaps she will be more suited as a lady's maid than she is to dusting."

Adrian swallowed his laughter. Tales of the red-haired maid's disastrous efforts with a feather duster had traveled from the house to the stables with amazing speed. Apparently the girl had rid her employer of numerous ugly inherited gimcracks. Adrian had a strong suspicion the maid's inepti-

24

tude was the reason she had been left at the task so long.

"Heavens, Aunt. Wasn't Gladys the maid who spooked Lionel's horses?"

"Unfortunately, yes. I now understand why her father was so eager to send her into service. The home farm would not have survived her. My difficulty is to discover where she is best suited." Heloise sounded perplexed.

"If I may suggest, ma'am, she wants to grow flowers," Adrian said. He felt compassion for the fourteen-year-old who initiated chaos each time she attempted a new task. To his dismay, the girl seemed to have misinterpreted his kindness, a problem he would have to address very soon.

"Gardening, is it?" Heloise replied, her tone thoughtful.

"Yes, of course," Chloe observed. "I don't imagine her father grows anything but useful crops. He wouldn't encourage Gladys to waste her time on such frivolous plants as flowers."

Her insight touched Adrian as much as it infuriated him. *Bloody hell! Why couldn't she be an ugly emptyhead?* he seethed inwardly.

"Your information is most helpful, Drury, although I doubt Ostley will relish the singularity of adding a female to his gardening staff. I shall have to exercise tact," she said, her inflection indicating this would be a new experience. "We must join Lionel, Chloe."

Ignoring propriety and convention, Chloe said, "I'll help Drury and be with you in a moment, Aunt."

The enchanting wrinkle in Chloe's brow as she wheeled the other bicycle alongside him warned Adrian that his own ease with his employer had aroused her curiosity. The interest with which she greeted everything she encountered was charming, but exercising such curiosity could be a dangerous activity for a young lady—particularly if she began asking questions about *him*.

As if reading his thoughts, Chloe said, "You appear to be on comfortable terms with my aunt, Drury. Most of the time she terrifies people, and she *never* allows anyone to question her actions. She also dislikes stupidity, which means you have impressed her in a very short time." She eyed him consideringly as he propped the first bicycle against the wall of the stall. "Have you always been a groom?" she asked.

Three years of gathering information for the government, followed by nearly two years of living in the shadows, sleeping lightly at night and guarding his tongue during his waking hours, had conditioned Adrian to easy falsehoods. Without a flicker of an eyelid he inhaled the comforting, familiar odors of horse and neat's-foot oil, then met her curious gaze and lapsed deeply into the country accent he had used among the servants since he arrived. He reached for the second bicycle.

"I worked with horses on me da's farm."

"That's not what I asked. Have you ever done anything else?" she persisted.

He sighed, averted his eyes, and concentrated on adjusting the bicycles. "I run away ter work in the shipyards, but a beam fell on me shoulder some months back, and I lost me job. A lady at the charity hospital sent me ter your aunt. She said Lady Heloise Lockwood took in people down on their luck but willin' to work."

"My aunt is very kind, but she can also be exacting. You must be quite exceptional, Drury. Particularly since you haven't talked with that accent since I leaped from the coach onto you."

Shards of gold light danced in her brown eyes, and her plump lower lip curved teasingly. Adrian wondered how he had ever been successful in his work for Fitz. The presence of this willful, wildly attractive girl erased any ability he had ever had to dissemble. With immense effort he willed his face and eyes to blankness and busied his hands with the bicycles. "If you say so, Miss Chloe."

The defeated expression on her lovely face was satisfying, even though he found himself resisting an urge to comfort her. Clearly, Chloe Lockwood was accustomed to extracting information until her curiosity was assuaged. She could probably succeed as a spy herself. Adrian imagined few people would refuse to tell her anything she might want to know.

He smothered a sigh. His present situation was uncertain, and Chloe's arrival, plus her inexplicable inquisitiveness, could endanger him with every passing day. Why was it so difficult to slam the door on her questions? Why did he feel so damned uncomfortable looking straight into her eyes and pretending to be as stolid and unfeeling as a piece of firewood?

He recognized her social smile as the one young women of good family were taught from birth when she said, "I'm sorry. That was very rude of me. Your background, or lack of it, is none of my affair. Forgive me if I crossed the line."

Adrian nodded in acquiescence, but he couldn't miss the determined set to her chin as she spoke. He had little problem interpreting the set of her shoulders as she made her way toward the house, even though he appreciated the graceful sway of her hips. Perspiration broke out on the back of his neck.

Heloise presided at the luncheon table spread with platters of cheeses, meats, and hot rolls as if she were serving a ten-course meal to royalty. She motioned to a footman to remove her nephew's soup bowl. "I was in hopes you would honor us with your presence longer than the time it takes to empty your plate, Lionel."

Lionel lifted his gaze for a moment, then returned his interest to the succulent slice of ham he had just served himself, answering, "Can't. Not this trip. Got to be at Ferdie's by tomorrow night. He has a mare I want to buy before the others arrive." He forked a neat portion into his mouth, chewed, and complained, "Coming out of the way to escort Chloe has been damned inconvenient."

"Be fair, Lionel. I didn't hold you back at all," Chloe protested.

An affectionate grin curved his lips as he buttered a cloverleaf roll. "No, but the weight from those two bags of books you stuffed inside the coach slowed the horses."

"Lionel, I do believe you're teasing your sister!" Heloise exclaimed.

Chloe laughed, recalling instantly her aunt's observations on his resemblance to his father at that age. As if by instinct Chloe had from early childhood patterned herself after her aunt, fulfilling the pattern of the Lockwood heredity, which produced twins with amazing regularity—twins invariably consisting of a male of somewhat limited intellectual ability and a female blessed with a bright, inquiring mind.

Lionel drained his glass and patted his mouth with his napkin. "Chloe's been teaching me. Says I have to learn to talk to women instead of horses. By the way, Aunt Heloise, you seem to have extra grooms. Could I borrow that fellow who helped this afternoon? I brought only the one, and he's not up to handling this many horses. I'd send your man back once I've arrived."

"I fear Drury is indispensable to me, Lionel, but I feel sure he can recommend one of his underlings," Heloise said smoothly, her modulated voice indicating the inflexibility of her decision.

"That'll have to do then. That turn-up this afternoon made me realize I need more help." He excused himself as he rose from his chair, then bent to give his sister a hearty buss on the cheek. "You behave, Chloe. Don't want you getting into any sort of a mess before we launch you."

He bade his aunt farewell with the air of someone whose mind is already on the next enterprise.

Heloise commented with asperity, "The boy knows nothing but horses. I suppose the importance of heirs won't occur to him until he reaches forty . . . just like his father."

Half an hour later Chloe entered her room to find Gladys Meadowes attempting to hold back a fit of giggles. The girl held up a black serge garment. "Miss Chloe, wot's this thing?"

"That's for my aunt. Hold it aside, please. She's taking her first bicycle-riding lesson tomorrow."

Gladys clutched the skirt to her short, sturdy frame as she looked at Chloe with excitement written across her broad face. "A bicycle! Kin I watch? I only seen one oncet, when me da took me to market."

"Of course," Chloe answered. The room looked as if a strong wind had just blown through. Gladys had obviously examined each garment in front of the cheval glass beside the ornately carved mahogany wardrobe. A stack of gowns lay heaped on the channel-back lady's chair next to the half-tester bed. Afternoon sun filtering through lace underdrapes flickered and danced across boots and slippers haphazardly dumped in front of the marble-topped dressing table. Lacy undergarments were strewn over the heavy crocheted bedcover. Gladys had indeed unpacked for her.

The red-haired maid's voice interrupted Chloe's survey of the room. "Yer corsets was bang on top in your dressing case, Miss Chloe. I put 'em in the top drawer so's they'd be where you could find 'em."

Chloe felt color rise in her cheeks and busied herself gathering folded shirtwaists. "You did exactly right." For all she cared, the nasty things could rot there.

"Don't rightly know how a body can do much o' anythin' wearin' one o' them things, but the gentry do look awful fancy all got up," Gladys observed.

Her arms full, Chloe clutched the clothing close for fear of dropping it. She kicked a riding boot out of her path. "I shouldn't think you see many. Upper Whiddlesby is out of the way of London society."

Gladys fingered the lace strap of a sheer batiste chemise longingly. "Folks used to come oncet in a while last summer. Ain't seen any since then, 'cept fer you, miss." She ran her hands over the filmy confection, her fingers caressing the unfamiliar textures.

"I wonder why. There certainly seems to be enough staff." Chloe closed the drawer on the shirtwaists and bent to retrieve the boot she'd kicked.

The maid cast the chemise aside and fell to her knees to gather footwear into an untidy heap. "There be four new ones, too. First that Drury come in the fall. Thomas come right after, with them two gardeners. Right queer types, some o' 'em."

"What do you mean?" Chloe inquired, seizing the opportunity presented by Gladys's mention of the intriguing groom.

"That Thomas is real hatchet-faced. Cook says he looks like he'd steal the gold out of yer teeth, but Drury says it ain't fair to think a body's dangerous just 'cause he's mortal ugly."

"He's right, Gladys. We mustn't judge a book by its cover, my old governess used to say," Chloe said, hoping she didn't sound preachy. "A person can't help his looks. Drury must be a fine friend for the man."

"Oooo, it ain't that Drury spends time with him or anyone. That Thomas follers *him,* he does. Sticks 'round like a shadow. Can't hardly ever get to talk to Drury without he's close enough to spit on."

Chloe pushed a smartly striped poplin skirt to one side and shook out the rose crepe lisse dinner gown heaped beneath it, her mind fitting the unknown Thomas into her mental equation. She returned to the subject of greatest interest. "Is Drury friendly, Gladys? He seems rather reserved." What if he was some sort of servant Romeo? The thought depressed her.

At her question, Gladys forsook all pretense of work. She clasped her hands, swaying from side to side as if she were dizzy. "He's ever so kind, Miss Chloe. And polite, too. Treats me like I was a real lady, same as he treats all t'other maids." She rolled her eyes heavenward in ecstasy.

"Gladys, he hasn't . . . he doesn't . . ." Chloe sputtered.

"He never did! Even when I tol' him he could. Even offered to meet him up in the loft," Gladys said dejectedly. "Me mum says some men are backward. Ye has to prime 'em like a pump."

Her head deep in the carved mahogany wardrobe, Chloe bit her lip to keep from laughing. In addition to information about Drury, she was privileged, courtesy of Gladys, to hear Gladys's mother's advice on courtship.

As she withdrew her head from the primrose-scented depths, Chloe cautioned, "Aunt Heloise would be disappointed to hear you were having such thoughts. A young girl can get into trouble meeting men in the hayloft. Or anyplace else."

Gladys received the reprimand equably. "That's all well and good fer ye, Miss Chloe, but not fer the likes o' me. Me mum says a bun in the oven has cooked many a man's goose.

31

That Drury be the best of the lot, even if he do talk funny sometimes."

Upon entering the stable, Adrian discarded his subservient posture much as he would shed a dirty shirt.

This time each day was his. Since both of the other grooms were family men, he performed the necessary duties during the dinner hour so they could be with their families. During this period he was Adrian, Viscount Harding, alive and in possession of all the freedom and privilege accorded a man of his station, even though he spent the time mucking out stalls.

Tonight he was uncomfortably aroused, and he was afraid the inner tension gripping him might become permanent—at least as long as Chloe Lockwood remained in residence.

The girl was too perceptive. He'd felt her clear, inquisitive gaze on him at every moment, and he'd dealt ruthlessly with the instinct to respond normally, to discover more about her. He thought he'd come to terms with his own death, but with each passing moment he was more aware he would never adjust to this shadow life.

He measured oats into a bucket from a large bin near the door and carried it to the stall of his favorite horse, a spirited gelding named Beau, dumped the grain in the trough, and rested his forehead against the horse's chestnut back. He hated constantly slumping his shoulders and carrying his head low. Even more depressing was the realization that he found the artifice had become almost second nature.

The mental discipline of maintaining a seamless facial expression seamless and blank eyes had seemed like a game when he accepted his first assignments, none of which had lasted longer than a fortnight; today he'd discovered that pretending substandard intelligence wore thin after months of the masquerade. He wanted his identity back.

Damn it, he wanted his old wardrobe back, even though everything in it was undoubtedly out of style by now. He wanted clothing that fit him and reinforced his feeling of worth; the oversized garments that blurred the lines of his body were cumbersome and became more so every day.

At least the clothes were clean, now that he worked for Heloise Lockwood.

Adrian let himself out of the stall and into the next corridor. He seized a pitchfork and hurled it like a javelin the length of the aisle between the stalls. It clattered to the cobblestones, disturbing the horses, who stamped their hooves and whinnied. Damn it, he wanted a woman. To his horror, the woman he pictured, gold-flecked brown eyes wide and glowing, her cheeks flushed with passion, was Chloe Lockwood.

"Sod it," he spat out. His hands trembled with frustration. He took a deep breath, held it, then exhaled resignedly.

Discipline, said an inner voice, the same voice that cautioned him each time he considered resurrecting himself without Fitz's permission and tracking down his betrayer.

Adrian took another deep breath, searching for patience. When he achieved his goal, he sighed and climbed the cramped stairway to his quarters above the stable. At least here he could pretend his life had normalcy. No one ever intruded on the two snug rooms containing his few precious possessions—the books that were his hold on sanity.

He stopped dead in the doorway, sweeping the tiny sitting room with a narrow-eyed gaze. Tidy by nature and accustomed to living alone, Adrian knew to an inch the placement of each piece of shabby furniture and each item the room contained.

With one quick, cautious movement, he stepped inside

and pulled the door closed behind him, leaning against it as if anticipating pressure on the other side of the solid oak portal. Spring sunlight, golden and clear, fell through the lone window, pooling in the center of the worn floor. He scanned his belongings again, his glance snagging on the tattered piece of paper protruding from the volume of Emerson on top of an ancient bookcase. The night before he'd left the book beside the lamp on his bedside table.

Crossing the room, he pulled the scrap free and moved to the window to read the precise handwriting marching across it. *The stone bridge. Midnight.*

Chapter Three

"I shall require your assistance tomorrow, Chloe."

"Of course, Aunt." Chloe dragged her thoughts from the romantic fantasy she'd been weaving. She focused instead on her discomfort in her reluctantly donned corset.

"The church has solicited my help with the Women's Institute jumble sale, which presents me with a problem." Heloise placed her knife at a precise angle across her plate.

Chloe grinned teasingly. "I suspect they couldn't manage the event without you."

Heloise nodded in agreement. "That is beside the point, however." She patted her mouth with a pristine linen napkin and placed it beside her plate. "McCandlish, the tenant on a local farm, was found dead last week. He was no great loss, but his wife is capable and honest enough not to grieve. Since she has been left penniless, I have hired her as underhousekeeper."

"How kind of you, Aunt."

"You need not interpret my intentions, Chloe. I'm being selfish. Jane McCandlish is a superior person, and finding suitable help in this rural village is next to impossible. Since I must be at the jumble, I should like you to drive to the farm, assist her in gathering her belongings, and bring her back here. Given the circumstances, she deserves what kindness we can offer."

"I'll be happy to. Will you tell her about Molly's past?" Chloe asked.

"I'll tell 'er meself. I don't 'old with secrets twixt folks," Molly said as she bustled in to clear the dessert plates. She paused beside Heloise's chair to demand, "Are yer goin' ta ride that contraption Miss Chloe brought ye?"

"I intend to make an attempt tomorrow."

"Well, be careful ye don't end up arse over tip. If God 'ad meant yer to ride like that, 'e'd 'ave put wheels on yer feet. Jist remember I told yer so."

Heloise cast her a repressive look. "I shall endeavor not to do so, Molly. Your concern is touching."

Bubbling with laughter, Chloe rose to her feet. "I shall take very good care of her, Molly. If she were to injure herself, people might think I'd tried to kill her to inherit her money." To Chloe's delight, her aunt's recent inheritance hadn't changed either her or Molly. Heloise still did as she pleased. Surely she'd understand her niece's wish to live the same way.

Molly chuckled as she carried the tray from the room. "If ye cut me in, I'll tell 'em it was ol' Budgley down at the pub. 'E done 'er in 'cause the beer was watery."

"That is quite enough about my late uncle's breweries. Aunt Caroline's husband's trade-tainted money will one day make Chloe a very wealthy woman."

Chloe rounded the table to hug her aunt. "I'd rather be penniless all my life than lose you, Aunt. Besides, you can't leave us until you confide the details of your mysterious past."

"I have absolutely no idea what you are talking about."

"Of course you do. When I was little, my father would look worried whenever you sent us exotic gifts from foreign countries." Chloe inspected her aunt's suddenly blank features. "Now where else have I seen such a wonderfully controlled face today? Why, here at your very own house. You remind me of Drury, that groom of yours."

"That is quite enough, Chloe. You are touching on matters that do not concern you."

"Aha! Since you choose to treat me as if I were still in the nursery, I'll leave you to spend the evening alone. I intend to walk in the garden before dark, then read myself to sleep."

"Stay within the grounds, my dear. Constable Pickens believes Ian McCandlish was murdered, and he has yet to apprehend the killer. The murderer could be anyone."

"I shan't wander out of sight of the house," she promised.

The idea of peril in this cozy rural village was as unreal to Chloe as being unsafe on her father's estate. Why should anyone harm her? As she slipped out the service entrance, the possibility added new dimensions to the fantasy she'd woven during dinner. If she were abducted, Drury could rescue her. Surely the queen would knight him. And then . . .

Her mind conjured up a picture of his long, lean-fingered hands. They belonged on the keyboard of a piano, or holding an artist's brush, or . . . She envisioned them touching her skin, and a delicious shiver heated her flesh.

Chloe didn't understand what had come over her. Her mind was obsessed with a groom—a man about whom she knew nothing. She looked across the twilight shadowed grounds toward the stable. While chatting with Molly in the kitchen before dinner, she had discovered that Drury lived on the second floor. "Wouldn't live in servants' quarters with the unmarried 'elp, not 'im," Molly had said, "Said as 'ow 'e sometimes 'as trouble with nightmares and gets up at all 'ours. Din't want ta disturb anyone."

Apparently, Drury had aroused Molly's maternal instincts, but her own feelings were a far cry from maternal. In spite of Chloe's limited experience, she knew a handsome man when she saw one, however much she might protest that her interest was only artistic. Her brother's rather burly good looks seemed to be "too much"—too much muscle, too much bristling male competitiveness, too much of everything. She straightened her back and assured herself only her artist's eye appreciated Drury's taut ranginess and the spare perfection of his features.

Yet she desperately wanted to bask in the charm and warmth she'd seen in his eyes while she was sprawled atop him. Had she merely imagined that special warmth? What would it take to break the rigid control he exercised over his facial expression and demeanor?

Fireflies, flickering pinpoints of light, flashed in the quickly falling dusk. Her soft slippers were soundless on the gravel path. She pretended interest in the sparrows twittering in the monstrous spruce tree to her right while she cast about for sight of Drury's lithe figure. The unexpected sound of voices ahead of her startled her so that she stubbed her toe on the border of an iris bed.

"Gladys, you know Molly will expect you as soon as it's dark." The smooth timbre of Drury's voice sent a little shiver of excitement through her.

"I'd druther stay in the stable wi' you. Yer must be lonely, 'n it's right cold sleepin' all by yerself."

A deep sigh prefaced his answer. "It's generous of you to offer, Gladys, but as I've told you before, the flat over the stable is very snug, and I'm not lonely."

"But . . ."

"Gladys, I like you very much . . ." The sentence ended abruptly with an inelegant exhalation.

Chloe peered cautiously around a clump of shrubbery, then suppressed laughter at the sight that met her eyes. Gladys, her red hair curling wildly around her head, had tried to throw her arms around Drury's neck at the same moment he had extended his arms to keep her away. She hung awkwardly from his elbows. Drury looked as if he wished himself anyplace but where he stood. "Leave off now, Gladys. Let me finish." He managed to disentangle her arms and hold her away from his body. "You're still very young. In a few years you'll meet some man closer to your age who'll marry you. I'm not marriage material."

"I ain't lookin' to marry. I jist want to have a little slap and tickle." Gladys sounded baffled.

Drury sighed again. When he spoke, his bitter voice astounded Chloe. "I'm not a likely candidate, even for that. You're better off with boys your own age, boys who are . . . more alive than I."

"But I—"

"Gladys," Drury said authoritatively, "Go back to the house. If I catch you here again, I shall report you to Lady Lockwood."

The threat sent Gladys away like a frightened rabbit, tears of rejection glistening on her broad, freckled cheeks as she pounded past Chloe's hiding place.

With sudden clarity, Chloe realized she was no better than Gladys. She'd come out walking in the near dark hoping for an encounter with her aunt's groom, for heaven's sake!

Chloe withdrew farther into the shrubbery, wincing as several branches stabbed into her back. She stared at the stable, which Drury had entered after Gladys's retreat. Moments later a light appeared in the white-framed rectangle on the second floor. A restless shadow moved across its warm glow. Giving up her vigil, she returned to the house and climbed the stairs to her corner room, where she peered out the lace-covered window at the stable in the distance. At that moment the lighted rectangle turned dark.

Hours later, Chloe couldn't pinpoint what had awakened

her. She lay still, straining to hear again the sound that had penetrated her confusing dreams. Silence. She eased from the high bed and crept noiselessly to the open window.

In the fading moonlight a shadow moved against the gray stone wall near the stable. Her heart pounding in her ears, she strained to discern any further movement. A figure that had been indistinguishable moments earlier detached itself from the wall. She had no trouble identifying his controlled movements as he blended into the darkness beyond the paddock.

Where could Drury be going at this time of night?

"What the hell do you want?" Adrian demanded in a harsh whisper that caused Fitzhugh Kent to jerk violently and brace himself against the rough stone arching above the spring-swollen stream. The reaction satisfied Adrian immensely.

"I do wish you wouldn't sneak up on a person like that," Fitz protested.

"Now we're even. I nearly turned and ran for the nearest constable when I discovered someone had been in my rooms."

"You'd never do that."

"Don't test me, Fitz. I'm sick and tired of this farce. My death didn't even serve a good purpose. That country has gone up in flames, and no one gives a damn but me. My God! This isn't like a war, where most of the casualties are soldiers. Women and children and . . . grandparents . . ." He had dreamed the horrors night after night.

Fitz stepped forward, hands out placatingly. "Adrian, we tried. We tried like hell, but no one wanted to take action."

Adrian turned away. "I don't believe you."

"You bloody well should! I offended bureaucrats from three countries trying to stop the bloody revolt. I nearly got the sack."

"What rot! You'll keep your job no matter what. Your files

stuffed with lurid details of Bertie's sordid indiscretions are solid gold insurance. You're still running the store. I'm so surrounded by incompetent agents pretending to be servants that I have half again as much work to do. *Someone's* still following your orders." He peered closely at Fitz, unpacified by his denial.

"It's not like you to be so bloody cynical, Adrian."

Rage bubbled up swiftly. "My dear Fitz, I'm dead, remember? And my death didn't stop a thing. I was damn near killed in that bloody shipyard, and your dog wouldn't live in the unspeakable kennel I called home. My parents are in mourning, and I don't see anyone breaking his neck to resurrect me."

Fitz snugged his coat around his neck; the night air had cooled noticeably. "Well, you've fallen into it now. I'm sure the work isn't arduous. The old girl's a bit of a dragon, but I've not heard any rumors of her starving her help."

"Don't play word games, Fitz. I'm still dead. And in any case, Lady Heloise knows who I am, as does the cousin who found me in the hospital. Surely Bess's husband, the vicar, is in on the secret. And of course there's Molly . . ." He seized his superior's exquisite lapels and drew him close until their eyes, shadowed in the moonlight, were inches apart. "What happens when too many people know a secret?"

Fitz pushed Adrian's hands away, then grasped his shoulders in a not unsympathetic hold. "I know. It's no longer a secret. I do take you seriously, and believe me, I feel damned inadequate. We simply haven't been able to turn up anything until now. The pot is starting to boil."

"I don't want to hear about it."

"You'd better listen, and listen well. Did you have any dealings with the man who was killed last week? Mc-Candlish?"

Adrian shrugged. "We might have been in the pub at the same time now and again, but we never actually spoke. According to the locals, he was a bit of a bounder. Rumor said he beat his wife." He pushed Fitz's hands away and turned to stare at the little stream. He exhaled loudly. "The news of his murder scared the hell out of me. The last murder in Upper Whiddlesby was twenty-five years ago. A jealous husband caught his wife's lover climbing out the window and shot him."

He spun back around, pushing his hands through his hair, hating the coarse feel of the dyed thatch. "Don't you understand? This place doesn't have mysteries. Now I'm here, and there's a murder."

"That blot McCandlish had been hired to kill *you*. We intercepted a coded message, but by the time I got through to my man in the village, McCandlish was no more. Who shuffled him off?" Fitz paced restlessly. "You're sure you didn't do the deed?"

"If I had, it would have been self-defense." Could he kill a man if his life were in danger? Deep down, Adrian knew he could. First spying, which he had taken up lightly, and now a calm acceptance of his ability to take a human life. How far had he fallen?

"Quite right. Actually, Fallonsby said you were nowhere near when McCandlish died. Adrian, we must ferret out who murdered McCandlish and why. Since you didn't kill him, there's an unidentified player in the game. This may trace back to whoever blew your cover in Armenia."

Adrian scarcely noticed his stomach muscles tighten. He'd lived with varying stages of fear for so long that the idea of someone taking money to kill him made little impression. "McCandlish's landlord was in a snit because of a botched harvest last fall, and several tradesmen wouldn't let him buy on the tick. Aside from his wife, I can't imagine why anyone would go so far as to do him in."

"Then find out. Ask Lady Heloise to apply herself to the task. Lord only knows she's more than up to the task," he added obscurely.

"Things have changed." Adrian withdrew further into the shadows. "Until now her ladyship's contented herself with terrifying the local gentry. Now her niece is here. The girl's mother broke her ankle, and her aunt's taking her into the social swim until her mother's recovered."

Chloe's vivid, laughing face flashed in his mind's eye, and for the first time in his life he regretted missing a London Season. Wide-eyed, marriage-minded innocents had never held any attraction for him. He kicked the nearest segment of the bridge, welcoming the jolt of pain that knifed through his toe and into his foot. "I'll leave tonight. I can't put people in danger."

"Indeed you will not leave," Fitz ground out as he swung Adrian around to face him. "The estate is overrun with bodyguards, and I've an agent in place in the village. If you move on, I'll have to secure another area—provided no one kills you first." Fading moonlight revealed his intensity. "Will you believe me when I tell you I'm doing my best to bring you back?"

Adrian swallowed to lessen the surge of hope Fitz's words caused. "Don't let me down, Fitz." He clasped the spymaster's shoulder and squeezed, then, embarrassed by his weakness, cleared his throat and said, "Molly might hear something."

"The housekeeper who used to be a prostitute?"

Adrian permitted himself a wry smile. Fitz had certainly studied the surroundings. "Haven't missed a trick, Fitz," he replied, amusement permeating his voice.

"Neither did she in her heyday. Lady Heloise believes in employing people with unfortunate pasts, which explains to the world why she took *you* on. She makes her own rules. She always did." Admiration rang in Fitz's voice.

"I'll see what I can find out. Could McCandlish have been hired by the Armenians?" Locating the remaining conspirators was the key. Adrian held his breath, afraid to hope.

"Not likely." Fitz pushed his shoulders away from the bridge and held out his hand. "Someone will contact you. Damn it, Adrian, I never meant for you to carry on this farce for so long."

Adrian shrugged away from Fitz's touch. "I don't want your damned sympathy. All I want is out of hiding so I can find the bloody bastard who identified me." Grateful the moonlight had vanished, he flung himself at the twisting path up the bank, calling softly, "Stay in touch."

"Just a minute. Aren't you forgetting something?"

Adrian paused and sighed. "All right. What's the ruddy password your man will use?" He expected something ridiculous. Fitz delighted in the absurd.

"Leather preserver saves leather's life." Fitz's voice held childish pride in its own cleverness. "I thought it suited your present status. You know, harnesses and all."

Adrian grimaced at the idiocy. "God save the Queen," he spat out before he faded into the darkness.

Chloe's knees were numb, the night chill had penetrated her batiste nightgown, and her head had nodded toward the sill several times before the stable door swung open with a low but harsh grating of metal on metal—the sound which must have wakened her earlier. Drury had returned.

Flexing her legs to restore circulation, she crawled into her bed, seething with curiosity. She discarded the idea of his slipping out to visit a woman. After all, he'd turned down young Gladys earlier. Minutes before, the downstairs clock had struck three, so the pub had been closed for hours. Where had he been?

She smiled in the darkness. Perhaps the adventure she'd been seeking when she left Bennington Hall was no farther than her aunt's stables. The next time Drury slipped away in the night, she intended to follow him.

"I just hope he forgets to oil that hinge," she murmured as she turned onto her side and nestled her head into the pillow.

The next morning Chloe stood beside a grumbling Molly as Drury and two stalwart footmen loaded an open wagon with donations for the jumble sale. "Don't know wot folks'll think of 'er gettin' rid of all 'em nice things. It'll look like she din't think too 'igh of 'er ol' auntie. And 'er leavin' 'er all 'er gilt."

"You're wrong, Molly. They'll think Aunt Heloise already has so many fine belongings of her own, she had to make room for them," Chloe contradicted. "This will increase her stature. I'm sure two wagon loads will be more than anyone else donates." She'd spent her short lifetime among the villagers near Bennington Hall. Molly, on the other hand, was London-raised.

"She is quite right, Molly, although my primary goal was to remove these eyesores from the premises. There are those who would have returned that disgusting bird cage to the sitting room, had the opportunity presented itself," Heloise said.

"Did Aunt Caroline have a bird?" Chloe inquired.

Molly's voice dropped. "A lovely one it was, too. Red an' green an' yellow, an' stuffed to a treat."

Giggling at the image Molly invoked of Aunt Heloise's reaction to the bird, Chloe made her way to the open carriage.
"A stuffed parrot?" she repeated breathlessly. Her eyes teared
with laughter, and she stumbled. A strong hand gripped her
upper arm, and she looked up into Drury's eyes. A smile
lurked in their indigo depths. She wanted to stand like this
forever, drowning in the luxury of his regard and sharing
laughter. His warm touch seemed to heat her whole body.

Her aunt's imperious voice broke the spell as she came up
behind them. "Jane is expecting you. I feel sure both of you
will treat her with kindness." Heloise directed a quelling
glance at her housekeeper as Drury opened the carriage door.
"Molly was quite taken with that monstrosity. She felt it
added a certain . . . air to the surroundings. Dead birds in the
parlor. Indeed."

Chloe's enjoyment of her aunt's disclosure didn't prevent
her from feeling bereft without Drury's touch. He'd released
her at the sound of his employer's voice, and his face had assumed the expressionless mask of the day before.

"I shall be at the sale the rest of the day. Please convince
Jane to rest after you deliver her here. I do not expect her to
assume her duties until tomorrow. And do not insult her by
expressing sympathy. None is required. I have already informed her that however violent her husband's death, it was
no more than the man deserved." Heloise cleared her throat.
"However, that's neither here nor there. Drury will bring you
home and then I expect him at the sale to assist me."

Laughter at her aunt's brusque dismissal of the late Mr.
McCandlish lodged in Chloe's throat. How like Aunt Heloise
to take the widow under her wing, but only after first assuring
her that the loss of her husband was of no importance. Chloe
climbed into the carriage and settled her rose-colored muslin
skirts with a joyous flip of her hands. Whatever the errand,

she would savor every moment of Drury's company.

Although spotlessly clean, the little cottage was damp, dreary, and dark. Chloe was sure Jane McCandlish must be overjoyed to leave such surroundings. Sharing these tiny quarters with an abusive husband must have been ghastly. "Shall I empty this cupboard by the fireplace?" she asked.

"Oh, Miss Chloe, surely Lady Heloise didn't mean for you to help. This will only take a few more minutes. I haven't much, and most of my things are already in those boxes." She gestured toward the pitiful collection by the front door.

Chloe was appalled by the distress her offer had caused. The poor woman looked as if she might cry. "Nonsense. The quicker we gather all this, the sooner we'll be on our way," she replied, unable to resist contrasting the new assistant housekeeper's politeness with the outspokenness of both Molly and Gladys. She pointed to a small cupboard in the corner and asked, "Are these your belongings?"

"No, that cabinet was Mr. McCandlish's, and he forbade me to touch anything in it. He kept private papers there. I . . . I suppose those things *are* mine now."

Wondering what kind of papers a crude, drunken lout would save, Chloe pulled the sagging door open and removed bulging envelopes containing yellowing bills and receipts from the front of the shelf. She deposited them in the small wooden box she'd brought from the shed. Behind the envelopes were two miniature burlap seed sacks tied at the top with twine. As she drew them toward her, the binding fell from one, and its folds sagged open.

Within the bag emeralds glowed and sparkled in the intricate gold filigree setting of a necklace tangled with a heavy collar of pearls, which curled around a diamond tiara. A heavy diamond brooch spilled out into her hands.

Chapter Four

Chloe's breath caught in her throat. She blinked several times, then reached out to touch the glittering cache.

"What's wrong, Miss Chloe? Did you get a splinter?"

Certain that Jane could have had no idea of the cupboard's contents, Chloe spoke quietly. "Jane, would you come here, please?" Jane crossed the room, and Chloe heard the shocked intake of her breath before she asked, "Where do you suppose all this came from?"

"Oh, my dear Lord! I never saw it before, miss." Jane stepped back, her dark eyes wide and tear-filled. Her thin fingers worried her faded cotton skirts. "I . . . I swear I didn't." Jane's voice shook with intensity and fear.

Hefting the two sacks, which were remarkably heavy for their size, Chloe was horrified when Jane's shoulders hunched protectively, as if she expected a blow. "You knew he had something secret in that cupboard, didn't you?"

Tears spilled down Jane's thin cheeks. "He . . . He came in one day when I'd moved the table from in front of it." Her work-worn hands clenched. "He beat me. Usually he'd stop when I began to cry. That time he didn't." She pushed her hair back from her forehead, revealing a raised red scar. " 'Twas the blood that finally made him stop, but he threatened to kill me if I ever touched the cupboard again."

"But where did he get these jewels?" Chloe demanded.

"I don't know. He used to disappear, sometimes for as long as four days. That's why he fell so far behind with the farm."

Chloe sank to a stool, the sacks clutched in her hands. "Jane, go bring Drury. I want him to see this." After Jane left the room, she realized she'd spoken impulsively. Could his clandestine trip the night before have had something to do with the jewels—or with McCandlish's murder?

Common sense told her Drury couldn't have any connection to the jewels or to the murder. After all, her aunt trusted him.

When Drury entered the room, she saw him glance immediately in her direction, his eyes narrowing at the sight of the sacks she held. She saw resignation, rather than the guilt she feared, in his eyes, and his gaze held steady. Chloe knew intuitively that his midnight disappearance had nothing to do with mysterious jewelry or Jane's husband.

"You wanted me, Miss Chloe?"

She extended the opened sack. His eyelids tightened marginally. Moving the flickering lantern to the scarred table, he emptied the sack onto its bleached surface. When Chloe held out the second bag he did the same. After studying the find, he turned to Jane and demanded, "Do you know where these came from?"

Guilt washed through Adrian as Jane flinched at his tone of voice. The sharpness had stemmed from his own fear of drawing attention to himself, and he had no business taking it out on this poor, terrified woman. He said gently, "Don't be afraid, Jane."

"They were in Mr. McCandlish's cupboard, the one I wasn't to touch. He said he'd kill me if he ever found me mucking about in his things."

Swinging his gaze back to the glittering array, Adrian said softly, "We'd better get the magistrate. He'll know what to do with stolen goods."

He wondered what the authorities would say if he told

49

them that the intricate diamond tiara was his great-aunt Amelia's pride and joy. In his isolation from the family, he hadn't been aware of its disappearance. The old girl's knickers must be in a twist over the loss.

Why would a would-be assassin possess stolen goods? Adrian asked himself as he returned the jewels to the bags. The fellow hadn't yet completed his assignment, so these couldn't have been payment. How had he gotten his hands on them? Was he so stupid as to think he could sell such jewels without drawing attention to himself?

Oh, God! Attention was the last thing Adrian himself needed. Adrian's mind scrambled for a way to dissociate himself from the discovery. His first instinct, to run, was unacceptable. No gentleman, he reminded himself, would abandon two females at this juncture. Besides, his sudden, unexplained disappearance would only fix Chloe's bright, inquisitive attention more solidly on him. *Bloody hell!*

"Stolen goods!" Jane's face blanched further. "They'll arrest me." She sank onto a crude wooden stool. "I didn't know anything about Mr. McCandlish when we married. His family owned a farm nearby. My father was a schoolmaster, and when he died, I was left penniless. I only accepted Mr. McCandlish's offer because I had no other choice." She pushed a lock of hair back into her tidy bun, and her body shook with her efforts to control her sobs.

Drawing a shuddering breath, she continued, "Shortly after we were wed, Mr. McCandlish's father threw him out because he'd been stealing from the family. This is the second tenancy he's had since then. He was tossed off the last place." Tears streamed down her face.

Chloe stood and threw her arms around Jane's shoulders. She looked at Adrian and said imperiously, "The constable wouldn't dare put her in jail. She's done nothing wrong, and

Aunt Heloise will tell them so herself." Tightening her hold, she said, "We'll fetch my aunt before we summon the magistrate."

Even though Chloe's voice remained soft, her expression was fierce. Adrian wondered if she might not, in forty years, be as formidable as her aunt. A lesser man would have been horrified. Adrian found it comforting. But then, he had developed a great fondness for Heloise Lockwood, and he knew she would not only protect Jane, but she would never mention Adrian's part in the discovery.

For more reasons than one, Adrian repressed a desire to seize Chloe Lockwood and kiss her soundly.

That evening, after a hurried dinner, Chloe followed her aunt into the sitting room and dropped wearily onto the blue brocade settee with a sigh. "I'm exhausted." She drew her legs beneath her, conveniently forgetting her mother's stricture that no lady sat in such a vulgar position.

"This has indeed been a day of many surprises."

"I've never seen anything quite like those jewels." Chloe giggled. "Some were so grand I can't imagine anyone actually wearing them. But the simpler pieces were nice. Is the magistrate competent?"

"I think quite highly of Sir Desmond Lowery." Heloise threaded a piece of dark green wool and drew it through the canvas in her hand. "I have suggested he make your discovery known. Otherwise that man's cohorts might think Jane still possesses the jewels and follow her here."

"Do you think her husband stole them?"

"My dear, the man's brains were sodden three-fourths of the time. He hadn't the intelligence to steal away in the night." Heloise set a precise stitch. "I suspect he was probably some sort of courier, trusted only to deliver the ill-gotten

51

gains farther along the trail away from London. He was an excellent choice. No one would suspect such a vulgar person of carrying anything of real value."

Chloe swung her feet to the floor and slid her hips forward on the seat. "Drury said much the same thing when I spoke with him after Sir Desmond left. Have the two of you had your heads together?" She watched her aunt narrowly.

"Since when do I discuss matters of importance with my groom?"

"You don't treat him like a servant, and, frankly, he doesn't behave or speak like any groom I've ever seen." Chloe watched her aunt's expression. There were secrets here.

Heloise dropped her needle and bent to retrieve it. When she straightened, her face was composed. "I'd quite forgotten that disconcerting habit of yours."

"What is that, Aunt?"

"Observing people. You're very acute, my dear, but in this instance I must ask you to keep your observations to yourself . . . and to refrain from being too inquisitive."

Delighted with her response, Chloe said, "Fine. I shall simply draw my own conclusions." She rose and crossed the rose-patterned carpet of the little sitting room to the door. "And now I think I shall go to bed with a good book. Adventures are wonderful, but they're terribly exhausting. Don't forget your bicycling lesson tomorrow morning."

"Chloe." Heloise's voice held a note of command.

Chloe turned, biting back a smile. "Yes, Aunt?"

"Since your visit is to be prolonged, I must ask that you obey several rules. One, you will wear a corset. You need not do so if the two of us are closeted in the house, as we are now. However, when you step out my door, you will be properly clothed."

"I thought you, of all people, would understand!" Chloe protested.

"I do. However, your mother has given you into my care, and we shall uphold her standards." Heloise stood and continued, "Secondly, and much more importantly, you will not draw attention to Drury. As you have already divined, things are not what they appear. Indeed, they are much more serious than you can imagine. For his safety, and perhaps your own, you will obey me in this."

Startled by the severity of her aunt's voice, Chloe assented and left the room. She would never betray Drury, but she had no intention of ignoring him, either. Not when the mere thought of him quickened her heartbeat.

Promptly at ten the next morning, Chloe called Adrian from his duties to help her bring the bicycles into the graveled oval in front of the stable. He couldn't decide whether he was disappointed or relieved by the reserve in her voice.

"I'll take this one, and you bring the other. Aunt will be along any minute," she said, wheeling the closest vehicle to the door. As they exited the stable, she spoke again. "By the way, Molly said a peddler came yesterday. He was selling a new brand of leather preserver that saves leather's life. Molly giggled when she passed on the message, so he must be a flirt. Anyway, he told her he hoped to catch you around noon today."

Surprise and relief weakened Adrian's knees. "Thank you, Miss Chloe." Damn Fitz and his little games. In the code they used, the time mentioned indicated a meeting twelve hours later than the stated hour, meaning he had another midnight trek ahead of him. Still, after yesterday's discovery it was imperative that he talk with Fitz.

As he followed Chloe, he was distracted from his dark thoughts by the delectable line of her back and hips in the trim divided skirt. His blood pooled uncomfortably in his loins. At least today she was wearing a corset beneath her lace-trimmed white shirtwaist. Perspiration dampened his palms against the metal handlebar as his body recalled the soft curves of her unconfined figure against him.

"Ready, Aunt?" Chloe called gaily to her aunt, who was walking toward them. "This is much like riding a horse. Just swing your leg over like this." She demonstrated. "See how easy it is?"

The sight of Chloe's long leg, clad in somber black gabardine, swinging over the rear wheel tightened the muscles in Adrian's groin even more. Without a doubt he had been away from decent society for too long. Sweat gathering on his brow, he held the second vehicle for Heloise.

"I doubt I shall be able to seat myself as easily as you, my dear. Perhaps you should have brought me one of those tricycles," Heloise said as she grasped the handlebar.

"Nonsense. Those are for people with no sense of adventure." Chloe pushed off with one foot and began to pedal away from them. "You're as limber as you ever were."

Adrian braced the front wheel between his knees. "You'll be fine, m'lady." He grunted as her weight shifted the bicycle against him but wasn't surprised to see his employer in the seat, her buttoned half-boots planted on either side. He stepped aside and put one hand on the frame behind the seat and the other on the handlebar. "I'll just run alongside to steady you."

In a very short time Heloise was pedaling slowly, if shakily, along the drive. From the corner of his eye Adrian watched Chloe, her cheeks flushed with exertion and excitement, riding in a circle around them and calling encouragement. Heloise pedaled faster, and he broke into a trot. Then, as he felt her gain her balance, he removed his hands and stepped back.

Heloise's posture was as erect as if she were receiving guests for tea. Her cheeks were nearly as bright with pleasure as her niece's. She had traveled some distance away from him before he remembered that no one had told Lady Lockwood how to halt the bicycle.

With stately dignity she rode in a straight line toward the blooming forsythia hedge. Chloe came to a stop, her mouth opened, but no sound came out. A look of horror spread across her face.

The bicycle rolled into the shrubbery and tipped to the right. Heloise remained in the seat, her hat still firmly pinned in place, her hands still gripping the bar.

Molly's shriek broke the silence that followed. "I tol' ye, milady. I tol' ye yer'd bust yer arse, and now ye've gone and done it!"

Laughter bubbling in his throat, Adrian turned toward Molly to hide his smile from his employer. Behind her, two serge-clad figures, bowler hats in hand, rushed to offer assistance.

"The inspector an' 'is man from Scotland Yard 'ave come ta talk with Jane," Molly added portentously.

Chloe paced the hall outside the morning room where Heloise had settled the men from Scotland Yard. They had been questioning Jane for two hours, and Chloe wanted to fling open the door and demand to know why they were frightening the poor, browbeaten woman. If they didn't release Jane soon, she intended to wrench open the door herself and warn them that if they thought they could arrest an innocent person for her husband's crimes, they would have Chloe Lockwood to deal with.

Her fingers had already curled around the knob when the door gave beneath her fingers and Police Constable Booth, a friendly-looking man with plump, beard-covered jowls, stepped out, closing the door behind him.

Chloe demanded, "What are you doing to her? Any fool could see she knows nothing. Her husband mistreated her shamefully, and now *you're* hounding the poor woman."

Booth smiled placidly. "Here now. McCandlish was a bad apple, make no mistake, just the kind to enjoy beating a gentle thing like her. The Yard's met him several times in the past. We're just going over everything now so's she won't have to talk about him again."

"You're not going to arrest her?"

"Not bloody likely. Begging your pardon, miss," he replied, his round cheeks reddening.

"Well, why didn't you say so at the beginning? I've worried myself sick for nearly two hours over nothing." Chloe turned away in disgust, then faced Booth again. "Why are you out here in the hall then?"

"I was looking for you. Inspector Willoughby wants to ask you a few questions about finding the jewels."

"Of course." Chloe stepped around him and opened the door. Jane, her face tearstained but calm, sat in the rosewood chair next to Heloise's sewing table. Across from her, rising from the love seat, was Inspector Willoughby. He appeared to Chloe as if his breakfast had disagreed with him. "I understand you wish to speak with me," she said.

She crossed to Jane, patted her hand, and sank into a channel-back chair. "You must understand, Inspector, that I can't tell you much at all. The jewels were simply there, in those little sacks."

Willoughby sat and motioned to Booth. He waited until the constable had opened his notebook and dug a pencil from his jacket pocket before speaking. "I would appreciate your describing the precise location of the jewels when you found them. The sacks should have been left where they were until we arrived. You may have disturbed valuable clues," he added in a sour voice.

"How ridiculous. I had no idea what was in the bags until after I pulled them out. Then one fell open. There was nothing else in the cabinet that could possibly be of help."

"You'll pardon me if I suggest that you wouldn't recognize clues an experienced detective might discover."

Chloe thought it odd that he didn't mention Drury's presence at the scene. Had Heloise and Jane neglected to mention him or did the police simply discount the groom? Either way, she had no intention of enlightening them. Instead, she stiffened her spine and looked down her nose at him, imitating Heloise's mien after the inspector freed her from the forsythia hedge. She hoped she appeared every bit as intimidating. "There was nothing to discover. The papers in front were bills for seed and supplies—nothing that would tell when or why the stolen goods were placed in the cupboard."

Willoughby scowled. "What made you think the jewelry was stolen?"

"How else could a drunken farmer have such things if they weren't stolen?" She decided she liked Constable Booth much better than the inspector, who appeared to think she should cower before him. Chloe had no intention of doing so.

"That is for the police to ascertain, my lady. In the meantime, you are not to mention your suspicion outside this room. We don't want the whole village talking." He flicked a piece of thread from his trousers and pushed his celluloid cuff, which had slipped down over the back of his hand, up inside his sleeve.

Chloe bit the insides of her cheeks to keep from laughing. Such an arrogant little man and so thickheaded. "My dear Inspector, the village has talked of nothing else since two hours after the jewels were discovered."

"I shall remember to reprimand your magistrate. He should have known better than to put the word about."

"Perhaps you should reprimand my aunt instead. As soon as she heard of our discovery, she urged Sir Desmond Lowery to spread the word. She felt Mr. McCandlish's cohorts might come here after Jane if they thought she had the jewels."

"Highly irregular," Willoughby said, his fingers stroking his neat mustache in agitation. "We shall have to work around it. Did you happen to notice a lock on the cupboard?"

Realizing he had no intention of confronting her aunt, Chloe decided to be helpful. "I suspect the cupboard door was warped. It appeared to be partially open, and I didn't see a lock."

Willoughby smiled thinly. "McCandlish was inept. That may help us apprehend this set of thieves."

"Then the jewels *are* stolen property?"

"Oh, yes. On the off chance, I brought with me a list of jewelry that's been stolen over the past six months. These are the first pieces to turn up. Your McCandlish was part of a successful band of burglars."

Jane spoke up. "Don't you call him Miss Chloe's McCandlish, nor mine neither. He was a mean, drunken man, that's what he was, and I wish I'd never met him."

Willoughby and Booth left shortly afterward. Since Molly refused to serve sustenance to Scotland Yard, luncheon had been delayed, Heloise having insisted it would be the height of rudeness to eat while the two Yard men cooled their heels. Adrian had overheard the argument in the servants' tiny dining room, and two hours later he smiled at the memory of the spirited exchange while he groomed the gleaming chestnut coat of one of Heloise's carriage horses.

The chore comforted him. His shoulder was now healed, and he savored the ability to drag the currycomb over the horse's sleek coat. He paused to stretch, inhaling deeply the homely odors of hay, horse, and leather.

"Oh, please, stand just like that for a few seconds more."

Chloe's voice startled him into dropping the currycomb. When he turned, he saw her perched demurely on the wooden box containing various items needed for the horses' care. Her right hand moved deftly across the page of the sketchbook resting on her knee. "What do you think you're doing?" he demanded.

"Sketching you," she responded, her eyes intent on her work. "You're a very good subject."

Adrian rolled his eyes skyward, then approached to look at the sketch. The drawing was not of a rangy man in loose corduroy trousers and rough twill shirt. The figure was strong and lean, with long back muscles flowing into clearly defined tight buttocks and contoured thighs beneath clothing that fit as if painted on the body beneath.

Any semblance of subservience fled. The woman drove him crazy. If she'd been his sister, he would have thrown her over his knee and spanked her. "What the bloody hell do you think you're drawing?" Since she herself had just overstepped the boundary of polite behavior, he saw no reason to apologize for his language.

"You," she responded, golden lights dancing in the warm brown depths of her eyes.

Adrian fought the temptation of such adorable impudence. "No well brought up young lady should know the male body in such detail." Adrian snatched the drawing. "Can't you draw proper clothing?" He was perversely flattered, but he could hardly tell his employer's noble niece that.

Cursing the invisible shackles of his situation, he realized the sketch depicted what she saw when she looked at him. His blood raced. If he were standing in the boots to which he'd been born, the beautiful Lady Chloe Lockwood would now be flat on her back.

His impulsive thought stunned him even more than did the sketch. Adrian thrust away the idea. "If your parents saw that drawing, they'd call you home and marry you to the first old peer they could find."

Chloe snatched back the sketch and, with quick strokes, filled in the length of Adrian's hair before looking up. "Don't be prudish. I've books on sculpture at home that are *much* more detailed than this. The human body isn't distasteful. It's beautiful. And I love to watch you move. You're graceful, like a dancer." She added another detail, then looked up appraisingly.

"If I painted you in oils, I would add the light blond hairs on your arms. Why do you dye your hair?"

The query caught Adrian off guard. Moving like a marionette, he folded his cuffs into place and buttoned them. Then he met her disconcertingly acute gaze. For one brief instant he allowed himself to imagine how she would respond if he threw caution to the winds and kissed her until she was mindless.

Chapter Five

Still reeling from the surprise of her question, Adrian backed up two paces. He'd been away from his own class too long. The content of her drawing didn't surprise him so much as the idea that she had seen beneath his disguise with such unnerving accuracy. Her observation about his hair brought home to him how closely she watched him—and his own stupidity.

Nerves Adrian had forgotten he possessed surfaced. He lifted a self-conscious hand to smooth his over-long thatch behind his ear. "And if I do?"

His cold response was intended to reprimand Chloe for her rudeness, yet he felt cruel when faint color spread across her damask cheeks. "I'm sorry. That was an incredibly personal question, wasn't it?"

"How clever of you to have picked up on that," he replied with trenchant sarcasm. One way or another he had to put as much distance between them as possible.

Her fingers trembled as Chloe gathered her sketch pad and charcoals. "My mother taught me that questions of that sort are impolite, but sometimes I blurt out whatever is in my mind. I suppose I'd best leave you to your work." She rose, then paused. "Why did neither my aunt nor Jane McCandlish mention to the Yard men that you were present when we discovered the jewels?"

His nerves tightened. "Perhaps you should ask your aunt. I gather you didn't see fit to mention my presence, either."

"I try very hard to do as my aunt wishes," she answered

righteously, then brushed at a wisp of hay clinging to her skirt before continuing with her normal ebullience. "It *did* occur to me, particularly since you aren't very forthcoming about your past, that there might have been a . . . reason you would prefer Mr. McCandlish dead." She stared at him intently.

The bloody sod was hired to kill me, he nearly said, but Chloe shouldn't know that. She'd been raised in a kind, simple world, a world where violence and lies didn't exist. "I can't imagine why. You really must read less melodramatic literature. Your suspicion sounds like something straight from Miss Brontë."

Recovered, Chloe teased, "Miss Charlotte or Miss Emily? Or perhaps Miss Anne?"

Disarmed by her delighted smile, Adrian realized that the average groom shouldn't even know of the Brontë sisters, much less have read their books. It was too late to pretend ignorance. "Any of them," he growled, then added, "Lady Heloise doesn't pay me to stand here and talk with you, Miss Chloe. If there's nothing more, I must return to my duties."

"Of course. Please do get on with your duties. I wouldn't want to inconvenience you."

"Would you mind terribly if we put off arriving at the Overton house party until Thursday, Chloe? I realize we are expected Tuesday, but I prefer not to leave until those two men from Scotland Yard have returned to London."

Knowing how much her aunt despised the idea of a house party anywhere in the world, much less at the Overton estate, Chloe wondered if she could convince her to cancel the obligation her mother had asked her to fulfill. Even a shortened attendance held no appeal; life here was much too interesting. "Of course not, Aunt. I've found several interesting views to sketch, so I shall have no difficulty entertaining myself."

Her words were uttered with honesty. Drury was a fascinating subject. She would spend the better part of every day simply looking at him, if that could be arranged. "Besides, there are your bicycling lessons to attend to."

"To be sure," her aunt responded, casting her a shrewd look before placing her dessert fork in the center of her flowered Limoges plate. "This morning's outing was but a mixed success."

Chloe grinned widely. "Those two detectives *would* arrive just as you rode into the shrubbery. I promise, tomorrow I'll teach you how to apply the brakes. Then you'll feel much more comfortable."

"I cannot imagine why I never inquired about that small detail before I embarked on that amazing vehicle."

"Because you were having a good time," Chloe said. "Come now, admit it. You were as eager as a child to learn."

Rising, Heloise smiled thinly. "I must admit to a certain . . . zest for the experience." Her smile vanished, and she said abruptly, "The vicar, Robert Shadwell, is calling this evening to discuss an outing for the young people from the village. Do you wish to join us?"

"Another time, Aunt. All the excitement of the past few days has tired me. I intend to read until I fall asleep." Chloe rose and pushed her carved rosewood chair back into place. She refused to meet her aunt's eyes; falsehoods had never come easily for her, and the keen old lady would know she was lying.

"I have always found Mr. Lytton's writings conducive to slumber." Heloise joined her on the way to the hall. "His complete works are in the library, should you require them."

The yawn Chloe covered with her fingers was not assumed; the past two days had been exhausting, and tonight she intended to stay awake well past midnight. Lytton would send her to sleep for a week. "I plan to reread *Jane Eyre*. Something today reminded me how much I enjoyed it." She leaned forward to kiss her aunt's cheek softly, then climbed the stairs to her room.

In spite of her determination to remain awake, she dozed off soon after climbing onto the bed. Clad in her black divided skirt and a dark blouse she'd changed into—minus the blasted corset—she had settled herself atop the counterpane, pillows propped behind her shoulders, the gas lamp next to her bed at its lowest point and the draperies nearly closed. A light in her room would be noticed by anyone on the grounds.

The squeak of the stable door roused Chloe. Still groggy, she wasted several seconds determining why she had gone to bed fully clothed. Then, senses alert, she crept to the window, arriving just as a shadow flowed toward the corner of the stable and disappeared into the darkness beyond the paddock fence.

Chloe ran quickly from her room in her stockinged feet. Half-boots in her hand, she padded silently down the stairs. The service door latch opened without a sound as she slipped out, and she paused only to step into her boots and fasten them.

She took the shortest route to the stable, having reconnoitered the area earlier in the day. The hedgerow beyond the paddock swayed as she reached the corner of the building. The fourth-quarter moon gave off such feeble light that she wondered if she had imagined the shift in the shrubbery, but she had little choice; she could see no other indication of life. She set out.

Dew wet the hem of her skirt as she entered the long grass beyond the hedgerow and peered across the field in time to catch a flicker of movement at the edge of the stand of birches across the meadow. She paused to give her quarry time to penetrate the trees before risking the move across open ground.

As she slipped between the ghostly tree trunks, Chloe had a strange sense of being followed. She paused and looked back, only to realize that the swaying trees cast ghostly shadows that trailed closely at her heels.

She was nearly through the grove, peering forward at what she hoped was Drury's figure in the distance, when the shadow disappeared over the steep bank of the stream. At that moment her skirt caught on a long bramble growing across her path. Hoping to escape the thorns' grasp, she quickened her pace. But the prickly arm stretched to its full length, then jerked her to such an abrupt stop that she lost her footing and fell, striking her head against a tree trunk.

Adrian finished his talk with Fitz's agent quickly. Something filled the air tonight—as if strings of electricity wove around his body. He felt edgy, filled with a sense of urgency.

He paused at the top of the sloping bank to scan the open meadow ahead of him. Seeing no movement, he eased across, his thoughts filled with the report he'd just received.

The information trail behind Ian McCandlish seemed to disappear in the bureaucracy surrounding intelligence operations, of which Fitz's branch was small and obscure, if vital part. No one seemed to know the exact source. Frustration ate at him—the same thing had happened when Fitz had attempted to discover who had leaked his identity to the Armenians. *What a mess!* Fitz had exercised his option to call in help from other sections when needed, which accounted for the small army that had descended on Upper Whiddlesby, and Adrian felt nearly suffocated by their presence. But it was necessary. Someone from his own government wanted him dead.

His thoughts raced so furiously he nearly entered the narrow wooded area without reconnoitering. During the past few days his finely-honed abilities had deteriorated to the point of carelessness.

The birch grove was occupied.

The husky feminine voice muttering words no polite young lady should know, much less utter, brought him up short. In spite of his dismay at Chloe's presence, laughter rose in his throat. Lady Chloe Lockwood was in a serious funk.

"Well, double damn and blast! Let go, you bloody monster! Bad enough that I banged my head, but you . . ." Her voice trailed off for a moment, then rose in volume. "If I ever get loose, I'm coming back tomorrow with a pair of clippers and sever your sodding thorns from your arms. Then I'll cut you off at the ground!"

Silence reigned, and Adrian drew nearer. He heard a sharp exclamation, followed by a choice selection of colorful stable curses, before deciding to announce his presence. He called softly, "Miss Chloe . . . are you all right?" Surely if she could swear so healthily she wasn't injured.

"This is all your fault." A thrashing sound met his ears. "If you didn't sneak out and wander the countryside at night, I wouldn't have to follow you."

Adrian wasn't sure whether to be angry or to laugh. His pride in his ability to slip unnoticed from the premises was shattered—yet another casualty of the presence of the intrepid young lady now wreaking vengeance on the local plant life. If not for the carnivorous bramble bush, Chloe would have followed him to his rendezvous. She might even have overheard their conversation, which would have led to an un-

comfortable explanation laced with lies he doubted such a
perspicacious and determined young lady would accept.

Adrian wished the very thought of Lady Chloe Lockwood
didn't cause his heart to speed up and his body to harden.
Her insatiable curiosity and her unreasonable anger toward
the plant filled him with tenderness. At all costs he must remain the gentleman he'd been before foolishly deciding that
serving Her Majesty's government would be a lark.

His eyes were accustomed to the darkness, and he had no
difficulty avoiding the brambles. And he could have located
Chloe by his body's stunning awareness of her presence.

Cautiously, so as to avoid unnecessary contact, he traced
the guilty branches from the sprawling bush to where they
had attached themselves to her clothing. "You *have* rather
entangled yourself, haven't you, love?" The casual endear-
ment slipped out without conscious thought.

"I didn't do any of this. The brambles did," she declared,
jerking at her skirt. "One of the bloody things caught me and
knocked me down, and that tree over there reached out and
bumped me on the head. As I lay there helpless, the other
bramble runners joined in."

Her self-deprecating humor was Adrian's undoing. He
dropped his hands from the offending vine and laughed.

"It's all very well for you to laugh. *You* weren't the one
wandering around in the dark without the faintest idea
where you were going. And don't imagine that I shall apologize for following you, because I have no intention of doing
so. But I still don't know where you went." Chloe peered up
at him hopefully and added, "I don't suppose you'd like to
tell me?"

Laughter cleansed Adrian of the bitterness that had filled
him for so long. Longing took its place. He touched her cheek
with gentle fingers. "No, brat, and it won't do you a bit of

good to demand to know." Removing his hand from further temptation, he busied himself freeing her skirt.

Once finished, he helped her to stand, then cupped her chin in his hand, fighting the urge to bury his face in the fragrant, tangled mass of her hair. "Show me where you bumped your head."

Chloe grasped his wrist with slender fingers and moved his hand to her scalp. "Right there. Ouch!"

Her silky curls flowed around Adrian's wrist, the contact causing the hairs on his arm to rise. Careful to touch only her head, he explored the swelling with his fingertips, then asked, "Are you sure you feel all right? No dizziness?" Immersed in solicitude and self-denial, he didn't bargain for his companion's resourcefulness.

"I do feel dizzy," she said, then promptly sagged against him.

For the second time in a week Adrian found himself the sole support of Chloe's slim, corsetless form. Lost in the bliss of her nearness, his arms instinctively clasped her close. As he lowered his head, her lips, parted and artless, were there to meet his.

Adrian groaned when her arms slid around his neck and her body nestled against his racing heart. Her lips were soft and eager and tasted of mint. So did the interior of her mouth, he discovered when she responded to the exploration of his searching tongue.

When she shuddered with pleasure, Adrian's body hardened from his head to his toes. In turn, he moved his hands restlessly down her back, learning the tender curve from her waist down over her buttocks. Before he could pull her hips against the raging heat of his loins she pressed closer of her own will, a little moan of satisfaction sounding low in her throat. He discovered firsthand that although Chloe lacked experience, her enthusiasm was boundless.

Hands shaking, he seized her shoulders and dragged his lips away from hers. "Miss Chloe, we shouldn't be . . ."

Not relinquishing her hold on his neck, Chloe asked innocently, "Didn't I do it right? I've never been kissed before. Does everyone kiss like that? With their mouths open? It's really very nice."

In spite of the earthshaking nature of the last few minutes, Adrian laughed. Against his better judgment, he pulled her close and inhaled deeply the scent of primroses—sweet, open, forthright English primroses. "Believe me, you did everything right," he groaned, "but . . ."

Chloe cut off his warning by burrowing against his achingly aroused body as if she wanted to become part of him and kissing his jaw softly. "Again, please."

Undone, Adrian lowered his head. He felt her smile of satisfaction against his lips and lost all capacity to think. The deprivations of the past two years, coupled with the frustration that had gripped him since Lady Chloe Lockwood burst into his narrow orbit, increased his greed as he drank from her eager lips and explored her exquisitely feminine body.

Her soft breast fit into his hand as if made for this moment. Frustrated by the barriers of blouse and chemise, he fumbled with the tiny bone buttons. He spread the material with one hand, his lips never leaving hers.

At the touch of his hard, callused fingers against her flesh, Chloe rose to her toes, offering herself more fully. She murmured against his lips, "Drury."

The sound of the assumed name penetrated his passion-numbed brain. *Damn it! She doesn't even know who she's kissing!* Adrian wrenched his lips free and rebuttoned her blouse with unsteady fingers. Then he stepped back, holding her at arm's length.

★ ★ ★ ★ ★

Chloe felt as if she had just run down a flight of stairs and discovered the last three steps missing. One moment she was drowning in the exquisite pleasure of Drury's kiss and the delightful explorations of his lean, knowing fingers, delirious with the joy of being in his arms. Now he held her away from him with shaking hands. "Drury, why did you stop?" She despised the tremor in her voice.

"Kissing you was undoubtedly the second most stupid thing I have ever done in my life."

His harsh voice and labored breathing confused Chloe even more. "What can be stupid about something so beautiful and perfect?" She reached for him, but he evaded her hands. "You aren't being an ass and remembering you're my aunt's groom, are you? Things like that aren't important. I know you haven't always been a servant."

Adrian groaned. "That has nothing and everything to do with this whole bloody mess. Your aunt trusts me. I owe her more than you could ever guess, and this is the worst possible way to repay her." He paused, breathed deeply, and continued sternly, "And just what in the hell do you think you're doing, anyway?"

"What do you mean?"

"Did no one ever tell you that well-behaved young ladies don't hang all over grooms, don't racket around the countryside in the dark, and don't have vocabularies that would send the stable lads home crying to their mothers? Where in God's name did you learn to swear like that? You sounded like a tart from the Haymarket. Why hasn't someone taken you in hand before this?"

Chloe bit her trembling lower lip. No one had ever before questioned her behavior; but then, she'd never before behaved as she had over the past few days. Since she'd leaped from the carriage into Drury's arms, she'd felt a strange compulsion to be with this fascinating, mysterious man who had just spoken to her as if she were a spoiled, reckless romp.

The truth tumbled from her lips. "I *do* know how to behave, but when I'm near you, I don't seem to have any choice. That day I arrived, my whole . . . everything in me responded to you as if you were the . . . the destination. Didn't you ever hear of meeting your destiny?"

"I told you before, you've been allowed to read too many romantic novels," he muttered.

Chloe heard the strain in his voice. Moments earlier he had been as aroused as she. "Actually, I've read very few novels. Mostly I read science, history, geography—anything that interests me. But people are more intriguing, don't you think? I watch and ask questions . . . and then I dream. Didn't you ever see a married man and woman and wonder how they met, what drew them together, what keeps them together? Sometimes I see strangers on the street and build whole lives for them. Exciting lives, with adventures . . . nothing like my own ordinary existence."

"And what have you imagined for me?"

The pain in his voice nearly broke Chloe's heart. Raising her hand to his cheek, she felt the muscle along his jaw tighten, as if he were afraid to hear her answer. "You've been difficult for me to assign a past to. Sometimes you're most ungroomlike, and then you overdo the entire image.

"You have beautiful eyes, but they're sad. Other times you look fierce, as if you're searching for a certain face. As if when you recognize it, you'll do something positively violent. You even stand differently when you get that look. Then again, I've noticed you fade into the landscape, even though I know that you're right in front of me. You would make a wonderful spy."

"Don't ever say that again," he ordered.

"What? That you act the way I imagine a spy would be-have?" She clapped her hands together. "That's it! You're a spy!"

"Oh, God help me," Adrian beseeched the heavens as he leaned against the nearest tree trunk. "You have just called me the lowest form of life."

"I'm right, aren't I," she declared, then added irrepress-ibly, "Aunt Heloise said I wasn't to make difficulties for you. Is your life in danger?"

"No."

Chloe decided he was lying and opened her mouth to pur-sue the subject when a rustling in the underbrush some dis-tance away startled her into peering suspiciously in that direction. "Let's go back, Drury. I don't like it here very much."

Recalled to their surroundings, he took her hand and led her back to the path. "I can't believe I've become so careless. Nearly as careless as that creature over there making his way home after a night of foraging."

She threaded her fingers through his. "Back at Benning-ton Hall, I spent my time reading and watching people. Since he's the heir, my brother, Lionel, dogged my father's foot-steps, learning to manage the estate, while I was expected to learn from my mother. She's a dear, but her only concern was that I behave like a lady. Do you know how boring it is to spend half a day planning an ensemble to wear for two hours?"

Adrian assisted her over a low stone wall. "I hesitate to point this out, but her lessons don't appear to have taken."

Chloe's sharp ears caught the wry undertones in his voice. "I know very well how to behave. It's easy to be stupid and prissy. But I ignore the rules whenever I feel like it. That's how I learned all those splendid curses. I hid in the stable and listened to the grooms and stableboys. Did you know . . . ?"

Adrian's hand covered her mouth. "I prefer not to learn the details of the lives and loves of your father's servants."

"*I* found them most educational," she said, her lips curving in remembrance of the day the head groom had confided to another groom a detailed description of his seduction of the undercook.

"I'm sure."

She heard the laughter behind his dry response. She wished he would kiss her again, but the determined set of his shoulders told her he had no intention of resuming that delightful activity. Now wasn't the time to attempt to change his mind, although she would definitely give the problem her attention very soon. The feel of his lips and the lean, hard strength of him pressed against her and beneath her hands had only made her yearn for more. A shiver passed through her at the memory. Chloe wanted to be with him in daylight, when she could read the passion in the endless blue depths of his eyes and see his expression as he focused all his attention on her. She wanted to touch his bare skin. She wanted to . . .

"I'll walk you to the service door, and you're to go straight to your room. Quietly. I won't return to the stable until your light flickers."

There was no mistaking the command in his voice. "If I don't signal, will you come up to make sure I'm all right?" she teased.

"No!" he answered roughly. "Oh, God, I don't envy your aunt the task of chaperoning you," he added in a strangled voice.

Before Chloe stepped over the threshold she whispered, "Maybe she'll ask you for help. Wouldn't that be delightful?"

Moments later, watching the dramatic flashes of light

from her window, Adrian imagined "chaperoning" Chloe Lockwood. The thought of it brought on both cold chills and an overheated libido. He had come close to taking more extreme liberties there among the birch trees, brambles or not. With a frustrated shrug of his shoulders, he traversed the silent formal garden and stable yard to his rooms.

She had been yielding and eager in his arms, as if she would trust him no matter what. The only thing that had saved him was her use of that damned name. For six months he had used his considerable skill to become a facsimile of a servile groom, but in less than a week, she blinded him to who he was supposed to be and why.

Someone had been hired to kill him. Now that the first assassin had been murdered, no doubt a replacement had already been selected to take his place. Tonight Fitz's man had shared his suspicion that one of the Armenian conspirators was in the area. Even *they* had found him. He was a target in plain sight, waiting to see which archer would hit the bull's-eye. And he could do nothing about it.

He should have remained at the shipyards. Damn fate for his bloody injury! He couldn't even see his cousin Bess; any contact whatsoever with his family was dangerous. Adrian slammed the door behind him and lit a candle. He watched the wavering flame. "God must hate me," he muttered despondently.

Now Chloe Lockwood had been thrown into the mix. In her quest for adventure, she had no respect for convention or propriety. And he wanted her more than he'd ever imagined wanting a woman. The dark-haired beauty was like that candle flame, a light glowing in the darkness of his existence. As he was tugging off his boots, the realization struck him. What if the assassins thought Chloe was more to him than merely his employer's niece? She would be in just as much danger as he.

Chapter Six

During breakfast the next morning, Chloe watched her aunt from beneath lowered lids, waiting for the right time to speak. She had spent the night tossing and turning and gazing into the darkness, reliving every touch, every caress of Drury's hands. Her body felt alive, her flesh tingled, and she wasn't the least tired. She had also made a decision. There remained only one problem—choosing a diplomatic way to approach her aunt. She toyed with the spoon from the marmalade pot.

"You're very quiet this morning, Chloe. Why do I have the feeling you intend to open a discussion about something unpleasant?"

The spoon dropped from Chloe's nerveless fingers and clattered against the plate beneath the flowered marmalade pot. She deliberately widened her eyes as she met her aunt's knowing gaze and blurted, "Must we really attend that odious house party? The Overtons' guests from London only want to escape the crush of social engagements for a week. Surely they won't miss my presence."

Heloise bit into her muffin and chewed thoughtfully before finishing her tea. "Your mother most particularly instructed me to accompany you to this function. I should be remiss if I went against her wishes." She stood, dropping her heavy linen napkin beside her plate. Her voice softened as she continued, "I have no more interest in those people than you do. However, you must mingle in society, if for no other reason than to learn to separate people of true quality from those who are unworthy."

She walked toward the door and paused before adding, "I shall meet you for our bicycle lesson when you have finished your breakfast."

Chloe grimaced at her teacup. Damn and blast. Who wanted to attend a boring house party with uninteresting strangers, when the most exciting man she had ever imagined meeting was here in Upper Whiddlesby?

The interlude in the birch grove had been a revelation. Internal wisdom told her that although she would sound like a naive little fool if she spoke the words aloud, a mystical bond connected her with Drury. There had been pain in his voice, and she desperately wanted to know the source, because she had felt it as keenly as if it had been her own. Why had her use of his name caused such a strong reaction?

Her heart beat faster at the memory of what had preceded his abrupt withdrawal. Warmth rose in her cheeks. Chloe hurried to finish her breakfast so she could see Drury.

Adrian returned the gelding's left hoof to the ground and eased himself out of the stall as Heloise entered the stable. "There you are, Drury. You will not be required to assist with the bicycle lesson this morning. I have some errands for you to attend to in the village."

Suspicious of her expression and tone of voice, Adrian replied cautiously, "As you wish, m'lady."

"And I have decided *you* will drive my coach to this Overton affair, not Peebles." Although she spoke authoritatively, her eyes were sympathetic.

Adrian was appalled. "I can't be seen there. I belong to the same clubs as Richard Overton." He sensed some purpose behind her change in plans and wondered what her devious mind was planning now.

"Don't be ridiculous. No one looks at servants. Their stables will probably be overflowing, so if you wish, you may deliver us and then repair to a nearby inn until we leave. Thomas will of course accompany us to protect you."

"I don't like it."

"If you must know, I abhor the thought of the whole affair. Felicia Overton was a simpleton when she was a girl, and I feel sure she has not improved with age. However, I promised Maude I would accompany Chloe, and therefore I shall."

"Someone will be sure to recognize me," Adrian insisted, his heart thudding in his throat.

Heloise favored him with a disdainful look. "You overestimate your importance. When you were declared dead, everyone relegated you to oblivion. However, you may adopt some sort of disguise if you wish. Nothing too bizarre, mind." Her features softened. "I'm convinced you would be in more danger here during my absence. No one would expect you to expose yourself to your own class."

He nodded reluctant agreement, capitulating in a battle of wills with the redoubtable old lady. He offered lightly, "Perhaps I can locate a false mustache and beard."

"Nothing too bushy, if you please." Heloise directed a sharp gaze at him as she turned to leave, "By the way, I prefer that Chloe not roam the countryside with you at night."

Two hours later Adrian returned from the village. As he entered the curving drive, he was conscious of Thomas riding some distance behind, his squat figure bobbing uncomfortably on his mount, four string bags bulging with packages fastened behind his saddle. Adrian carried several himself.

He had come to appreciate the humor of his stolid bodyguard's presence. Thomas's one weakness worked to Adrian's advantage. He slept soundly, rather like a contented babe, in the tack room, blissfully unaware of his charge's nighttime excursions.

On the other hand, Lady Heloise knew everything that occurred within her orbit, not just during daylight, but at night also. It was probably just as well, since she had the unenviable job of chaperoning the spirited Lady Chloe.

As if he had conjured them up, Chloe and Heloise pedaled their bicycles slowly toward him. He guided his bay gelding to the verge. At the sight of Chloe's slender form, frustration gripped him. She turned to her aunt and said something, and her bubbling laughter rang out, reminding him how innocent she was, in spite of the remarkably diverse information she'd stuffed into her head. He knew too well what type of young men frequented the Overton set, and Chloe would be out of her depth, and he would be unable to protect her.

Adrian tightened his hold on the reins. If he ever got out of this mess, he would seize control of his life, and God help anyone who got in the way.

Heloise demonstrated her newly acquired mastery of the bicycle's brake, then looked his way benignly. "There you are, Drury. I trust you had no difficulty locating Sir Desmond to notify him of our approaching absence."

Adrian avoided looking at Chloe, who had greeted his arrival with flushed cheeks and an eager smile. She looked adorable. "No, ma'am. He promised to ride over each day." From the corner of his eye he saw Chloe's lips droop. *Damn it! It would never do for me to greet her the way she seemed to expect.*

"Fine. Then we shall depart Thursday morning. I leave it to you to make the arrangements we discussed this morning."

"Very good, m'lady." On top of his frustration over the situation with Chloe, the muscles in his jaw ached from biting back a suggestion of what Heloise could do with her high-handed assumption that he wasn't competent to protect himself if left to his own devices. "Will you be needing me now?"

"We are progressing quite well, are we not, Chloe?"

"Yes. We're doing splendidly all by ourselves. We don't need anyone." Her voice was aggressively cheerful.

Adrian had no difficulty interpreting Chloe's response. She was miffed. At least *he* remembered his status. An errant breeze brought the scent of primroses to his nostrils. Ignoring his body's enthusiastic response, he said, "Then I'll be in the stable should you need me."

From the corner of her eye Chloe watched Drury ride down the drive. The idiot had all but pulled his forelock. She felt an urge to find the heaviest object within reach and bring it down on his head. Surely he could have given her the tiniest of smiles. Was the vitality and strength she had held in her arms last night an illusion? Just now he could have been a . . . stick, for all anyone knew. She gripped her handlebar and looked up to meet her aunt's shrewd gaze.

"You recall our discussion concerning Drury, do you not, Chloe?"

"You told me to leave him alone and not to pry, Aunt. It occurs to me that your advice was excellent, and I have every intention of following it," she answered. "Shall we finish our ride to the road?"

A week later, Adrian drove the empty traveling coach away from the Overton estate. As soon as he was out of sight, he reached up to wipe perspiration from his forehead.

The oversized wool livery jacket Heloise had furnished was entirely too warm for the balmy spring day. Sweat trickled down the middle of his back, and he wanted nothing more than to rip the bloody rag off and drop it into the nearest ditch. The stiffened burgundy fabric hung below his hips, and the upstanding collar nearly reached his ears, disguising not only his body but the lower part of his face, if he tucked his chin down far enough. And he had, much to Thomas's amusement. His physical discomfort was only one link of many in the unending chain of pain he'd experienced the last week.

Chloe's recent coldness hurt far more than his fear of recognition; since that encounter on the carriage drive, she had treated him like a servant. But wasn't that what he wanted? A dead man who had seen too much of the seamy, dishonest side of life even before his demise had no business becoming entangled with a girl who greeted every day with the excitement of a kitten on its first journey through a meadow, a girl who was fresh and young and beautiful and real—and in as much danger as he was, if his enemies discovered she was important to him.

He had no business even thinking of Chloe. Their encounter in the stand of birches had been comparable to offering food to a starving man and then snatching it away after his first bite. She would lead a much happier, more fulfilled life if she never saw him again. Holding her in his arms had been like grasping a tiny bit of heaven, like opening a magical golden gate into a kingdom overflowing with fulfilled dreams. Now the gate had swung closed in his face. "Dead men have nothing to offer the living," he muttered to himself.

Automatically curbing the tendency of the lead horse to break stride, Adrian continued brooding. Even the danger stalking him had increased. At last count, two separate groups appeared to be intent on making his demise a reality. The Armenian was no surprise; Fitz's minions would see to him. But Ian McCandlish had nearly slipped past their vigilance, and no one had yet discovered who had hired the man or, worse, if a replacement had been sent.

The stupid sod had deserved to be killed. As far as Adrian was concerned, any assassin so inept that he called attention to himself by drinking too much and beating his wife deserved whatever punishment that fell his way.

As he guided the horses into the courtyard of the unobtrusive inn, he mumbled an addendum to the words he'd muttered earlier. "And dead men have no futures." A man pursued by assassins had very little hope of returning to the land of the living. Dreaming of a life filled with love and happiness was foolish.

"Lady Heloise! I can scarcely believe my eyes! Although I'm sure poor dear Maude is suffering excruciating pain, that particular ill wind has brought us a miracle! It sent *you* to us!" Felicia Overton kissed the air beside Heloise's cheek before turning to Chloe. "And little Chloe! It seems only yesterday you and your brother were toddling about, dressed alike!"

Chloe promised herself that if her hostess continued to deliver each sentence as an exclamation, she would leave before nightfall. Not knowing how to respond to so much feverish gaiety, she said brightly, "Yes, here I am."

Felicia Overton gushed, "I'm sure each and every eligible young man present will be delighted to hear you are finally in the market for a husband! One can't imagine why your father has kept you buried in the country all this time! In another year you would have been quite too old to have any claim to beauty."

"Then I must be grateful to him, mustn't I?" Chloe answered, her annoyance growing.

Felicia grasped Heloise's arm, ignoring Chloe's reply.

"I'm sure you'll require a rest after such a long journey, Lady Heloise! Let me assist you to your room and send along a maid to make you comfortable. The others are out and about, but they'll be back soon, since we're keeping country hours for meals."

Heloise pulled away, drew herself up, and fixed a glacial gaze on her hostess. "I am most capable of climbing the stairs by myself, Felicia. If you wish to accompany me, then you may do so. However, I do not require a nap. I intend to walk out my stiffness from riding in the coach in your gallery. I've heard many compliments on the paintings Richard's family has accumulated."

Mention of the gallery brought an angry flush to Felicia's rouged cheeks. "Walking is all you'll do there. Only those musty old portraits of Richard's ancestors remain. The Gainsboroughs and everything else of value were stolen two months ago, along with my favorite jewels! One might almost think the thieves knew exactly where to find our most precious belongings!"

"How unfortunate, Lady Overton. What jewelry was taken?" Chloe asked.

"My ruby necklace. The stones were set in a gold filigree collar." Her thin, restless hands drew an outline of the piece. "The necklace was not only extremely valuable, it was an anniversary gift from my dearest Richard!"

From the description, Chloe recognized the necklace from the cache in Jane McCandlish's home. She realized Scotland Yard must not yet have notified her hostess that her jewels had been recovered. "Such a great loss for you."

"A most disagreeable man from Scotland Yard informed me the setting had probably already been broken up and the stones sold. As for the paintings, I'm sure we shall never see *them* again! Over the last two years nearly everyone I know has been burglarized. One would think the Yard would be capable of catching such terrible people! What do we pay them for?"

Chloe watched her hostess's hand caress her throat, as if recalling the cool caress of the gold and rubies, which must have disguised the signs of aging beneath her chin.

"What, indeed? This is England, after all," Heloise said, directing a quelling glance at Chloe.

"Chloe, I understand we're to play a role in matchmaking this weekend," Felicia said coyly.

"I've no idea what you're talking about, Lady Overton," Chloe said.

"You needn't be shy with me, my dear. When your arrival was delayed, I felt sure you had already been alerted that Lord Roderick would not arrive until tomorrow morning."

A horrible suspicion formed in her mind. Chloe looked at her aunt, who refused to meet her eyes. "Actually, I have no idea about whom you are speaking, and I know nothing of his delay. But then, the village where my aunt lives is quite remote." She patted her lips delicately, as if disguising a yawn. "I am much more weary from traveling than I thought. Aunt, won't you come up with me? A short rest before dinner will be much healthier for you than walking in the gallery." She gave her aunt a hard look.

Heloise smiled thinly. "Perhaps Chloe is right, Felicia. I believe a brief nap is what I need."

Felicia turned and with quick, nervous steps, led them toward the stairs. "I'm sure your trunks have already been taken to your rooms. Colfax is most efficient about such matters."

After leading them up the curving staircase, Felicia motioned them to the right, down a broad, carpeted hall. "Your rooms are in the west wing. The afternoon sun is so delightful at this time of year! I'm sure, at your age, you prefer not to be awakened by the sunrise." She opened a paneled oak door and waved them into their suite of rooms.

Once the maid finished unpacking and left, Chloe rapped on the connecting door. Not waiting for a reply, she turned the knob and entered. Heloise stood before the window, gazing down into the garden. "And just who is Lord Roderick? Come now, Aunt. Was this why you were so determined to chaperon me here?"

Heloise turned from the window, her features composed. "As you know, I live my life by my own rules, but that does not apply to you. I cannot interfere with your parents' wishes. The Earl of Twyford approached your father last winter concerning a match for you with his son, Roderick."

Chloe made no effort to stifle her outburst. "No! You, of all people, should understand! An arranged marriage, without so much as a word to me. How . . . gothic!"

"You're leaping to conclusions. The final decision will be yours and yours only. When you were but a baby, I made your father promise that your wishes would be paramount in any marriage contract." Heloise's face softened in a way Chloe had never seen. "My own father attempted to force me into a match I despised. When I refused, he washed his hands of me. I have never regretted my decision, but I did not want you to suffer the same fate. I didn't tell you about the offer because I felt you should meet the boy with no prejudices."

"Then who told Felicia . . . ?" Chloe's thoughts whirled.

"Lord Roderick is most likely to have done so. I must say, this colors my expectations of him."

"Then I'm free to refuse him or anyone else who doesn't please me?" Chloe demanded hopefully.

"Within reason, my dear. I've done the best I can for you," her aunt replied sympathetically.

* * * * *

That evening at dinner, Chloe toyed with the rich trifle on her dessert plate. Peeking sideways through lowered lashes, she catalogued once again her blond dinner partner's features. He was pleasant, with excellent manners, and when Felicia had partnered him with her for dinner, he assented with good grace.

Throughout the meal, Chloe had noticed his gaze straying in the direction of the tiny, reddish-haired beauty seated across the table. The glances that pouting damsel sent her way had been arctic. Chloe wondered how she could inform the girl that David Mountjoy, although attractive enough, didn't appeal to her in the least.

What fascinated her was the sense of familiarity she felt for her dinner partner. Something about the set of his eyes and the line of his jaw nagged at her, but she was unable to make a connection. She was clever about keying in on facial similarities, but tonight she was baffled, even though she had concentrated, she could not recollect who David Mountjoy resembled. Lost in her thoughts, she failed to hear his question when he spoke.

"I say, Lady Chloe, you seem miles away. Am I such dull company?"

Caught, Chloe offered him an apologetic smile. "I'm so very sorry. Please forgive me, but you remind me of someone, only I can't seem to recall who that might be. I'm afraid I was mentally sifting through all my acquaintances, which aren't very numerous, in hopes I'd remember." She placed her hand on his arm apologetically. "The name will probably come to me in the night, and I'll realize there couldn't possibly be a connection." The arm beneath her fingers tensed, and she felt, rather than saw, nervousness in his blue gaze. Chloe removed her hand quickly, amused by the relief she saw on his face. "I promise not to think of it again."

"Can't imagine who it could be. There's not much left of my branch of the family. Just several female second cousins. The only male of my generation died tragically a few years ago, which is why I'm in line for the earldom."

"Oh, dear. Had you been close?" As a child she had listened to her mother's friends gossip about unexpected deaths and inheritances in the most distressingly shallow way. Inheriting was everything—never mind the poor person who had died or the bereaved loved ones. The whole idea depressed her, reinforcing her belief that she couldn't fit in with people who thought that way.

"My cousin Adrian was one of my favorite people, and his family has always been very generous to my mother and me. They've put up a good show, but I know they're terribly broken up. Actually, I feel rather guilty about the whole thing." He grimaced. "I never cared much for titles or rank, although I can't deny I look forward to the income from the estate."

Felicia stood at that moment and signaled for the ladies to withdraw, and Chloe smiled up at David as he held the back of her chair. Gathering the pale pink silk folds of her skirt, she rose to her feet. "I know how you feel. I'm Aunt Heloise's heir, and I hope she lives forever."

The understanding in his eyes warmed her as she made her exit, but a cool voice close to her ear dispelled the glow. "You'll do well to concentrate on Lord Roderick Derwent and forget David Mountjoy, Lady Chloe. He and I have an understanding."

She turned and encountered the cold blue gaze of the girl from across the table. Too forthright to pretend misunderstanding, she said, "How fortunate for you, Miss . . . Fenton, is it not? I feel sure that if I were planning to attach someone, Mr. Mountjoy would be an attractive candidate. As to this

Derwent person, he might suit me, and he might not. I'm in no hurry to marry, but you obviously are. You're perfectly welcome to him."

"You don't fool me for a minute with that game. Women who pretend disinterest are the most dangerous." Lelia Fenton's small teeth showed briefly in a tight smile. She stepped back for Chloe to precede her into the drawing room. "I guard what is mine, no matter what is necessary to do so."

Chloe looked beyond her adversary's shoulder and encountered her aunt's sardonically amused gaze. The scene was so melodramatic that for a moment she thought she might giggle. "Please don't exert yourself needlessly, Miss Fenton."

"There you are, Lady Chloe!" Felicia's light voice caught her attention. "Do you play or sing? I'm attempting to arrange an impromptu concert to entertain the gentlemen."

"If I were to sing or play, I fear your drawing room would empty very quickly, Lady Overton. Perhaps Miss Fenton is more accomplished."

As Felicia's feverish gaze shifted to Lelia's pale face, Chloe slipped away with Heloise close behind.

"What on earth provoked that little scene?" Heloise demanded.

"I don't think I enjoy society, Aunt." The encounter had shaken Chloe more than she realized. Her cheeks were warm, and she knew her color was high. What on earth could she have done to deserve such an attack? "She accused me of trying to steal David Mountjoy from her, and all I did was sit with him at dinner. At Lady Overton's insistence."

Heloise's bright, knowing gaze swept the room from their vantage point on the carved love seat. "Felicia is mischief-making. David Mountjoy is the new heir to the Warnham earldom, which comes with a great deal of entailed property.

Lelia's father is a commoner who has risen to a post of some importance at Whitehall, I believe." Her eyes swung to Chloe. "Many will claim that noble birth may not matter as it once did, but for Miss Fenton, marrying into the Mountjoy family is a step upward."

"I can't imagine why she should care, unless she's unsure of him. Or if all she's interested in is the title."

An amused smile curved Heloise's lips. "The only reason you feel titles are of no importance is that you are accustomed to your family's status. When one is born to rank and privilege, one tends to forget how out of reach they are for those who don't possess them. You've read your history books. Surely you know people have even murdered for wealth and status."

Chapter Seven

The next morning, Chloe went down to breakfast reconciled to the prospect of a day spent listening to meaningless conversation about events and people in which she had no interest. The previous evening had been interminable. After the men had joined the ladies, Lelia had made a great production of appropriating David Mountjoy and hanging on his arm like a pet pug, much to Chloe's amusement.

Even more entertaining were Felicia's efforts to pry David loose from the clinging young beauty. As her hostess passed Chloe, she had whispered in a shaking voice, "I was counting on you to detach David from that poisonous nothing. He's much too good for the little trollop."

Pretending innocence, Chloe had whispered back, "I thought I was here for the purpose of meeting Lord Roderick." Felicia had gone on her way pouting.

Chloe felt rebellious. As far as she was concerned, she'd been brought here under false pretenses, and a tiny corner of her heart resented her aunt's complicity. The only entertaining aspect of the whole affair was that when her erstwhile suitor finally arrived, he would have no idea that his prospective bride was measuring him against a standard set by her aunt's groom.

As for David Mountjoy, he seemed nice enough, and he was certainly handsome. His mane of dark gold hair glinted in the candlelight, but even though his lean features were intriguingly aligned, he held no attraction for her. She wished she could recall who it was he resembled.

Two plump maids had just placed an array of silver serving pieces over the spirit lamps when she entered the dining room. No other guests had yet come down, which suited her fractious mood. She filled her plate and settled herself at the far side of the table.

When her aunt entered, Chloe teased, "I've taken all the best bits. You'll have to make do with my leavings."

Suspending her china plate over the scrambled eggs, Heloise contemplated the kedgeree, as if unable to decide between the two. "Felicia may be a scatterbrain, but she at least has the sense to employ a decent chef. Dinner last night was superior."

Darting a look at the door, Chloe replied in a low voice, "The food may be the only enjoyable part of the whole weekend. I didn't realize I was expected to attach both David Mountjoy and Father's eligible prospect, if he ever turns up."

"I suppose it is fruitless to remind you that the choice is entirely up to you. As to Mountjoy, Felicia's ambitious. Mountjoy's a distant cousin of Richard's on his mother's side, and now that he's in line for an earldom, she wants him to marry someone who will add to the family prestige. Felicia is quite aware the Fenton girl will drop her as soon as the knot is tied."

"I can't imagine worrying about something so trivial." Chloe applied butter to her muffin with such vengeance that it crumbled between her fingers. Curiosity got the best of her, and she inquired, "Why did Felicia invite Lelia?"

Heloise seated herself beside Chloe and contemplated the kedgeree on her plate. "She had little choice. Richard needs Robert Fenton's influence for the political entree he wants."

"If that isn't the most ridiculous thing I've ever heard. People should keep their noses out of other people's business.

And to use social relationships to gain political power . . ." Too disgusted to continue speaking, she paused and looked at her aunt accusingly. "I certainly have no intention of being part of such a nasty little scheme."

Raised voices and the sounds of scurrying servants from the hall outside the breakfast room interrupted her.

Heloise lifted her teacup and said dryly, "Unless I'm mistaken, your suitor has arrived." She sipped reflectively and then continued, "There's little to be gained by punishing me for misleading you about the reason you're here. Your father may appear to think only of cattle breeding and fertilizer, but he *is* aware of the necessary qualifications for any candidate seeking the hand of a duke's daughter, and the Twyford connection would be excellent. He's serious about this, Chloe."

Felicia's entrance on the arm of a tall, darkly handsome man in his thirties cut off Chloe's attempt to respond to her aunt's words.

"Here you are! Lord Roderick thought it might be too soon to seek you out, but I assured him you were an early riser. Lady Heloise, Lady Chloe, may I present Lord Roderick Derwent." She patted his arm familiarly. "Isn't he every bit as attractive as you hoped, Lady Chloe?"

By the time an hour had passed, Chloe found herself desperately scrambling for excuses to avoid Roderick Derwent's company. Her first glimpse of the pomaded, carefully combed, thinning hair atop his head as he'd bowed over her hand had nearly sent her into whoops of laughter. His country tweeds were too new, and for some reason, he'd had the laundry starch his soft linen shirt which fit too tightly at the neck. Everything about him offended her.

Immediately after his introduction, her suitor had prepared a plate, settled himself to her right, and proceeded to monopolize the conversation. "And I told Bertie the other night at Carlton House . . ." prefaced every fourth sentence.

His talk of the dissipated prince and his fast-living friends, combined with the way he stared pointedly at the bodice of her lilac morning gown, sent a chill over her flesh. Chloe had smiled brightly and murmured polite comments, all the while counting the minutes until she could leave the room.

Finally she said, "I'm disappointed I was not in town to attend Mr. Wilde's party, but since we've never met, I doubt he missed my company."

"My dear, he's already eager to make your acquaintance. I told him of our prospects, and he's looking forward to welcoming you when you arrive in London." Lord Roderick's white teeth gleamed as he bestowed an approving smile on her.

Chloe thought she could survive quite nicely if she never met Oscar Wilde's coterie. Lord Roderick's lecherous looks sent shudders up her spine. The man was handsome in a flashy way, but he was going to seed; the gold signet ring he wore was too ornate and too shiny. Her father must be out of his mind. "I'm deeply flattered," she said. "However, you must excuse me now. I need to change before we set out on the picnic Lady Overton has planned."

Derwent hurried to pull out her chair. Since Heloise was also preparing to stand, he appeared torn between deferring to her superior rank and Chloe's eligibility, nearly tripping over his own feet in his attempt to assist both women at the same time.

Chloe contained herself until they reached their rooms, then fell into her aunt's arms and laughed until tears ran down her cheeks. "Whatever can Father have been thinking?" she said after she drew back and mopped her face with a linen handkerchief.

"I believe Sir Roderick's father is what my brother George calls 'a sound land manager,' " Heloise said sardonically.

"Well, he should have planted his son deeper!" Chloe gasped before she collapsed, laughing, on the bed.

Her aunt surveyed her with an approving eye. "You're taking this very well."

"Of course. Now I have no reason to stay. The man is a disgusting, lecherous loose fish, don't you agree?" That Heloise's mouth twisted in distaste as she nodded was all the answer Chloe needed. "If I try very hard, I should be able to struggle through the picnic and dinner."

Heloise said grimly, "I shall send a message to Drury to come for us in the morning."

In spite of her flippant words, the prospect of a rustic afternoon in Lord Roderick's company nearly caused Chloe's stomach to clench. "I've never before been treated like the prize cow at the fair. Do you suppose he'll ask to check my teeth?" she asked her aunt as they left their rooms.

"He has undoubtedly been told that you will inherit my money and is delighted to discover that, as Felicia pointed out, you haven't lost your looks at your advanced age," Heloise replied.

Chloe grimaced. "Rather two for one, am I?" She looked to the foot of the stairs and felt her stomach tighten. "There he is, the little wart. I hate this, Aunt."

"Do not, under any circumstances, allow yourself to be alone with him." Heloise cast an unsmiling nod in Sir Roderick's direction.

"I've already told him it will be necessary for me to ride in the barouche so I can assist you." She smiled at her aunt, hoping she appeared merely solicitous. "Can you manage to look frail and doddering?"

"I fear I neglected to bring my cane."

Chloe held her aunt's elbow as if Heloise might stumble at any moment. "I also told him I only mount a horse if I can wear breeches and ride astride, and I didn't want to shock the other ladies."

"Such unconventionality should recommend you to his friends," her aunt commented.

"Don't even suggest such an idea," Chloe muttered as they descended the last few steps. Looking up, she said brightly, "There you are, Lord Derwent. I do hope we haven't delayed everyone's departure."

David and Lelia rode horseback, arriving at the picnic long after the barouches and other riders. Lelia's hair looked hurriedly pinned back into place, and she showed no embarrassment at her disarray. While Chloe didn't envy her, as she'd honestly told the reddish-haired beauty the night before, she coveted the other woman's glow and her openly displayed infatuation. An image of Drury's face swam through her mind. Somehow, she would manage to get through the day.

Later that afternoon she entered her room, tugged the pins from her hair, and flung them gleefully onto the dressing table. Kicking her slippers to one side, she unfastened her bodice and loosed the waistband of her skirt. Her annoyance with Drury's rejection forgotten, she thrilled at the thought of seeing him again. Her happy anticipation was interrupted by a perfunctory rap at the door to the adjoining room. Then her aunt's figure appeared behind her in the mirror. "These people are as dull as ditchwater," Chloe told the reflection. She removed her skirt and shrugged out of her bodice.

"I heartily agree. One hopes there will not be another musicale this evening. The Enswater girl who sang 'Poor Little

Buttercup' last night was frightfully flat. If Mr. Gilbert or Mr. Sullivan had heard that twit, they would have begged forgiveness for having written the wretched song."

Chloe stepped out of her petticoats and unlaced her corset, breathing a sign of relief as air circulated beneath it. "I discovered another reason Felicia is so upset. Her sons, Nevil and Oliver, have been sent down from Oxford for introducing a flock of ducks to the Ashmolean building. Richard has punished them by arranging for them to spend a year in his company's Australian office." She sighed. "I wish Father would send me to some foreign country, instead of to London for the Season. After only a day and a half in society, I feel as if I've been sentenced to Bedlam."

Heloise walked to the connecting door, facing away from her niece as she spoke. "This irregularly arranged circus bears no resemblance to civilized entertainment. You will find your own style in London."

"If I survive this evening, London society can hold no terrors for me," Chloe said. Tomorrow she would see Drury, not to mention escaping from her erstwhile suitor and Lelia Fenton's poisonous glances. The irony of her situation prompted a gurgle of laughter. Drury might ignore her, but she intended to seize every opportunity to be in his presence, even if she had to fabricate reasons, in an attempt to pierce his cold reserve and unveil the mystery that surrounded him. Conversely, Roderick Derwent pursued her, and she wouldn't be disappointed to hear he had ridden off a cliff on his journey home.

"Aunt, let me remain in Upper Whiddlesby until the Season is over," she said impulsively.

Heloise turned to face her. "That is impossible. No matter what your plans for the future, at least a year of exposure to society is necessary for a woman of your birth."

Chloe moaned at the prospect, then brightened. She wasn't in London yet, and any number of things could occur that might cancel the dreaded trip. "If I must, I shall bear it. After all, it's not as if I'm going to die of society," she agreed, her fingers crossed behind her back.

"I should hope not. Death is scarcely a reasonable alternative," Heloise said, watching her niece from hooded eyes.

"True. One can hardly change one's mind and come back from the grave, can one?" Chloe said airily.

The next morning, a laughing group of riders set out for an early ride as Heloise's traveling coach rolled to a stop at the foot of the broad graveled approach to Overton House. Adrian shrugged his shoulders more deeply into the scratchy jacket and pulled his hat farther down over his forehead. Today of all days he needed to employ the skills which had helped him survive this long.

In the past it hadn't taken superhuman effort to assume any role he wished to play; the shift had come to him as naturally as breathing. Fitz had frequently marveled at his ability to blend into varying backgrounds and identities. Today Adrian chafed at the necessity.

The butler marched stiffly down the front stairs and motioned him toward the side entrance, where the ladies' luggage would be brought down. Adrian flicked the reins and guided the horses behind the bank of shrubbery that shielded the stables and carriage house from the formal entrance. Thomas leaped down, and Adrian threw him the reins before climbing from the box. He removed his hat to rub his handkerchief over his perspiration-streaked forehead.

"Oh, my God! My God! Can that be you, Adrian! But you're . . . you're dead!"

Dismay filled Adrian as he recognized the voice of David

Mountjoy. Despite Heloise's assertion that none would look for him among the servants, he had been recognized. He rested his face against the neck of the lead horse, feeling as if all his blood had just seeped out the tips of his toes. The familiar odor of horseflesh revived him to the extent that he quickly spat, "For God's sake, be quiet!"

As Adrian had hoped, the sharpness of his command slowed David's enthusiastic approach. His cousin paused, shock, surprise, and something Adrian couldn't interpret written in his eyes. When David spoke again, his voice was pitched low, but the words rang with emotion. "It *is* you, isn't it? Adrian! What the hell's going on?"

Adrian surveyed their surroundings cautiously. They were alone except for Thomas's stolid presence and that of two grooms walking a pair of saddled horses not twenty feet away. He drew closer to assure he couldn't be overheard. Keeping his voice soft and controlled, he said, "David, if you value my life, forget you've seen me."

"But you're alive! Now I don't have to inherit the title or any of that rot!"

The shining relief on his face drew a reluctant smile from Adrian. "Not for many years, I hope. Even if I don't return."

"What do you mean? You're alive. Come home!"

"God, I dream of it at night." The side door swung open and a footman balancing a small trunk on his shoulder stepped out. "There's no bloody time to explain. Get out of here, and forget you saw me," Adrian hissed, and he turned to assist the footman.

From the corner of his eye he watched David hesitate, then walk toward the grooms and horses. As he finished supervising the loading of the luggage, Adrian saw a petite, reddish-haired young woman in a topaz riding habit round the corner of the shrubbery and approach his cousin.

★ ★ ★ ★ ★

Chloe hastily climbed the stairs to the second floor, prepared to tell anyone who inquired that she intended to check her room for anything she might have forgotten. Closing the door firmly behind her, she hurried to the window and parted the underdrapes. Peering far to her right, she saw her aunt's coach, with Drury and Thomas strapping the trunks into place. Her gaze focused only on Drury, drinking in the ease of his strong, controlled movements, while her heart beat wildly from the shock of what she had overheard.

She hadn't intended to eavesdrop, but she'd gone down ahead of the footman to open the door for him, and parts of the conversation between the two men outside had filtered to her through the open portal. Surprise had locked her hand on the knob and frozen her in place. Following their lowered voices had been difficult, but she'd recognized Drury's—a far different Drury from the one she thought she knew. The rough speech and half-educated cadences he affected occasionally were missing. In their place was an authoritative upper-class accent.

By what name had David called him? To her frustration, the syllables had blurred as the man turned his head from her.

She pressed her flushed cheek against the cool glass and whispered, "I was right. He isn't really a groom. He's related to David Mountjoy somehow. That's the resemblance that puzzled me so the other night at dinner." But why would Drury's life be endangered if the truth were known? And she'd pried. Had made him uneasy. She closed her eyes and tried to think.

The mystery of someone hiding sounded like a farfetched plot from a novel—something dark and dangerous created by the drug-clouded mind of Edgar Allan Poe. But this was real. Although her first impulse was to confront Drury and demand to know who he really was and why he was hiding, Chloe knew he would refuse to answer. But that didn't mean she couldn't protect him. Whether Drury wanted it or not, she intended to insure his safety, whatever desperate trouble he was in.

At the sound of Heloise's footsteps in the next room, Chloe hurried to the washstand and splashed cool water on her cheeks and wrists. She was patting the moisture away with a linen towel when Heloise opened the adjoining door.

"I'm coming right down, Aunt. I just wanted to check to be sure we had everything."

"There was no need. I looked through both rooms before I went downstairs. You're quite flushed, my dear. Did that bounder Derwent attempt any unwanted advances at breakfast?"

"If you call his insistence on knowing your address so he could visit next week an unwanted advance, yes, he did." Chloe dropped the towel on the washstand and leaned toward the mirror to tuck in a lock of hair that had fallen loose in her mad rush up the stairs. "I told him you enjoyed a very retired existence and discouraged guests."

Heloise's mouth curved in a wry smile. "Did you indeed? I suppose I must be grateful. As soon as we return, I shall write George to tell him Roderick Derwent clearly will not do. After breakfast, he had the temerity to inquire as to the yearly income from my aunt's estate. After, of course, he assured me how much he admired her boldness in marrying so far beneath her."

Grateful for the diversion, Chloe took her aunt's arm and drew her into the hall. "I suppose it's to his credit that he would condescend to enjoy the fruits of a brewer's labors. So very democratic of him, don't you think?"

Chapter Eight

Shaken by his encounter with David Mountjoy, Adrian was so buried in his thoughts that he failed to notice Chloe's sympathetic glances as she descended from the coach for luncheon at a country inn, and then again that evening when they reached Upper Whiddlesby.

His mind searched frantically for a means to end his masquerade. The description Fitz's agent had furnished of the newcomer now in the village could fit only one man. Josef—memorable for his zealotry, the quintessential radical firebrand. He would have to find Josef and silence him before he could carry out his mission.

As he and the other grooms curried the weary horses, he considered, and tossed aside, various plans for locating and dealing with the revolutionist.

"There's a new stable lad over ta Sir Desmond's," Willie Upton remarked.

Adrian continued his rhythmic strokes with the currycomb. "I expect that'll be a help. They were shorthanded last I heard."

"Looks like a wrong 'un ta me." Willie paused to spit out the stalk of straw he'd been chewing. "Swarthy. Looks like a Gypsy, and he talks funny."

Suddenly Willie's words had his undivided attention. "Funny how?"

"I dunno. Like he's readin' from a book. Stiff like, y'know?"

As if he'd learned the language in a class from someone who didn't know how people in England spoke during daily intercourse. Adrian felt his heart leap inside his chest. "Big fellow?"

"Not so's you'd notice. Only 'bout as tall as Miss Chloe, and thin. One o' those wiry blokes, y'know? He's a dab hand with horseflesh, so Roger says." Willie's brother was assistant head groom at the Grange.

"Well, then, I'm sure Sir Desmond is glad to have him." Adrian lifted a hoof to clean it, and his eyes nearly crossed from the effort it took not to ask if the stable hand's forehead was noticeably low and whether or not the lobe of his left ear was missing. He would have to see for himself.

"Well, I tried. You told me to 'get my toes wet.' I did, and I've decided I'll be better off keeping my shoes on," Chloe observed as she pushed off her left slipper with the toe of her right shoe and propped her stockinged foot on a needle-point-covered footstool in her aunt's private sitting room. She nursed a fragile cup filled with fragrant green tea between her hands.

Heloise snorted, a decidedly unladylike sound for which she offered no apology. "A blind man would have known that mixed bag was not precisely the cream of society."

Drawing a deep breath, Chloe said, "You forget, I've also met an example of the kind of man my father thinks of as an eligible husband." She pushed off the other slipper and crossed her slender ankles. "Once Mama is recovered, I shall announce a truly ambitious purpose for my life. One that supports my refusal to go to London for a comeout."

Heloise cast a horrified look at her niece. "Surely you cannot believe that a two-day participation in a country house party qualifies as experiencing polite society. As for that Derwent creature, I have already written my brother George a stinging letter concerning his unsuitability."

"You're not really listening to me, Aunt. I went. I heard the talk. And I was bored to tears and nearly pawed into the bargain. That's sufficient exposure, if you ask me." Chloe's dark eyes sparkled with mischief. "Father will understand when I explain. Dear Aunt, you may have me on your hands for far longer than you wish." At least until she discovered Drury's true identity. Until she understood the reason for the joy she felt when their eyes met, the inexplicable weakness that occasionally overtook her—weakness that wasn't really weakness but a helpless desire to be held in his arms.

"You're behaving childishly, Chloe. If, after a full year of society, you still wish to pursue a different path, I shall speak with your parents on your behalf." Heloise set her cup and saucer on the marquetry table beside her chair. "I expect you to be sensible about this."

"I've already been sensible enough. What is wrong with experiencing something wildly romantic and adventurous? Must one always set a proper course?"

Heloise was unyielding. "Yes, because that is what separates us from the savages. I have traveled all over the world and, on occasion, behaved unconventionally, but I never embarrassed my family. And never have I disgraced myself." Her gaze sharpened, and a grim smile crossed her lips. "I always acted for the good of my country."

Eyes sparkling mischievously, Chloe encouraged her to continue. "I knew someday you would tell me."

"Not tonight, however," Heloise said as she rose. "I intend to retire."

Disappointed but knowing she would hear no more, Chloe yawned mightily, covering her lips with slender fingers and stood also. She wanted to see Drury. Alone. "I believe I shall take a ride before breakfast tomorrow."

The remaining guests at Overton House trickled up the stairs to their respective rooms. In his chamber, Robert Fenton dismissed his valet and loosened his cravat. He poured himself a snifter of brandy and inhaled the fumes of the amber liquid appreciatively. The last few days had proceeded according to plan. Only one other matter required his attention. He despised the necessity of reassigning tasks that he had assumed already executed, but in this instance, he couldn't take any chances.

The door to his room burst open, interrupting his thoughts, and he tilted the contents of his glass dangerously. As he turned, the portal swung closed with an angry thud. "He's still alive, Papa."

Robert's lids closed wearily. He'd hoped his daughter wouldn't discover that Viscount Harding was alive until he'd rectified the mistake. "I know, my love. I've made . . . other arrangements."

"You told me he was dead," Lelia said accusingly.

"I did. Unfortunately, the, ah, chosen instrument deceived his associates in connection with another matter, and he was murdered before he could undertake my commission." He added soothingly, "Don't worry, I have contracted another individual. The matter will be in hand in a matter of days."

"David saw him today. The fool claims to be delighted that Adrian Harding is still alive. He could be troublesome."

Robert looked at his daughter, the daughter he could never deny anything, and foolish pride swelled in his breast. She was magnificent in all ways. "He'll come around, my dear. No one will ever connect Harding's second demise to us. In fact, no one will even be aware he didn't die the first time." Reaching out, he patted her cheek. "I promised you a title, didn't I? Have I ever failed to give you anything you've wanted?"

Chloe smoothed the dark blue poplin riding habit over her hips and eyed herself in the mirror. How ridiculous to wear a corset to ride a horse! Then she reminded herself of her real purpose in riding this morning. The despised undergarment enhanced the trim outline of her ensemble, and since her objective this morning was to appear as desirable as possible for Drury, it was worth any discomfort.

Scooping up her dashing red felt hat, she hurried out the door. Fifteen minutes had passed since she'd sent a footman to the stable with word that she intended to ride. She hoped Drury was wondering what was keeping her.

Only Drury wasn't there when she arrived. Willie, his pale hair damp from a quick wetting and combing, held the reins of her mare and those of another mount. "Where's Drury?" she demanded.

"Lady Heloise sent him on an errand, Miss Chloe. He said as how I was to ride with you today."

Chloe bit back the language that had so affronted Drury that night in the birch grove. She favored Willie with a pained smile and placed her foot in his cupped hands. As she swung into the saddle, she warned, "You'll have to keep up the best you can. I feel like a real gallop this morning."

Half an hour later she drew rein and looked back. Willie had fallen behind and was out of sight, so she slowed the mare to a walk. The furious pace had eased her disappointment, but her aunt would be furious to discover Chloe had lost her escort.

Sunk deep in her thoughts, she allowed the mare to nibble at the weeds while she waited. Last night had seemed endless.

Her thoughts whirling furiously, she had conjured reason after reason to explain why Drury might be trapped in this bizarre no-man's-land. Her imaginings had fueled nightmare after nightmare. Toward morning her fevered dreams had lessened, and reason had returned. Philosophical now, she decided that if Drury continued to avoid her, she would simply have to make it impossible for—

Rough hands seized her and pulled her from the saddle. As she parted her lips to scream, a foul-tasting cloth was crammed into her mouth and tied behind her head, and she was thrown over the back of a horse. The leather ridge of the saddle dug into her stomach, forcing her breath out in a dizzying, sickening gust. She felt her hands being fastened behind her back with some kind of soft cloth.

Before she could strike out with her feet, her captor leaped onto the saddle behind her and clamped his hand in the middle of her back. The horse lurched into a ground-eating canter. "Lie still. You will not be hurt."

In spite of the reassuring words, his guttural voice and stiff speech struck fear into her, and Chloe wasn't sure what he meant by *still*. Since she couldn't clutch the edge of the saddle, her upper body bounced against the horse's withers. She felt as if her head would snap loose at the shoulders, and the saddle dug into her stomach and ribs at each stride of the horse. The kippers she'd eaten for breakfast worked their way upward. If she threw up now, she would strangle on the filthy cloth. Suddenly Chloe was mortally afraid.

They traveled for what seemed a short distance; then the horse's pace slowed, and its hoofs crunched through endless dry underbrush. The zigzag journey ended, and Chloe's captor dismounted, pulling her off the horse and to her feet. Before she found her balance, he seized her bound hands and twisted them upward. Pain shot through her

105

shoulders; she screamed silently.

"If you do not try to run, I will leave your legs unbound."

A not ungentle shove at her shoulders urged her toward a small, ramshackle hut twenty feet away. Chloe darted quick looks left and right in an attempt to place where she was but saw only brambles and the aged oaks and elms whose branches arched over the tiny hovel as if conspiring to hide it from curious eyes.

Her tender stomach made walking torture. She wanted to curl up into a ball and clutch her bruised midsection, but the hand at her back was inexorable, and she forced her feet to carry her toward the hut.

Her abductor remained behind her. Reason told her not to attempt to see him. His speech had been curiously unaccented, as if he had rehearsed the words. She watched as his gloved hand reached in front of her to pull open the hut's rough door.

Then she was thrust into the dark interior and pushed gently to her knees. Her face broke through spider webs as she fell, and the odors of sour earth and rot met her nostrils. She shuddered uncontrollably. Even though her mind told her to resist the curiously considerate treatment, her body was compliant. Groping hands pushed aside the hem of her habit, and another piece of cloth was jerked around her ankles and tied snugly.

With a courtesy that seemed grotesque, her captor pushed her into a sitting position, her bent knees in front of her face. His voice was muted in the murky gloom. "Your friend, Mr. Drury, will come for you . . . after he and I have a little . . . how do you say it . . . visit. Yes. He will be anxious to save you, and now he listens to me. Not to worry."

Worry? Chloe thought. *Why on earth should I worry?* A spider that had just discovered her presence walked down the bridge of her nose. *Worry? Of course not.*

As self-imposed punishment for his cowardice in sending Willie with Chloe, Adrian sat on a rough wooden box, polishing the brass on the carriage harness. He knew why he'd played craven. The maelstrom of conflicting emotions he'd experienced since his encounter with his cousin the day before left him far too vulnerable to Chloe's unaffected charm.

Cleaning brass took effort, but not enough to erase his frustration. The sound of horses approaching at breakneck speed added to his ill humor. He dropped the cloth and the harness, prepared to give Chloe and Willie the dressing down they deserved for pushing their mounts so hard after a long ride.

Chloe's horse was riderless.

Panic nearly froze him in place. "Where's Miss Chloe?" he shouted to the white-faced groom.

Breathless and shaking, his only answer a wheezing rasp, Willie slid from the gelding and fished in his pocket. When his hand reappeared, Adrian grabbed the wrinkled scrap of paper from him and turned away from the lad to read it.

> *I have the Lady Chloe. She will be safe if you come within the hour to the stone bridge where you have met others.*

Adrian cursed under his breath. "Where did you get this?" he demanded of the shaking groom.

" 'Twas tucked beneath the saddle o' Miss Chloe's horse. She rode too fast. I couldn't keep up," Willie answered defensively.

Only fear for Chloe's safety kept Adrian from seizing the stringy young lad by the throat and choking him. Lips tight, he spat out, "Where did you find the horse?"

"T'other side o' Barnhill Farm, on the path by the woods. At the top of the rise, where the trail turns at the boulders."

Adrian raced into the stable and saddled a young gelding, his mind working rapidly. Striding to the tack room, he unlocked the padlock on a storage box and removed a pistol. When he had loaded the gun, he tucked the weapon into the back of his waistband. "Take the note to Lady Heloise and tell her I've set out after Miss Chloe," he ordered. Then he mounted and rode off furiously.

Adrian had no intention of meeting with the kidnapper until he found Chloe, no matter how long it took. As he rode, he visualized the trail Willie had described. In an excess of precaution, he had memorized the surrounding terrain. He knew every way out—in case Fitz's protection should prove useless.

The wording of the note could mean any of several things, one of which was an ambush. If the bastard meant to kill him, there had been dozens of opportunities over the past months. Why would he decide to talk now?

Chloe. Chloe of the clear, laughing eyes that invited him to share her delight. Chloe, who had become a symbol of survival to him, a vision of the life possible beyond the limbo he inhabited. No matter how much he wanted to meet with her captor, he had to find Chloe first.

Chloe fought back the tears crowding behind her eyes. Dampness from the earthen floor seeped through her riding habit. The smells of mold and decay revolted her bruised stomach, and her body shook uncontrollably. Gritting her teeth, she willed her breathing to slow, her muscles to relax. As she felt she was gaining control, she heard a scrambling sound behind her. *Oh, God, it's a rat. I know it's a rat.* Her heart beating in her ears, she pounded the earth with her feet. The rather pathetic thump she produced silenced the creature. *Until next time,* she told herself. *Well, there bloody well won't be a next time. I'll free myself if I break an arm in the attempt.*

Leaning until she tipped onto her side, Chloe looped her arms over her bottom and stretched her fingers toward the knots of the binding around her ankles. Because of her boots, the cloth lay smoothly against the leather. Her cheek grinding into the pungent packed earth, she arched her back and dropped her shoulders while she shifted her ankles against each other in an attempt to work the taut fabric closer to her hands. Her joints protested the unnatural position, but she ignored the pain.

She damned her gloved hands. If her fingernails were free to work at the knot, she would have no trouble. Arching farther to give her fingers more room to work, she felt like the contortionist she had seen at the May Festival. After several fruitless minutes she ceased her efforts and lay still, her muscles screaming from abuse, her heart pounding wildly.

I can't give up. Drury may be in worse danger than I. Fear for him fed her resolve, and she arched again, this time approaching the knots methodically. Moments later the first twist came free; the remainder opened as if by magic. She nearly fainted with relief.

The binding around her wrists gave way when her fingers found one end that pulled the hurriedly tied knot loose, and she laughed weakly at her own idiocy in not attempting to free her hands first. *Some kidnapper,* she jeered inwardly. *He would never have made the grade as a sailor.* She jerked the filthy gag from between her teeth and spit out bits of foul-tasting cloth.

Rolling to her knees, she peered into the musty darkness and fumbled her way to the sliver of light around the ill-fitting door. Seizing the diagonal board holding it together, she pulled and pushed, but the rickety-appearing portal wouldn't budge. Grateful now for her gloves, she searched the barren room for a weapon of some kind. A sticky cobweb brushed her cheek, and she scrubbed at her face with frantic fingers while shudders wracked her body.

When her search proved fruitless, she pulled off her boots and clutched the top of one in each hand; a boot heel would be a better weapon than nothing. She then positioned herself to one side of the door, hoping to surprise her captor when he returned. After that, Chloe reasoned, she would have to improvise.

Adrian searched for a trail in the straggly growth around the formation of boulders left by some cataclysmic upheaval millions of years earlier. He found what he sought: hoof prints to one side of the narrow path, and, farther on, yet more evidence that a horse had turned north.

He was so intent on the ground ahead that he nearly missed the broken dogwood branch, its blossoms waving in the breeze like a flag. His quarry had turned into the forest.

After that, it was almost too easy. If he hadn't been frantic with worry, Adrian would have laughed aloud at her abductor's ineptness.

Any desire to laugh fled when he came upon the dashing hat he had seen days earlier securely pinned atop the braided knot which confined Chloe's mass of curls.

Minutes later he came to a small, roughly built hut.

Reining in behind a screen of undergrowth, he scanned the area. Seeing none, he dismounted and looped the gelding's reins around a branch. As he edged forward, he searched left and right, watching for movement. When he noticed none, he paused. Birds, silenced by his approach, resumed calling to each other. The hut stood silent, dilapidated and overgrown with wild grape. Adrian was afraid to consider what it might hold, but he strode forward.

Inside the hovel, Chloe stood beside the door holding her breath. The birds had quieted moments before, and she thought she had heard the creak of saddle leather.

A shadow crossed the light creeping through the crack beside the door. Someone was out there! She flexed her knees, tensing her body to race through the opening as soon as her captor stepped inside. When the door swung open, she flung both boots at the shadow falling across the opening and barreled through at a dead run, only to collide with a solid wall of muscle and tendon and bone.

"Oh, God, Chloe. You're safe." Strong arms enveloped her, but she struggled violently within the confining hold, ceasing only when her senses identified Drury's voice and touch. She fell against him, throwing her arms around his back to hold him.

Chloe inhaled deeply the heady combination of leather and clean male perspiration that clung to him, seeking to banish the smell of mold and damp earth from her nostrils. She wanted to tell him she had never felt so wonderful in her life, but her first attempt came out as a croak. Giving up, she burrowed against his strength and warmth.

"Are you all right? That bastard didn't hurt you, did he?" Drury's hands ranged up and down her back, his ministrations accompanied by a colorful description of her abductor. "Answer me, Chloe," he commanded.

She moved her lips experimentally. As she looked up into his worried gaze, she felt a prickling behind her eyelids. She whispered, "Why is it that I didn't cry when I was kidnapped and thrown into that wretched hut, and now that I'm safe I feel as if I'm going to weep all over your shirt?" Tears rolled down her cheeks.

Chloe had never felt more like a helpless female, yet she didn't care. She gave in to the feelings of terror and futility that had gripped her during the last hour. She nestled against his reassuringly solid body while she sobbed out her fears.

When her tears were spent, fury surfaced. "He kidnapped me! That bloody . . ." Chloe was too angry to come up with sufficiently insulting epithets for her assailant.

Drury glanced around the tiny clearing, then picked up her boots. "We can't stay here. He might come back at any time." He scooped her into his arms, carried her to the patient gelding, and swung her up into the saddle before helping her slip her feet back into her boots and swinging up behind her. Then he guided the horse through the forest in another direction.

"Where are we going?" Chloe demanded.

"We're putting some distance between us and that hut. The path ahead leads to the lane."

Ten minutes later they were free of the trees. Dismounting behind a stone fence, he held up his hands to assist her to the ground. He led her several feet away, leaving the horse to graze. "Now, tell me what happened. Did you see him?" Adrian demanded.

"No, but he talked to me." Forced to relive the event, Chloe suddenly realized that although she had been terrified, she had never felt in real physical danger. "He was . . . almost solicitous. Except for forcing me to ride facedown over the saddle." She grimaced. The ache in her bruised stomach was a graphic reminder of that jouncing journey.

A confused expression appeared on Drury's face. "Solicitous?"

Chloe concentrated before speaking. "After he tied me up,

he tried to make me comfortable. He said you would come and free me . . . once he had talked with you." Suspicion flared. "You've already met with him, haven't you? Why did he do this?"

Drury's reaction shocked her. His expression closed in on itself, and his eyes became opaque, as if his thoughts were far away.

"No, wait," she continued, "Before . . . you asked what he looked like. You haven't seen him yet. How did you find me?"

Drury focused on her once more. "I tracked you from where Willie found your horse and the note." He shoved shaking fingers through his hair, then reached out to drag her against him, his hands traveling over her as if to reassure himself of her safety.

Chloe wanted more than comfort. Where his hands touched her, warmth spread; want pooled low in her belly. Her fingers, splayed against his chest, registered the sudden acceleration of his heartbeat, and his thighs, pressed against her own, had become taut and hard. She felt the ridge of his arousal against her stomach. The memory of her brazen response the last time he had kissed her made her hesitant, but her body didn't appear to carry similar guilt about their earlier encounter. With a little involuntary movement, that rebellious entity nestled closer, seeking contact.

When Drury raised her face for his kiss, Chloe sighed with relief. She threw both arms around his neck and in one fierce movement pulled his head down. When he tried to pull back, she probed the line between his lips with her tongue, seeking entry.

Chapter Nine

Helpless against her demand and his own accelerating desire, Adrian slanted his head and molded his mouth to hers. He cupped her buttocks and dragged her against his aching arousal. Any thought of restraint fled at the contact. His groan was part ecstasy and part despair.

The feel of Chloe's fingers threading through his hair, learning the contours of his head, heated his blood. And then her lips parted still more beneath his. Each thrust of his tongue took him further from sanity, and when her hips pressed forward, he ground against her. Her immediate response told him where this would lead.

Dredging up the last vestige of his self-control, he gripped her arms and wrenched her away from him. Her confusion-filled eyes pleaded, but he held firm, resting his forehead against hers. He couldn't seem to draw enough air into his lungs. When she attempted to embrace him again, he clamped her arms to her sides. "Don't. Don't pull away from me again," she said, her voice shaking.

His own voice, halting and breathless, came to his ears as if from a distance. "In fifteen seconds I would have lifted your skirts and been inside you. Is that what you want?"

Adrian nearly broke when she laid her palm along his cheek. None of her reading, and certainly not her upbringing, could have prepared her for the passions awakening every part of her. He felt so in tune with her that he sensed her confusion before she spoke.

"I'm not sure what I want, Drury."

His body jerked as if she had struck him. He pushed her hand away and stood tall before her, his eyes full of resentment. "My name isn't Drury."

"I know."

Adrian was thunderstruck. "What the hell do you mean, you know?"

"She stood. I overheard you . . . with David Mountjoy. He thought you were dead. But I don't know why, and I couldn't catch the name he called you." Chloe seized his shirt and wound her fingers in the fabric. "I don't care who you are or what you did."

He grasped her fisted hands and closed his eyes, fighting for control. "My name is Adrian, Viscount Harding. I was . . . in Armenia, where I eavesdropped on a meeting to which I wasn't invited. Before I could gather more information, someone betrayed me. Her Majesty's government felt it safer for me to be dead, so I disappeared."

"You should have chosen another disguise. You're a highly unlikely servant."

"I didn't set out to be one. I really *was* hurt working in a shipyard. It's all been . . . ." His words trailed off as he remembered. He pulled his watch from his trousers pocket and eyed it. "Willie returned with the note over an hour ago. Your kidnapper won't wait forever for our meeting. It's imperative that I hear what he has to say. Come on."

Before she could protest, he seated her crosswise on the gelding and mounted behind her. "Where are we going?" she demanded.

"To the stone bridge to see if he's still there. The note under your saddle demanded that I meet him within the hour." Adrian guided the horse to the road. "If I cut cross country, we may be able to catch him before he leaves. I've been expecting the blighter to try to kill me, and this still may be an ambush, but the note said he wanted to talk."

"Kill you?"

"He's one of the Armenian conspirators. The worst of the lot, actually. Hold on," he cautioned as he guided the horse down an incline. "It's too complicated to explain right now."

"I wish I'd seen his face."

Relief that she hadn't done so washed over him. "The less you know about him, the safer you'll be."

"He talked funny."

Adrian grinned. "Did you ever hear anyone speak Armenian?"

"Not that I know of."

He repeated his question in the language.

Chloe frowned in confusion. "You speak Armenian?"

"How do you think I landed there in the first place?"

Chloe wrapped her arms around his middle and pressed her cheek against his taut chest. "Does Aunt Heloise know?"

Adrian allowed himself a burst of rueful laughter. "Of course. She always knows more than she tells."

"She would make a good spy herself. Or a queen. She certainly has more presence than Victoria," Chloe mused.

Adrian grinned in agreement, then stopped the horse behind a hedgerow and dismounted. Handing the reins to Chloe, he dug out his watch and placed it in her hand. "I'll walk from here. If I don't return within half an hour, or if you hear anything suspicious, ride back to your aunt's and tell her what happened. Take the way you followed me that night." A smile pulled at the corners of his mouth.

"But what if he tries to kill you?"

"He said he wanted to talk. If not, I'm prepared." He reached behind his back to assure himself he hadn't lost the pistol, then he pulled her head down and kissed her tenderly.

"Wish me luck." The tears in the golden-brown depths of her eyes touched his heart. Incredibly, she smiled, her dimple wavering uncertainly. Adrian knew then that he would move mountains, with his bare hands if necessary, to hasten his return from the dead by as little as five minutes.

"Good luck, Adrian." He was conscious of her anxious gaze following him as he strode toward the rippling stream in the distance.

The walkway beneath the stone arch was uninhabited, and Adrian positioned himself in a shallow niche. He had an excellent sense of the passage of time, and after twenty minutes he gave up on his adversary. He'd arrived too late. What had been the purpose of this morning's little exercise? After two years of living one step ahead of extinction, Adrian trusted his instincts. Yet, if Josef meant to kill him, he'd surely had other opportunities.

Nothing made sense. He trudged alongside the Whiddlesby, oblivious to the soothing sound of rippling water lapping against its banks. If he could neutralize this one adversary, then he could concentrate on the second threat—the one he suspected was responsible for his original betrayal. He could return from this damnable shadow existence. He could claim Chloe, court her as she deserved. He could . . .

Adrian dragged a hand over his face as if to wipe away such optimistic thoughts. Counting success in advance never worked. He was no better off than before. No, things were worse, because now there was Chloe, who couldn't be told Josef wasn't the only person stalking him.

He found her exactly where he had left her, eyes intent on the watch in her hand. He wished he could build a sturdy wall around her to preserve her innocence forever.

Chloe's head came up as she sensed his presence, and the

relief he saw on her face weakened his knees. How long had it been since he'd been greeted with such joy?

"Adrian!" She slid from the gelding's back, ran to him and threw her arms around him, her hands searching his body as if to assure herself he was whole. "Did you see him?"

"Josef must have left before I got there. I wonder if he's discovered that his hostage has disappeared." Adrian basked in the warmth of her embrace and his self-satisfaction at her rescue. It wasn't the time to warn Chloe how much danger could lie ahead.

She loosened her arms and drew back. "While you were gone I thought about your situation. It's quite possible that this man really did wish only to talk with you. Has it occurred to you there may be more than one person who wants you killed? Whoever it is probably betrayed you in the first place, and he could be taking advantage of the Armenian threat to accomplish his own goals."

When his brain stopped spinning, Adrian said, "Would you repeat what you just said?" Even the second time, he had difficulty believing how accurately she had assessed his dilemma. "And why would anyone else want me out of the way?"

"Well, it is said that the most powerful motivations are love, power and money. Did you have a wife or lover when you 'died?' "

Adrian laughed. "Why would they want to kill me a second time?"

"Laugh if you like, but . . . say you were married. A certain type of woman would be disappointed to discover you were alive, particularly if you were extremely rich," Chloe explained patiently.

"Well, I'm not married, nor even close to it. Does that make you feel any better?"

She smiled generously up at him. "Immeasurably. In books, the villain is usually the heir, except David doesn't want the title. He told me so when I sat next to him at dinner."

David had told him the same thing. "Why would a woman rather have a dead husband?"

"Because the freedom of widowhood, plus a great deal of money, could be very heady. She might not want to relinquish her independence if you came back."

Suddenly serious, Adrian said, "I left no wife, no fiancée, although there was a woman who hoped she and I might match. Not even a mistress. Just my family, and we were close." Chloe's objective recital of human frailties had been frightening. Although he had searched his past many times for reasons someone might want him dead, he had never considered anyone close to his family. His memories of those he loved best had kept him sane. Surely no one he loved . . .

Chloe scooped up the horse's reins and led it to him. "You know your family best, of course. One thing I *do* know is that Aunt Heloise will call in Scotland Yard if we don't return soon."

Driven by sudden urgency, he rose, backing her up to the gelding's side and caging her against the warm horseflesh with an arm on either side of her body. At the welcome he saw in her eyes, his need to possess receded to tenderness. He kissed her softly and smiled. The joy he saw in her face replaced the worry that had been there earlier. "Have I told you how wonderful you are?"

Chloe's dimple flashed as she grinned at him. "Not in so many words, but you may tell me anything you like—after your resurrection." A frown crossed her smooth brow. "You *will* let me help you unravel this mess, won't you?"

"Not on your sweet life. I want you someplace safe."

Adrian raised one of her hands and pressed a kiss on the soft skin of her inner wrist, just above the edge of her glove. "Chloe, you were uncannily accurate when you said more than one person might be after me. Although I wish you were wrong, you may also have put your finger on a reason some-one besides Josef wants me dead. My father is disgustingly wealthy. Do you mind?"

Adrian's implication that his future inheritance was signif-icant brought Chloe's thoughts to a standstill. She looked into his eyes for a long moment. In spite of his flippancy, Adrian, who seemed unsure whether he would be alive in six hours, much less six years, had spoken as if her reaction to his future wealth mattered. That *she* mattered to him. Really mattered.

Stunned, she took refuge in teasing. "If the money became a burden, you could always give it all away."

Adrian swung her up onto the gelding and mounted, an-swering, "Of course, there's always the chance some other chap will drag you to the altar while I'm searching for villains so I can restore myself to the public eye."

His answer both annoyed and reassured Chloe, and she settled against his chest with a long-suffering sigh. "If you must insist on doing everything without my help, please don't take so long that I become tired of waiting."

The wretch didn't alleviate her annoyance when he pulled her closer and pressed a kiss on the top of her head, then maintained a preoccupied silence for the remainder of their journey, his rejection of her assistance causing her to fume in-wardly.

"Oh, Miss Chloe, wot a relief! Yer aunt's been like an old tabby without a tom, she has. Them Yard men were back this mornin', too!"

Gladys's jumbled greeting did little to calm Chloe as she trudged, hatless and wrinkled, into the house. She wanted only to remove her filthy riding habit and immerse herself in a tub of scented water.

"I feel sure the inspector and his friend can hear you from the village, Gladys," Heloise said. She stood behind Molly at the door of the servants' hall with a relieved smile on her face. "Drury found you."

Chloe's composure crumpled under the wealth of affection in the three words. "Oh, Aunt! . . ."

Heloise's arms wrapped her in a rare embrace.

"So much has happened. I don't know where to begin. And I'm sure I've spiders in my hair," Chloe mumbled.

"Go along and let Gladys run a bath for you while I speak with Drury. I felt sure he would find you, so I didn't mention your disappearance to the inspector. He brought some shocking news about that McCandlish person."

"He *was* a thief, wasn't he?"

"Oh, indeed he was, but they brought other, more distressing news."

Chloe paused in the act of removing her stained leather gloves. "What could be worse than stealing?"

Glancing around, Heloise said cautiously, "It has to do with Drury."

"That fiction is no longer necessary around me, Aunt."

Heloise eyed her cautiously. "I rather thought his identity might surface during today's events."

Memory of the circumstances of that disclosure warmed Chloe all over. "The situation is clear in my mind. Although I'm sure you know much more about what is going on than he would ever tell *me*."

"Don't be petulant, Chloe. It doesn't become you. You're

speaking of a young man who has been cut off from his family and forced to live in hiding for two years." Heloise patted her arm to remove the sting from her words. "Among McCandlish's effects from the farmhouse was an anonymous letter complaining of his delay in completing a commission he had accepted."

Her hand tightened on Chloe's shoulder. "Someone had paid Ian McCandlish five hundred pounds, in advance, to murder Adrian. Fortunately, the fool was killed before he made the attempt."

Chloe scrubbed vigorously at her hair and scalp. It had been one thing to theorize about the danger to Adrian. It was yet another to discover how close she had been to the truth. Her aunt's revelation that Ian McCandlish had been paid to assassinate him was enough to bring on an attack of the vapors, whatever they were.

Her mind's eye pictured Adrian's bleak expression when he'd spoken of his exile, and she realized she was angry enough on his behalf to face down an army of Armenian revolutionaries if that was what it would take to restore him to his family . . . and perhaps to her.

Chloe dried her hair, then secured the thick mass of damp curls at her nape with a yellow ribbon to match the simple cambric gown she selected. She fastened the last button and whisked into the hall, taking a detour through the kitchen to provide herself with a wedge of cheese and a hard roll to nibble on her way to the stables. She was finding that adventures stimulated the appetite, and luncheon wouldn't be for another hour.

She came to an abrupt stop when she saw Adrian in close conversation with a tall, gangly, bewhiskered stranger clad in jacket and trousers of glaring plaid. The visitor was listening intently, his frequent intelligent nods belying his garish appearance. When Adrian finished speaking, the man nodded again, picked up the square case at his feet and left.

Chloe watched him disappear around the corner of the house before she joined Adrian. "Did Aunt Heloise tell you about McCandlish?" she demanded as she reached him.

His eyes had darkened to a shade of blue so dense as to be almost black. His thoughts appeared to be a millennium away in a sterile land devoid of warmth and light. Chloe repeated her question hesitantly.

When Adrian's attention focused on her, his expression warmed, but a certain bleakness remained. "I already knew."

"Then why didn't you tell me?" she demanded.

The stern set of his mouth softened, shaping into a rueful smile that didn't reach his eyes. "I saw no need to frighten you any more than you had been. And sometimes it's safer if only one person knows everything."

Undaunted, Chloe pursued her interrogation. "Who was that man? You looked as if you were telling him something important."

Adrian looked at the tin in his hand. "Just a peddler."

"I don't believe you for one minute. You were giving him instructions of some kind, and he didn't act the way he looked."

For the first time since she had joined him, he gave her his full attention. " 'Act the way he looked?' "

"Even *I* could tell the man wasn't what he seemed." A world of disgust filled Chloe's voice. She wasn't so innocent she couldn't note the contrast between the stranger's behavior and his blatant clothing. Adrian was shutting her out as surely as if he had sent her away. "Perhaps I've read too much into our . . . encounters, but I'd hoped you would confide in me." A sob caught in her throat. She would not cry. "Don't you dare treat me like a weak female who can't keep a secret. *I'm* not the one in danger."

"You were in danger this morning," he reminded her, his voice bleak.

Chloe wanted to hit him. "Of course I was. But if you hadn't come, I would have gotten away on my own. I'd already freed myself, and my boots were excellent weapons."

She stepped close to glare into his eyes, which were now alight with enjoyment. "Go ahead. Keep information from me. But remember, I'm the only other person who knows what Josef's voice sounds like. If I should come across him, I may just decide to take care of him on my own!"

With that she turned and marched toward the house, her head high and her spirits low. For a few short hours she'd believed Adrian felt something for her, something wondrous. She'd hoped that this time he would welcome her help. She was a naive idiot. She prayed her composure would last until she'd climbed the stairs.

Heloise's voice hailed her as she passed the drawing room. "Chloe, I wish to speak with you."

"Perhaps later, Aunt. I'm exhausted." Chloe continued on her way, then slowed as the crisp whisper of Heloise's taffeta petticoats sounded behind her.

"The only shock you're suffering is the discovery that Adrian neither requires nor wants your assistance."

Whirling, Chloe demanded, "How did you know?"

"He told me much the same thing not an hour ago. Now come sit down and allow me to explain."

Chloe realized that the need to cry out her frustration would have to wait. No one disobeyed her aunt's commands without retribution. She sat on the edge of the plum-colored velvet settee, willing to listen but prepared to argue.

"You are very young, Chloe."

"Not really, Aunt. Most girls my age have come out and been married for two years or more. Some are even mothers."

"Very well. Inexperienced, then. Your father and your brother are the only men you know, and neither of them are particularly complex. I do not mean to disparage either of them, but they are remarkably unambitious and single-minded. Not only that, they live quite boring lives."

"The whole world knows that. What has this to do with anything?" Chloe demanded impatiently.

Heloise sighed. "The point is, Adrian is very different from my brother George or your brother Lionel. He has quite rightly informed me of your attraction for each other and, in view of your abduction this morning, has asked that I send you back to Bennington Hall for your own safety."

"That's positively medieval!" Chloe declared, jumping to her feet.

"My dear, I agree with him."

"And what excuse will you give my parents when you bundle me home out of the blue?"

Heloise appeared amused. "I could tell them their daughter has formed an attachment for my groom, who is being pursued by persons unknown."

Picturing their reaction, Chloe choked back sudden laughter.

"Your mother would succumb to shock. Perhaps the information that a member of a notorious band of jewel thieves has recently been murdered in the village would serve the purpose. I could say I fear for your safety."

"They'd only insist that you come with me to Bennington Hall," Chloe retorted, adding, "for your *own* safety."

"I quite seriously doubt that. My brother knows I am the equal of anything I encounter."

Her argument deflated, Chloe resorted to defiance. "I

won't go. You'll have to bind me and throw me into the coach, and I doubt either you or Adrian have the stomach for that. Besides, I discovered this morning that I'm very good at rescuing myself. I promise you, I'll not stay away." She squared her shoulders. "Adrian might not want me involved, but I am, and I intend to stay here until he is safe." She turned to leave the room.

Heloise managed to have the last word. "Please do not underestimate Adrian's ingenuity in convincing you to leave Upper Whiddlesby."

As she ran up the stairs, Chloe muttered to herself, "Ingenuity indeed. What will he do? Put snakes in my bed?" If either Adrian or her aunt thought they were going to send her home, they had better think again.

Informed of Chloe's refusal to depart, Adrian smiled wryly. He'd expected nothing different. But even as his lips curved, his heart clenched with fear. He harbored a very real suspicion that the next attempt to reach him would harm Chloe. "Could you restrict her to the premises?"

"She will defy me," Heloise responded. "Confinement will only encourage her to slip away on her own. I would have done the same at her age." She had joined him in the arbor behind the kitchen garden after dinner. Wisteria vine twined the latticed enclosure, its newly unfurled leaves providing the privacy they required.

Adrian's restless gaze searched their surroundings for movement. "There's nothing she can do. Don't think I haven't made inquiries about everyone who has come to the district since I arrived here. Three of Fitz's men are on the estate, and there's one in the village. I had no idea he was covering me so thoroughly."

"She doesn't know that. Perhaps I should enlist Bess

Shadwell to speak with her. As your cousin, as well as being the vicar's wife, she might be more persuasive."

"Don't bring Bess back into this. That would only place *her* in needless danger. Let me speak with Chloe again." Adrian struggled with his own ambivalence. He didn't want her to leave; seeing her each day would give him added incentive to resolve his situation and return to the life which had never before had such value to him.

"Do you think you will succeed?"

Adrian jammed his hands deep into the pockets of his twill trousers. "I suspect I must have been indirect before. This time I'll be specific."

"And I'm afraid I have been a rather lax chaperon. These encounters between the two of you are extremely improper."

"I fear I've been playing fast and loose with correct rules of behavior." Adrian regarded her with lowered eyebrows. "But can you honestly tell me that petty convention has ever influenced your own actions?"

"Only when it suited me," Heloise replied, her lips curving in a reminiscent smile.

"Staying alive and assuring Chloe's safety are far more important than any rules. I'll ride with her tomorrow morning."

Chapter Ten

Robert Fenton smiled to himself. This time he had selected a worthy instrument to remove the bothersome viscount. When the job was done, his daughter would have what she wanted—a title and riches beyond any man's dreams. He clipped the end of a smoothly wrapped Havana and ran its length beneath his nose, savoring the rich, pungent fragrance of the tobacco.

Satisfaction made him swell with pride. His daughter would be a viscountess, and eventually a countess. His grandchildren would be members of the peerage. As he scraped the match against the rough rock bordering his meeting place, he felt triumphant. A more than satisfactory achievement for the son of an obscure tailor from Leeds, he told himself as he climbed the low bank leading upward from beneath the stone bridge.

Ten yards away a slight figure crouched behind the protection of a mound of underbrush where he had retreated after listening to the muffled conversation beneath the bridge.

Josef couldn't comprehend the hypocrisy of the English mind. Officials from both England and France called him and his co-conspirators bloodthirsty for rebelling against the tyranny of their country's leaders—for trading the lives of several thousand peasants in exchange for the future of Armenia.

Here in England, men plotted to kill another man for something as trivial as status.

★ ★ ★ ★ ★

"I thought you didn't intend to be seen with me now that I know too much about you," Chloe commented as Adrian wheeled her aunt's bicycle from the stable.

Pretending reluctance, Adrian replied, "Willie doesn't know how to ride a bicycle."

Chloe tightened the ties of her wide straw hat and slanted him a sidelong look. She repressed the smile tugging at the corners of her lips. "There now. If I'd known that yesterday morning, I'd never have been abducted. I'd have ridden my bicycle, and you would have had to accompany me. Don't you find it fascinating the way life has a way of settling the order of events?"

"If you had any sense, you'd return to your parents. Think about that while we ride. Just put your feet on the pedals and push them in a circle. The movement will stimulate your brain in the right direction. Meanwhile, I'll keep a properly respectful distance behind you."

Deciding Adrian didn't sound nearly as severe as he hoped, Chloe slowly worked her left glove down each finger. She risked a glance over her shoulder, hoping to see frustration. Instead, Adrian stood astride the bicycle, his forearms resting on the handlebar and his head forward as if he were looking for gold nuggets among the gravel of the carriage drive. Swallowing her laughter, she said, "I'm ready now."

"No hurry," came his reply.

Without looking to see if he followed, Chloe set out. As they passed between the gates, she turned left. Once on the smoother surface, she pedaled faster and smiled. She acknowledged that Adrian was right. Her brain felt stimulated, and she'd come prepared with a way to punish him for his gothic ideas. Send her home, would he? She smiled happily. He deserved a reminder that such an idea was absurd.

During the three-mile ride, Chloe plotted the revenge she would heap on Adrian in the village. So lost was she in her plans that she almost didn't see the plain black gig approaching. Suddenly aware of the equipage, she braked and pulled to the side of the road. Horses disliked bicycles, and horse-drawn vehicles had an unwritten right of way.

Instead of passing them, the driver reined in his horse. He lifted his hat obsequiously and said, "Do I have the privilege of addressing Lady Chloe Lockwood?"

Startled, Chloe turned a questioning glance to Adrian, then looked back at the tidy, black-garbed little man holding the reins. His light blue eyes were set rather too close; his sandy whiskers matched his wispy hair. In a voice modeled after her aunt's when she considered someone overly familiar, she said, "Have we met, Mr. . . . ?"

"Inspector Moon of Scotland Yard. I apologize for being so forward, but I wonder if you might be so kind as to assist me."

Still imitating Heloise at her most intimidating, Chloe replied, "I've no idea what possible assistance I can offer."

"I've been sent to make further inquiries of you and Mrs. McCandlish concerning the jewels you found. I recognized you from the description I'd been given." His gravelly voice rang with authority.

Chloe could almost feel Adrian relax behind her. "I'm sure I can be of very little help, Inspector. I discovered the jewels when we were packing Jane's belongings."

"Yes, well, that's one of the little questions I'm puzzling over. How did Mrs. McCandlish react when you made that discovery?"

"She was extremely upset, but that can be no surprise to anyone. Ian McCandlish was a brute. He beat her," Chloe said aggressively, daring him to refute her words. "She could hardly dance for joy at his death, but I am sure she felt very little grief. From what I could gather, the presence of stolen jewels only reinforced what she already knew. She'd married a blackguard."

Moon stared at her fixedly as he asked, "Are you quite sure she didn't know about the jewels beforehand?"

Chloe gripped her handlebar tightly to keep from hitting the officious little man. "Jane McCandlish is now part of my aunt's staff. Needless to say, her honesty has never been in doubt. Two Scotland Yard men have already questioned her. If you intend to browbeat Jane again, you must contend with my aunt first."

"I have no intention of upsetting an innocent lady. Surely your aunt's word that Mrs. McCandlish is innocent will suffice."

"I should think so. Now. I have several important errands. Good morning."

Chloe nodded haughtily and rode off, glancing swiftly back to be sure Adrian followed. Seeing his open amusement, she said stiffly, "I'm sure I have no idea what could be so funny."

As they entered the village, Chloe halted in front of the dressmaker's. "It is very unservant-like of you to find my best imitation of Aunt Heloise so amusing. I'll have you know I plan to be exactly like her when I grow up," she said firmly.

Adrian now laughed out loud, his voice echoing along the quiet, cobblestone street. Several children playing in the next yard came to the edge of the road to stare. Even after his chuckles subsided, his eyes sparkled. "Finish your errands as quickly as possible. Please. We must talk."

Aware of what he wished to discuss, Chloe decided to continue with her plans to annoy him. "Of course. I shall be only a minute."

She dawdled at the dressmaker's for nearly fifteen minutes, leaving Adrian to cool his heels on the street. When she descended Mrs. Redding's shallow steps, she discovered the dressmaker's maid of all work had brought Adrian a currant bun from the morning's baking.

In response to her frown, he swallowed hastily and thanked the girl, who flashed him a dimpled smile.

A ten-minute stop at the library drew yet another giggling maid, who paused on her way to the butcher's to pass the time of day with Lady Heloise's groom. Chloe gritted her teeth. His customary lack of expression was missing. She wanted to wipe the fatuous smile off his handsome face. The fool was encouraging the attentions of every maid in the village.

Her plan to keep him dancing attendance on her throughout the morning as punishment for insisting she leave had backfired. Without a word, she mounted her bicycle and rode off. She heard Adrian's flirtatious farewell, then the sound of his bicycle tires on the gravel following her to the small post office at the end of the street.

Mary Sinclair greeted her politely, but an expectant smile appeared as she spied Adrian. The postmistress's daughter's broad, plain features took on a rosy glow. "And Mr. Drury. So much bin goin' on out ta the big house I were certain yer couldn't get free ta pick up them cigars I bin carryin' regular ever since ye came. Maybe I shoulda' delivered 'em meself."

This last was delivered with a wink, and Chloe bit back a groan. The red tide creeping up Adrian's neck looked about to engulf him.

"After you've taken care of my letters, you may attend to Drury's needs," she said firmly.

"Kelly at the livery stable said as how a different Yard man come from Lunnon t'day," the girl commented as she

132

counted the coins Chloe placed on the counter.

"Yes, we encountered him on our way to town," Chloe said. "Did he tell Kelly why he was here?"

"Kelly said he thought mebbe the inspector would take Jane McCandlish away."

"Oh, surely not." Chloe was horrified.

"Well, 'twas Jack Lifton found McCandlish's body near the stone bridge. He said the man had been hit on the head and left with his head in the water ta drown. Me pa says as how it coulda' bin a woman did that, and ev'ryone knows McCandlish beat her."

The stone bridge—the same place her abductor had summoned Adrian. "I'm sure they'll find that the murderer was another person, someone with a grievance, Mary. Are there many newcomers in the village?" Chloe inquired.

"Not so many. Folks want ta go where there's somethin' lively happenin'." Her eyes filled with longing. "Now Lunnon's the place. Always a good time goin' on, partic'ly fer a girl like me. Me pa says it's wicked there, but I'd sure like ta see fer meself." She sighed.

Chloe bit back a gurgle of laughter. While she was doing everything in her power to keep from being sent to London, Mary spent her days longing for the bright lights of the City. "You might find London noisy and smelly. I've heard the streets are unsafe, and in some sections people never go to bed."

"Don't it sound wunnerful?" Mary enthused, her glance drinking in Adrian's handsome profile.

Adrian frowned at Chloe's back as they left the tiny post office.

He yearned to cast off this ridiculous masquerade and return to his own world, where every maid and farm-girl he met

133

didn't throw herself at him. Then he recalled numerous well-bred young ladies who had offered him the same wares as had Mary Sinclair.

He stepped close to hold Chloe's bicycle while she mounted and asked dryly, "Have we played enough games this morning?"

Chloe's eyes rounded with feigned innocence as she leaned against her handlebar, the divided skirt swinging gracefully from her hips. "I have no idea what you're talking about."

Adrian nearly ground his teeth in frustration. "I beg your pardon, Miss Chloe. Have you any other errands?"

"No, I believe that's everything. Are there any serving girls in the village you haven't greeted?"

He stepped closer and said tersely, "Don't be sarcastic. If you think I enjoy their attention, you're sadly mistaken."

"I know only what you tell me," she shot back. "So I know precious little, don't I?"

She was jealous. The discovery pleased him so much that he wanted to kiss her, now, this very instant, in the middle of the village. Adrian stepped back. "Then perhaps you'll honor me by granting me a few minutes' conversation after we return. We can discuss arrangements for your journey back to Bennington Hall." He released the frame of her bicycle and stepped over to his own.

Before he could swing his leg over the seat, she pedaled away, calling over her shoulder, "I've no intention of returning home right now. I'm having a perfectly *lovely* time here in Upper Whiddlesby."

Adrian raced after her and fell in line several feet behind her, where he tortured himself by picturing her long, graceful legs and gently undulating hips without the demure skirt. As they approached a graded curve in the narrow road, her pedaling became more labored, and he gained on her. As his muscled legs propelled him into the lead, he sighed in relief. Watching her without being able to touch was a painful process.

At the curve he glanced back to be sure she had pedaled safely up the incline, then returned his gaze to the road ahead, only to have the sun blind him. When his vision cleared, he saw the glint of sunlight reflecting off a thin wire stretched taut a foot above the roadway.

"Turn aside, Chloe!" he shouted as he braked and steered toward the hedgerow. He wasn't quick enough. His bicycle tire struck the wire at an angle, and he sailed through the air toward the verge, where he landed in a heap against the base of a budding hawthorne hedge.

Shaking his head to clear it, he rose on his hands and knees and looked around for Chloe. She had avoided both the wire and his bicycle but had rolled to a stop with her front wheel wedged in the thicket. "Are you all right?" he called.

"I'm fine," she answered as she dismounted and hurried toward him. "Are you hurt?"

"No." As Adrian straightened, his eyes caught movement on the other side of the growth behind him. Before he could call a warning, a shot broke the silence. He threw himself to the ground, dragging Chloe with him and covering her body with his.

A second shot echoed through the clear air. There was a sound of branches breaking, and the hedgerow swayed. The shrubbery shook as a heavy object crashed against the branches and fell to the ground.

Pressing Chloe's face onto the grassy verge, he felt her heartbeat vibrate through her back against his chest, matching the accelerated rhythm of his own. "Stay down. Someone's shooting at us."

"I noticed, you idiot. For heaven's sake, let go of my head. I'm breathing ants," was her disgruntled reply.

They lay flat, listening intently for the sound of approaching footsteps in the dry grass. The hedgerow shielded them on one side, and Adrian scanned the road anxiously in both directions, only to find it deserted. After several moments Chloe stirred against him. To Adrian's discomfort, in spite of their danger, his body reacted to her nearness.

"You've crushed my favorite straw hat," she grumbled.

Unperturbed by her uncharacteristically feminine complaint, Adrian braced his arms on either side of her and levered himself upward. Once the fright of the gunfire and his stark fear for her safety had passed, his body was betraying him in a shocking manner; she had to have noticed. Her rounded bottom had been pressed against his loins. He rolled away from her.

Chloe drew herself cautiously against the base of the thick shrubs. "If you want to look around, I promise to be small and invisible."

Adrian inspected the roadway. He felt sure their assailant had fled. If someone had wanted to do away with them, those moments when they were sprawled on the verge had presented an ideal opportunity. He stood cautiously and sighted down the hedgerow until he spied an opening thirty feet to his left. Moving quietly, he edged toward the break in the shrubbery, his head down and his body close to the prickly branches.

He peered carefully into the field beyond. All he could see were rye shoots attending to the business of growing. Adrian doubled back along the hedgerow toward the point where he had landed on the other side. Now he knew what had made the branches snap. A man's body was crumpled against the hawthorne.

"Damn! Why did whoever shot him have to kill him?" Adrian grumbled as he looked down at the tidy hole in the back of the victim's head. Its very tidiness matched the discreet black suit. His memory nagging him, Adrian turned the dead man's face to one side. "Damn! Thomas picked a hell of a time to lose me."

"Adrian! Adrian, are you all right?"

Chloe's voice penetrated the shock that had engulfed him at the sight of Inspector Moon's blank countenance. "For God's sake, stay back. You shouldn't see this."

His command was too late. Chloe breached the hedge and ran to him. Adrian seized her upper arms, shielding her from sight of the body. "Don't you ever do anything you're told?"

"You were quiet for so long. I was afraid something had happened to you." She peered around him. "That's the Yard man we met this morning!" She pulled from his grasp and bent close to the body, then said, "He's dead, isn't he."

"Very." Adrian had seen death before, but he was quite sure Chloe had not. "You're not going to faint on me, are you? Go back to the road and sit down."

"Don't be ridiculous. I knew there was something strange about him. He didn't sound official enough. I'll bet he's an imposter. Did you search his pockets?"

"Forgive me. I've been too busy trying to protect you from the sight of a body. So much for chivalry," he muttered as he turned over Moon's corpse. Adrian unbuttoned the black coat and withdrew a flat wallet and a card case from the inside pocket.

Chloe crouched beside him, surveying the scene. "Look, there's a gun next to his hand. And a coil of wire over there. Adrian, he must be the one who booby-trapped the road! He was waiting to kill you."

Her observations could hardly be more shocking than the

warrant card, issued by Scotland Yard to Inspector Cecil Moon. "He's who he said he was, Chloe." Adrian held out the card.

She looked at it with disbelief. "Then why was he trying to kill you? And who killed him?"

"But why must Adrian leave?" Chloe demanded for the third time. She had never seen her aunt so adamant.

"Through your own inquisitiveness and interference, you are now enmeshed in this abysmal situation, which puts you in danger. You are now vulnerable through Adrian. I want you gone as soon as possible, preferably before Scotland Yard descends on us. The investigation of this sordid affair will destroy Adrian's anonymity." Heloise's voice was low, even though they were closed snugly in the tiny upstairs sitting room that adjoined her bedchamber, the door of which was locked.

"I want to go with him," Chloe said stubbornly. The thought of a separation made the future everyone had decreed for her even more distasteful.

Heloise rolled her eyes heavenward, as if asking for divine protection from her niece's impulsiveness. "I have no idea where Fitz will send him, but there may be hazards. He will be backtracking and constantly looking over his shoulder, directing all of his wits toward staying alive. Do you want him killed because he is distracted by fear for you?"

The tears in Chloe's eyes threatened to overflow her lower lids. "I . . . I want to help him."

"You have no more idea of how to go about such an enterprise than that witless Gladys. And don't tell me you learned how by reading a book. I've heard quite enough of that," Heloise said briskly. She leaned forward as if to give her niece a comforting hug, then apparently thought better of it. "He must disappear. And I want you packed and prepared to leave for Bennington Hall tomorrow morning. I shall accompany you there myself and supply your parents with a suitable explanation for your return."

"Not unless I can say good-bye to Adrian," Chloe bargained, unaware that her expression was suddenly as unyielding as her aunt's.

"I don't like this."

"If someone attempts to drag me away without seeing him I shall fall into a fit of hysterics."

A grim smile tightened Heloise's lips. "If you persist in such idiocy, do not doubt there are ways to remove you against your will."

For the first time since Adrian had hurried her home and thrust her into her aunt's care, Chloe smiled widely. "I'm sure there are, but I suspect you would have scruples about using drugs or violence against your own niece . . . even to insure her safety. Besides, my father wouldn't approve. You know he can't bear for me to be unhappy."

"The prospect horrifies me," Heloise answered dryly. Her gaze measured her niece's will. "I can't permit it. Fitzhugh gave me specific instructions in an event such as this. Adrian is under guard until his orders arrive." Her gaze shifted to a point beyond Chloe's shoulder. "However, Fitz will not be here for hours yet. Molly is to deliver Adrian's dinner as soon as dusk has fallen. Make your arrangements through her. I prefer not to know anything more about them."

Chloe threw her arms around her aunt and delivered a smacking kiss to her wrinkled cheek. "Oh, thank you. I'll never forget you for this, Aunt. And I promise I'll leave whenever you say."

Chapter Eleven

An hour later Molly pulled the ruffled cotton cap down over Chloe's hair and straightened the bib of the coarse cotton apron over the maid's dress she had appropriated from the laundry room. " 'Tis a good thing that Ellen's a tall one. The other maids're short little things. Ye'd have stood out like a sore thumb in one o' their dresses." She lifted the linen-covered basket from the pantry shelf. "Now, carry this like so. And walk gawky-like. Ellen has a hitch in her gallop." She handed Chloe the basket, its contents concealed by a checked towel.

Grimacing, Chloe altered her naturally graceful stride and made her way to the door.

"Ye'll do."

As she left the house, Chloe smiled at Molly's brusque instructions. She knew her aunt was aware that the plump housekeeper could never deny Chloe anything, not since Molly had nursed her through chicken pox during one of her aunt's visits. The maid had entertained the fretful five-year-old with carelessly edited tales of her London street-life.

Only in the past five years had Chloe realized how unsuitable some of those stories had been.

Careful to stay on the grass so as not to make a sound, she slipped through the shadows near the hedge. The memory of that first night, when she'd witnessed Adrian's gentle rejection of Gladys, played before her eyes. How kind he had been to the red-haired maid—almost fatherly, as if he cared about her feelings. Chloe paused beside a mock orange in full bloom. The scent was acrid in her nostrils.

Adrian was leaving, and the wonderful new world of love she had just discovered was about to be snatched away from her. Tears welled in her eyes. Chloe believed strongly in fate, and she knew she had met the other half of her heart. The sense of connection she'd felt that first day was real. Since then, all her dreams for the future had revolved around the one thing she had thought to exclude from her life: Love for a man.

She shifted the weight of the basket to both hands and continued on her way.

As she entered the side door of the stable, a horse shuffled its hooves restlessly in freshly strewn straw. A shadow drifted from one of the stalls and approached her. A low murmur pierced the darkness lightened only by the faint glow of the lantern hung from a hook near the tack room door.

"Is that for me?" the guard asked in a gravelly voice.

"No, it's for your sick cousin," she whispered as Molly had instructed. In spite of the silly code, her heart beat wildly in the base of her throat. "I'm to make sure he gets it."

The shadow stiffened a moment before its voice said, "I'll take you to the stairs. The door's at the top."

Chloe followed him to the enclosed stairwell and continued upward. Her guide remained behind in the shadows. She knew if she met the man tomorrow, she would never recognize him.

She knocked as Molly had instructed. The bolt slid back and the door swung inward, revealing a room lit only by a lantern sitting in the middle of a sturdy pine table. The single window was snugly shuttered. She jumped at the sudden appearance of a hand from behind the door, then clutched the wicker handle tighter as seemingly disembodied fingers tugged at the basket.

Adrian stepped from his hiding place, a frown creasing his forehead. "Isn't that my dinner?" He held a businesslike revolver in one hand. Gone was the subservient droop of his shoulders and deferential dip of his head. He had the appearance of a dangerous opponent, his knees flexed as if prepared to spring. Chloe stood frozen.

She heard a muttered curse before his hand clamped over her arm and dragged her into the room.

The door swung to behind her, and the bolt shot noisily, breaking the brittle silence between them. Adrian whispered harshly, "What in the hell are you doing here? My God, woman, have you no sense at all?"

"I had to see you once more," she said, her voice tight with tears.

Moving precisely, his face expressinless, Adrian turned from her and laid the revolver on the table beside the lantern before walking to the shuttered window, where he braced his hands on either side of the frame. "No, you didn't. You'll be better off if you never see me again."

"No!" Chloe sobbed, her heart in her voice. She dropped the basket and hurled herself against him, wrapping her arms around his unyielding torso. She pressed her cheek against his shoulder and wept into his coarse cotton shirt, nuzzling her face against the rough weave while her hands explored the lean, muscled contours of his chest, memorizing them for the bleak future. "I'll never believe that. You must come back to me or I'll . . . I'll wither and die."

Adrian was angry with himself for exposing her to danger. Still, he'd just spent the last hour pacing the room like a caged panther, wanting so desperately to see her one more time that he wondered if he had willed her arrival. More than breath, he needed her, warm and open and loving, in his arms.

His fingers clutched the uneven surface of the window frame convulsively while Chloe's heart beat strongly against his back. His body throbbed with each pulse, as if they were one. Her touch had weakened his resolve, but her tears were his undoing. With a groan he twisted within her grasp and crushed her against his chest.

"God, Chloe, why are you doing this to me?" Tilting her head back with his fingers beneath her chin, he gazed deeply into her eyes. They glowed like drowned topazes. With infinite care, he brushed her tears aside.

"Because I didn't realize how terribly I loved you until I thought I might never see you again." A single teardrop rolled down her cheek.

"I don't want to leave, but I must . . . for both of us." He buried his face against her neck, his lips pressed to the fragile skin beneath her ear, and whispered, "And I can't return unless we identify whoever is after me."

Adrian could scarcely recognize his own voice, harsh and cracking with strain. He was focused on his splayed fingers meeting at the center of her slender back, his thumbs bracketing her rib cage. She was heaven between his trembling hands, and only the scruples bred in his blood prevented his seizing paradise for his own.

"A track handicapper wouldn't even give odds on my life right now. How can I ask you to wait? For what? A body surreptitiously delivered to my parents so they have something tangible to mourn? A cautiously worded commendation letter from the queen? Or better yet, no word at all, because I've been disposed of with such skill and because no one knew I was alive to begin with? You're in danger because of me. I should be flogged."

He closed his eyes and rested his forehead against hers. When he spoke again, his voice was laced with pain. "You're young and so damn beautiful I can hardly sleep nights thinking about you. You deserve much more."

Chloe moved her head back and forth in denial of his words. "You don't understand. I'd rather hope . . . because without that I'll have nothing. Oh, Adrian!" she sobbed, swaying against him.

Gathering her close, Adrian cursed the fates that had brought them together and were about to tear them apart. Then he threw his scruples to the wind. "I love you, Chloe. Even if you should be told I'm dead, always remember that."

Chloe's arms were anchored firmly behind his back, and her face was buried just below his left collarbone. She pressed against him as if she were attempting to burrow beneath his skin to his inner soul. Her silence alerted Adrian that she was thinking rapidly. "Damn it, Chloe, you can't come with me. I want you safe."

Her reply was muffled. "What if the worst happens, and I never see you again?"

Adrian wrapped her more tightly in his embrace and forced himself to say firmly, "You'll meet another man. One with a future. You'll marry him and live happily ever after. I insist on it."

Chloe tilted her head and kissed the underside of his jaw. "Then I want memories. Real memories of the two of us together. Adrian, please make love to me." She pressed her lower body into the cradle of his hips.

"Chloe, I can't," he moaned, his heart breaking.

"I think you can," she said, a knowing smile curving her lips. She thrust her uncorseted body closer, against the proof he couldn't disguise. "In fact, I'm sure you can."

"No."

As she rose on her toes, her upward movement nearly sent Adrian over the edge. Her lips, open and sweet and warm,

claimed his, and her tongue naively stroked his. Forgetting his resolve, Adrian grasped the delicious curve of her bottom, gathering her against him. He pulled his mouth away long enough to murmur through gritted teeth, "I said no, Chloe. We can't." His control was slipping at an unnerving rate.

Her breath was light and mint-scented as she whispered against the corner of his mouth, "Oh, yes, we can. Please, Adrian. I want this to remember during the long dark nights and sunless days we're apart. And you'll remember, too. You'll know I'm waiting for you and praying for you. You'll come back to me."

Her words and her hungry kisses were Adrian's undoing. When she pulled his shirt from his trousers, he found his own fingers busy disposing of the apron and bodice buttons of her borrowed gown. Even as her dress opened, she wrenched his shirt over his head. All the while a voice deep within him reminded him he was behaving irresponsibly. Pausing to relish the sight of Chloe's quivering breasts beneath the sheer batiste of her chemise, he mumbled, "You're trampling all over my conscience, Chloe, but God help me, I can't resist you."

Chloe threaded her fingers through the golden whorls of hair covering Adrian's chest, mesmerized by the silky texture. She rubbed her cheek against him, luxuriating in the unfamiliar sensation. Locating one flat male nipple with her lips, she kissed it tenderly, then touched her tongue to the nub. When he shuddered, she threw her arms around his neck and arched against him, rocking from side to side. "I'm so glad, Adrian, because I'm about to explode with wanting."

His responding groan vibrated against her breasts. Each time Adrian deepened his kisses, each time his fingers explored a new and untouched patch of skin, spirals of sensa-

145

tion pooled in her lower body, making her clench her thighs together and push against the intriguing ridge of his erection. She'd read objective scientific analyses of the mechanics of what they were about to do; she'd seen drawings and photographs of statues with quite unbelievably proportioned male bodies. None had prepared her for the wondrous mix of lassitude and excitement overtaking her body.

"Copulation sounds so cold," she babbled, scarcely able to form the word with her kiss-swollen mouth.

Her gown slid to the floor as Adrian swung her up into his arms, his laughter sounding light and rather shaky in her ears. "Only if you're presenting a paper on animal husbandry, darling. We're about to make love." The laughter fled his voice, and his eyes were dark and haunted as he whispered, "These few hours may have to last a lifetime for both of us. Love it will be. Oh, yes." He lowered his head.

The reverence in his kiss contracted Chloe's heart, and her nerves fled. She wished there were some way to banish the bleak loneliness she'd seen in his eyes. Tears tightening her throat, she whispered, "Love for a lifetime . . . and beyond." She clung to him as he carried her into the tiny, slant-ceilinged sleeping room, his narrow iron bed a shadowy outline in the faint light from behind them.

As he gently lowered her to the coarsely woven sheet, Adrian said, "I only wish I could surround you with the satin and lace and flowers you deserve."

Her lips quivered with feeling as she answered, "I have you. There's nothing else I could ask for. The sun is shining on us right now. This very minute."

Chloe watched his trembling hands pull off his scuffed work boots and unbutton his twill trousers, dropping them where he stood. He came down beside her and caressed her cheek. "I swear I'll move heaven and earth to return to you.

146

When I do, we'll have sunshine all day and every night of our lives."

Speaking around the lump forming in her throat as she turned her head to kiss the callused skin of his beautiful hand, she said, "I intend to remind you of that promise at every single opportunity. Forever and ever."

"I'll cherish every word," he murmured as he reached for the hem of her chemise.

His fingers skimmed her body as the sheer garment inched upward. Chloe moved eagerly beneath his touch, arching from the bed to rid herself of anything that separated them. Even before he released the chemise, she pulled him against her. "Good, because I intend to nag you," she said breathlessly as, without shame, she rubbed her body against him, glorying in the feel of hard muscle and sinew.

Adrian stayed her hands. "Much more of that and this will be over before it begins," he cautioned. "Do you know how long it's been since I've . . ."

"I'm so glad to hear you've done this before," Chloe interrupted, her breathing shallow and her husky voice breathy. "I've only read about it in . . ."

"Books," he finished for her before dipping his lips to her breast. He slanted a glance upward. "We'll muddle through somehow."

Chloe felt her nipples contract as he suckled first one, then the other. Tiny nerves beneath her skin quivered as his lips moved lower, and she arched upward against him when his warm breath dusted her tight brown curls and lower. "I read about this in . . ." The sentence hung unfinished as an inner explosion of exquisite feeling shattered her ability to speak.

Adrian raised his head, sure he would remember until the

day he died the bliss that contracted Chloe's features at that moment. His gaze fixed on her face, he positioned himself and eased carefully into her narrow passage until he reached the frail barrier of her innocence. He kissed her deeply and surged through, drinking her little cry of surprised pain and folding his arms around her tightly.

"I'm sorry, darling. I tried to be as quick as possible, but then, I'm sure you've read about that, too." Even though his lips were tight with the need to hold back, he felt a smile tug at the corners.

Her lips curved against his, and his body shuddered as she wrapped her legs around his hips. The simple, trusting movement shattered his control. He pulled back and plunged deeply within her over and over until release racked his body and he collapsed against her, his face buried in the dark silk of her hair. He closed his eyes and allowed himself to dream, if only for a few moments.

Chloe's fingers, light and graceful as shadows drifting over water, grazed the damp skin of his back, bringing him back to reality. Adrian shook his head in denial, as if awakening from a long sleep. With a groan, he lowered his forehead to hers. An incredulous shudder shook him, and guilt flooded his senses.

"If you're going to begin apologizing and calling yourself an inconsiderate oaf, I'll never speak to you again. At least until the next time I see you."

Chloe's voice was slightly disgruntled, but her fingers had resumed their delightful explorations. He pushed her dark curls from her cheeks. "You didn't read my thoughts accurately. I was calling myself a thoughtless sod," he said.

Her fingers strayed upward, smoothing perspiration from his forehead. She frowned. "Whatever do you use to dye your hair? It feels so . . . rough."

Deserting his abandoned principles, Adrian smiled. "Rather like walnut bark, I'd hazard. I don't think the dye is far removed from the tree." He kissed her gently. "Chloe. I . . . I've never felt so . . . exalted. I love you." He kissed the misplaced dimple on her cheek before grazing upward to the dark oval of eye lashes fanning her cheek. Reverently, he pressed his mouth to one eyelid.

"And I love you, Adrian," Chloe whispered. Her jaw tightening, she added, "And you *will* come back to me. Soon. Because making love is ever so much more wonderful than any book ever said."

"Totally irresponsible! I shall never forgive you for this, Adrian," Heloise snapped.

So fierce was her expression that Adrian pictured blood flowing from the wounds where her gaze raked him, but he stood his ground. "You've every right to be angry, Lady Heloise. I'm not feeling very proud of myself, either. All I ask is that you notify Fitz immediately if Chloe should be pregnant. If so, I'll come back to—"

"And should that be the case, how am I to explain the pregnancy to her parents? I am responsible for her, you know."

Adrian managed a bleak smile. "They might understand better than you think. After all, she's been tricking them into giving her her own way for years."

Heloise stood in the shadow of the stable beside Adrian, whose hands were thrust deep into his jacket pockets. A short distance away, Thomas held the reins of two horses. She said resignedly, "I suppose I was even more headstrong at Chloe's age. Lockwood women demand everything life has to offer. Never doubt I'll take care of her, Adrian, but come back soon."

Leaning forward, she brushed his cheek with her lips.
"I've become quite fond of you." Then, as if surprised by her
own gesture, she gave him a little shove toward the restless
horses. "Go."

A night spent in vigil at her window proved poor preparation for the next morning, when it seemed to Chloe that half
of official London was making her aunt's house its unofficial
headquarters.

A Scotland Yard inspector pursued his inquiries from the
seldom-used blue sitting room. Uniformed constables bustled back and forth and interrogated everyone who had set
eyes on Inspector Moon from his arrival until his death.

Of far more interest to her was the elegantly dressed, mysterious figure she had observed entering the stable at two in
the morning. He had remained there a very short while, then
walked to the house and disappeared within.

Early this morning he had entered the breakfast room,
where he bowed graciously over Heloise's hand and con-
versed with her in a soft, indistinguishable whisper. Chloe
pretended disinterest, even though she was aware of the
piercing glances he cast in her direction, and concentrated on
spreading quince jam to the edges of her toast, which she was
quite sure she could never force down her throat. He had
then disappeared into her aunt's private sitting room.

Even more intriguingly, Heloise had immediately ordered
a breakfast tray for two, then announced to Chloe that their
departure for Bennington Hall would be delayed until the
next morning. With that she had left to join the mysterious
stranger.

Determined not to miss one detail, Chloe had lingered in
the hall after breakfast, and now she sat with her aunt at the
dining table picking at a light luncheon, her position opposite

the open door to the foyer providing her an unobstructed view of all comings and goings.

"My dear, you will benefit from your meal only if you actually consume that food rather than shred it," Heloise pointed out.

"I'd eat if it weren't necessary to spy to discover what's happening. Or, of course, if you could see fit to tell me what all this activity means," she retorted. The man her aunt's butler had just admitted was the shambling fellow she'd seen with Adrian a day or two earlier. Putting down her fork, she craned her neck to see his destination.

Lemasters directed the guest to her aunt's private sitting room, then approached and placed a silver salver before her. "This just arrived for you, Lady Chloe."

One look at the telegram's contents and Chloe stared accusingly at her aunt, who was calmly pouring tea into a fragile flowered cup. "You wired my father."

"I had no choice, Chloe. You have been both reckless and headstrong, and I needed your parents' weight behind what must be done. Both you and Adrian are in dire peril." She twisted a wedge of lemon over her cup. "Those words are, of course, somewhat melodramatic, but they seem to be the only description that comes to mind. I have had an extremely busy day and night."

Chloe wanted only to throw herself into Adrian's arms and sob. But he was gone, his destination unknown. "I won't leave until I hear from Adrian."

"You said something similar yesterday, and look where *that* led," Heloise pointed out.

Before she could continue, an amused voice interjected, "Adrian is presently quite busy attempting to preserve your precious hide, and his own, for that matter." For the first time that morning the double doors swung closed, and the willowy, fashionable figure earlier closeted with her aunt moved gracefully toward her. He drew out the chair closest to Chloe, said, "May I?" and, without awaiting permission, seated himself.

First he busied himself with preserving the crease in his wool broadcloth trousers. That settled to his satisfaction, he leaned toward her and said, "Allow me to introduce myself. I'm Fitzhugh Kent. For my sins, it's my duty to unscramble this hurly-burly. First, I must tell you that the victim yesterday was an imposter. The real Inspector Moon retired fifteen years ago and is busily cultivating begonias in Cornwall."

"I *said* he wasn't really from Scotland Yard! Wait until I tell Adrian!" Chloe exclaimed. Her excitement drained away abruptly when she recalled she would be unable to share anything with Adrian for the indefinite future. For a moment desolation threatened to consume her; then, reaching deep inside for strength she didn't know she possessed, she turned her attention to Fitzhugh Kent and distracted her morose thoughts by allowing her curiosity full rein. His appearance was that of a Bond Street lounger, but in spite of his surface affability, his bright hazel eyes surveyed her shrewdly.

"To be sure. I shall make every effort to ensure that he is informed. For now, Lady Chloe, you have already forgotten Adrian was ever here. I feel confident you understand why I make that request."

"I hope you do a better job of hiding him this time than you have so far," she responded fiercely.

He exchanged an uncomfortable look with Heloise, then rose to stand before Chloe. "Adrian warned me you would be unhappy with me, but I had very little choice. I'm pledged to keep him, and now you, alive. We're quite sure two separate parties are in the hunt for him, and only one has a name. No one wants Adrian back from limbo any more than I. He's my friend."

Chloe aimed a scathing look at him. "Some friend. He could have broken his neck yesterday. Or been shot."

"My dear, that is why Adrian is much better off elsewhere . . . where he needn't concern himself with your safety. If he were to remain here, you would be in as much jeopardy as he." Frowning, he shot his cuffs back into the sleeves of his exquisitely tailored coat. "All you need know is that I've sent him out of the country, and although I hope that now he's gone you're in no further danger, there will be people in place to assure your safety."

He reached for her hand and smiled, his expression showing warmth for the first time. "If you could manage to pretend you have no interest in his destination or his future, both parties should lose interest in you." He patted her hand and said coolly, "By the way, if we should encounter each other socially in London, please pretend you have never seen me before. Unless, of course, I acknowledge our earlier meeting first. Should you wish to communicate anything vital to Adrian"—he paused meaningfully—"I shall, of course, do my best."

Chloe felt hot color rise to her cheeks and pulled back from his touch. *Oh, God. He knows!* With a sudden flash of clarity, she realized the possible consequences of her rash behavior the night before. Then she swallowed a smile. She could think of nothing more wonderful than to have Adrian's baby. Still suspicious, she demanded, "What do you intend to do now?"

"Track down that blasted Armenian. And attempt to discover who hired our dead man to impersonate an officer of the law. Succeeding at either task could provide further clues about the intriguing mystery of why at least *one* of Adrian's pursuers wants him dead." He smiled, his eyes taking on the concentration of a terrier who has spied a rat. "Actually, the entire exercise is a fascinating little puzzle. Quite keeps one from becoming bored, don't you think?"

Chapter Twelve

Three weeks later Chloe found herself comfortably installed in the London home of her mother's sister, Lady Ashton. The time since Adrian was spirited away in the night had passed in a daze. At times she wondered if the interlude in Upper Whiddlesby had actually happened.

But memories of Adrian's eyes darkening from indigo to black with arousal, memories of his tenderness as he made love to her, haunted her dreams, and when she awoke each morning with tears on her cheeks, she knew her dreams were reality.

Since their arrival in London, her mother and her aunt had talked of nothing but fashion. How ridiculous to worry about the cut of a bodice or the angle of a bonnet's brim when Adrian was in exile, in danger—in misery.

The sound of her mother's soft voice from across the tea table in the little sitting room reminded Chloe that her thoughts had strayed far afield, and she returned her attention to the present.

"It's so helpful to visit your aunt while we order our gowns. Not opening the new town house until we're here to stay will conserve my strength. The modiste now has our measurements and requirements and can do the final fittings this week, then deliver our new gowns directly to Portland Place when we arrive." Maude Lockwood sighed at the thought of even this much effort.

"Mother, I've told you before that you needn't put yourself to all this trouble." Her prayer that she might be pregnant had gone unanswered, but Chloe saw no reason to suffer the rigors of a presentation and to attend an endless string of ridiculous entertainments. Adrian was sure to return at any time.

For one breathless moment she thought her mother looked relieved. Then Maude replied with martyred resolve, "I shan't hear of it. You will never marry suitably if you don't meet eligible young men. At least launching you after the Season has begun will be much easier. As it is, your father's title procured us the last of the available presentation dates."

Chloe fingered the ribbon ties of the Olivia bonnet she'd cast aside. Its high crown made her appear even taller. She would tower over the majority of other young women.

Defiantly, she perched the bonnet in front of the curls clustered on the back of her head and crossed to the oval mirror above the white marble fireplace. Cocking her head to one side, she peered at her reflection. Intimidating. Perhaps affecting an air of disdain would keep eligible young men at a distance until Adrian rescued her from this madness.

Her gaze fell on the lace-covered bustle perched atop a stack of bundles, and she grimaced. She had reluctantly given in on corsets, but she would not tolerate this latest abomination.

A light tap on the door was followed by, "Here you are, my dears." Lady Ashton whisked into room. "That bonnet is dashing, Chloe, but perhaps we should select something softer. Gentlemen might find the Olivia daunting on someone of your height."

Chloe turned from left to right, nodding at her reflection. "Certainly not. I can't imagine having any interest whatsoever in a man who is put off by something so trivial as a hat."

Lady Ashton looked for help from her sister, who sighed

and wriggled her silk-stockinged feet, which she had freed from her high-heeled laced boots. The recently healed ankle was still rather swollen. Receiving no assistance, Lady Ashton commented, "Dear me, how you remind me of your Aunt Heloise."

"Good," Chloe said, reaching up to remove the hat. "And while we're at it, Aunt Mary, I really must tell you that I refuse to wear that thing sitting over there."

"But, Chloe dear, the bustle is back in fashion. Everyone wears them."

"Then we'll tell the dressmaker to design my gowns another way. I can't imagine walking around with a cushion attached to my bottom. How on earth do people *sit?*"

Lady Ashton spread her arms helplessly and pointed out, "The bustle isn't placed exactly . . . there, Choe." Then she pleaded, "At least allow Madame Deucet to make up a few of your new gowns to accommodate the figure improver."

Her aunt's look of despair reminded Chloe how much she owed her. "Dear Aunt Mary, you are so kind. You mustn't suffer because of my vagaries. I'll speak to the dressmaker myself."

"Oh, no. Let me talk with her. If she becomes upset, she might refuse to finish your wardrobe." Discouraged, she turned toward the door.

Chloe raised her eyebrows and answered, "After she's cut all that perfectly good cloth? I should think not. We are, after all, the reason she's in business. She'll be agreeable."

Without speaking a word, Maude rose from the settee, picked up her discarded shoes, and joined her sister. As the two left the room, Chloe heard her mother lament, "Exactly like Heloise. Whatever shall we do?"

Her good humor restored, Chloe looked forward with pleasure to confronting Madame Deucet. As she headed for her bedchamber, an idea blossomed in her inventive mind. She needn't look like every other girl. Over the past year she had read many writings by the Pre-Raphaelites, who for years had advocated a free, healthful mode of dress. A small, daring number of women had adopted less constricting, flowing gowns—dispensing with the corset she hated so much. Dress reformers had denounced the return of bustles, and she would do the same.

And she would continue to hope for a miracle. Any day, Adrian would surely return and rescue her from the tediousness of society. She was convinced Adrian would let her wear anything she chose—even bloomers.

She had no wish to impress society; conforming to its silly foibles would be stupid, because she didn't care. She never had.

The idea grew to full bloom in her mind. Chortling with glee, Chloe whirled in a circle. She would be an original, and people could accept her as she was or not at all. If she scandalized society, her mother might be forced to take her home, where she would wait for Adrian. Forever, if need be.

Only one thing dampened her spirits. Why had there been no word from him? Her excitement dissipating as rapidly as it had arisen, Chloe threw herself across the bed. Did the mysterious Fitzhugh Kent really exist, or had she imagined him? And if he did, why should he trouble himself with her? Why had he and Aunt Heloise seemed so cozy? Her aunt had refused to answer the second question, and she had no idea how to reach the mysterious gentleman.

For the first time, she felt discouraged and lost.

Four months later, Adrian huddled over a smoky fire in a crofter's cabin deep in the Scottish Highlands, seeking relief from the mid-October damp and cold. Whenever he allowed himself to rest, his mind resumed the ritual of searching the past. Each time his thoughts were distracted by the memory of the dancing golden lights in Chloe's eyes, of her tall, slender body, and of her ingenuous acceptance of his love.

Chloe must be in London now, exposed to flirtations and social obligations. She might be impetuous and headstrong, but she had too much common sense to be impressed by the false gaiety of the social scene. The corners of his lips quirked when he recalled her matter-of-fact response when they discovered the bogus Yard man's body. Any other well-bred young lady would have fainted, or at least have had hysterics. Not Chloe.

Adrian poked the fire with the toe of one scarred boot. It was raining steadily, the same drenching downpour that had fallen for the past week. He was convinced Scotland existed in a state of permanent rainfall, and there were sheep everywhere. *Please, God, if you allow me into heaven, let there be no sheep.* He'd been offering the same plea ever since his arrival.

Imagining His response to that prayer, Adrian grinned. Sheep appeared to have significance for God; witness the references in scripture. Perhaps the Lord's sheep were intelligent. Those he tended were the stupidest animals Adrian had ever encountered. The day before he'd found an old ewe who had fallen onto her back. He'd turned her over, aware that if he didn't, the stupid animal would remain belly up until she died, making no effort to right herself.

"You blend nicely into this bucolic setting."

Fitz's brittle baritone brought Adrian to his feet. "It's about time you showed up. I've come damned near setting out to look for you."

"Now, now, old chap, no need to embarrass me with your enthusiastic welcome. I know you've been having a jolly time working with my uncle's sheep." Fitz brushed a straw from the sleeve of his damp herringbone overcoat. "He says you're a great help, by the way."

"By Jove, I'm delighted to hear that, old man," Adrian replied bitterly, irritated by his friend's impersonation of a social gadfly. "Since I've been left here among the rocks and hills for so long, it's nice to hear I'm carrying my weight."

"I should think so. My uncle's not wealthy, you know. Can't afford a careless shepherd." Fitz shook out his linen handkerchief and spread it on a wooden stool before seating himself at a safe distance from the smoky, smoldering fire.

"Put a sock in it. I'm bloody tired of being buried in the wilds." With three long strides he crossed the room to tower over Fitz's seated figure. "I want out *now*. Your convoluted little mind may not accept the concept, but I'd like to have a life apart from all this cloak-and-dagger nonsense."

"Something to do with the Lockwood chit, I suppose." Pretending indifference to Adrian's belligerence, Fitz unbuttoned his coat and dug into an inner pocket. "Charming young woman, Lady Chloe. She's become rather an enigma to me." He pulled out an envelope. "Thought you'd like to know how she's going on."

Arrested by the amused undercurrent in Fitz's voice, Adrian returned his stare and made no effort to open the envelope Fitz thrust into his hand. "What are you trying to tell me?"

"Become quite the rage, has Lady Chloe. She doesn't dress like anyone else. She doesn't give a damn whether she has partners for dances, the theater, or for rides in the park. The result is, everyone wants to be seen in her company. At least that's what I hear. Haven't been in town myself. Went to South Africa on a rescue mission," he added absently. "At Heloise's she was green as grass. Four months later the world dances to Lady Chloe's tune."

Adrian removed the contents of the envelope and leaned toward the flickering lantern for enough light to read the newspaper column from the top of the stack.

Since her arrival on the social scene late last spring, Lady Chloe Lockwood has set her own style, wearing draped, unstructured gowns in unconventional colors other women would eschew, thumbing her elegant nose at established customs. One must allow that her height and form lend themselves admirably to such individuality. Even the most hopeful of her rivals for the unofficial title of Trendsetter is handicapped by a lack of the joi de vivre and cheerful disdain for public opinion that characterizes this young lady.

"Sounds to me as if Chloe's still doing things her own way." Adrian grinned, recalling how relentlessly she had swept aside his scruples that night over the stables.

"Oh, she's all the rage. Read on."

Something in Fitz's voice alerted Adrian to read the next clipping with greater attention. It was a gossipy account of a house party in Devonshire where the young woman who had entranced him with her ingenuousness had apparently led three eligible sophisticates, each of whom Adrian knew, around like puppies.

The rest of the articles only reiterated the first two. Adrian's rage grew with each word he read. When he'd finished, he crumpled the newsprint in his fist. "If I hadn't gone into hiding with the misbegotten idea of drawing attention away from Chloe, this would have never happened!"

"Adrian, old sod! Can this be true love? You've not even asked what other enlightening information I brought." Fitz smiled broadly. "For instance, would you have guessed it was your Armenian friend who murdered that ersatz Scotland Yard inspector?"

Adrian turned from his inspection of the crude mantel, his attention diverted from dark thoughts of Chloe's unexpected metamorphosis from naivety to gossip fodder in a few short months. "Josef?"

Fitz answered, "Poor chap had been waiting for a chance to tell you he bears you no grudge. He was the only conspirator left after the military stepped in and took control of the revolution. He watched you at Heloise's, following you when you met with me or my operative, but he dithered about whether or not to confront you. He even told me about the night Lady Chloe joined you on your outing." He waggled his eyebrows suggestively.

"You're obnoxious, Fitz," said Adrian, suppressing an urge to smash his fist into his friend's grinning face.

"He told no tales. I rather got the idea Josef admires you."

"Where is he now?"

"Haven't the foggiest. He floated into my orbit several weeks ago. He'd been searching for you since you did the flit from Lady Heloise's. Afraid that other set—not that he could identify them, alas—had done you in." Fitz shivered and pulled his collar closed. "My sainted aunt! It's cold as Greenland in this place."

Adrian turned to face the dubious warmth of the fire and spoke over his shoulder. "And here I thought you'd come to change places." At that moment he wished Fitz would return to his clandestine operations and leave him to brood over the loss of Chloe's innocence.

"Actually, I came to take you back with me."

When Fitz's words penetrated his mind, Adrian turned to stare at his friend, his tongue incapable of forming words.

"Damn it all, Adrian, did you hear what I said? I came to

take you back. You're going to recover from being blown to bits or drowned, whichever version suits you."

"Why?"

"Because Josef told me more about the anonymous tip the conspirators received about you. Could have come from anywhere, but he thought the wording was British. He reads the language well." Fitz grimaced. "On another front, we discovered the counterfeit Cecil Moon was a down-on-his-luck actor who'd been hired to kill you. No family, few friends. A dead end, if you'll pardon the pun." He stood and drew close to Adrian. "Someone wants you taken care of permanently. Waiting hasn't drawn him out, so we'll use you as bait. You're to return to your family . . . and to the dashing young lady."

Adrian's features hardened. "My family, yes. But I fear that Chloe has some explaining to do."

"This time you needn't rush off and abandon her. Perhaps she'll be able to reassure you."

"No more innocent trips abroad?" Adrian arched his left eyebrow and looked at Fitz straight on.

"Would you go if I asked?"

Adrian clapped his friend's shoulder a trifle harder than necessary. "I'd tell you to go directly to hell, and I'd mean it."

"That's what I thought."

Your package arrives tonight.

Chloe frowned at the crumpled note. She held the missive up to the gaslight, looking for other marks on its clean wrinkled surface. Nothing caught her eye.

The note had fallen from her reticule in the carriage during her return to Portland Place that afternoon. She had managed to snatch up the paper before the dour-faced chaperon her mother had hired shortly after they'd settled in could notice it and comment. The message must have been slipped into her bag during her visit to Mudie's Select Library.

Closing her eyes, she reviewed that visit, trying to recall if she had let her reticule out of her sight at any time. Then she traced her path through the library. She'd perused the latest books from America. Who had been near her?

Was it the scholarly old gentleman with a fascination for the novels of Nathaniel Hawthorne? The flighty young matron who pushed ahead of Chloe to check out her books? Perhaps the tiny white-haired old lady, a connection of Lady Ashton's who had prosed on about her aunt and her mother as young girls, had tucked the message into her purse.

"Well, it hardly matters. I'm not expecting a package. Perhaps I picked up one of the clerk's papers by mistake," she decided.

Chloe tossed the note aside and walked restlessly to the window, where she parted the heavy lace underdrapes to stare moodily at the street below. Nothing was turning out as she wished. Her scheme to make herself unacceptable to society had failed. Instead of being an outcast, her outrageous dress and frank, open manner intrigued people, had placed her in the position of turning down more invitations than she had been able to accept.

With disregard for her fresh manicure, she nibbled the end of one finger. She was unbearably lonely, her life was hollow, and she could see no hope for the future. Each time she allowed herself to think of her naive infatuation for Adrian, she burned with embarrassment. She had actually demanded that he make love to her. Wherever he was, Adrian, that profligate bastard, was probably still chuckling.

Chloe could name the day and even pinpoint her whereabouts when she had discovered his true nature. She had been on the verge of entering the billiards room at the Heathridge estate when she heard Adrian's name and withdrew behind the doorframe. Gerald Winrow had been ragging his friend, Thomas Wakefield, about his conquests over the past two years. "Take care, old man. You will be surpassing the rec- ord Harding set before he died."

"At least I leave the ladies on good terms," Wakefield defended over the clack of the ivory balls. "That disappearing trick of Adrian's was damned good. Thalia Fairfield haunted his mother's drawing room until Lady Warnham fled town."

"Bit fishy, that. Some thought Thalia might be preggers, the way she carried on. Particularly after she accepted Reginald Fell so fast."

A ball thudded softly against the padded edge of the table. "Well, she wasn't, but it don't matter. By the time Harding surfaced again, she was married. Remember Helen Worth? She and Adrian lived in each other's pockets for weeks. Everyone said it was a match. Then he disappeared. Helen didn't waste any time attaching that American chappie. Was at the dock myself to see them installed in the bridal suite before they left the country."

"Sheer coincidence, of course, that Adrian arrived back in town two days after the boat departed."

"He always was a spooky sort. Women ate it up. Followed him in droves. Too bad about the last one, though."

"Caroline Satterfield? That wasn't Adrian's fault. He'd been gone two weeks when she broke her neck fox hunting."

Chloe had fled to her room, where she smashed every piece of bric-a-brac within reach, causing a minor uproar when her hostess discovered the wreckage.

Lelia Fenton's observation when Georgina Lefton and her husband, Lucas, won a doubles tournament was also engraved on her memory. She shuddered. "Georgina played her best tennis with Harding. Lucas had to come up with a sapphire necklace to get his wife back."

Adrian had even pursued married women! The knowledge was like a knife in her heart. How naive she had been! She was not only brainless; she was a fool. Recalling the instant passion that had overwhelmed her, she told herself she was probably a wanton as well.

In seven months, the year in society she'd promised her aunt would end. By then she would have to have reached a decision about a concrete plan for her future to present to her parents, or Heloise would refuse to support her cause. Surely by then the pain of betrayal would fade.

"Damn and blast," she cried, releasing the curtains. A soft knock at the door interrupted her thoughts. "Who is it?"

Her mother's voice was muffled. "My dear, I must speak with you about what you plan to wear this evening."

"Tillie is pressing my gown at this very moment."

The door opened, and her mother entered the room.

"Surely you're not wearing another of those outrageous draperies. And that ridiculous excuse for a corset—why, it has scarcely any boning."

"You sound exactly like Aunt Heloise, Mama." Chloe hugged Maude affectionately; it wasn't her mother's fault that her daughter was so miserable. "Of course I am. Why should I suddenly become conventional after going to so much trouble to establish my own style?"

Maude's determination seemed to desert her. "Oh, dear. I can't help but think your father would be displeased if he knew how you're behaving."

"Don't worry, darling. I'll tell him it was all my idea, which is the truth. He'll surely believe *that*." Chloe knew, without any lack of respect, that she could convince her father black was white if she chose. Hadn't she persuaded him to delay her comeout for nearly four years? If she'd entered society at the proper time, by now she would undoubtedly be married to some pleasant, unimaginative man and have produced at least one child. The thought depressed her even further.

Maude looked at her daughter piercingly. "I'm well aware your father is besotted with you, Chloe, but your unconventional behavior distresses me. People are talking."

Her mother's expression dragged Chloe's attention from her own self-pity. "Darling, you know I'd never do anything to embarrass the family."

"I know you wouldn't, but I do worry about you."

"In what way?" Chloe sank into the slipper chair beside the fireplace, her knees suddenly weak. Her mother had seldom taken her to task.

"You appear to behave outrageously on purpose. Your dress is influenced by intellectuals you have never met. And your free and easy speech and manners are being copied by girls who are too young to know better. Their parents are dismayed." Maude sank into the chair opposite her daughter.

"Ever since you were a child," she continued, "your father has encouraged your independence. But society has certain rules, and you can't continue to break them without any regard for others. When people tire of you, they won't hesitate to discard you, along with the rest of the family."

Chloe covered her face with her hands. Even though she didn't give a fig what society thought of her, she realized that while she had been flaunting convention—first waiting for, then later, she had been, in effect, thumbing her nose at Adrian, who wasn't even there to see—she'd never given a thought to her family. Chloe suddenly felt like a spoiled, willful child. "I'm so sorry, Mama," was all she could manage through trembling lips.

Maude knelt and pulled Chloe's hands away from her

cheeks. "Darling, I've never really understood why you balk at looking for a husband. But I've reluctantly come to realize that simply because I think of marriage as the only suitable goal for a woman doesn't mean it suits you. Shall we return to Bennington?"

Her mother's unexpected offer only intensified Chloe's shame. "I'd like that more than anything, but I won't run away," Chloe declared, dashing the tears from her cheeks.

"I'm only distressed because I don't understand. So many eligible young men have shown interest in you. Why do you treat them as if they were . . . engaging boys, instead of possible suitors? I know I'm not observant, but I do notice *some* things."

Chloe rose and crossed to the dressing table, where she lifted a cut-glass perfume bottle. As she pulled the stopper, the scent of primroses reached her nose. How could she explain her brief, ill-judged romance with a man who'd been declared dead? On the other hand, her mother would probably prefer that version to the truth—that the man was Aunt Heloise's groom. She settled on a carefully edited version.

"I . . . while I was visiting Aunt Heloise, I met a man."

Maude settled into her chair, an expectant smile tugging at her lips.

"There were some . . . difficulties I was sure we could overcome." She bent her head and added abjectly, "He apparently doesn't share my optimism, for I've not heard from him."

"Surely he wasn't married!" Horror contracted Maude's pleasant features. "Free-thinking as your aunt is, she would never countenance such a connection."

Chloe sighed. "No. Nothing like that. I wish it were that simple. But others are involved—people who could be hurt quite badly. Since I've been in London, I've heard tales about him. Just rumors, but obviously I never knew what he was really like."

Since David Mountjoy was accepted everywhere, his status as Lord Warnham's heir became a topic of discussion, and thereafter, comparisons between David and Adrian were inevitable. These, plus the damning gossip, had increased her disdain for society's morals—and for Adrian, Viscount Harding in particular.

"Put him behind you, then, Chloe. He doesn't sound worthy of your loyalty." Maude rose and embraced her. "And decide as you wish when to return to Bennington. Roderick Derwent's father still hopes you'll look favorably on his son."

Laughter dispelled the last of Chloe's tears. Her mother wasn't going to give in easily. "Roderick Derwent is what Lionel would call a blister. When he looks at me, I feel dirty. Aunt Heloise's fortune, even though it is derived from a brewery, is the real attraction for him."

"To many, gold outshines everything else in life," Maude observed with unexpected insight. "One day you'll find someone who doesn't care about the money. Someone who values you because of who you are inside."

Chloe wasn't accustomed to this side of her mother. In that moment she wondered about the accommodations her mother must have made to insure a peaceful marriage. Surely her dear, bluff father must have had some uncomfortable moments with someone so surprisingly acute. "Perhaps you're right. Darling, I promise to behave this evening. And I'll think about what you've said. There's more than enough time to decide whether to stay in London."

Chapter Thirteen

Nerves ate at Adrian like tiny insects nibbling every inch of his flesh. He tried to ignore the feeling by studying the sheen of his gleaming dress shoes. Then he scrutinized his pleated evening shirt in the mirror over the fireplace, carefully inspecting each jeweled stud for possible imperfections. Moments earlier he had peered at his face, fresh from the ministrations of a skilled barber. The sight of his cap of blond hair still surprised him. The shaggy dyed mane was history.

In moments he would appear, reincarnated, before society. One part of him was eager. Hadn't he dreamed of this? His reunion with his parents and sisters had been tear-filled, the suffering etched on their faces tempering his own joy. Tonight he would face an uncertain welcome.

At Fitz's insistence, no one in the ballroom knew of his return. "I want several faces under observation when you appear. Give me a few minutes to get my people into place, then I'll send for you," he'd ordered.

Somewhere out there in that bejeweled crowd was Chloe. Closing his eyes, Adrian pictured her against the backdrop of an azure sky, the sun burying itself in her breeze-tossed hair, her sherry-colored eyes sparkling and her head thrown back as if life were a celebration that would never end.

Fitz's clippings had tarnished that vision; they told of a willfull young woman out of control. The more he had thought of them, the more anger welled up inside him. During the long months in Scotland, only his dreams of her had

170

kept him sane. Chloe had been his talisman and his prayer, and the discovery that she was as faithless as any society flirt had shattered those dreams. He couldn't resist torturing himself by wondering how many other men she'd slept with since that night above her aunt's stable.

Unable to stand still any longer, he tugged the formal broadcloth coat into a more comfortable position across his shoulders and adjusted his already perfectly tied cravat.

A discreet knock sounded on the gleaming walnut panel behind him. Adrian squared his shoulders, drew a deep breath, and left the room.

Chloe sat with her erstwhile dance partner in a corner of the ballroom. She'd mentioned the recent death of Charles Darwin, choosing the subject in hopes of launching a rumor that she had something beneath her hair besides empty space.

"But I read that Mr. Darwin at one time considered entering the ministry. What do you suppose his thoughts were as he faced death? He surely was aware of the uproar his theories caused."

Thomas Edgely looked at her blankly. "My dear, what possible difference can it make? The man all but proclaimed from the hilltops that the creation as described in Genesis is humbug. I say let him rot."

"That will happen to all of us. My concern is with his soul."

"The man had no soul. He set himself beyond the line of decent thought."

Chloe could have cried with disappointment. She had tried to hold an intelligent discussion, and Edgely discounted her ideas as if she were an idiot. "It must be wonderful to be so sure of what you believe."

"You'll find I'm a rational chap, my dear." His eyes, which

were rather too small for his face, gazed at her appreciatively. "Heavens, a woman has no business reading Darwin in the first place, much less trying to fathom the man." Shouts from the entrance to the ballroom caught his attention. "There seems to be some excitement, Lady Chloe. Shall we see what it's about?"

"Of course." Rising, Chloe rested her gloved hand on his arm. She had resolved to appear docile this evening, but Edgely's pomposity caused her to wonder if such a state might be fatal.

He peered over the heads of the crowd and cried, "I say, it's Harding! But he's dead . . ."

The buzzing in Chloe's head threatened to drive her into the first faint of her life. She covered her face with her hands. Her knees felt like water.

"Lady Chloe, are you quite all right? Shall I find you a chair?"

The buzzing subsided, only to be replaced by raised voices and waves of nervous laughter spreading through the crowd. She looked toward the entrance. In the center of the confusion she saw an unfamiliar golden head of hair above a familiar face with a strong, straight nose and high cheekbones. Her memory supplied the laugh wrinkles at the corners of his eyes, the sharp lines of tension at the corners of his chiseled lips, and the bleakness that had often dulled his expression. But here in the environment where he belonged, he was self-assured and confident. An almost princely aura surrounded him, as if he had cast off a cocoon and emerged a brilliant, glittering butterfly.

His evening clothes were impeccably tailored, his blond coloring reminiscent of angelic cherubs. Even from a distance she could see the nonchalant grace with which he accepted enthusiastic greetings from friends both male and female.

A similar but less handsome face beneath a darker gold mane appeared nearby. David Mountjoy. He was no longer the heir; Adrian had displaced him.

Adrian's return would alter many lives. But not hers, she vowed silently. She tugged her escort's arm to get his attention. When he turned to her, she said, "You needn't stay with me. I can tell you're dying to join the crowd around the Prodigal Son."

As Edgely deserted her with a mumbled apology, Chloe watched the gathering crowd. She had little doubt Adrian had forgotten her existence. Why did the thought make her feel like a piece of used goods?

She desperately wanted to confront him with a litany of his past sins, not the least of which was encouraging her infatuation, but she doubted she would ever have the opportunity. People thronged around him, and her pride was too great to allow more than faint interest to show on her face. Her effort would have been successful if a soft voice behind her had not murmured, "I notified you your package would arrive tonight, Lady Chloe."

She whirled and surprised a small, satisfied smile on Fitzhugh Kent's fine features. As their gazes met, his lips firmed, as if he had never revealed the emotion.

Collecting her dignity, she said coldly, "I thought I wasn't to acknowledge you if I met you in society, Mr. Kent. And for your information, this particular package is not mine. I've known for some time that Adrian never had any real feelings for me." The lie almost stuck in her throat, but she would be damned if she would show weakness to Fitzhugh Kent.

"The gossips have been at work, I see," he replied dryly.

"I have no reason to disbelieve what I've heard. You and he enjoy the clandestine so much, you've probably no idea how to be straightforward. You've no thought for the flesh-and-blood people involved." Chloe felt tears rising behind her eyes and blinked rapidly. "I wish you both great happiness."

She turned from him, her shoulders stiff with suppressed anger, but he seized her arm. "My sainted aunt! You'll draw more of a crowd than Adrian if you keep that up." When surprise brought her drowned gaze to his, he removed his gloved fingers from her arm. "Here now, let us at least give the appearance of cordiality." He held her gaze a moment, then gestured toward the milling crowd across the ballroom.

"As soon as you've recovered your composure, we'll join the welcoming throng. With very little fanfare I shall introduce you to Adrian as if you've never met before. Then you will express the proper surprise and amazement."

"Indeed. And what fairy tale are we telling this week?"

He grinned like a schoolboy and responded, "A fascinating saga of drifting to shore with the flotsam and awakening in a fisherman's cottage with no memory of his past. Of nearly two years spent working side by side with the family who rescued him. A month ago he slipped and struck his head while climbing a cliff. Eureka! The blow restored his memory."

The patently ridiculous tale restored Chloe's balance. "How very touching. I'm sure the legend will become a standard in nurseries across the country. Perhaps even around the world."

Fitz arched a mocking eyebrow. "The most unbelievable tale is always the one most readily believed." He inclined his head toward the excited crowd milling around Adrian. "Do you see any skepticism abroad?"

Studying the chattering, animated people, Chloe said disgustedly, "No, you're quite right. People will believe anything—if you tell your lies with a straight face. What a cynic you are, Mr. Kent."

"Quite right. Understanding the means of manipulating one's fellow man can be diverting." He took her arm once more. "And now I'll take you over for an introduction."

"I have no intention of accompanying you anywhere," Chloe retorted stubbornly.

"My dear, Adrian is well aware of your behavior since you've arrived in London. Did you really turn down four proposals in one week? And what about that scandalous excursion to Bath?" His smile reminded her of a satisfied cat. "In spite of all this, or perhaps because of it, you're one of the reasons he has, shall we say, risen from the dead."

"Have you any idea of the number of stories I've heard about his scandalous past since I've been in London? Nothing, not one single thing I have done, compares with the exploits of Adrian Harding. You and he are free to muddle along on your own. I refuse to have anything more to do with him." She attempted to tug her arm free.

"Too late. Now you're both in danger once again. His enemy is aware you and Adrian know each other. If you snub him, questions might arise in that person's mind, and we can't have that."

His gaze deadly serious, he continued, "If you two conduct a casual flirtation, you might draw the villain out, cause him to expose himself."

Chloe's head began to spin. She was furious with Adrian, and the thought of being in his company once more made the blood drain to her toes. "Don't be ridiculous. Aunt Heloise is the only person besides you who knows about our . . . past connection. And why should it mean anything to anyone else?"

"What makes you think that bogus Yard man intended only to eliminate Adrian? Why couldn't he also have meant to kill you?" A sardonic smile curved Fitz's lips. "Actually, your aunt suggested that possibility. She has a rather . . . interesting view of the situation. In fact, she was involved with information-gathering for my father, who was my predecessor. Why do you think I stashed Adrian at her estate? She knows the drill."

"Aunt Heloise?"

"The one and only. An amazing lady. Legend says she and my father had a bit of a romance years ago. Shortly before he married my mother." With a practiced, graceful gesture, Fitz raised her hand and kissed it. "Believe me, someone in this room knows the two of you have met. Therefore, for the next few months I want you to pretend a mild interest in our modern-day Lazarus. You should have no difficulty pretending to be an empty-headed beauty. From all accounts, you know the role well. Don't worry. You'll be well protected."

She stiffened, so angry at the insult that she couldn't speak.

"Good. I see I've banished those tears you were about to shed down my coat front." He nodded his head toward the crowd around Adrian. "Lady Chloe?"

Chloe despised Fitzhugh Kent for accusing her of behaving like a wanton. Even as her sense of fairness told her it would be unforgivable to leave Adrian vulnerable, she felt ill-used. Unable to disguise the distaste she felt for the spy master, she rested her fingers on his extended forearm. "I suppose I have little choice."

Over the heads of dozens of excited well-wishers, Adrian saw Fitz leading Chloe toward him. Her disdainful expression told him what he had already guessed. Now that she had experienced the heady power of social success, the young heiress wanted no part of him. Like any other shallow debutante, balls, parties, picnics, and flirtations filled her every waking hour; the seductive call of frivolity had triumphed over her dreams of adventure.

His mind might condemn her, but Adrian's body responded as enthusiastically as ever. If anything, he admitted to himself, she was lovelier than before. The graceful lines of her simply draped amber gown needed no embellishment other than the willowy form beneath it.

Her shining dark hair was gathered artfully high on her head, and her skin glowed like fine damask. Suppressed anger turned her eyes dark and stormy. His desire gave way to fury at the thought of other men dancing with her, their hands resting on her supple body—a body unprotected by the cage of steel stays and muslin that encased the other young women in the room.

The bewhiskered man at his left broke into his thoughts. "Seeing you gave me a hell of a start, old man. Be at the club tomorrow? I'd give half a year's rents to hear the whole story, but maybe you'll settle for a drink."

"Sounds like a golden opportunity to fleece you, Grosvenor. Some brandy will do," Adrian said, shaking his friend's hand. If he collected half the drinks he'd been promised this evening, he'd be drunk for the next quarter century. Ten years earlier he would have done his best to follow up on every offer. Now the idea bored him.

Fitz's mocking voice sounded to his right, and Adrian turned, steeling himself. "I say, Adrian. Such a dust up. One might almost think these people had given you more than a passing thought the past two years."

"I'll cease to be a Seven Days' Wonder as soon as someone comes to town with a two-headed calf. How have you been, Fitz?" he inquired, as if he hadn't seen him forty-five minutes earlier.

"Worthless, as usual. Wanted to present Lady Chloe

Lockwood to you. She hadn't yet come to town when you were here last, and she's eager to hear your story."

"How do you do, Lady Chloe. I've met your brother, but I wasn't aware he had a sister," Adrian lied. He watched her eyes, seeking something other than the glittering anger in their depths.

"I had convinced my father to delay my comeout for some stupid reason or other. Now that I'm here, I wonder why I waited." Her defiant glance clashed with his. "Mr. Kent says you've been believed dead for two years. Where have you been all this time? In purgatory?"

The pointed jibe slammed into Adrian like a physical blow. Chloe had changed more than he'd thought possible. Determined to match her callousness, he smiled. "There have been times in the past year when it was more like hell. I have ghastly nightmares."

Chloe's lips quivered briefly, then tightened. "One's imagination can be powerful. I feel sure you have a wealth of fascinating stories about your adventures."

"Haven't you heard? A gentleman never tells, Lady Lockwood." Adrian refused to believe her vulnerable in any way. "Allow me to obtain some punch for you, and I'll confess everything. You'll excuse us, won't you, Fitz?"

"Why is it that the hero of the hour always walks away with the most beautiful woman in the room?" Fitz lamented. "Take her with my blessings, Adrian. Just remember, like Cinderella, you have an appointment at midnight."

Her full lower lip caught between her teeth, Chloe watched Fitz drift away, then turned to Adrian. "There's no need for us to continue this charade. We've been seen together. That should suffice. I wish you good luck . . . and good health."

"Not so fast." Adrian caught her wrist lightly, a harmless gesture that anyone who might be watching could interpret as playfulness. "We have matters to discuss."

Chloe tugged ineffectually at his hold. "If this hare-brained scheme is all you and your asinine friend can come up with, you have my permission to hatch another plot. We had a . . . dalliance last spring. You disappeared. That was the end of it."

"We were both present when a man was murdered. You were kidnapped because of me, for God's sake," Adrian muttered between his teeth. He guided her firmly toward the terrace. The punch could wait. "That fake Scotland Yard man's death put me in danger, with your sweet little hide next in line." He guided her deftly through the French doors and into the shadows.

"Your imagination is exceeded only by that of your friend, Mr. Kent," she declared. "Where do you think you're taking me? If you don't care for my reputation, I do! Besides, it's cold out here."

Glancing around, Adrian realized that five months earlier he would have given all he would ever possess to be alive and here on the terrace with Chloe. But there was no romance in the expression on her face. She was regarding him as if he had just emerged from a primeval swamp.

The irony slashed through him like a sword thrust, and he said coldly, "What reputation? Look at you! You're dressed like a reject from a poetry colony. Damn it, you're not even wearing a proper corset beneath that dress." His earlier fury at the idea of anyone but himself touching her spilled out. "If you weren't in line to inherit half the money in the Bank of England, decent people wouldn't allow their sons to associate with you."

Chloe felt as if she had been struck. Her first impulse was

to retaliate, but her mother's gentle criticism of her behavior haunted her. Of course she behaved outrageously, at least by rigorous standards. But while many of her actions stemmed from rebellion, the rest were the result of her growing sense of emptiness. With no reassuring message from Adrian, her feelings of ill use had grown. The gossip concerning his propensity for wooing and deserting women only intensified her defiance. She had been naive to allow herself dreams, dreams she now knew were fairy tales. And Adrian was no fairy prince.

Although she wanted nothing so much as to turn and bolt through the crowded ballroom, such a scene would precipitate gossip that would mortify her mother. Perhaps now was the time to return to Bennington Hall. For good. She clenched her hands into fists so tight that her fingernails bit through the thin silk of her gloves. Chloe refused to give Adrian the satisfaction of knowing how heartbroken she was. She shivered, drew a deep breath, and said frigidly, "Think what you like. Now, if you'll excuse me, I must find my next partner."

"As soon as we settle the terms of our relationship, you're welcome to go inside and resume whatever flirtation you're conducting this week." Adrian rested one arm on the wall beside her head, imprisoning her. "It's crucial that we appear mildly attracted."

The rough stone scraped Chloe's elbow through her crepe silk gown. It crossed her mind to wonder if he were insane. She braced herself, shrinking as far from his unnerving touch as possible. "That's ridiculous. I want nothing more to do with you."

"I'll enjoy this no more than you, my dear. As little importance as you apparently attach to our little 'dalliance,' you're in danger, and I feel a certain responsibility toward you. If we ignore each other, someone might think the separation is intentional to protect you. A casual flirtation will suffice."

"That's the most ridiculous idea I've ever heard." In her annoyance, Chloe forgot the cold.

"Not at all. As I recall quite clearly, you enjoy sketching. I shall call on you Monday afternoon to escort you to the British Museum."

Chloe despised his remote manner, his clipped speech. He seemed detached, as if he weren't part of the absurd situation into which he had thrust them. She remembered vividly his ability to tamp down his personality. Even as she quivered with awareness, she wanted to destroy that aloofness. Surely he knew that the museum's less popular exhibits were notorious trysting places. "Aren't you afraid such a shameless flirt as I might lure you into a deserted room and compromise you?"

An expression of distaste crossed Adrian's face, and his arms fell to his sides, affording her the opportunity she sought. Satisfied, she walked away from him. "I might be at home when you come for me, or I might not, you . . . you unspeakable bounder," she spat over her shoulder.

Reentering the ballroom, Chloe scanned the dancers and clusters of laughing people. Since no one appeared to notice her, she paused at the edge of an animated group, only to have her ears assaulted by the excited speculation of Adrian's return and the incredible story of his amnesia. Interspersed were laughing recollections of his past romantic entanglements. She wished she were elsewhere, anywhere at all.

"I wouldn't be surprised to hear he seduced the fisherman's daughter before he left," Cecelia Singleton purred.

Chloe wondered what the gossiping group would say if she announced that *she* was the fisherman's daughter and confirmed that she had been thoroughly compromised. Their raucous laughter and the swirling mixture of fragrances worn by the four women seemed to penetrate her skull, and she was wondering how to extricate herself when rescue came from an unwelcome source.

"There you are, Lady Chloe. We never did have that dance you promised me."

Although Fitzhugh Kent was the next to last person she wanted to see, and she had certainly never promised him a dance, Chloe seized on his offer. As the waltz began, she said coldly, "Is there no end to this evening's unpleasantness?"

"Now, now. No need to be testy. After all, I'm the fellow who's slogging away to keep you safe. And I did bring Adrian back, didn't I?"

Bitterness so thick she could taste it rose in Chloe's throat. "From what I hear, you've orchestrated Adrian's freedom for a number of years. All in the guise of patriotism, of course. I'm sure you'll now attempt to convince me that Adrian's involvement with me was serious and that you'd no intention of separating us. Ha!"

Chapter Fourteen

"In case you haven't heard, he's the toast of the town—a man returned from the dead. People flock to entertain him, and he's carrying on openly with that stupid Lockwood woman. You've failed again." Lelia Fenton's lips drew back from her teeth in an unattractive snarl. "Because you hired bumblers, Adrian slipped through our fingers, and now Kent's brought him back."

Robert Fenton scrubbed his rumpled linen handkerchief across his forehead, then down his cheeks. Although he refused to admit it, his daughter was exactly like her mother; she could reduce him to near idiocy with a few well-chosen words. "Don't worry, m'dear. The problem is in hand . . . and will be taken care of before the month's out. We've plenty of time."

Lelia's ivory fan closed with a snap. "I've heard that fairy tale before. Harding's like a cat with nine lives. And I don't like the way that girl keeps cropping up. Disposing of her may also be necessary. An heir will ruin all my schemes."

"Of course. Of course, Lelia. Have I ever denied you anything?"

Her smile chillingly childlike, she rose on her toes to kiss her father's cheek. "Never. But remember, if you fail, I shall be very, very unhappy . . . and you don't want that, do you, dear papa?"

Adrian's father, Lord Warnham, traveled extensively, overseeing business interests throughout the world, and when he was in England, the family much preferred life in the country, so they seldom used the tidy mansion tucked at the end of a secluded Mayfair *cul de sac*. Before Adrian disappeared, he had used the town house as his own. Now, a quickly engaged staff had opened the residence so efficiently, it seemed he had never been away.

Adrian eyed his guest warily. There had been a time, years earlier, when Fitz's arrival brought a sense of anticipation. Patriotism and the potential for a dangerous assignment were an irresistible combination. That time was past. Now he found himself inexplicably annoyed when Fitz made himself at home before the fireplace in the cozy study. His elegant presence only reminded Adrian that he himself had lost two years of his life.

He had sworn not to allow the change in Chloe Lockwood to affect him, but the vision of what might have been, had he not disappeared to insure her safety last spring, filled his thoughts.

"Stop brooding, Adrian. Your Chloe's not stupid, nor is she as wild and wicked as she'd like the world to think." Fitz held his brandy snifter up to the light and swirled the contents, watching the movement of the dark amber liquid through narrowed eyes.

"She's not *my* Chloe. She never was. I merely worked in the bloody stables at her aunt's," Adrian reminded him. He'd be damned if he'd allow Fitz to know how deeply Chloe's transformation had hurt him.

"Of course you did. But the old girl and three operatives all reported a grand passion in the making."

"She was different then."

"Only on the outside. It's my opinion she's heartbroken. She'd have to have carried her head in her pocket not to hear gossip about your past. She as much as told me she suspects we have a diabolic agreement that enables you to break hearts the width and breadth of England without commitment. Accused me of helping you escape your romantic entanglements for years. And she had tears in her eyes when she spoke. I was quite touched."

Adrian snorted as he set his glass next to the pipe stand. He picked up a ledger from the corner of the desk and leafed through the pages aimlessly, then closed the book and set it aside. "Had I known tears affected you, I would have tried them myself long before this. You aren't the only one on the hook, old sod. It appears my romantic adventures grew both in quality and quantity after I died. According to Chloe, my antics are legendary. She intimated that I was a cad."

"At least she only made me *feel* like a cad. She really has no clear idea of what kind of work you did for me, does she?"

"Would she believe that much of the information I brought back was gleaned not through derring-do but mostly by listening and observing the man on the street? Not bloody likely." Adrian leaned back in his chair and frowned. "I never told her what I did. I simply let her assume I was the most successful spy in history, that my reputation struck fear into the hearts of men and nations the world over."

"Of course you did. Makes a chap feel important."

Adrian sipped his brandy and looked solemnly at his friend. "You're probably the only one who knows I was the worst spy who ever slipped into an alley. My heart was in my throat every time, and I bumbled my way through every assignment. Perhaps that's the real reason I was finally discovered and nearly caught."

"You simply lurched into your successes?"

"If that's how you wish to describe it. Whatever, I'm finished. Done with the whole bloody mess." Adrian tossed back the remainder of his drink, savoring the spreading warmth as the aged liquid hit his midsection. He reached for the decanter and refilled his snifter, then raised it in salute. "Here's to the end of a misguided career. I intend to become sodden and to remain so."

"I wouldn't. Drunks are extremely vulnerable."

Adrian leaned forward intently and demanded, "What the hell is that supposed to mean?"

Fitz rose and crossed the room to move the half-empty decanter. "We discovered your new chef cleaning and loading a nasty-looking pistol in the butler's pantry tonight. You were to have been the victim of a break-in sometime before morning."

Suddenly cold sober, Adrian demanded, "Who hired him?"

"Do you know, he hasn't the foggiest notion. He thinks the bloke worked for the employment agency. He was recruited there. Need I explain that the deal was concluded in a dark room?"

"Chefs aren't likely assassins, unless they're adding ground glass to the soufflé." Adrian swallowed nervously.

Fitz collapsed gracefully in his chair, a faint smile on his lips. "This one usually specializes in poison. Seems there were unexplained deaths in a family he cooked for in Sussex. He swears his innocence, but I doubt it. Only the agency knew his past, but since there's a shortage of chefs during the Little Season, they assured him they believed his denials and cautioned him to be more careful about his choice of herbs and spices. He encountered the unknown blackmailer just before being engaged to work here."

Unable to sit still, Adrian lunged to his feet and paced the room. He stopped suddenly and flung the contents of his snifter into the fireplace. The cozy fire flamed, its leaping fingers flaring bright blue. The acrid odor of burned grapes filled the room.

"Damn it, when will this end!"

As if to show his own faith in the purity of the brandy, Fitz drained his glass. "For some obscure reason, someone appears to be in a hurry to shuffle you off, beginning with the betrayal in Armenia. But he's getting more careless all the time. If we sit tight, he'll make a mistake, and we'll snare him."

"The Lockwoods. Did they bring their own staff, or did they hire one here in town? Have you checked?" Adrian demanded.

"Why should you care? You said Lady Chloe didn't mean anything to you." Fitz's eyelids drooped, giving him the appearance of boredom. "Apropos of nothing, that murdered tenant farmer—seems he was eliminated by his cohorts because he was attempting to take his cut off the top of the loot. Dead end."

"The bastard deserved what he got."

"True. Very true. The burglars have been rounded up, by the by. The brains of the crew was a waiter with a catering firm. He had an inside opportunity to . . . evaluate the premises of their victims."

Adrian made no response. Theft seemed a minor offense at the moment.

"Care to talk about where you really stand concerning Lady Chloe?"

Adrian glared at him. He was tired of Fitz's prying. A vision of Chloe as she had walked away from him this evening came to him unbidden. She'd looked fragile and unsure, but she had held her head high. Only the tremor in her hand when she pushed back an errant lock of hair gave her away. He'd gripped the balustrade to keep from following her and kissing her senseless.

He wondered if he were going mad.

187

"Get out, Fitz. I'm going to bed."

Two days later Chloe rose after another sleepless night. Insomnia and irritability had plagued her since the Skeffington ball. She looked at the ornate crystal clock on the mantel and mumbled her favorite curse word. In approximately four hours, His High and Mightiness Viscount Adrian Harding would arrive.

The possibility that he wouldn't appear never crossed her mind. Adrian had said he was coming, and he would. Give the impression they were mildly interested in each other indeed! Chloe clenched her teeth to keep from screaming.

She had been unable to invent a reasonable excuse to cancel the engagement. If she attended the card party at Lady Candida Morefield's, Adrian would in all probability appear and make a great show of whisking her away. No one would dare criticize the behavior of the Toast of London, and she would also be leaving herself open to a lecture from her chaperon.

"Damn that Ogilvie woman," she said, not for the first time. Lady Claudia Ogilvie was the dour widow her mother had hired as her companion. Chloe never left the house without a sharp inquisition concerning her destination. With Lady Maude at Bennington Hall for the week, Claudia was keeping Chloe under even keener observation than before.

Reconciled to her fate, Chloe finished her breakfast chocolate and bathed. The primrose-scented steam rising from the claw-footed tub revived not only her spirits but her active mind.

Moments after she had submerged herself in the water, she sat straight up. "Why didn't I think of it before?" The prospect of an afternoon with Adrian had been daunting until this inspiration.

"Tillie," she called to her maid, "In the guest room wardrobe is a plaid walking dress Madame Doucet included in the first wardrobe she designed for me. Would you please press it?"

Three hours later Chloe clutched the bedpost while the maid tugged on the strings of her corset. "Tighter, Tillie," she panted. "Otherwise I shall never fasten the buttons. I'm afraid I've gained some weight since the seamstress fitted the waist."

"*I'm* afraid you've lost your mind," said Tillie, with the familiarity of a long-time family servant. "After fretting your mother all this time, you've suddenly decided to dress like a Christian. You're planning mischief, and I want no part of it."

Ignoring the maid's grumbling, Chloe closed her eyes against the dizziness. After a moment, her vision cleared, and she breathed as deeply as she was able. "This will have to do. Now the figure improver." She stepped into a stiff hair-canvas petticoat, waited for Tillie to attach the lace-covered cushion at the back, then donned a silk petticoat before topping the layers with a heavily quilted dark red underskirt. "At least if I fall backward, I shan't bruise," she said weakly.

"Don't blame me if you faint," Tillie said, jerking the underskirt into place. "A body can't leap into a corset after not wearing one for over three months. 'Tisn't normal."

"Hush. I'll be fine. Now hand me my bodice." She refused to acknowledge the little frisson of excitement that ran over her skin at the prospect of seeing Adrian once more.

Adrian's stilted visit with Lady Ogilvie lasted only a few brief moments; his first sight of his companion for the afternoon stole the remainder of his conversation from him. Her mincing entry, swinging a red Olivia bonnet by its ribbons, announced precisely what she intended, and rather than feeling intimidated, he found himself looking forward eagerly to her next move.

"How kind of you to be so prompt, my lord."

Chloe's voice sounded wispy, as if she were unable to breathe. Recalling his caustic criticism of her unconventional dress, Adrian smiled inwardly. "I would never be so rude as to keep you waiting, my dear Lady Chloe. You're looking extremely fine this afternoon."

"I suppose I must thank you for inviting me to the museum. No one else has offered to escort me there," she said grudgingly, setting the hat on an occasional table.

Adrian bowed politely, waited until Lady Ogilvie left the room to fetch her cape, then grinned at Chloe. "No one has thought you intelligent enough to appreciate the exhibits. Must I thank you for dressing so conservatively for our outing?" he teased.

His eyes swept the tight, buttoned bodice and narrow sleeves of her tartan plaid gown. The overskirt draped deeply across the front, then swept up in the rear, where it gathered into a modified train. The dark green and blue tartan contrasted richly with her stiff red underskirt.

Chloe said glumly, "This . . . abomination makes me walk like a chicken." She busied herself with pulling on thin leather gloves and fastening the tiny buttons at her wrists. "Wait until you see me in that ridiculous hat," she added.

He watched her walk across the room to retrieve the aforementioned article. "You know, I do believe you're in the right of it. Shall I follow three paces to your rear and look like a rather cowed rooster?" Adrian recalled his mother's outspoken comments on the absurdities of fashion. He had never before realized why women walked so awkwardly. He compared Chloe's present stilted steps with a clear memory of her graceful movements at the Skeffington ball.

At last he understood his mother's contention that fashion was a nefarious male plot designed to keep women corseted, restricted and useless, as if they had nothing to do but select a gown for the next occasion, which was frequently the case. Concern overcame his chagrin at being trapped in his own hypocrisy. "Look here, if you're that uncomfortable—"

"Certainly not," Chloe broke in. "God forbid you should suffer the embarrassment of being seen with an unconventional woman. Allow me to redeem myself."

At the stubborn note in her voice, Adrian dug his heels in. "Very well." He took her dark cape from the patiently waiting footman and placed it over her shoulders, then watched as she tied on the bonnet. Its crown rose above the top of his own head; somehow the absurd ensemble amused him. "I intend to enjoy myself immensely, as I'm sure you shall also."

"Of course."

As she preceded him through the door and down the steps, Adrian grinned at the determined glitter he'd seen in her eyes. Even Lady Ogilvie's dowdy presence at the foot of the staircase couldn't diminish his anticipation of an entertaining afternoon.

Two hours later Chloe grumbled, "I assume we shall not remain long enough for me to study the Rosetta Stone." With her chaperon's reluctant permission, they had parted ways to pursue their own interests. Adrian had drawn Chloe from room to room, allowing her only a glimpse of the exhibits contained in each, as if he were in a hurry for another appointment.

"Had you plans to decipher it?" Adrian's hand rode lightly at the base of her spine as he guided Chloe from the marble hall into another dimly lit room.

Chloe responded to his comment with the silence it deserved. The oaf was impervious to sarcasm. She reconciled herself to a cursory perusal of the many treasures on display. *I shall come back by myself one day soon and make Ogilvie cool her heels while I look my fill,* she promised herself. For now she intended to take what pleasure she could.

As they rounded the corner of a mahogany case displaying ancient coins, Adrian stopped abruptly. His hand on her arm stayed her steps, and Chloe followed the direction of his gaze. At the end of the aisle a man and a woman stood locked in a desperate embrace, their lips meeting in a passionate kiss. Without asking permission, Adrian grasped her waist and dragged her back to the end of the display. Leaning so close that his warm breath raised goose bumps along the side of her neck, he murmured, "I don't want them to see us."

Forgetting her annoyance, Chloe turned in his loose embrace, rose on her toes, and whispered back, "Is it someone you know?"

"Lelia Fenton and my cousin."

Out of necessity, the breathy exchange brought their bodies together from shoulder to thigh, forcibly reminding Chloe of what had passed between them. She risked an upward glance, then wished she hadn't. How could she have forgotten how his thick lashes tangled at the corners of his eyes or how his eyebrows tilted ever so slightly upward at the corners? The nearness of his lean, close-shaven cheek sent her heart high into her throat. Her corset-constricted body suddenly craved air. She inhaled his clean, familiar scent deeply, relishing the hint of a woodsy male cologne. The heat of her memories nearly overcame her, and suddenly she was panting. She couldn't stop.

As if able to read her mind, he gripped her arms and murmured, "Breathe slowly."

Secure in his hold, Chloe counted as she inhaled, even though the action only furnished more of his scent. Still, the threatening dizziness disappeared. As her mind cleared, the rustle of taffeta reached her ears. "They're coming this way."

Adrian bundled her around the corner into an adjacent aisle. He held a finger to his lips as Lelia's tortured words broke the stillness.

"Please don't speak of it anymore. I can't bear the thought of you leaving for America. I shall be desolate."

"Then come with me." Passion deepened David Mountjoy's voice. "It's our only chance, Lelia. Adrian's return makes it necessary for me to find a position, and the New York bank won't make this offer again. I never wanted his title in the first place. You know that."

"David, you can't leave England. You'd be a nobody in America, and I couldn't bear that for you. And what would my father do without me? I'm all he has."

Chloe could hear the calculated pathos in Lelia's voice. She wondered why David was deaf to such whiny manipulation.

"Your father is so busy with affairs of state that he would hardly notice your absence. Besides, he could visit. Steamships travel back and forth regularly."

The voices came no nearer. Chloe attempted to peer around the corner of the cabinet, only to be dragged back against Adrian's hard chest. A glance over her shoulder revealed his face, his eyes darkened to midnight blue. He was too close; she needed to put some distance between them. But as she pulled away, he cautioned her to silence with a firm shake of his head and pulled her back.

"David, I won't go to America! I refuse to exile myself in a country where a man's worth is measured only by his wealth. Birth means nothing there. Think of the common people you would be forced to acknowledge!"

"Wealth matters in England, too. And I have none. Lelia, I'm *excited* about this opportunity. I have a chance to make something of myself by my own efforts."

Stupid twit, thought Chloe. *Can't he understand she's not thinking of him at all?* She shook her head. The conversation only confirmed her assessment of Lelia's selfishness.

All the while her attention was consumed by the drama taking place in the next aisle, Chloe remained in Adrian's embrace. Little by little she became conscious of the heat from his body burning through the layers of wool, silk, lace, and stays. Her skin felt unbearably sensitive and alive; a film obscured her vision.

Her interest in eavesdropping vanished. Belatedly, she tried to inch away from him, but his arm, wrapped around her from behind, held her fast. As breathing became more difficult, she inhaled slowly, desperately concentrating on each breath. She'd never fainted in her life, and now was not the time to develop such a despicable weakness.

"Please wait another week, David. I implore you. I have an idea that could assure your future."

Lelia's words were the last sound Chloe heard before she fainted in Adrian's arms.

Chloe's slender body was suddenly a dead weight. Adrian's attention swung between the delicious warmth in his arms and the low-voiced conversation in the next aisle. The scent of primroses filled his nostrils as all his senses responded to Chloe's unconscious form. To his chagrin, his body hardened painfully.

The reaction was so complete and immediate that with a flash of honesty, he realized he wasn't merely carrying on a casual flirtation with Chloe to lull the suspicions of his enemies. He still wanted her with an intensity that left him shaken.

His memories of their brief romance had been no figment of his lonely imagination during those months in Scotland. As soon as this business was cleared up, he intended to marry her, even if she fought him every step of the way. In fact, he looked forward to the battle. His wooing skills might be rusty, but this time he would, at least, be alive. And expecting to stay that way, God willing.

It occurred to him that the process would have to include an unexpurgated recital of the kind of work he had done for Fitz. He winced. In spite of his disclaimer to Fitz, many of his activities had been hazardous. The task of insuring her discretion would be his and his alone. Adrian pressed his lips to her pale temple and the thick lashes fanning her cheekbones.

"I wish Adrian were truly dead!" Lelia wailed, tearing his thoughts from the beatific prospect of a future with the woman in his arms.

"Don't even *think* that, Lelia. Adrian isn't simply my cousin; we're friends. We grew up together. God, I was never so happy in my life as when he returned! It was a miracle."

"Oh, darling, I didn't really mean that. You know I didn't. It's just that I love you so much!"

Lelia's voice held a sensual intensity that had been missing before. The rustle of petticoats, followed by a low masculine moan, broke the ensuing silence. Adrian wasn't sure he could listen to much more of this, not with Chloe's unconscious body resting against him. She ought to be laid flat, her feet raised, her stays loosened. This last sounded so pleasurable he nearly commenced the task of reviving her on the spot.

"I must go. The museum will close soon, and your chaperon will be looking for you," David said, his voice full of regret.

The reminder of Lady Ogilvie's convenient absence provided Adrian with a whimsical mental picture of a cloakroom where couples checked chaperons.

"Don't worry about the conventions, darling. I left the old dear so engrossed in the Elgin Marbles, she probably doesn't even know I'm gone. You'll come to tea tomorrow, won't you?"

"If I'm able."

"Promise you won't make any important decisions without me, David."

"I promise. Oh, Lelia, I still can't believe I've found someone like you. You're everything I've dreamed of."

"I plan to take very good care of you, David."

Sharp, short footsteps, overlaid by the rustle of silk, told of Lelia's departure. Moments later, Adrian heard the dull thud of a man's leather heels tracing the same path.

Chloe stirred in his arms, and Adrian lowered her to the floor, then knelt beside her. Her color was returning, but he began to loosen her bodice in hopes of speeding her revival. He was to the third buttonhole when footsteps, accompanied by a curious thumping sound, rounded the corner of the display case. Adrian fanned Chloe's cheeks, shielding her partially opened bodice with his shoulder.

"Fainted, did she? Don't know what the world's come to when these young gels lace themselves so tight they can't breathe."

Adrian looked over his shoulder and breathed a sigh of relief. Lady Muriel Harding was his great-aunt, as doughty an old bird who'd ever insulted a prince, which legend said she had done on more than one occasion. "She's coming around, Aunt Muriel."

Shrewd, pale blue eyes surveyed him from beneath bushy, graying brows. "Finish with those buttons, you idiot. You ought to loosen her corset, but you're probably too proper for that. A pity. Shouldn't wonder if she's still in shock from the surprise of seeing you the other night at Skeffingtons'. Heard you disappeared with her on the terrace. Did you kiss her?"

His fingers, suddenly clumsy, slipped inadvertently inside the stiffened bodice, encountering the warm, pulsing skin beneath Chloe's collarbone. He recalled that mind-shattering night above the stable when he had burrowed his lips against the same spot, and he withdrew his fingers as if he'd just touched hot coals. "Certainly not."

"More fool you." She clutched the knobbed head of her cane and pushed him aside with the tip. "Her eyelids just fluttered. Don't sit there like a lump. Go get her a cup of water."

Chapter Fifteen

Chloe opened her eyes to the astonishing sight of Adrian running down the aisle as if fleeing the hounds of hell. Standing above her was a short, dumpy woman with wild white hair escaping around a black bird's nest of a bonnet and surveying her as if she were something the dustman had forgotten. She thought she might faint again.

"Come along, gel. You're awake. I saw your eyes open. I'm Harding's great aunt. No one'll dare make too much of your dress being open as long as I'm here."

Chloe looked down at her partially opened bodice and gasped. Adrian must have undone the fastenings. She fumbled with a buttonhole. Did he think her a weak-minded fool for fainting?

A deep, cackling laugh escaped Lady Harding. "I sent Adrian for some water. Surprised me to see you trussed up like a Christmas goose. Heard you had more sense." Her bright, darting gaze focused beyond Chloe. "Here he comes. Dependable sort, if he'll stay alive this time."

"One of the guards gave me his own mug," Adrian announced as he knelt beside her. "Here. Let me help you sit up."

Chloe welcomed the strength of his arm behind her shoulders every bit as much as the cool water in the pottery mug. "I can't imagine what made me do that. I've never fainted before."

"Corsets—that's what does it. Should burn the bloody

things." Lady Harding smoothed the shapeless tweed skirt hanging from the middle of her body over her thick waist. "Glad I'm too old for that foolishness."

Chloe decided she liked the abrupt old woman. "They are dreadful, aren't they? I wore this because your nephew told me my other clothes were scandalous. *This* is scandalous." She pulled her legs beneath her and tried to stand. She realized she was wobbly and accepted Adrian's support with reluctant gratitude.

"Can't imagine why he's suddenly become so stiff-rumped. The whole family's ramshackle—always has been." Lady Harding stumped to the end of the aisle, her cane thumping with each step. "Well, I'm off. Have m' nevvy bring you to tea."

Chloe looked at Adrian. His laughing eyes were so beautiful, she nearly forgot how positive she was that she hated him. "You certainly had very little to say to your aunt."

"Not much point in it. She says everything herself. And she's always right."

"I like her," Chloe said. She checked to make sure her bodice was returned to respectability, then reassured herself that her bonnet hadn't been bent out of shape.

"Here. Stand still." Adrian fingers tucked an errant curl back into her fashionable coiffure.

Annoyed by a sudden, overwhelming desire to lean into his touch, Chloe pulled away. "It was extremely rude of us to eavesdrop on your cousin and Miss Fenton."

"Would you rather we'd walked up and tapped David on the shoulder while they were kissing?" His look was one of teasing wickedness.

Chloe wanted to hit him. "Certainly not, but we could simply have turned and left."

"I found their conversation most enlightening. This

morning David left a message inviting me to dine tonight. Said he had exciting news. About Lelia or the job offer? Of the two, I think the latter shows more promise."

"I can't imagine what he sees in her. She's . . ." Chloe stopped. David Mountjoy's fiancée was none of her business. Talking of them reminded her that she and Adrian had been in the exhibit room nearly an hour. She looked nervously left and right. "I must get back to Lady Ogilvie. She'll be anxious."

A delighted smile creased Adrian's face. "Fine. Have we been in here long enough to raise eyebrows?"

Anger made it difficult for Chloe to speak. "Beast! You did this on purpose, so people will believe in our flirtation," she finally managed. Spinning on her heel, she sped toward the arched opening.

Adrian followed at a leisurely pace. He wondered if Chloe realized her rapid exit would cause even more talk than if they had come from the room arm in arm with their hair and clothing in disarray. Admiring the sway of her hips as he followed her down the hall, he recalled her deliciously vulnerable and yielding body in his embrace—corset or no.

Was his enjoyment of her fainting spell a sign of depravity? Eavesdropping on his cousin and Lelia Fenton had been simply a happy bonus. Fitz, who regarded David as a possible suspect, would be enthralled to hear of the new development. His curiosity concerning David and Lelia was endless. He caught up with Chloe as she paced nervously near the heavy front doors.

"Has it just now occurred to you that we arrived in my carriage? James was to meet us in front at four-thirty." He looked fixedly at his pocket watch, then opened the portal to peer out. "It's precisely four-thirty-seven, and there he is, just as I requested. We've made him wait. Where's Lady Ogilvie?"

"I don't see her anywhere! She was to keep an eye out for us." Chloe looked thoroughly irritated by the woman's defection. "I'm sure I'm not responsible if she doesn't follow instructions. She can simply find her own way home."

Since the mousy woman's absence suited his purposes, Adrian extended his elbow. "Shall we?"

Chloe's stony acceptance of his courtesy amused him. She looked so delightfully mutinous that he wanted to kiss her in full view of the attendant on duty at the door.

When he helped her into the carriage, she cast him a challenging look and said, "I refuse to take on any more of these little outings with you."

Adrian patted her hand as he seated himself beside her in the carriage. "Why not think of them as assisting Fitz's men to maintain surveillance? When we're together, he needs only half as many."

"Ridiculous! I haven't seen one person who looks like an agent this entire afternoon. Are they invisible?"

"Who do you suppose is driving the carriage?"

"Your coachman," she spat back.

Adrian settled into a corner of the carriage, stretched his long legs in front of him, and smiled. "You of all people should know coachmen and grooms aren't always what they appear."

She drew herself up even more stiffly, as if to rebuke his lazy posture.

"You'll be extremely uncomfortable sitting on the edge of the seat all the way home," he said, inching toward her.

She moved closer to her side of the compartment. "Get away."

"But I want to apologize," he said. The slight pinkening of her cheeks encouraged him.

"For what?" she asked disbelievingly.

201

Adrian moved until his thigh brushed hers. "For criticizing your clothing. My temper goaded you into that getup you're wearing, so your faint today was my fault."

"If you think I dressed this way because of something you said, you flatter yourself," Chloe said haughtily. "I merely wanted to show you how ridiculous current fashion is. This bonnet nearly sent you into whoops of laughter," she challenged. "Admit it."

"I hoped you hadn't noticed," he answered unrepentently. Adrian wondered what she would say if he told her the hansom cab behind them was the same one that had pursued his carriage since he set out to pick her up. After assisting Chloe into the carriage, James had assured him he'd taken note of it, and another agent was now following their pursuers. "I was most . . . ah, taken with your entire ensemble. May I say that only someone of your height and excellent carriage could carry it off."

"I intend to burn these clothes as soon as I remove them. And I shall throw this abominable . . ."

Adrian glanced through the window as they turned a corner. The vehicles behind them followed as if in a parade. When Chloe's sentence stuttered to a stop he cheerfully supplied, "Corset." How paradoxical that she had difficulty saying the word, considering the extent of her vocabulary. Adrian rather enjoyed the dusky rose color creeping up her cheeks.

He glanced behind them again. This time he was rewarded by the sight of a third cab neatly cutting off their pursuer and blocking the street in front of the hansom.

"And the figure improver also," Chloe continued, unaware of any disturbance behind them. "How can they call it an improver when it makes you stick out in back like a . . ."

"Chicken," Adrian supplied, remembering her earlier

comparison. His thoughts abandoned the contretemps behind them. The militant sparkle in her eyes filled his world, and he edged closer, entranced. "Am I to deduce that you intend to spend the rest of your days dressing like the wife of a Cambridge poet?"

"Perhaps I shall shock my peers even more by *marrying* a Cambridge poet. I'd fit right in, would I not?"

The carriage rolled to a stop in front of the Lockwood town house. As he stepped down, Adrian glanced at the line of vehicles carrying fashionable residents home for late tea. There was no sign of their pursuers. Perhaps this time Fitz's men would discover who had hired them.

He assisted a defiant Chloe to the cobblestone road and drew her hand firmly within the crook of his arm. He bit his tongue to keep from informing her arrogantly that it would be a cold day in hell before he would allow her to throw herself away on a daydreaming scholar and the life such a marriage would provide.

He decided to take another tack. "I'm sure you would derive great pleasure from living in an attic and discussing intellectual matters while the rest of world goes its merry way. However, you'll be much more comfortable married to me."

Chloe digested his statement with narrowed eyes. Her reply seemed to explode from her lips. "I have no bloody intention of marrying you!" The near shout caused a passing couple to stop and stare.

Adrian leaned close and whispered, "No matter what *you* intend, I've decided to hold you to the promise we sealed with such enthusiasm last spring." He lifted her gloved fingers to his lips and kissed them.

She snatched her hand away and turned to the stairs. "Don't be ridiculous. That was merely . . . infatuation. We both know we don't . . . we aren't . . ." As her reply trailed into nothingness, she stopped three steps from the top, confusion written on her countenance. She drew a deep breath. "I don't even like the real you."

"Let me help you overcome your aversion, love. A promise is a promise. I'm convinced we're meant for each other." Adrian retreated when he spotted her right foot swinging back as if to connect with his shin on its return flight. "Breach of promise suits are so untidy, Chloe. You don't want to cause further scandal."

"Why, you arrogant ass!" She advanced, colliding with him just as he reached out to hold her upright.

Adrian smiled at the glittering amber light in her eyes. He would never have to question Chloe's mood after they were married; when she was angry, her eyes glowed golden, while passion had the opposite effect, turning them dark brown and slumbrous.

Above them, the door swung wide, and the butler stood ready to admit Chloe. She pulled free of Adrian's grasp and stalked toward the opening. "I never want to see you again."

The effect of her exit was spoiled when she caught her toe on the top step. Adrian caught her by the waist to prevent her from falling. "On the contrary, I shall see you Sunday. Your mother plans to return from Bennington Hall on Saturday, and she sent me a gracious note inviting me to join you both for the afternoon."

Before she could protest further, Adrian smiled and said, "Amazing how the news of our dalliance reached Bennington Hall the day after the Skeffington affair. The servants' grapevine is ever so much better than Fitz's information system," he added before he turned away.

Chloe rushed up the curving staircase, her mind outrunning her feet. At the ball Adrian had treated her as if she were beneath contempt. At the museum he had been deliberately provoking. During the ride home he had alternated between amused condescension and distraction; his attention seemed elsewhere half the time. Why had he decided to hold her to promises made during that impulsive, besotted interlude at Aunt Heloise's?

Recalling the way she had responded to his passionate lovemaking made her dizzy, and Chloe slowed her steps, remembering clearly how insistent she had been. Her cheeks burned with embarrassment.

Reaching her room, she slammed the door behind her and ripped at the buttons of her bodice. She removed it and unfastened her skirts and petticoats, then struggled with the hooks on the front of her corset.

By the time each offending piece of clothing sailed to the hearth, she was flushed and trembling. A tightly laced corset hadn't been the true cause of her dizziness. The reason she'd been light-headed was the presence of Adrian, Viscount Harding.

Surely, she should be immune to him. The man had stolen her heart, made promises, then disappeared. Reminded of the hopes she had naively cherished, her anger built. Throughout the last months Adrian should somehow have sent word. For all she knew, he really *could* have been dead.

Now he had reappeared from nowhere, looking more handsome than anyone had right to, criticized her dress and her morals, and audaciously announced his intention to wed her.

And her dear, unenergetic mother was at this moment preparing to rush back to London to further a courtship Chloe had been promised was nothing but a sham.

She pulled her cashmere dressing gown on over her chemise and knickers and fastened the satin ties at her waist. Stalking to the heap of rumpled clothing, she seized the lace-covered bustle and threw it into the fire. The silk ignited with a satisfying burst of flame.

Chloe knelt, dry-eyed, watching the pathetic little conflagration. She couldn't risk letting herself care for Adrian again. Loving him would be far more dangerous than the physical peril he spoke of so offhandedly. She refused to allow her heart to be a pawn in the grotesque chess game he and Fitzhugh Kent played.

When Sunday arrived, Maude Lockwood's plan to encourage the wonderfully eligible suitor who had appeared from nowhere didn't include sufficient energy to both accompany her daughter to church Sunday morning and entertain the gentleman that same afternoon. She maintained that she needed to conserve her strength, which meant sending Lady Ogilvie to church with her daughter.

Chloe had been most outspoken on the subject. "Really, mother. Adrian Harding has no more intention of marrying me than has Tillie. You're overreacting."

"Everyone's talking about the way the two of you disappeared onto the balcony at the Skeffingtons' not an hour after he stunned society by rising from the grave. Your father said it sounded as if the young man wasn't wasting any time."

Maude smiled muzzily before pushing her breakfast tray aside and swinging her feet to the floor, sighing both from emotion and the effort needed to exit her bed. "I thought the whole affair most romantic. Your father would be here, but Miranda has gone into labor, and Queen Victoria herself couldn't summon him from his favorite cow's delivery."

"Well, bloody hell," Chloe mouthed as she left the room. Throughout a night of frenzied thought she had been unable to contrive any means of escaping the day ahead. She was stuck, and although she might be forced to spend the afternoon in Adrian's company, she daren't risk enjoying one second of it.

As she rose from her church pew later that morning, Chloe realized she had been so immersed in her dilemma that she had missed the message of the sermon. Lady Ogilvie had twice angled an admonitory glance in her direction to still her fidgeting. Worship over, the fashionable congregation filed toward the door. Her thoughts elsewhere, Chloe responded perfunctorily to the few acquaintances who greeted her. So distracted was she that she became separated from Lady Ogilvie. Almost immediately she was approached by a hard-faced couple who claimed to have met her at a tennis party in early July.

"Sir Drake and I played the match after yours. You can't possibly be expected to remember our names," gushed the woman.

Chloe smiled politely, wondering how quickly she could escape their unwelcome company and search out Lady Ogilvie. She felt a sense of claustrophobia when they bracketed her, offering small talk as they progressed down the crowded aisle. Near the exit, she looked around for her companion, expecting to see her pacing the aisle. The dreadful little woman had disappeared.

Sir Drake and his wife supplied helpful comments, all the while carrying Chloe along between them. "I believe I saw your companion going out this side entrance," he said.

"Is your carriage meeting you here, my dear?" his wife asked, her elbow hard against Chloe's arm as the door swung open. Glancing at the would-be Good Samaritans, Chloe sensed an underlying resolve in their manner. She attempted to turn away, but the portal closed behind them with an ominous thud. She was trapped between the pair as they descended the steps.

Stifling a surge of panic, Chloe stopped and announced calmly, "You've been quite kind, but I shall await Lady Ogilvie at our carriage. It's surely back there in that crush of traffic."

All pretense of affability deserted Sir Drake's features. His grip on her arm tightened. "Don't make this more unpleasant than necessary, Lady Chloe. If you'll notice, my wife has her hand in her reticule, where she is holding a pistol pointed at your lovely body. She won't hesitate to fire if you precipitate a scene." Holding her arm close, he moved forward.

Chloe felt deserted by God; it had never occurred to her that attending church would be unsafe. How she wished she hadn't discounted Adrian's warnings. Surely Lady Ogilvie was searching for her. If only she could stall her abductors.

She allowed her rising hysteria full rein, "What do you mean? I don't understand. Why must I go with you?"

Sir Drake propelled her viciously along the walkway. "Don't pretend innocence, my dear. Up until now your protection's been better than the queen's. Otherwise we'd have made off with you long ago."

Pretending ignorance, Chloe protested, "I have no idea what you're talking about. Where are you taking me?" She dragged her feet, only to be jerked painfully forward. One look at the face of the woman at her side dissolved any hope of escape.

"You're going on a little trip, Lady Chloe. Just think, an ocean voyage and new experiences in a foreign land. And the fat fee you'll bring will enrich our bank account nicely. You're a little tall and spirited for most tastes, but there are those who prefer a challenge," Sir Drake explained.

As he led her toward the closed coach at the corner of an alley, Chloe saw a soberly clad man weaving his way toward them through the crowd. Recognizing Adrian's coachman of the day before, she felt a sense of relief, and with it came new strength. She jerked her arm away from Drake, then dropped to her knees and rolled into the woman at her side, knocking her off balance.

"Little bitch," the woman said, striking Chloe on the side of the head with her heavy reticule.

Chloe reeled with pain; her arms and legs went weak. She felt Drake's hands seize her by the waist and heave her unceremoniously into the coach, where she sprawled on the floor between the seats. In her half-stunned state, she thought, *Dear God! Why do people keep kidnapping me?*

"How in bloody hell did you manage to lose her?" Adrian demanded. He refused to apologize for his language, since Claudia Ogilvie's face revealed none of the anxiety that had already prostrated Maude Lockwood. The woman had glared back at him defiantly in response to all of his questions. Adrian compressed his lips into a grim line and towered over her. "Or perhaps you didn't lose her at all. You delivered her."

The companion's close-set eyes flickered. "Lady Chloe is headstrong. She darted away from me. I thought she wished to speak with someone she knew. When I looked to follow her, she was nowhere to be seen." She edged toward the door. "I believe I shall retire to my room for a restorative."

With insistent courtesy Adrian grasped her arm and guided her to the ornately carved rosewood sofa. He bowed slightly, gesturing for her to sit. "I prefer to keep you in sight until my friend arrives. He's not as polite as I, so perhaps your answers to his questions will be more forthcoming."

After casting him a vicious look, Lady Ogilvie lowered her round, tightly corseted frame to the sofa.

Adrian paced the room restlessly, his anxiety growing with

each second that passed. Chloe had vanished. For one frenzied moment he wished hysteria would bring Chloe back. He had to keep a clear head, in spite of the fear squeezing his heart. The need for physical action vibrated within him, but he felt almost paralyzed. He needed direction. Damn it, where was Fitz?

As if in answer to his silent demand, the butler ushered Fitz Kent into the room.

"What the hell took you so long? Did you have difficulty matching your handkerchief to your cravat? Your damned people lost Chloe! God only knows what's happened to her!"

Fitz's cool manner appeared to have deserted him. His movements were hurried, a far cry from his customary lounging grace. "I've had no reports as yet. Neither agent who was in the church has sent word, so I'm in hopes they're on her trail." His gaze paused at Maude Lockwood's puffy cheeks, then settled on the stolid face of Chloe's chaperon. "And this is . . ."

"Lady Ogilvie, Chloe's supposed companion," Adrian growled.

Fitz shrugged, settling his worsted suit jacket more comfortably on his shoulders, and became his usual languid self. " 'Supposed?' "

"Because I suspect she was sent by the same people as those who sent the chef."

"Ah, yes, the chef," said Fitz, a genial smile creasing his features. He strolled across the flowered carpet and politely offered his hand to her. "There's no need to distress Lady Lockwood further." He gestured toward Maude, who had calmed somewhat. "Allow me to escort you into the study, ma'am. If you would be so kind as to describe Lady Chloe's disappearance one more time? I feel sure you will furnish a detailed accounting."

Lady Ogilvie evaded his glance as she stood. "I've already told Lord Harding everything," she said defiantly.

"Yes, well, perhaps I'll be able to jog your memory for additional details." Fitz turned to Adrian. "I gave the butler instructions to send anyone who asks for me directly in here."

"In that case, I may be gone when you return. If news of Chloe arrives, I'm not waiting around."

"Patience, my dear boy. Patience." Fitz focused a cold smile on the woman by his side. "If I learn anything helpful, we may be able to take action without any further information."

Chapter Sixteen

Chloe's knees buckled as Sir Drake pulled her from the coach. She'd spent the jolting ride sprawled miserably on the foul-smelling floor, but the acrid aromas of dust, dirt, and other things she didn't want to think about had revived her senses. She nearly fell when she stumbled out of the coach, but he jerked her upright. Looking around, she demanded, "Where are we?" Ancient buildings leaned against each other and crowded the narrow, cobblestone street where they stood. The air was redolent with the scent of damp wood and smoke.

"Look all you like, my dear. Memorizing your surroundings won't be of any help. Where you're going, no one will be interested. We're near the waterfront." Drake's mirthless laughter grated on her nerves and exacerbated the headache Madge's blow had given her. He twisted her arm cruelly. "Forget that trick you used back at the church. You won't take me in a second time."

As his hot gaze swept her face, Chloe felt dirty. She swallowed a sob and gritted her teeth to keep her lips from trembling. Her thoughts were a jumbled mixture of regrets and yearning. *Oh, Adrian, why didn't I listen to you? I never really stopped loving you . . . and now I may never see you again to tell you how much.*

Madge's harsh voice interrupted her half-prayerful internal litany. "Keep your trousers buttoned, Harry. Can't you keep your hands to yourself for two hours? Damaged goods won't bring us as big a fee." She inspected Chloe through narrowed eyes and added, "I wonder if the little bitch is still a virgin anyway."

From the corner of her eye Chloe sensed movement at the rear of the coach. Almost afraid to hope, she swiveled her head a fraction to her right. James, the coachman Adrian said was an agent, clung to the vehicle like a barnacle, his feet braced against the luggage rack. He smiled around the finger he held to his lips. "I'm not," she said defiantly, drawing both Madge and Harry's attention before continuing, "so why don't you just let me go?"

"You'll still bring a good fee. White women always do," Madge pointed out.

Still, hope flickered in her heart as Drake pulled her toward the broken steps of a clapboard house that looked about to fall in on itself. James wouldn't leave her to such a ghastly fate. Adrian would kill him.

"Wait for me, Harry. You aren't to be alone with her."

"Shut your trap, Madge. I know what I'm doing."

In spite of her desperate optimism Chloe was numb with terror; she could scarcely move her feet.

Madge continued talking as she followed them. "I'm just reminding you. Remember what I told you would happen the next time you let your eyes rove? I'll whack off your dickey bird."

The ancient door swung open at his touch, the creak of its rusty hinges nearly obscuring his reply. "Bugger off, Madge. I'm sick of your yapping." He dragged Chloe into the house.

Unaffected, Madge followed, spewing obscenities that were answered in kind. Chloe was amazed at how quickly the veneer of civility had peeled away from her captors, but at least their verbal skirmish helped her resist looking back over her shoulder for one last, reassuring glimpse of her only hope for rescue.

Still brangling, the two bundled her into a musty-smelling sitting room. Could James summon help quickly enough? The dock area was dangerous. She knew Scotland Yard had been unable to make more than a small dent in the myriad crimes committed in the dank, poorly lit alleys and side streets. Were constables near enough to be summoned?

Her first look at her surroundings sent a frisson of revulsion down her spine. She was even more repelled when Drake released her to hold a match to the wick in a filthy oil lamp. He and his wife continued haranguing each other, their voices rising as accusations flew. Sir Drake paced the filthy room and hurled countercharges at his mate.

Chloe edged toward the door. She had remained standing, unwilling to sit on any of the mold-covered chairs.

"Oh, no you don't, bitch. Put your arse down over there or I'll—"

"No marks, Harry. You'll drive her price down."

"Might damn well be worth it. The slut tried to escape." He turned aside and reached inside his heavy overcoat, bringing out a flat metal bottle. "Bleeding cold in this dump. If you won't let me warm myself against our high and mighty damaged goods, this will have to do." Opening the flask, he poured some of the contents into his mouth.

The piercing odor of gin joined the sickening odors of decay. Chloe's stomach lurched, a metallic taste filled her mouth, and she knew she would disgrace herself within minutes. "I'm about to be sick. Is there a bathroom of any kind?"

"Would you listen to the little lady? Madge, did you put out the monogrammed towels? Since you're so afraid I'll cop a feel, you can take her to the jakes out back yourself." Drake tilted the flask once more.

"Shut up, you fool. And lay off the gin," Madge said angrily as she lit a lantern. She reached into her reticule and brought out her pistol, then waved it toward the cramped entryway. "Come along, your highness. I'll take you out through the kitchen, but no funny business or I'll put a bullet in you in a Yorkshire minute. Bugger the money you're worth."

Chloe walked ahead, cringing at each prod of the pistol. With trembling fingers she pushed aside the tattered baize curtain covering the doorway and stepped cautiously into the kitchen. Something brushed against her boot, then skittered away; her other foot slid when she put it forward. Cold perspiration broke out across the back of her neck. A scuttling sound from across the room made her close her eyes, afraid to look. She'd never seen one, but she *knew* the scrabbling paws belonged to a retreating rat. Her stomach lurching more strongly than before, she raised her hand to her mouth.

" 'Tain't the Ritz, my lady, but chucking the bunny's the same for you as it is for me. The sink's over there."

Chloe saw the outline of a pump against the filthy window over the chipped sink and murmured, "Get out of my way, rats, because I'm coming through." With bravado born of desperation, she fled across the dimly lit room, reaching the sink with no time to spare. Madge's derisive laughter echoed off the peeling walls. When her spasms ceased, Chloe remained bent over the sink and reached into her reticule for a handkerchief. As she did so, a shadow moved outside the dust-streaked window.

Before she could straighten, James burst through the sagging back door, which banged against the wall and fell from its hinges. Instinctively, Chloe crouched lower. A shot rang out, closely followed by another. Chunks of rotting plaster fell from the ceiling. The lantern in Madge's hand swung wildly, and Chloe felt, rather than saw, her rescuer rush past.

Although weak with relief, Chloe ran to help James subdue Madge. "Her husband's in the parlor," she told him, her voice sounding weak in her own ears. She held Madge's wrists together while James stuffed a gag into her mouth.

"My partner's taking him out," he grunted. "Turn her around so I can tie her arms."

Footsteps hurried toward them down the narrow passageway. A stocky individual with wild whiskers sprouting from the lower half of his face appeared with a strangely still Harry thrown over his shoulder. "There's noise in the street. Either coppers or the neighbors. Kent don't want either of 'em involved," he warned.

Hoisting the woman over his shoulder, James subdued her flailing legs and hurried toward the door. "Then let's be off. Did you send a message to Kent?"

The second agent hustled Chloe behind the first. "Hired a hackney driver to track him down. Told him we had things in hand and to meet us at The Thirsty Camel."

James thrust aside a trash bin that leaned into the doorway and stood back. "Here you go, Lady Chloe. We'll have you all right and tight before you can say Bob's your uncle."

Adrian watched impatiently as Fitz closed the study door behind him, allowing only a glimpse of Lady Ogilvie tied to a chair, her mouth neatly stuffed with a paisley print silk pocket handkerchief. Just then, a cadaverous-looking hackney driver was ushered into the foyer. The spy master smiled sunnily at the bearded man and said, "I presume you've a message for me?"

The barely intelligible Cockney recital reached Adrian where he stood at the open door of the sitting room. When he saw Fitz press several pound notes into the man's hand, he said forcefully, "I'm going with you."

"Of course you are, old man." Fitz slipped his arms into the beautifully tailored tweed coat the butler held for him, then gave instructions to the hackney driver while the servant performed the same service for Adrian.

As they hurried out the door, Adrian demanded, "Ogilvie cracked, then?"

"Loathsome old biddy," Fitz announced as Adrian's carriage approached. "Just let me have a word with my man. I want him to take her back to the office for questioning."

Adrian leaped into his carriage and sat, his impatience growing, while Fitz conferred briefly with his coachman. When his friend joined him, Adrian demanded, "Is Chloe safe? Did Ogilvie say who'd hired her?"

"Another damnable dead end. Ogilvie doesn't know who hired her, either. She might recover her memory, but I doubt it. My men will work on her." He added, as if in an afterthought, "Lady Chloe's safe. James and his partner have her. They were also able to capture the couple who kidnapped her. Good thing they all got out in one piece. The toughs at the docks would turn on my people at the drop of a hat."

The day had delivered enough emotional blows to Adrian. "You bastard. I don't care about your hirelings. The important thing is that Chloe's alive and unharmed. She's not to be used as live bait any longer, Fitz. I'm taking over from here on."

The spy master propped his ankles on the cushion of the opposite seat, leaned his head back, and closed his eyes before saying languidly, "This should prove vastly entertaining."

The stench of moldering plaster and musty carpet still lingered in Chloe's nostrils as she sat, absorbed in her own misery, in the private upstairs room of the unobtrusive pub. Part of her yearned to be ten years old once again and safe at Bennington Hall. James and his partner had promised her the ancient place was safe, but she wasn't sure she would trust anyone ever again.

All her life she had read and dreamed of the new experiences and adventures she would have, but she never could have imagined The Thirsty Camel. The padded chairs were threadbare, and the room smelled of stale spirits and even staler cigar smoke. To the publican's credit, the place was at least clean. And there weren't any rats—at least up here.

"I thought Mr. Kent was to meet us," she demanded of James, who stood peering through the shutters.

"That he will, once my message finds him. He probably wasn't in his office, so the hackney driver had to scout him out."

"I didn't mean I wanted to see *him!* I just want out of here. Take me home. My mother must be frantic." Adrian would surely be with her by now. The knowledge that her disappearance would disturb him brought her a spurt of pleasure. What wouldn't she give to see him walk in the door.

But what if Adrian had also been abducted? Or attacked? She paced the crowded little room impatiently, pushing aside small tables and knocking a stack of yellowing newspapers from the rack next to the door. If anything happened to Adrian . . .

A discreet knock startled her. She jumped at the sound, her nerves jangling. James, pistol in hand, walked to the door, rapped out a signal, and pressed his ear to the panel. Seconds later he fumbled with the lock and eased open the portal.

"Adrian!" Chloe cried as he burst into the room, closely followed by Fitz.

She threw herself into his arms as if into sanctuary. It didn't matter that the last time she had seen him she had been

218

tempted to push him off the front steps. What mattered was that Adrian was safe and holding her close. She inhaled deeply the fragrance of outdoors clinging to him and rubbed her cheek into the rough herringbone of his topcoat.

"Touching."

Fitz's dry comment took a moment to register. Chloe pulled away long enough to frown at the spy master. "Those two waltzed me out of the church in front of several hundred people. Where were your watchdogs?"

"Why in God's name did you go with them?" Adrian demanded, refusing to relinquish his crushing hold.

Chloe eyed him crossly. "They looked respectable, and they spoke politely. We were out of the church and away from everyone before I realized something was wrong. By then the woman had a gun pointed at me." Her temper building, she turned on Fitz. "I even lost that poor Ogilvie woman."

"Who is presently being transferred to a safe place for intensive questioning," Adrian answered. "Fitz didn't get a chance to screen her before your mother hired her, either."

"Either?"

"My ex-chef," he answered obliquely, then pulled her back into his embrace. "Darling, Fitz's people can't be everywhere at once. I'm taking you where no one can get to you."

"I'm tired of being kidnapped, Adrian. I want to go home to Bennington Hall. Please," she entreated. Although the reassuring beat of his heart beneath her ear made her feel secure, she was weary of being moved around like a chess piece.

"I suppose you're thinking of Warnham House," Fitz said over her head.

"Of course. My family knows everyone within miles. If a stranger rides through the village, the villagers have vetted him before he passes the last cottage."

Chloe pulled free of Adrian's arms, planted her hands on

her hips, and shouted, "No one's listening to me! I said I was tired of being dragged from pillar to post. I've decided where I want to go, and that's Bennington Hall."

Adrian hauled her up and kissed her soundly, much to the enjoyment of the other occupants of the room. "My dear fiancée, you have no choice. Believe me. My parents will be delighted."

Wriggling free once more, Chloe folded her hand into a fist and landed the right hook her brother had taught her on Adrian's handsome jaw.

The closed coach rumbled through the night. Faint moonlight pierced the dark. Fields and villages flew by, an occasional glowing cottage window the only other illumination, but the occupants of the coach had no interest in the scenery.

"I haven't any clothes with me," Chloe grumbled.

"Wardrobes all over the house are filled with my mother and sisters' clothes," Adrian replied equably. He smiled and massaged his jaw, reflecting that his love certainly had a healthy right hook.

"Fat lot of help *that* will be," she grumbled, shifting to a more comfortable position across from him. For the last hour she had fidgeted and protested her latest abduction.

Smiling in the darkness of the coach, Adrian said, "Since my return you've accused me of desertion, coldheartedness, high-handed arrogance, philandering, and of making you dress like a chicken. I must say, you're not exactly behaving like the other half of any love affair I ever imagined."

She clutched her arms more tightly across her breasts before saying, "And that's another thing. Did you and Fitz really plan those escapes from all the women you were involved with? Lelia said one of them was even married!"

Angered for a moment, he explained tightly, "There weren't

many, and if I decide to break off with someone, I don't need Fitz's help. Lelia lied about the married woman."

"I'm supposed to believe that?" she demanded, her militance undaunted.

Adrian folded her hands into his and cherished her fingers. "The longer I was thought dead, the more gossip grossly embroidered my exploits. It took me four days to realize that your outrageous behavior was retaliation for those exaggerations. I confess I was just as bad. I made assumptions about you based on gossip." His grip tightened. "I swear I have never led any woman to expect more than I offered, and I never intentionally broke anyone's heart."

Her muffled response was unintelligible, but when she pressed a tear-damp kiss against his fingers, Adrian nearly sighed with relief. She believed him. As he leaned forward to kiss her more satisfactorily, she reminded him, "News that I've been carried off to Warnham House won't calm my mother . . ."

His lips twitching, Adrian pulled back and sprawled lazily against the corner of the opposite seat, enjoying her protestations. He could have used any of several methods to calm her nervous state, but the fear that had pierced him after hearing of her abduction had abated little since she'd launched herself into his arms in the dingy parlor above The Thirsty Camel. He sympathized with her uncertainty. His own still ate at his soul.

Did she love him? His hands shook with the desperate desire to touch her; his nerves stretched more finely with every mile. He wanted the words; he wanted her in his arms. "Chloe, love, you're not to worry about another thing."

"Oh, am I not?" Chloe shifted once again on the cushion, leaning forward in the darkness. "Have I heard any talk of love? Has anyone asked what *I* want? Certainly not. I've been bundled off against my will. I'm tired, and I'm hungry, and my clothing reeks of that wretched place. I'd give anything for a bath and clean clothes, even if they're borrowed."

"If I may quote Fitz, 'Patience, my dear, patience.' " He smiled in the dark, his senses so attuned to her that he sensed her response before she spoke.

"Don't ever mention his name to me again. He's a loathsome, bungling snake. He may have kept you alive for the last two years, but after we're married, I refuse to allow him into the house."

The words were grudging, as acceptances went, but they revealed a great deal. Discarding his lazy pose, Adrian dragged her from her seat, pulling her into his lap. "Love, I wondered if you'd ever get around to acknowledging your fate." Frustrated by the battered bonnet that impeded access to her face, he ripped the bow loose and threw it across the carriage.

With trembling hands Adrian cupped her face and touched his mouth to hers, delicately, then firmly, and finally deeply, drinking in her warmth and sweetness. He felt, rather than heard, her breath escape in a luxurious sigh. When her arms crept around his neck, anchoring him close, Adrian turned into the squabs and slipped his hands within her heavy cloak. She was soft and warm and vital beneath his touch, from her slim back to her narrow waist and the splendid subtle curve of her hips. When her lips opened to give him access, he slid farther down and gathered her hips against his aching need. The coach bumped over a rough crossing.

A gurgle of laughter escaped Chloe's lips as she jostled against him. "I do love you, Adrian. But once, just once, couldn't we be together someplace conventional?"

"Again," he murmured blissfully into her hair. Throughout his estrangement from everything he held dear, Adrian had despaired of ever achieving happiness. For over two years, all he'd known was a desperate struggle for survival. Now, miraculously, in spite of all odds, he had found his dream, and she was in his arms.

"The 'love' part?" she whispered shyly.

He inched backward, settling her more securely against him. "The 'love' part."

"I love you, Adrian." She kissed him sweetly. "I lied to you at the Skeffington ball. I was nearly frantic because I'd had no word of you. I hated everything about entering society, and the gossip about you made me ill. Nothing was right. Have you ever noticed how boring most people are?"

He was silent for a heartbeat. "That's why I allowed Fitz to talk me into working for him. After Cambridge, I had assumed my father would involve me in his international interests. He surprised me by insisting I sow a few wild oats first. I tried, but that became old after a few months."

He kissed the sensitive skin just beneath her earlobe, inwardly cursing the high-necked bodice of her gown.

"When I returned last week, my father offered to let me run his shipping companies." He teased the delicate whorls of her ear with the tip of his tongue. "I'll have to familiarize myself with our foreign offices. How does a honeymoon trip to China sound?"

"Say something to me in Chinese." Chloe's voice was thick and strangled, as if she were having difficulty speaking.

Adrian's hands moved over her, caressing each pliant inch while he whispered tenderly in her ear. At each sibilant syllable, she melted closer against him.

"What are you saying?" Chloe broke in, her voice husky and languorous.

"I love you, my heart. You are the sun on the water, the

moon on the birch tree, the fire in my heart. I love you," he said tenderly.

Her body shuddered against him. Chloe kissed her way across his cheek to his mouth, drew back a fraction of an inch as if considering, then said grumpily, "Well, I'm glad you finally got around to saying so, even if I had to ask for a translation."

Adrian closed the minute distance between them himself, smiling against her lips. He was one step from paradise.

The decanter of single malt whisky shattered against the mantel on its downward arc. The redolent odor permeated the confines of Robert Fenton's book-lined study. "*Damn Kent!*" he raged, oblivious to the glittering fragments of crystal scattered across his precious Persian carpet. So intent was he on his anger that he failed to notice his daughter's entrance.

"From the smell of this room, I gather you've failed again, Father," Lelia said coldly.

Fenton kept his back to her. His head throbbed; pain tore through his chest. He responded through clenched teeth, "Worse. Kent not only interfered, but he has all three in custody: Lady Chloe's companion and the pair who specialize in furnishing girls for the white slavers."

"If they failed, they deserve whatever happens to them," Lelia said coldly. Wrinkling her nose at the pungent odor, she edged inside, closing the door behind her. "I'll take over from here. I intend—"

"You don't understand, Lelia," her father broke in. "One of them has seen me."

The flat of her hand cracked against his cheek. "You fool! You careless fool!"

"She doesn't know my name. I was there for just a moment. I . . . I'm quite sure she couldn't possibly have known who I was."

"Don't be an idiot. Kent will keep at her until she gives you away. The man is much more clever than he looks. Where are Harding and the girl?"

"They're headed for Warnham House."

"I made a mistake. When we discovered Harding's activities and reeled David into our plot, I should have anticipated the dashing viscount's uncanny ability to survive. The fool could marry her before we get the situation in hand." She stood thinking for a moment, then clapped her hands and smiled maliciously. "I believe I'll convince David to take me to visit his dear relatives. A courtesy call before our engagement is formally announced. And before moving to America, which I've let him believe I might do."

Lelia picked her way through the shards of crystal. At the door she paused. "You always think in terms of separation and death, but there are more devious ways of preventing Harding from marrying, if I arrive in time. Of course, if a wedding takes place, we'll have to fall back on a fatal ending. For both of them."

Chapter Seventeen

Drowsy and intoxicated with unfulfilled passion, Chloe allowed Adrian to carry her up the broad stone steps into Warnham House, grateful they were arriving long after dark. Minutes earlier Adrian had awakened her and helped her restore herself to a semblance of neatness. Unable to locate her hairpins, she had tied her tumbled curls at her nape with her bonnet ribbon. The bonnet she had consigned to the floor of the carriage.

"What will your mother think, Adrian?" she demanded as they reached the third tread. Her body still quivered from his skillful touch and the memory of her own unrestrained response.

"She'll be delighted to believe you've been well and truly compromised. Then she'll set about welcoming you to the family. My mother's a remarkably sensible woman, as you'll soon discover." His smile flashed briefly as if at a secret joke, his teeth gleaming whitely in the glow of the gas sconces on either side of the door. "I think you'll find the two of you have a great deal in common."

The carved double door swung inward to reveal a broadly smiling man in dark blue livery. Disconcerted, Chloe said, "Adrian, your butler is staring at us. Is it necessary to look so *pleased* with yourself?"

Adrian roared with laughter, and she saw him wink in the direction of the fatherly-looking servant. Holding her tightly, he answered, "But I am, love. Why should I hide it?"

"The least you could do is allow me to walk in like a lady."

Adrian squeezed her reassuringly, then lowered her feet to the ground. The portly butler, still wearing a beatific smile, divested her of her wrinkled cape. Chloe glanced down to assure herself that her bodice had been rebuttoned correctly during that hurried refurbishing in the dark interior of the coach. She'd burned her bridges on the road from London—and had enjoyed every minute of it.

In spite of the late hour, the house was aglow with lights, and servants of varying levels had discovered urgent reasons to be in the front hall, the ceiling of which soared three stories high. Twin curved staircases bracketed a wide hall leading toward the rear of the house.

Chloe's high spirits diminished as she took in the grandeur of her surroundings. Bennington Hall was rambling and comfortable. She loved it, but even her months in London hadn't prepared her for the elegance of Warnham. A quick glance down at her bedraggled skirts made her feel even more out of place.

"Everything will be fine, sweetheart," Adrian whispered close to her ear.

His intimate gesture in the presence of so many strangers brought heat to her cheeks just as Chloe heard feminine footsteps and the rustle of silk.

The newcomer, a stunning blonde in a tea dress consisting of multiple layers of diaphanous blue silk, descended the left staircase. Behind her floated a much younger edition similarly garbed in pink.

In London, no one wore tea dresses at this hour of the night. Even in their own homes. Suspicious, Chloe raised her eyes searchingly toward Adrian's face. The only expression she could discern was joy at the sight of his family.

"Adrian, I could scarcely believe your telegram. Your father and I are delirious with happiness." A cloud of lavender scent surrounded Dorothy Warnham, and as she embraced her son, it spread to encompass Chloe as well.

Adrian's mother's gown and her fresh, clean fragrance made Chloe miserably aware of her own crumpled appearance and of the noxious odors that must linger in her burgundy broadcloth skirts. Before she could distance herself, Dorothy turned and enclosed her in a loving embrace. "Two wonderful surprises in one month are almost more than I can bear. To have Adrian alive is a miracle. And now we're to gain a beautiful daughter-in-law. I've already planned the wedding, just as Adrian asked."

Chloe saw the glitter of tears in the dark blue eyes so like her son's. Her jangled emotions threatened to furnish her with tears of her own. What had the countess said?

"Wedding? What wedding?" Once again she had a sense of being caught in a whirlwind, with unprecedented events sweeping her along. From the shelter of her brother's arm, Lady Dinah Harding said excitedly, "Yours and Adrian's, of course."

Chloe saw guilt in her beloved's eyes. His rueful smile and self-conscious shrug told her more than words. "Perhaps hunger has made me rather more dense than usual. Would you be so kind as to tell me when I'm to be married?"

Before anyone could answer, a voice from beneath the carved arch proclaimed, "Bloody hell! I've missed Adrian's arrival. I should never have stepped into the garden to enjoy a cigar."

Apparently oblivious to tension, Edwin Warnham strode across the black and white tiled floor to seize Chloe in an exuberant embrace. Holding her by her shoulders, he pronounced, "My dear boy! I do believe your young lady more than upholds the family standard for beauty. Just think! I can look forward to dark-haired grandchildren to play with all those little blond beauties your sisters are sure to produce. What a wonderful portrait they'll make!"

Adrian saw a glazed look in Chloe's eyes. He should have prepared her for a great deal more than his ebullient father, but he'd been flush with success—and too cautious to spring his brainstorm on her. Glancing at the enthralled expressions on the faces of the butler, the footman, and two downstairs maids, he sighed.

"Mother, do you suppose Antonio could produce something to eat? Neither of us has had a bite of food since just south of London." He avoided Chloe's attempts to look him in the eye and placed his hand at the small of her back to guide her down the central hall. From all appearances, his bride-to-be would soon fall over from exhaustion or explode with anger at his high-handedness.

"Darling, the poor man has called me to the kitchen six times since we received your wire. He designed and then threw out five different menus before settling on one that pleased him." Dorothy drifted alongside, casting anxious looks at Chloe. "You both must be exhausted."

Adrian led the way to the family sitting room, rejoicing in its slightly shabby welcome. If only the homey ambience of their surroundings would affect Chloe the same way. Once inside, he settled her among the pillows of a settee at right angles to the fireplace. Then he sat close by her side and reached for her hands to warm them.

Within moments the family chef, his saturnine appearance more pronounced than usual, directed a maid to place highly polished fruitwood tables in front of them. At a snap of his fingers, another maid set linen and flatware in place, while still another wheeled in a serving cart laden with covered platters.

"I honor you and the beautiful *signorina, Signor* Adrian. I, Antonio, will serve you myself."

"By God, Antonio, I've paid your wages for fifteen years, and you've never yet so much as handed me a glass of water," said Lord Warnham.

Adrian winked at Antonio. Through the years he'd enjoyed many a glass of wine on the portico off the kitchen wing while conversing in the chef's native language. "You've never been rescued from a fate worse than death, Father. And even though Mother thinks you're pretty, you're not a beautiful young woman."

"For the *signorina* I shall create a wedding cake so beautiful the stars weep," the chef declaimed dramatically as he served Chloe a flat bowl of fragrant broth.

She looked longingly at the food, then folded her arms over her chest. "I refuse to eat a bite until someone explains why you all act as if Adrian and I are stepping to the altar before the sun sets on another day."

Adrian's beaming parents and his sister, who could barely tear her adoring eyes from her brother, turned toward her.

"Adrian's telegram said . . ." Dorothy sputtered, while Dinah added, "You'll *have* to marry him after being alone with him in the coach for so long. Please say you will."

Edwin's eyes sparkled shrewdly. "My boy, I think you tried to jump the fence before your horse this time. You must have forgotten a few facts about females while you were, ah, out of commission. Women like to have some say about their weddings."

The condemning gaze Chloe turned on him gave him the feeling of a schoolboy who'd been called to the headmaster's office.

Unperturbed, Antonio ladled soup into a second bowl and placed it before him.

Chloe stared fixedly at Adrian as she demanded, "What did you tell your family, Adrian?" She twirled her spoon slowly between her fingers. In spite of her exhaustion, her back was very straight.

"I told them I was bringing you here and that we planned to marry within the week." There was no other way. Since Fitz and his men had failed thus far to protect Chloe, he himself would now guard her night and day. The way to do that was to marry her as soon as possible.

"You didn't ask her first? Oh, Adrian, how could you!" Dinah cried. "*I* would leave you flat."

Adrian said forcefully, "No one asked you, Dinah."

The earl glanced from Chloe to his son, then shepherded his wife and daughter toward the door. He nodded sharply at Antonio, who appeared fascinated by the little drama. Reluctantly, the chef headed for the door. "We'll leave you two alone to sort this out. Whatever you decide, Lady Chloe, be assured I will offer you the same assistance I provided for my daughter Evelyn and will give Dinah in the future."

Chloe shot a glare at Adrian, then said graciously, "Thank you, Lord Warnham."

As the door closed, she dipped her spoon into her broth. "Explain your high-handedness while I eat. I prefer my soup hot."

Adrian forced himself to remain calm. "Darling, I didn't want to discuss the wedding until I explained why it's imperative we marry immediately." When her only response was to swallow another spoonful, he continued wildly, "We can't have the wedding until your father arrives. Believe me, I'm trying to do this properly."

Chloe looked up calmly. "Is my father coming here?"

"Of course he's coming. I haven't even bloody asked his permission to marry you yet! Fitz was to arrange transport for him and your mother as soon as your father arrived in London."

"Fitz again. Does he pick out your socks and tie for you each morning?"

Adrian removed the spoon from her fingers. Lifting her hand, he pressed his lips against the vein pulsing just beneath the skin of her wrist. "I love you, Chloe," he murmured against her satin flesh. "I want our life together to be perfect, which means you're never to be in danger again."

Chloe removed her hand from his grasp and returned her attention to her soup. "I suppose Fitz is bringing a special license?" she asked dispassionately.

Adrian resisted a compelling urge to run his finger beneath his rumpled cravat to loosen it further. "Well, yes. He also wired your Aunt Heloise. I knew you'd want her to be here." He offered this last in hopes of gaining favor.

For one moment, Chloe contemplated her empty bowl. Her stomach growled, and she cast an inquiring look at the cart with its platters of food. "I wonder what else there is to eat."

Adrian choked back a desire to laugh. They *were* marrying in rather indecent haste, and she obviously intended him to suffer for it, no matter how pure his intentions—or how great his passion.

"Don't strangle yourself. I can't imagine what you find so amusing," she said as she rose to investigate the fragrances wafting from the vented covers.

Caught, he chuckled. "You are. Chloe, I know this is a hole in the corner affair, but I want the right to protect you. And I don't intend to wait six months, or even three, for that right. If you're uncomfortable about the rush, I promise you I'll try to find another way." He followed her to the trolley and supplied her with a china plate.

She looked from the fragile porcelain to his face. "Aren't you afraid I'll break this over your head? Really, Adrian, you *must* acquire some self-confidence. Decision-making will come quite naturally after a while." She lifted the first cover and inhaled deeply. "However does he do that with chicken? Mama will spend her entire stay in the kitchen. Other than fashion, food is her only other passion."

Dazedly, Adrian watched Chloe replace the silver lid, then set her plate aside. She reached for his lapels and tugged sharply, pulling him against her soft curves. "Adrian, you darling idiot, I don't care when the wedding is, or where, but the sooner it takes place, the happier I'll be." Rising on her toes, she kissed the corner of his mouth before adding, "I just wanted to help make the decision. What happened yesterday made me understand the danger we're in, and I never want to let you out of my sight again. Surely if we're together, we'll be safe."

Relieved, he buried his face in her hair. "I promise to never again make a single move without consulting you." He threaded his fingers beneath the thick fall of her dusky curls and turned her face to his. Gazing into the golden glow of her eyes was like falling into the sun.

Adrian was so enraptured, Chloe's next words took a moment to penetrate his thoughts.

"I will ask one thing of you. You must promise never to work for Fitz again."

Fighting his way back from his sensuous dreams, he said, "I beg your pardon?"

"Promise me never to work as a spy again."

Lowering his lids so she couldn't see the teasing light in his eyes, Adrian pretended to consider. "Well, I don't know. If we're in the Orient for our honeymoon, I might pick up some useful information to send back. Perhaps we could swing around to the United States on our return trip. There's always turmoil of some sort there, and Fitz will want someone to keep him abreast of matters." Conscious of Chloe's fixed stare, he suppressed his grin before raising his gaze to hers.

For one long moment their glances held. Distress had damped the golden lights in her eyes to somber brown. She was quiet beneath his touch, but her heart beat shallowly against his. He heard her slight intake of breath as she opened her mouth to protest, and he relented.

"Forgive me for teasing you. The night of the Skeffington ball I told Fitz that I was through with his nasty little business, and I meant it."

"See? They're kissing," said fifteen-year-old Dinah as the door swung open minutes later. "Father said we shouldn't interrupt, but I couldn't hear any voices through the door, so I knew you'd made up. After all, you would never kill each other." She grinned at them. "At least not quietly."

Chloe was becoming inured to interruptions during tender moments. Since young Dinah was as open and outspoken as she herself was, she felt none of the shyness she had expected to experience at being thrust on his family with so little notice. Reluctantly, she withdrew herself from the shelter of Adrian's embrace. "You may as well all come watch me expire. Adrian seems determined to let me die of starvation."

Antonio, muttering threats against anyone who dared to deprive such a beautiful lady of sustenance, prepared a heaping plate of food, which he placed before Chloe with great ceremony. Conscious of the chef's anxious eye, Chloe applied herself to her meal and listened intently while Adrian and his father talked, admiring the way Adrian timed his questions so he could chew while his father supplied the answers. She smiled inwardly, guessing he must have learned the technique in self-defense.

"Have you discovered any newcomers to the area?" Adrian asked as he applied butter to a warm roll.

Lord Warnham chuckled. "As soon as your wire arrived, I enlisted old Agnes at the village grocery. Within three hours she had reports from every merchant and land agent within a day's ride. Not a one." Edwin chuckled and propped his feet more comfortably on an upholstered ottoman. "She has her eye out for strangers, particularly gypsies and peddlers. She's never trusted them. She'll probably stop the stages and ask travelers to produce identification."

As they ate, Chloe watched Adrian's tension recede. The coziness of the homey, gaslit room invited relaxation. Drawing a deep breath of the fragrant scent of applewood blazing on the hearth, she sensed his family's lavish love. Their emotional embrace would help her heal Adrian's spirit, scarred by the past two years.

Her hunger finally satisfied, she bestowed a grateful smile on Antonio as he whisked her plate from in front of her, then moved closer to Adrian, who immediately clasped her hand in his while he continued to eat and talk with his father.

"Has anything else unusual happened?"

Lord and Lady Warnham exchanged questioning glances. When Edwin nodded, Dorothy offered, "I received a wire from David Mountjoy today. It seems he and his fiancée plan to marry and migrate to America next month. They're arriving tomorrow to say their farewells."

Chloe nearly cried out when Adrian's grip on her fingers tightened excruciatingly. His tension flowed through his fingertips into hers. She struggled to recall any facts from the overheard conversation at the museum that could cause the imminent arrival of Lelia and David to affect him so strongly.

His voice taut, Adrian said, "I dined with David just the

other night. At that time he was undecided about America because Lelia was unwilling to leave England. She must have changed her mind."

"I don't mind admitting I'm the one who put his name forward in New York. When I was there two months ago, they said they were looking to train a likely fellow who'd eventually set up their London branch," Edwin said. "I wouldn't have suggested him if he were still the heir, but when you returned, I wired them immediately. David's mother did a fine job of raising him after his father died. This is an excellent opportunity for him."

"That trust you settled on them helped Edwina. I remember you mentioned at the time that David would need a good start." Lady Warnham's voice broke, but she continued, "Then, when we were convinced we'd lost Adrian, David *was* the heir. He must have been bitterly disappointed when Adrian returned."

"David told me he had never wanted to inherit," Chloe contributed.

"No, I don't believe he did," Adrian said. His gaze was fixed on his plate, his face expressionless, as if his thoughts had turned inward.

"Well, no matter. He and this Lelia person plan to arrive sometime tomorrow," Dorothy said brightly, her eyes sheened with tears, as if she was recalling the years she'd thought her son was dead. "Should I wire them not to come?"

"Of course not, my dear. David is family, after all," Lord Warnham reassured her.

"Are you hearing all this, Antonio?" Adrian said suddenly to the chef, who had covered the platters and was transferring their soiled plates to the food trolley.

"Family may come, but no strangers. Be assured no one will reach you through my kitchen. My knives are the sharpest on this heathen island." His dark eyes glowing, he left the room.

Chloe found herself awaiting comment on the chef's outrageous claim.

Dorothy leaned forward, her eyes alight with laughter. "We didn't hire Antonio in the usual way, Chloe. He interviewed *us,* to see if we were worthy of him. Once he decided we were, he made it known that he would personally guarantee the perfection of every bite of food we ate—but only if he were considered a part of the family. You might say he adopted us."

"That soufflé last week was better than anything I've eaten in Paris," Edwin commented.

"What's David's fiancée like, Adrian?" Dinah asked eagerly.

Chloe watched Adrian's face as she waited for him to speak. She considered Lelia a cold, selfish cat, but David was the person whose happiness mattered. Still . . .

"I only met her once or twice *before* I . . . went away, Dinah, so I really couldn't say. David thinks she's the sun and the moon," Adrian answered. The disinterest in his voice indicated his own lack of enthusiasm for his cousin-to-be.

Before anyone could ask her opinion, Chloe politely covered an immense yawn.

"You poor darling. I'm sure you're desperate for a bath and a comfortable bed." Dorothy was on her feet and across the room in a swirl of silk before Chloe could do more than blink. "I've put you in the yellow room, overlooking the gardens. The flowers aren't much this time of year, but the windows face west, and the morning sun won't awaken you. Come along."

Half an hour later, rid of the gown that had begun to feel

like a rather filthy second skin, bathed and clad in a borrowed lace-trimmed batiste nightgown, Chloe crawled gratefully between the sheets of the high bed. Even though she was exhausted, she wished she had been able to kiss Adrian good night. The day, which had started so prosaically with church attendance, had taken her from fear and anger to rescue and passion—and now to the prospect of marriage within days.

She understood Adrian's seizing the opportunity to visit with his family. Still, she wanted to see him, to feel one last touch of his lips reassuring her all would be well through the night and into the morning. Her wedding! She quivered with excitement. Chloe couldn't wait. Adrian had sacrificed so much over the past two years. She intended to spend a lifetime making up to him for what he had missed.

She studied the flower-sprigged silk wallpaper shimmering in the glow of the firelight for a brief moment, then reached out to extinguish the little lamp by her bed. The door opened a scant inch, and Adrian's voice reached her as she turned the switch.

"Are you decent?"

Her joy at hearing his voice made Chloe giggle with delight. "Would it make any difference if I weren't?"

He slipped cautiously into the room. "Actually, I was half hoping you wouldn't be." His shadow loomed large against the opposite wall as he sank down on the edge of the bed and cupped the side of her face with one long-fingered hand. The soft light from the crackling logs in the fireplace shadowed his deep-set eyes, casting his cheekbones into sharp relief. "Will you have trouble sleeping after your experience today?"

"I may only lapse into a coma for forty-eight hours," she teased, nestling her cheek into his palm. "How did you know I was lying here wishing you would come kiss me?" If she lived forever, Chloe was sure she would never forget the sweetness of his smile as his mouth lowered to hers.

His lips were firm and smooth and warm, pledging and promising and draining her of any thought other than of Adrian and that moment in time.

When he withdrew his lips, her whimper of protest drew a rueful smile from him. "I spent too many years of my life taking my family for granted and caring only for myself. Sometimes I wasn't sure I was worth much effort. Then you came into my life and I was complete. I intend to spend the rest of my days attempting to anticipate your slightest wish. Believe me, I've only begun to love you."

After his noiseless exit Chloe lay drained and humble, her senses flooded with his touch, his voice, and the intensity of his love. The terrors of the day never had an opportunity to invade her dreams.

Chapter Eighteen

Adrian awoke suddenly, perspiration drenching his body. His breath came shallowly, almost panting. He shifted uncomfortably in the familiar bed; nights were the worst.

During his enforced absence from everything he held dear he had suffered nightmares depicting his homecoming. In each horrifying scenario, one or both of his parents was dead, his sisters somehow banished to obscurity. Since his return, the dreams had subsided, but Chloe's abduction yesterday must have triggered the foreboding lurking deep in his mind. Adrian forced himself to breathe deeply and slowly, counting with each inhalation.

He turned over, allowing the smooth slide of finely woven linen against his bare skin to soothe him. *Lord, how I've missed sleeping on sheets smelling of sunshine and lavender.* The thought reminded him of Chloe's soft, silken body, the fragrance of primroses that clung to her. He shifted to his side with a bittersweet sigh, yet a smile curved his lips. Conjuring up the feel and scent of his beloved presented him with a different reason for discomfort, and, God forgive him, he relished it. The need for sexual release reminded him he was truly alive.

Staring into the darkness, he counted the hours, superstitiously afraid to speculate on the shortest possible time before they could marry. Then he doubled the total he came up with, knowing that her father's arrival and consent were essential before the ceremony. He'd never even met the man, Adrian realized. *Please, just this once let things fall into place,*

Adrian petitioned, adding, *Please, God,* for good measure.

Once Chloe was truly his, he would take her where no one could touch them. Let his enemy's hatred consume him; the man could burn in hell, for all Adrian cared. He punched his feather pillow into a more confortable shape.

A voice spoke from the darkness. "Really, old man, the thing is harmless. Let me light the lamp and show you."

Adrian lay silent for a moment. Then he growled, "Damn you, Fitz. How in hell did you get in here?" He squeezed his eyelids tightly closed against the sudden blaze of gaslight, then eased them open after Fitz lowered the flame to a steady glow.

"I 'rode 'cross hill and dale' and threw myself on the mercy of your chef. Interesting fellow, Antonio. I've always liked him," his friend said jauntily, showing no signs of exhaustion after spending long hours on horseback in freezing weather.

Adrian pushed both pillows against the headboard and propped himself against them. "I'm sure he even fed you. Hell of a lot of help the man is if he lets people like you into the house."

"Oh, he waved one of his knives around when he found me picking the lock at the kitchen entrance. Then he recognized me and welcomed me like a brother."

"I thought you were to arrive with Lord and Lady Bennington." Adrian snatched the quilted velvet robe from the chair next to his bed and wrapped it around his bare shoulders.

"Adrian, you must know I'd do anything for you, and your Chloe is a remarkably bright, charming, and resilient young woman. I find her parents delightful—in small doses, as I'm sure you'll discover. They decided to take the train to Brighton and then dogleg back by carriage, and I simply could not bear the thought." He sprawled on the sofa in front of the fireplace. "Picture me trapped in a compartment, even first class, with the two of them. I know diddly about cows, and I'm convinced Lady Lockwood's perpetual exhaustion would be contagious in such close quarters."

Adrian found no reason to disagree with his friend. His thoughts focused on his wedding day. "Do you have the license?"

Fitz patted his breast pocket. "Would I fail you? What are your plans for afterward, or shouldn't I know?"

"No, you shouldn't. I've no intention of taking you along on my honeymoon." Sleep had deserted him; when necessary, he had survived for days on brief catnaps. His thoughts reverted to the offer his father had made him before he slipped into Chloe's room to bid her good night. At the memory of her sleepy, passionate response, his body tightened. "If you don't know, you won't slip and tell someone."

Surprisingly enough, his slur on Fitz's discretion drew no rebuttal. "You're quite right. By the by, one of that trio who connived at the kidnapping knows something. Before I left, we hadn't convinced her to share it, but I'll receive word as soon as she empties her cupboard."

"Then you'll rush to apprehend the bastard who's been making our lives a living hell?"

"Come now. Look on the bright side. If it weren't for these attempts, you and Chloe would be looking at a minimum engagement of six months, perhaps a year."

Adrian tossed the robe aside and slid contentedly back beneath the covers. He smiled, even though a shudder shook him. "We'd have to do the whole social whirl. From what I've observed, Chloe's mother would complain the entire time about the effort involved. And Chloe would hate the endless entertainments." The thought of avoiding a lengthy pre-wedding period relaxed him as no amount of tossing and turning could have. "I find the idea so satisfying, I've become sleepy again, Fitz. Go away so I can put the rest of the night to good use. There should be an empty room on this floor. Make yourself at home."

Late the next morning Chloe entered the breakfast room in a swirl of borrowed azure silk, refreshed after seven hours of sleep. Her thoughts were almost celestial, and her body vibrated with excitement. To her surprise, everyone was still seated at the long mahogany table, a hum of spirited conversation playing a musical counterpoint to the clink of heavy silver against fragile china.

"Good morning," she called gaily, heading toward the covered dishes on the sideboard. Antonio's early-morning supper was but a distant memory; she was famished. She lifted a silver lid and inhaled blissfully.

Adrian was beside her in an instant, whispering in her ear and managing to brush his fingers against hers each time he served her a new delicacy.

She had never imagined the intimacy of choosing between bacon and kippers, eggs and kedgeree, muffins or toast, with her lover's assistance. By the time she sank into the chair at Adrian's side, she was delightfully flustered, aware that her condition drew grins from Adrian's family—and a small, cynical smile to Fitzhugh Kent's lips.

Registering his presence, Chloe nearly dropped the strawberry she had just dipped in clotted cream. "When did *you* slither in?" she demanded.

Lord Warnham choked on a bite of toast. In the pregnant silence that followed, Fitz favored her with an approving nod that acknowledged her insult, then said, "I brought the license."

Weighing the necessity to apologize against nursing what

she felt was a very real grievance, Chloe chose the middle ground. "Well, then. It's about time you made yourself useful. I hope it's properly executed." She popped the strawberry into her mouth and smiled at Adrian. Even Fitz's presence couldn't spoil her happiness today. She felt like a cat basking in sunshine. In an attempt to steer the conversation to safer ground, Adrian's mother said, "You look lovely in that gown, Chloe."

"You were so generous to lend it to me, Lady Warnham. Mother will bring my trunks, so I shouldn't have to impose on you much longer. The parish can have that dress I wore yesterday." She picked up her fork and attacked the food on her plate.

"Fitz tells me your parents will arrive this evening. Your brother, Lionel, is escorting your aunt. They should all arrive at nearly the same time." Lady Warnham sipped her tea, her face serene. "David Mountjoy and his friend are also expected sometime today. Really, we'll have quite a little gathering. If Adrian can spare you for a few minutes after breakfast, we'll discuss how you would like things arranged, Chloe."

Adrian chose that moment to rub his ankle against hers, and Chloe returned the pressure while demurely spreading marmalade on her toast. Heat spread from the point of contact; her breathing quickened. She would do anything to hasten the ceremony. "By all means. As long as the marriage is legal . . . and soon." She flushed at the laughter her remark drew, then grinned helplessly at her future in-laws.

"Don't rush your fences, Mother. There's always the possibility Chloe's father will refuse his permission." Adrian continued the delicious pressure against her leg.

"Hah," said his father. "Can't see why he would. Heloise will bring him into line if he becomes difficult."

"I didn't realize you knew my aunt." Chloe smiled broadly

at her future father-in-law. "But we shan't need her help. If this is what I want, my father will not object." She swung her attention to Fitz. "Of course, when he hears how poorly I've been protected, he may demand to know who was responsible."

His composure unruffled, Fitz replied, "Then your aunt will vouch for me, I'm sure."

Confused by a conversation that meant nothing to her, Dinah stood and excused herself, then said, "Adrian, would you like to look around the stables with me? There wasn't time when you were here before, and we've some wonderful new horses."

Adrian squeezed Chloe's hand and stood. "I'd love to, Dinah. Why don't we go now? We'll take Fitz along, so Chloe can finish her breakfast in peace." He lifted a dark, shining curl from Chloe's shoulder and rubbed it between his fingers. "Mother won't keep you long, darling. Come join us when you're finished."

Heat from his fingers traveled through the lock of hair to the very heart of her. Chloe felt flushed and feverish. She had never felt so aware, so alive, and at that moment she wished the other occupants of the breakfast room would vanish into thin air. "Yes. I mean, yes, I'll be with you as soon as I can," she answered weakly.

As Adrian left the room, Dorothy reached across the embroidered linen to squeeze Chloe's fingers. "You've made us very happy, Chloe. I've never seen my son so content. His father and I have always wished for someone like you for him. This more than makes up for all those months when we thought he was lost forever." Her voice broke, then strengthened. "Then we had nothing to hope for. Now we have everything."

Chloe recalled Adrian's mother's words two hours later as

they watched Fitz and Dinah set out on horseback. "Adrian, did your parents know you were spying? Before you had to 'die,' I mean, not after. I suppose then Fitz had to tell them *some* of the truth."

"The news was a surprise to them. If I'd told them what I intended to do, I knew they'd have locked me up if necessary, to prevent me from working for Fitz, so I didn't tell them. It broke my heart for them to believe I was dead. My only consolation was that Father didn't have to worry about Mother's being turned out of her home if he were to die suddenly. The title and the estates are divided by a mass of legalities, but this house isn't included in the entail, and she would have been left with enough money to continue living just as she has." He tugged her hand. "Come with me. I want to show you one of my favorite places."

Eagerly following his lead, Chloe pulled a heavy paisley shawl more tightly around her shoulders. His reference to the inheritance intrigued her. "She would inherit Warnham House?"

Adrian held back the branches of a spruce tree overhanging the path. "This isn't the ancestral seat. The real Warnham House, the first earl's seat is on thousands of acres in Cumberland. This land came to my great-grandfather when he married a rich heiress. They had only the one son, so he in turn got the entire package." The path narrowed considerably, and Adrian pulled her close so they could pass side by side between the encroaching tree limbs.

"My grandfather despised Cumberland. He hated the Scots, so being that close to Scotland made him furious; he hated the cold, and he hated everything about the family seat—called it a pile of stone falling down around its ankles. He decided to build here. The land has been in the family long enough that we think of Warnham House as ancestral, but it's not."

"What about the shipping line and your father's other business interests?"

Adrian stopped and eyed her quizzically, one brow cocked. "Why all this sudden interest in my prospects?"

His question brought a blush to Chloe's cheeks, but she wouldn't be swayed. Something, some fact she'd forgotten, was trying to surface in her mind, and she intended to fit all the pieces into their proper places. "Since I'm heiress to an inheritance larger than nearly anyone you know, you know perfectly well I'm not mercenary."

She pressed a kiss at the corner of his mouth and dragged her lips along the clean line of his jaw, savoring his taste. When Adrian turned his head to meet her lips with a hungry kiss of his own, she returned his ardor, then pulled back. "We both know where *that* will lead. You'll distract me, and I'll forget what I wanted to know."

"You started it," he answered, his hand caressing her breast.

"I did, didn't I," she said smugly. Nestling her cheek against the hard plane of his shoulder, Chloe formulated her next question. "I'm just trying to sort things out. If you had been truly dead, and something happened to your father, what all would David inherit?"

Groaning, Adrian set her from him and turned her toward the path ahead. "I've seen my father's will. In the event of my death, Mother and the girls receive everything that isn't entailed. David would be saddled with a rotting castle in Cumberland and land as far as he could see. It's very beautiful, but the bigger half of the estate is mountains and trees. Tenants eke out their livings with sheep and crops on the rest, but the returns aren't great. With the castle and the estate needing constant improvements, the place is lucky to pay for itself."

"Then all he would end up with is the title and an estate in

Cumberland. That doesn't sound like much of an inheritance." A squirrel darted across the path ahead of them, breaking her concentration. "Where are you taking me?"

Adrian guided her up a gentle rise to a clearing. "Not down the garden path, no matter what either of us might prefer. Let's finish this discussion before we reach the top, because I've more interesting things to tell you once we're there. The estate also includes a couple of properties in Carlisle, but the rent from them doesn't allow for much profit. Once again, there are always necessary improvements. And the death taxes would be exorbitant."

"If he were to inherit, could David sell the Cumberland land for money to live on?"

Adrian chuckled, then suddenly sobered. "I've no idea." His steps slowed, and his eyes fixed on the trunk of an ancient oak as if he were seeing through it. "You may have hit on something, Chloe. I'll ask my father. He'll know the legalities."

Satisfied, Chloe returned to the present. "What is it you want to show me?" She tugged on his hand, pulling him toward the crown of the hill.

A vista had been provided by a cut through the thick growth on the slope before them. At the bottom lay fallow fields already plowed in preparation for the spring four months ahead. Clusters of barren trees dotted the landscape, and tidy stone walls turned the land into a checkerboard. Far beyond were tidy cottages; the few people traveling on the single main thoroughfare looked like moving dots.

"Is this all?" she demanded. Adrian's narrowed gaze was fixed beyond the wide opening in the wooded hillside. His thoughts appeared miles away. A slight smile curved his lips. She studied the vista, narrowing her eyes to focus her vision far beyond the little village.

"It's moving! Adrian, that's the sea!"

His smile widened to a delighted grin, and he drew her tightly against him.

"It's the Channel!" Chloe felt a thrill of excitement. The British Channel led to the ocean, to the world. The hours she'd spent poring avidly over maps and histories of other countries had furnished tantalizing glimpses of places she'd despaired of ever seeing. Adrian had promised her the world, and the sea was the gateway to anywhere she wanted to travel. Standing here, snug against the warmth and taut excitement of Adrian's body, she felt her cup of happiness overflow.

"Right you are." He gestured with his free arm. "Our yacht is anchored in a harbor a few hours' ride south. A large, ocean-going yacht, sweetheart." Adrian dragged his lips across her temple, dislodging a tendril of hair. Wrapping his hand around her slender waist, he turned her into his full embrace. His voice, a breath from her ear, was low and seductive. "After the ceremony, we're sneaking off to the yacht. The trip will take three or four hours, but once we're on board, we can sail wherever you wish. Unless you're in a hurry to return to England."

"Together?"

"Always."

The subtle tremor in his voice affected Chloe more than she could have believed possible. She saw the sheen of moisture behind the thicket of dark, gold lashes guarding his shadowed eyes. "I love you, Adrian. I'll go anywhere with you, and I promise to keep your heart safe. You'll never be alone again." She raised her lips to his.

His kiss was tender, molding and shaping her mouth until she felt as if they were one being. A delicious languor spread through her, and she wondered if it were possible to expire from joy. When he lifted his lips from hers, she felt bereft. She consoled herself by burying her head beneath his chin.

He pulled her hips against the tautness of his thighs. His voice was wryly embarrassed. "I'm supposed to be protecting *you*. And a precious poor job I've done so far."

Chloe threaded her fingers through the hair at his nape, rubbing the taut tendons beneath the skin, luxuriating in the feel of him and the fact that he was hers to touch whenever she wanted. "We'll take care of each other. We could even stand back to back to watch for attackers—although but that might be inconvenient from time to time." She rocked gently against him.

Adrian returned the motion. "*Very* inconvenient."

Given a choice, Adrian would have thrown his jacket down on the prickly grasses and made love to Chloe in full view of God and anyone who happened by, but a sharp gust of icy wind reminded him of the discomfort of such an indulgence. He kissed Chloe one last time, lingeringly and thoroughly. "We'd better get back." Frustration rode him as they descended, but the past two years had taught him patience. He counted the dwindling hours until Chloe and he would be safe on the yacht, far from shore and harm. He even allowed himself the naive hope that by the time they returned, their unknown enemy would have lost interest.

He laughed aloud at such optimism; he was too aware of the dangers that could still beset them.

"What's so funny?"

He tightened his arm around Chloe's shoulders and said evasively, "Only my father knows where we're going. You mustn't tell anyone. Even Heloise."

"You don't think . . ."

His quick, hard, kiss stopped her words. "Not in a million years, but sometimes even the walls have ears." God only knew he'd learned that particular lesson in Armenia; it had almost cost him his life.

"Well, then, I won't. But I can't imagine why we must be so secretive, since only family members will be here for the wedding. Aside from Fitz, of course." Her nose wrinkled in distaste.

Adrian steered her to the right fork of the path ahead. "He didn't corrupt me, Chloe. I leaped into spying like a rat into a sewer. I was frantic to escape the boredom of life in London. When my grandfather built this estate, he spent every penny he had. My father had to work like a navvy to rebuild the family fortunes, and he mistakenly believed I needed freedom from responsibility for a few years. I didn't have a place anywhere."

"For your sake, I'll be polite to Fitz. Just don't ask me to *like* him." Chloe shaded her eyes to peer ahead to the graveled stable yard. She gave a little bounce of excitement. "Look, a carriage is leaving. Who do you suppose has arrived? If my father's here . . ." She pulled free of his hold and ran ahead.

Her excitement was contagious. Adrian followed, lagging slightly behind to watch her. Chloe's hair had escaped its combs and flowed down her shoulders above the unrestrained movements of her body beneath the clinging folds of his mother's dress. He was almost disappointed when she slowed to a decorous walk.

"Goodness, I hope it's my parents or Aunt Heloise who arrived in that carriage."

Chloe attempted to push her luxuriant dark curls behind her ears without great success. Her cheeks were flushed, and her mouth gave every appearance of having been recently and thoroughly kissed. Adrian wanted very much to kiss her again, right now, but he understood her eagerness to discover who had arrived.

"Do I look too much of a fright?"

"If your father sees you as you look this instant, I won't have to ask permission for our marriage. He'll demand I make an honest woman of you," Adrian teased. He adjusted the shawl around her shoulders before opening the service door.

Chloe's delighted giggle preceded them down the narrow passage to the main part of the house, announcing their arrival.

"Here they are now," Lady Warnham said brightly to the other occupants of the foyer before turning toward the newcomers. "Your cousin and Miss Fenton are here, Adrian. Isn't it lovely they've arrived in time for the wedding?"

"Wedding?" Lelia said blankly.

"Aren't you the quiet one, Adrian! You never said a word about getting married when we dined the other night." David Mountjoy blinked several times and peered at Adrian's companion. "Lady Lockwood. What a pleasant surprise."

Adrian chuckled at the way Chloe's tongue tripped over itself trying to explain. "It's all quite complicated, Mr. Mountjoy. You see, Adrian—"

"Can't wait to marry you and carry you off," Adrian finished ruthlessly. He extended his hand to his cousin. "I understand you've accepted the post in New York."

"Yes, well, I thought my news was exciting, but I can't quite match yours, old man. When is this wedding?"

"As soon as the bride's father arrives to give the bride away. When we saw your carriage, Chloe and I were in hopes you were her parents." Still clasping Chloe's hand, Adrian nodded to Lelia. "It's been a long time, Miss Fenton."

Lelia smiled tightly, her little cat's teeth showing white between her pink lips. "Since before you disappeared, Lord Harding. I'm thrilled to be here and take part in such a wonderful family occasion." Her eyes were sharp and bright as she continued, "I'm relieved to hear you've given up that unfortunate connection with Fitz Kent. People were concerned your preference for each other meant you would never marry," she purred.

Before Adrian could counter the spiteful implications of her remark, his mother demanded, "Whatever are you talking about, Miss Fenton?"

"She's probably heard rumors that Fitz and I are spies, mother. Lockerbie began spreading that one years ago on a bet. Of course, most people know better than to believe it."

Chapter Nineteen

Chloe's breath caught in her throat. Had Lelia just implied there was something not "normal" between Adrian and Fitz? And Adrian had all but admitted to spying!

Why on earth would David's fiancée say such a thing? She observed her companions from beneath lowered eyelashes. Lady Warnham's features had tightened with anger. Chloe could only guess at her feelings. One would have to be blind not to notice how lovingly her gaze followed Adrian or her tendency to touch him whenever possible. She'd spent two years believing her son dead, and her joy at his return was beautiful. Lelia's insinuation could break her heart.

Then Chloe realized she herself was the real target of Lelia's venom. For some obscure reason Lelia didn't want Chloe and Adrian to marry. She tightened her grip on his hand and felt reassuring pressure in return.

David looked devastated. When no one else spoke, he broke the uncomfortable silence engulfing the little group. "I say, Lelia—"

Adrian, his face a picture of boredom, interrupted his cousin. "Actually, I wish I could tell you I *had* been spying. In the name of a just cause, it's actually quite an honorable activity. Even biblical. Remember Paul pleading with his adherents to inform him of their progress and the events in the countries where they were spreading the Word?" He chuckled. "Although Fitz will be miffed to hear that someone has accused him of actually being useful."

Chloe was amazed by Adrian's cool response, aware, not for the first time, of his uncanny ability to disguise his feelings. What was he thinking beneath that bland facade?

Adrian continued, "Her Majesty appears to be most grateful to those who monitor activities and attitudes in other countries. Keeps the Empire financially healthy, as you, Lelia, should be aware, since your father's been working with foreign economies for some years now."

"What in the name of sense are you all doing standing in that drafty foyer talking politics? I just noticed there's a roaring fire in the blue parlor, and here you stand, nattering on with our guests in the hall." Edwin's voice boomed from where he descended the curving staircase. He was the picture of vigor, looking only a few years older than his son. His bluff voice conveyed welcome, but Chloe thought his eyes narrowed when his gaze settled on Lelia.

If he had overheard the awkward little encounter, Lord Warnham made no other sign. Like father, like son. She wondered if *he* had ever been a spy.

She tightened her hold on Adrian's hand.

"Good to see you, David, and your young lady, too," the earl said as he joined the group. "Fenton's daughter, aren't you?" Without waiting for a reply, he shepherded them through the tall doors to his left. "Come and get warm. Tea and Antonio's special anchovy paste sandwiches should arrive any time now."

Anxious to share her momentous discovery, Chloe held Adrian back until the others had filed into the blue parlor. Adrian's hand clutched hers, and he seemed to be staring into space, his eyes unseeing and unfocused. For the space of a heartbeat she thought she might have to commit violence to gain his attention. She waved a hand in front of his face, and he blinked, abruptly aware of her. His features tight, he demanded, "Chloe, do you believe that filth Lelia just tossed into the midst of my family?"

Chloe rose on tiptoe and kissed the corner of his mouth, teasing his upper lip with her tongue and welcoming the clean scent of outdoors that clung to him. "It would be impossible for you to have made me as happy as you have if your heart preferred Fitz. Besides, I'm much prettier than he is."

The tension drained from Adrian. The corners of his mouth quirked with the beginnings of amusement. "Modest, aren't you?" He wrapped his arms around her and held her tightly. "I'm afraid David has a real piece of work on his hands."

Chloe hugged him back with equal enthusiasm. "Ha! From the look he gave her, she's just managed to scratch some bloom off the rose. Adrian, do you think your father heard everything she said?"

"Of course. You didn't notice him falling over himself to welcome her, did you?"

Leaning back within his embrace, Chloe looked up at him intently and whispered, "I'm convinced Lelia's despicable innuendo was aimed at me. But why?"

His mouth curved in a humorless grin. "A whiff of anything of that sort would be likely to put a damper on your enthusiasm." All teasing vanished as he said seriously, "I'm beginning to think there might be an excellent reason, and you may have pointed your finger right at it this afternoon."

He turned Chloe toward the parlor door, removing her shawl as he did so. Bending to kiss the sensitive skin below her ear, he whispered. "Make my excuses in there, will you? I want to send several wires off to London." His lips browsed her temple and her eyelids, filling her with yearning. "Try not to forget me while I'm gone."

* * * * *

Half an hour later, Chloe excused herself from the awkward conversation taking place around the tea table and climbed the stairs to her room, intent on a warm bath. Her parents could arrive anytime, and she wanted time to herself.

Although Lelia's vicious insinuation hadn't been mentioned during tea, she knew everyone was thinking of it. The countess had treated Lelia with an icy civility that contrasted strongly with the warmth she showed Chloe.

David Mountjoy had been quiet, brooding over his cup when he wasn't studying Lelia, who spoke vivaciously to everyone in the room and acted as if she had never inferred something so despicable. Chloe wondered if the woman cared that she had crossed the line of good taste.

Shedding her clothing, Chloe donned Lady Warnham's silk dressing gown and sat on a petit-point upholstered stool to brush her hair. The wind had snarled her curls mercilessly. She winced as she brushed each lock loose from its fellows. So intent was she on her task that she nearly missed the faint rap at her door. "Who is it?" she called.

"It's Lelia. May I come in?"

Chloe grimaced. She set the brush on the gleaming marble tabletop, pulled the folds of ecru silk more closely about her, tightened the belt, and called, "Come in, Lelia."

Still wearing the fashionable twill traveling dress in which she had arrived, Lelia slipped furtively through the door. "I had to talk with you before dinner."

"I can't imagine anything we need to discuss."

"Of course there is. You're marrying David's cousin, the future head of his family." She crossed to the needle-point-covered slipper chair beside the fireplace and sat. "I think it would be well if you and I became better acquainted. After all, we shall probably see a great deal of each other."

257

Chloe was quite sure she didn't want to know Lelia any better than she already did. After her outrageous insinuation, the woman was no longer worth noticing. On the other hand, perhaps she could discover why Lelia had spoken as she had. Crossing her fingers behind her back, Chloe said, "Of course. Since Adrian and David are close, it's essential that you and I get along."

"How very sensible you are. But I guessed as much. I felt I should explain more fully why I said what I did this afternoon." Lelia's eyes were wide and sincere. "I never believed the rumors about Fitz and Adrian, but you should be aware they existed." She fluttered her hands expressively and leaned forward. "Even before he was believed dead, the gossip was ugly. Truly. But Adrian courted so *many* women that both Fitz and he were always invited to the most select gatherings, regardless of the talk. Naturally, people like that are ostracized by careful hostesses."

Chloe bit the inside of her lip to keep from either screaming with laughter or slapping the woman. As seriously as possible, she asked, "I suppose you did your best to quash such gossip?"

"Yes. But even then, one always wonders . . . just a little. You *do* understand, don't you, Chloe? I'm frightfully embarrassed that I didn't stop to think before I spoke today. The trip from London had been so tiring. It was all a dreadful mistake." Lelia twisted a striking cameo ring around and around her finger.

"Yes, it was," Chloe said bluntly. "I felt particularly embarrassed for the countess. She's been through so much, and hearing something like that, whether or not it was true, could have been devastating." She looked directly at Lelia, dropped her voice confidentially, and continued, "Of course, I could reassure her that Adrian is very . . . shall we say, normal, but then, that would create a rather embarrassing situation for me."

Lelia's nervous fingers stilled, and the color drained from her face. A brittle smile appeared on her lips. "That explains such a hole-in-the-corner wedding. Congratulations are doubly in order."

The insinuation shattered Chloe's calm. "Don't be ridiculous. I'm not increasing. It's just that neither of us gives a bloody damn about a society extravaganza. We're wildly in love, so why wait?"

"There's no need to be crude, Chloe." Lelia rose, the picture of virtuous outrage. "I'm simply thinking of appearances."

"Then take your bloody concern for appearances out of my room and go make an effort to turn David up sweet," Chloe said heatedly. "You may have your work cut out for you. It was obvious that *he* was uncomfortable with your bloody little lie."

"Listen to you. You're nothing but a common . . ." Apparently struggling for the proper insult, Lelia settled for "Farm girl!" Then she spat, "What a pity Lord and Lady Warnham can't witness such coarseness. They'd throw you out and forbid Adrian ever to see you again, much less marry you."

Chloe realized with dismay that their voices had risen. She clenched her hands tightly at her sides to keep from striking her uninvited guest. With an effort she controlled her volume but not her tongue as she said, "Maybe he's relieved he's chosen a graceless, provincial, *honest* woman who loves him with all her heart rather than someone like the vicious little gold digger who's ensnared his cousin."

With an outraged shriek, Lelia leaped for her. Chloe caught her wrist just before her hand made contact with her cheek. The smaller girl tugged wildly to free herself.

A soft rap at the door broke the tension. Chloe released Lelia and said softly, "Leave. Right now. I have another guest." She couldn't remember ever being so furious.

Lelia shook out her skirts with a righteous twist of her hips and hissed, "It's probably Adrian, coming to continue your disgusting, immoral . . ."

Chloe sighed as she walked to the door, "Out, Lelia."

The blonde flounced through the opening, brushing against the countess in passing. When Lelia had disappeared, Adrian's mother stepped into the room and pushed the door closed before she said conspiratorially, "I had no intention of eavesdropping, but I couldn't help overhearing the two of you. As hostess, I was afraid it might become my duty to rescue Miss Fenton, even though my heart wouldn't have been in it." She held out an amber velvet gown trimmed with rich black lace. "And to think I only came to bring this for you to wear this evening."

Chloe clapped a hand over her lips. She wished she were invisible.

With a delighted laugh, her future mother-in-law embraced her. "Wait until I tell Edwin. When Adrian was very young, he was such a straitlaced prig, I quite despaired of him. Then during his first year or two in town he became so wild, I found myself wishing he were a prig again. Suddenly he became dashing, charismatic. Little did I know the evolution was the result of his missions for Fitz. The mere idea would have given me spasms." She carried the dress to the bed and spread it across the counterpane, then turned to face Chloe. Her blue eyes were bright with unshed tears.

"When Adrian was reported dead, we were devastated. After Fitz came to us and finally told us the truth, everything fell into place. Poor Edwin felt quite guilty, as if he had driven Adrian to risk his life for adventure." She pressed her hands to her cheeks and laughed shakily.

"In spite of those terrible years, now that they're over, I find the idea of spying rather exciting." She took Chloe's hands in her own. "When Adrian wired that he was bringing you to us, I was afraid he had chosen a wide-eyed innocent who would leap to obey his slightest command."

Relief swept Chloe like a spring shower. She sank back onto the embroidered stool. "I don't quite fit that description."

"My dear, you're magnificent." Lady Warnham enveloped Chloe in an exuberant hug. "I'll tell you another secret. This afternoon in the foyer I came quite close to smacking Lelia's nasty little mouth."

Adrian bathed and shaved quickly, chafing under the necessity for formal dress. If Chloe's family wasn't due to arrive at any minute, they would have dined casually in the cozy breakfast room. As things stood, he could scarcely approach the duke for his daughter's hand wearing tweeds. Even the "Farmer Duke" deserved deference at such a time. Fortunately, the ladies would take longer to prepare; he would have time to keep his appointment with Fitz in the library.

As he slipped down the stairs and along the hall, he thought he heard retreating footsteps. A quick glance assured him he was alone, but he listened carefully for a moment before entering the masculine room. Bookshelves lined the walls from floor to ceiling, and heavy burgundy velvet draperies were drawn over the windows overlooking the formal garden. A welcoming fire crackled on the hearth. Fitz held out a low tumbler half-filled with amber liquid.

Adrian took the glass and raised it to his lips eagerly. He choked on his first swallow.

"Not much soda in there. I heard what happened earlier,"

Fitz said sympathetically.

"You mean well, I'm sure, but I can hardly arrive at dinner three sheets to the wind," Adrian replied as he crossed the room to the siphon. He turned to his friend. "Chloe put her finger on something this afternoon. She wanted to know what David stood to inherit if I were actually dead. We've been so busy searching for a connection to the Armenian affair we never looked as closely at the personal angle."

"But why kidnap Chloe?"

Adrian considered his glass meditatively, then drank. "The first time, when Josef took her away, had nothing to do with Chloe herself. He was merely using her as a way to meet with me." He paced to the fireplace and stared into the flames. "The second time was an attempt to separate us."

Fitz nodded agreement. "I haven't a report yet on the interrogation, so we still have no idea who hired them, but the pair who took her from the church let something slip about turning Chloe over to slavers. I'll wager she knew that but didn't choose to tell us."

Horror washed through Adrian at the unspeakable fate Chloe had so narrowly escaped. "Then the second attempt was meant to dispose of her. What would happen if I lost Chloe? What if she disappeared?"

"You'd be brokenhearted and quite possibly never again consider marriage, although that seems rather extreme. She's a lovely girl, and I know you're idiotically attached to her, but I can't imagine myself in that state," Fitz said coldbloodedly.

"When you meet your match, I'd give half my prospects to be there," Adrian said cheerfully. "Anyway, what would happen if I died an old, brokenhearted bachelor . . . or perhaps a young one?"

Fitz dropped onto the overstuffed leather couch. "Do you

know the trouble with playing international chess twenty-four hours a day? One tends to see everything as complicated." He tipped his head back and looked at the ceiling as he said, "Have you any idea how many times I've reviewed your missions, looking for an enemy from the past? I never gave the obvious enough consideration. You're a target because you're the heir to a fortune."

"Not quite. David wouldn't inherit the fortune, just a title and some rather lovely but remote ancestral acres of mountains and farmland." Adrian frowned into his glass. "Somehow, I find it next to impossible to suspect David."

"No one's above suspicion. Particularly if they're in line to inherit anything more than twenty pounds."

"Not David," Adrian insisted stubbornly.

Fitz closed his eyes and contemplated the problem. When he opened them, he said shrewdly, "Lelia, then?"

"I wish you'd heard her this afternoon. Any woman other than Chloe would have broken our engagement. With less evidence, I might add."

"Ah, faith *and* love. You're truly in a bad way, my friend."

Adrian turned to study the fire once more. "Fitz, what if for some reason the Cumberland estate should be more valuable than we think?"

"Is it?"

"I engaged a private investigator today. Instinct tells me our land agent might know more than he's told my father. If there's a hidden asset . . . say, minerals of some sort . . . it would be worth the agent's while to withhold the information . . . if he were promised a cut."

Fitz's beatific smile gave him the appearance of an impish choirboy. "Pure speculation, of course, but such a promise could corrupt nearly anyone."

The sound of voices and of people hurrying toward the

foyer filtered through the door. "The detective in me says we have arrivals." Rising, he bowed and swept an arm toward the door. "You first, my boy. Step out and seal your fate."

In the billiards room later that evening, Adrian reflected on how very simple the entire affair had been. The duchess had apparently informed her husband of what had occurred in London, probably implying that Chloe never would have been recovered in one piece without Adrian's heroic efforts. Throughout an interminable dinner she had adroitly directed everyone's attention to the extraordinary events that had brought Adrian into Chloe's life.

Heloise, who, along with Lionel, arrived immediately after Chloe's parents, had maintained a Sphinx-like silence throughout, while Fitz had seen fit to excuse himself from the dining room on several occasions, his shoulders shaking.

The anticipated interview with Chloe's father never actually took place, although Adrian knew a routine discussion of settlements was scheduled for the following morning. As soon as the dessert wine was poured, the duke had toasted the newly engaged couple, then inquired as to the hour of the wedding. Chloe, her dark hair and damask cheeks glowing above the drape of amber velvet, had deferred to Adrian's mother, who announced a brief ceremony scheduled for the following afternoon. Antonio was already hard at work on the reception.

Now, Adrian wished Lionel, David, and Fitz were at the ends of the earth. The ladies had scurried upstairs following dinner, their mission a search of closets for a suitable wedding gown. The duke and the earl were in the library discussing commodities. He hadn't even had an opportunity to kiss his beloved good night.

Fitz's voice returned him to the present. "Come back,

Adrian. You look as if you were planning someone's funeral
. . . or murder."

"I was considering how to rid the house of everyone but
Chloe."

Lionel snorted. "You'll have more than enough of my sister after tomorrow." He removed a rather vile-looking cigar
from his mouth, set it in a brass bowl on the sideboard, and
proceeded to chalk his cue. "I hope you're prepared. My
mother gave up trying to teach Chloe to be a proper lady
shortly after she went into long skirts. She's done exactly as
she pleased all her life. Has she told you she used to run wild
on the estate wearing my outgrown trousers?"

Adrian chuckled at David's shocked expression. "She's
graduated to divided skirts," he said, making a mental note to
provide Chloe with a pair of trousers. At the thought of her
long, slender legs and delightful derriere encased in tailored
worsted, his own trousers became uncomfortably smug. He
shifted in his chair.

"Surely she'll conform once she's married," David said soberly.

"I devoutly hope she doesn't," Adrian answered.

The loud smack of one ivory ball hitting another preceded
Fitz's shout of laughter. "The more I hear and see of your
bride-to-be, the more I approve. If you should change your
mind about marrying her, Adrian, please let me know first."
He bent to line up his cue stick for another stroke.

"Find your own woman, Fitz. Maybe you should try dying." Yet another ball made its way into the corner pocket.
"Entirely too uncomfortable. The idea leaves me quite cold,
if you'll pardon the pun."

David said heavily, "This isn't a joking matter, Adrian.
The last two years must have been beastly for you. I don't
suppose you'd care to tell us more about them."

Adrian refused to discuss his experiences. His accounting to his parents had been brief and undetailed; only his sojourn at Heloise's estate had been described with any accuracy, and he'd omitted several significant interludes from *that* story.

"Rejoining civilization has been nearly as stressful," he said evasively.

"Must have been a shock to meet my sister again after meeting her at Aunt Heloise's. I hear she was traipsing around in draperies and thumbing her nose at society," Lionel observed. "Have you convinced her to dress like a lady?"

Adrian chuckled. Lionel was a good man with horses, but when it came to understanding his own twin, he was a loss. "I tried it once, but I'm afraid the cat's about to escape the bag about the women of my own family, Lionel." He glanced at Fitz, who was leaning against the billiards table laughing. The damned idiot was having a wonderful time at the expense of everyone in the house. "My mother and my sisters think the same as Chloe. She's probably learned the truth by now."

"Chloe, we can simply let out the hem, as we did with the gowns you wore before." Lady Warnham passed the ivory satin gown to Chloe. "This was in fashion ten years after Victoria came to the throne," she said nostalgically.

Chloe shook out the pearl-encrusted ivory folds reverently. "You'd let me wear your wedding gown? What about Dinah?"

"We'll simply shorten it when her time comes. Evelyn wore it, but she is my size, so it's never been altered." Lady Warnham sighed. "I do wish she and her husband hadn't left for the Mediterranean last week. She'll be livid when she hears she missed Adrian's wedding."

Lady Lockwood patted her hand sympathetically, then

turned to Chloe with a practical air. "Your corsets are in your trunks."

A pregnant silence settled over the little group of women in Lady Warnham's sitting room. Setting her chin, Chloe scrambled for a polite way to present her case without offending her mother-in-law-to-be. She said, "Mother, you know—"

She was interrupted by Lady Warnham. "Corsets? My dear Lady Lockwood, I've never worn one in my life. I consider them unhealthful." Taking the gown from Chloe, she turned the bodice inside out. "See? Quilted crinoline gives a wonderfully firm look to the fabric. Chloe's so slender, no one will be able to tell the difference."

Chloe couldn't decide whether to murder Adrian directly after breakfast or to wait until she wore his ring. The devil had known all along! Yet he had encouraged her to think he expected her to truss herself up like a Christmas goose.

Tacitly excluded from the group dressing the bride, Lelia had retired to her room. Ellen, her traveling companion, whom she referred to as her chaperon when such an explanation became necessary, also served as her maid. Previous hostesses had been known to err on the side of politeness and include Ellen in their seating arrangements, only to regret their decision. The dark, wiry woman had a forbidding air and no conversation. More than one person had observed that someone with such an unpleasant demeanor must be extremely efficient; otherwise there'd be no reason to keep her around.

"Pack my trunk," Lelia said as she entered the room.

"As you wish."

"Nothing has worked as it should. I was sure I could force Chloe to cry off, but she's either stupid or so besotted, she doesn't care. The wedding is tomorrow. And now David's turning stuffy about my comment this afternoon." She unhooked her heavy satin bodice and stripped it off.

Ellen nodded knowingly. "Good thing I overheard Lord Warnham direct the chef to prepare hampers for the yacht."

"I'm taking matters into my own hands." Lelia removed the pins from her hair and peered at her face in the mirror. "Tomorrow I'll claim the women snubbed me this evening, which isn't far from the truth. I'll play martyr, then leave in a huff." Lelia unfastened her skirt and petticoats and stepped out of them, tugging at the hooks of her corset as she did so.

The maid picked up the clothing. "Can you convince Mountjoy you were misunderstood?"

"He'll come 'round easily enough." She preened in front of the mirror. "Besides, I must be away from here to follow them myself. I don't trust anyone else. Adrian's become so secretive, I'll wager he hasn't told even Fitz Kent where they're going. This time there'll be no one to come to his rescue."

Chapter Twenty

With one glance Adrian deducted that the aggressive jut of Lelia's chin when she entered the dining room for breakfast bode ill for someone. Since David was the room's only other occupant, he resigned himself to the kind of scene that never failed to ruin his digestion.

Rising out of courtesy, he debated the possibility of making a quick escape. His hopes were dashed when Lady Maude entered directly behind Lelia. One could hardly flee the room just as one's future mother-in-law entered.

Across the table from him, David apparently recognized the signs of a storm brewing and hurried to assist Lelia. "Here, darling. Let me get you some kippers and eggs."

"Are you sure there will be enough kippers for everyone? I don't want to be accused of taking the last ones," she said petulantly.

"A fresh platter just arrived," he assured her. "Would you care for fruit?"

Outwardly oblivious to any undercurrents, Chloe's mother selected two slices of dry toast and seated herself beside Adrian. "I eat only toast and tea in the morning," she announced to no one in particular as the footman filled her teacup. "More than that simply drains my energy for the rest of the day."

Adrian thought Chloe's mother rather enjoyed her lack of vitality, but he nodded sympathetic agreement—a move that earned him a recitation of the multitude of imaginary tasks

requiring her attention before the ceremony. Not for anything would he have reminded her that his mother had the affair well in hand.

Throughout Maude's narrative he could overhear the
murmured conversation on the other side of the table. David's voice alternated between conciliatory and impatient,
neither of which appeared to be having an effect. Lelia was
aggrieved and sounding more so by the second.

"She didn't even speak to me, David. No one speaks to me
but you. They don't like me."

Adrian was willing to wager a thousand pounds that the
whine in her high-pitched voice would drive David to drink
before the year was out.

"Lelia darling, you're imagining things."

"Then why wasn't I invited to the countess's sitting room
last night with the others?"

Adrian, one ear tuned to Lelia's recital of ill-usage and the
other giving token attention to the duchess, buttered his
toast. He wondered why he and Chloe hadn't simply taken a
train to Scotland, established residence for three weeks, and
married without any fuss. He'd been born there, a fact he had
just remembered.

He hesitated to remind his cousin's fiancée she had retired
to her room long before the ladies adjourned to his mother's
quarters. When Lelia's broken mumbling turned to sobbing,
he had to restrain himself from throwing a glass of water in
her face. Fascinated, he watched Lelia cast herself against
David's chest and employ the ultimate weapon: tears.

"I wish I'd never come here. I should have known your
family would look down on me," she wailed between sobs.

David patted her shoulder ineffectually. "Of course they
don't, darling. You're simply overtired."

The earl stepped through the door, saw the emotional

storm on one side of the table and Adrian trapped on the other, turned on his heel, and disappeared. Until now Adrian would have given a great deal to follow his father, but Lelia's performance had reached such a pitch that he was riveted to his seat.

As if realizing she had taken the performance as far as it would go, Lelia withdrew from David's arms and carefully patted the tears from her face, careful not to flaw the perfection of her pink-rouged complexion. "I'm leaving after breakfast."

David opened his mouth to protest, and she patted his cheek. "No, you must stay here to attend the wedding. This is your family, and you're important to them. I feel sure I will be more comfortable in London." She pushed back her chair and walked toward the door before David could spring to her assistance.

"Lelia, you can't run away like this! What about America?"

She turned and said sadly, "We'll talk about it when you return, David. If you've changed your mind, I'll understand."

At the suffering in her voice, David mumbled his excuses and hurried after her.

"That young man would be better off if he never saw her again," Lady Lockwood commented.

Adrian saw the bright wisdom gleaming in her eyes.

"No man should ever consider marrying a woman who manufactures guilt to achieve her ends," she observed.

Surprised by her astuteness, he absorbed the surprising knowledge that he liked his prospective mother-in-law very much.

The day passed quickly for Chloe, who busied herself

repacking the clothing her mother had brought from London and undergoing final fittings of the borrowed gown. When at last her mother and the countess lowered the shimmering ivory satin over her head for the final time, her heart nearly burst with excitement.

Seeing the sentimental tears in the eyes of the older women, she said brightly, "Well, at least I've something borrowed."

Adrian's mother laughed shakily as she fastened the last of the dozens of tiny pearl buttons that ran down the back of the gown. "It's also old, so you've filled two of the requirements." She turned and lifted a velvet case from the dressing table. "Adrian sent this for you. His wedding gift."

Chloe was suddenly struck by the immensity of the step she was taking. In a startling moment of clarity she asked herself how well she really knew Adrian. Vignettes of their unorthodox courtship flashed through her mind. She recalled landing in his arms as she leaped from the coach, her unabashed pursuit of him, the moonlit night the brambles had captured her in the birch grove, their passionate joining the evening before he left for Scotland . . .

Embarrassed color flooded her cheeks. She'd chased the man and compromised him. Did Adrian really want to marry her? Or was he simply fulfilling the demands of his honor? In a turnaround from her joy of a moment before, Chloe covered her face with her hands and moaned.

Maude chuckled, a watery sound that brought Chloe's eyes wide open. Her mother was laughing at her. Laughing!

"Dorothy, my daughter is having an attack of bridal nerves."

"I must say, I'm glad," said Lady Warnham. "It wasn't natural for her to approach her wedding as if it were afternoon tea." She nudged the flat velvet case. "Open this. I'm dying to see what Adrian thinks is wonderful enough for you."

Unreasonably embarrassed, Chloe turned away while her fingers fumbled with the intricate catch. The case opened easily, and tears blurred her vision at the sight of the magnificent double string of pearls with a glowing sapphire clasp. She removed the sheet of heavy cream notepaper from the lid and placed the case in her mother's hand. Then she walked to the window and read.

> *Beloved,*
>
> *You are what I have dreamed of all my life. Today we embark on the greatest romantic adventure of all—together. I can hardly wait.*
>
>

I love you now
and forever,
Adrian

Her heart contracted. Then she turned and remarked brightly, "Adrian is so clever. His gift is both 'new' and 'blue.' "

Minutes later, Adrian's gift fastened securely at her throat, Chloe descended the curving staircase. Her father, his eyes suspiciously shiny, awaited her at the foot and held out his arm to escort her to the formal drawing room Chloe had not yet seen.

Banks of deep red and pale pink hothouse roses flanked the local vicar, Adrian, and Fitz. Dinah met her at the door, pressed a nosegay of primroses into her fingers, and preceded her.

The ceremony passed in a blur, yet later Chloe could have recited every word from memory. Throughout it all her eyes never left Adrian's face, loving his intent expression and then his smile, which was nearly as wide as her own, when he placed a diamond-studded gold band on her third finger.

Later, standing in an alcove near the buffet table, she smiled at the memory, then took another sip from the crystal champagne flute. Her eyes met those of her Aunt Heloise, and she laughed out loud, pleased with the world and everything in it.

"I must say, I have never before witnessed such a . . . happy wedding," her aunt observed, raising her own glass in an informal toast. "I quite expected the two of you to burst into laughter during the ceremony. There are those who would consider the whole affair quite inappropriate."

Her words sobered Chloe. "Think of all those months when Adrian had nothing to laugh about and no one with whom to laugh. I intend him to be happy always."

A sound indicating sympathy escaped Heloise's thin lips. "Indeed. Well, I must say the occasion has been a great deal more joyous without the presence of David's fiancée. The girl does not improve with acquaintance. If he should be so bubble-headed as to marry the little wretch, I suggest you maintain your distance. Adrian and David can easily remain friends without their wives present."

"Dinah says she flounced off this morning in a state of self-pity."

Heloise frowned. "Men are extremely susceptible to women who claim ill use. Particularly if they're pretty and blond." She looked at David. "He appears to be a nice enough young man, although I should be surprised if he wins any prizes for intellect."

"I don't want to hear another unpleasant thing today," Chloe said, throwing her arms around her aunt and nearly spilling the remains of her champagne on the nosegay clutched in her other hand. "The whole world is perfect, and everyone must be happy. That includes you, most favorite aunt." She leaned closer and whispered, "After we return, you must tell me about your adventures while spying for the Crown."

As Adrian approached, he watched Heloise's features shift. On a more vivacious person, her expression would have passed for mild surprise. After months in her employ, and with the knowledge he had gained since, he could hazard a guess at what his impertinent bride had whispered into Heloise's ear. Not for the first time he thanked the benign fate that had thrust him into the shrewd, capable hands of Heloise Lockwood and thus into the path of her beautiful, impetuous niece.

His eyes met Heloise's. Adrian had no difficulty interpreting her suddenly fierce expression, and he mouthed, "With my own life," in answer to her unspoken demand. He laid a hand on Chloe's narrow waist, drawing her close. "The coach will be at the door in less than an hour, love. Can you be ready?"

Chloe released her aunt and turned to him with a lavish smile. "I'll run up and change before saying good-bye to everyone. Oh, Adrian, I can't believe we made it!" She rose on tiptoe and pressed an exuberant, passionate kiss on his lips before slipping gracefully away.

Adrian watched her leave the room, his thoughts already skipping to the night ahead.

"Must I remind you that it isn't considered decent for two people to look at each other in that manner publicly?" Heloise asked.

"You're quite right, Lady Heloise," Fitz said as he joined them. "They should develop more sophistication. Love is highly overrated."

Before Adrian could reply, Heloise said with asperity, "You, young man, may speak for yourself. Surely you are not deluded enough to believe I have lived all these years without experiencing that exhausting state?" Turning to Adrian, she demanded, "Are you quite sure you will be safe?"

"Only my father and the coachman know our destination, and we have outriders. Once we've arrived, believe me, no one will be able to reach us." Heloise's concern was no greater than his own.

Adrian looked around to make sure no one else could overhear before saying to Fitz, "Replies to my inquiries concerning the matter we spoke of should arrive any time soon. My father has instructions to give them to you for the necessary action."

"Poor Chloe ate hardly a thing after the wedding," Lady Warnham said, a delighted smile on her face. "I was quite relieved to see her abandon her *sangfroid.*" She smiled happily at her houseguests, who had were gathered in the homey family parlor in various stages of exhaustion.

The duke had removed his coat and was tugging at the knot of his cravat. He, too, smiled indulgently. "Never thought to lose her this suddenly, but she couldn't have done better."

"Neither could my son," said Lord Warnham as he propped his long legs on a cushioned footstool. "By Jove, this feels good! Even simple weddings are wearing."

Just then a young footman peered hesitantly through the open door, then entered at a wave from his master. "These just arrived from the village, my lord." He delivered one envelope to the earl and another to Fitz.

Seconds later Lord Warnham leaped to his feet and motioned to Fitz to follow. Cursing beneath his breath, he led the way to his private study. Once inside, he crammed his message into Fitz's hand. "That damn Stubbs. I trusted him completely, and all along he's been feathering his nest."

After scanning the contents of the two telegrams, Fitz felt an irrational foreboding. Chloe's astute observations and Claudia Ogilvie's grudging identification tied things together nicely. His mind working at top speed, he commented, "If I may be so bold as to say so, sir, you're a much better businessman than you are a landowner."

Edwin grimaced and nodded agreement. "But how could the iron deposits on the Cumberland property have been discovered three years ago without word reaching me before now?"

"The wire I just received covers that. Lelia's father used his ministry position to suppress the information, then searched for a way to dispose of Adrian. All so his daughter could attach David and reap the benefits. Buying Stubbs's silence would have been a simple first step."

He read the messages once more, his mind turning over possible action. "Now Fenton wants both Adrian and Chloe out of the picture. I suppose his greatest concern is that Adrian not leave an heir, and he's concerned she might already be pregnant, which explains Chloe's abduction. Fenton must also have engineered that debacle in Armenia, though I'm damned if I know how he discovered my department's activities."

The earl paced the room, his earlier exhaustion forgotten. "But now Adrian and Chloe are married."

"I'm afraid we shall have to interrupt the honeymoon," Fitz said. "Where were they headed from here?"

"To the coast to board my yacht. It's capable of ocean travel. Adrian thought to simply leave the country until he felt it safe to return."

"Lelia Fenton made rather a production of her departure this morning. At the time, her theatrics were amusing. But could she have discovered the yacht was their destination?" Fitz demanded.

"I'm the only—" A look of self-disgust crossed Edwin's face. "I was in the kitchens last night instructing Antonio to prepare hampers of delicacies for them to take on board. I trust Antonio implicitly, but that companion of Lelia's was in the hall when I left. She could easily have listened at the door."

"Is there any way we can intercept them before they arrive at the coast?" Fitz demanded.

Lord Warnham's eyes narrowed in thought, then closed while he calculated travel times. "We can cross the coach's path on horseback in just over two hours of hard riding."

Fitz strode to the door, his lazy elegance abandoned. "Well, what are we waiting for?"

The carriage wheel hit another rut, and Adrian held Chloe firmly on his lap, bracing his booted legs against the opposite seat. "Why are the roads always so rough that it's next to impossible to make love in the carriage?" he complained.

"You promised me romantic adventure. Maybe this is it." Chloe wiggled seductively on his lap.

Adrian wondered how he could be so aroused and want to grin like an idiot at the same time. He couldn't remember ever feeling such contentment. "If this is your idea of romantic, your education has been sadly neglected." He buried his lips in the tender skin just below her ear. "When we're on board, I'll teach you the difference," he whispered.

Chloe turned and murmured against his lips, "I hope the lessons are *very* thorough." She ran a forefinger along his lean jaw, around to his nape, and back again.

"We've at least another hour before we arrive." Adrian slanted his lips against hers with an intensity that left no question as to his intentions. Her response made him shake like a young boy in the throes of his first romantic encounter. "Nothing says we can't at least *begin* them."

In the light from the carriage lamp, her eyes were dark with passion as she met his gaze. She smoothed a lock of hair from his forehead. Her primrose scent surrounded them, and the brush of her ungloved hand against his brow was unbearably erotic.

"I'm feeling very adventurous," she purred before pressing her lips against his.

The prim jacket of her silk poplin traveling suit was already unbuttoned, and Chloe's uncorseted body was open to his searching fingers. Her breasts seemed to swell as his hands molded and caressed them, and her nipples thrust against his palms through the sheer batiste of her blouse and chemise. Her little sound of contentment vibrated against his lips.

The eagerness of her response nearly unmanned him. Her avid mouth and inventive tongue left no crevice of his mouth unexplored. Adrian stopped stroking, focusing all his concentration on their kiss. She drew back slightly, her wine-scented breath brushing his lips as she said huskily. "Do I receive honors for that?"

His loins throbbed against her rounded bottom as she nestled closer. For seconds that seemed like hours, Adrian was incapable of speech. He finally drew a deep, steadying breath and said, "Where did you learn to kiss like that?"

"My father never inquired as to the subject matter of the books I ordered. The bookseller's catalogue listed an extremely informative one on Arabian love practices." She giggled. "As I recall, it arrived tucked between a volume on landscaping and one on Russian architecture."

Adrian twisted, lowering Chloe to the seat beneath him. "Do tell me more about this book." Just then the carriage hit a rut so deep that it felt as if the road had recently been plowed for planting. Unable to brace his legs, Adrian tumbled to the floor, Chloe clutched to his chest. They clung together, laughing and attempting to scramble to their knees, when two shots whistled through the coach windows, sending slivers of glass flying across the seat they had occupied seconds earlier.

Fitz's mount followed Lord Warnham's over a low stone fence at the edge of a barren field. Looking back, he could make out Lionel, David, and Lord George Lockwood, all, like himself, mounted on Edwin's prized hunters, racing across the open field surrounding a thatch-roofed farmhouse.

The riders had been traveling for nearly two hours. If the earl's calculations were correct, they should catch up with the carriage within the half hour. Then the group would provide an added escort for the remainder of the journey. The moonlight was fading, however, and Fitz wondered if they would be able to keep up their bruising pace. Although the horses had been bred for stamina, his mount's stride had roughened.

Each member of the party carried pistols and rifles, which Edwin had dispensed from the locked cabinet in his study. Fitz surveyed his companions. "We look like a band of brigands," he muttered to the night air flowing past him.

Their pace slowed as they descended a rocky incline to a wide, shallow creek murmuring in the quiet coldness of the night. Lord Warnham brought his mount to a halt after they crossed and climbed the bank, waiting until Fitz moved alongside. "The road's just ahead, beyond that copse. The carriage probably passed here not ten minutes ago."

Fitz was impressed; the earl knew every twist and turn of the route.

The others paused, the sounds of their horses' heavy breathing and the creak of saddles almost cozy. Fitz spoke authoritatively. "We don't want to catch them yet. Three of my men are with Adrian, two disguised as outriders and the other as a coachman. If we burst out of the night, they're likely to shoot before they ask who we are."

Fitz glanced at David Mountjoy, whose worried face gleamed white in the fading moonlight. Revealing to him the lengths to which Lelia and her father had gone to provide him with wealth and a title had been painful. At first disbelieving, David had finally accepted the truth and had insisted on joining their rescue mission as a way of retrieving his honor. "I'll ride ahead to locate them. Then we'll hang back far enough that we don't cause alarm. We can join them when we reach the coast." He didn't mention his desperate fear that the coach might already have been attacked.

The others set off at a ground-eating trot, while Fitz urged his horse into a gentle canter. The route Lord Warnham had described led through a tiny sleeping village, then forked to the right. He was grateful for the detailed directions; the moonlight had disappeared by the time he turned down a narrow, winding road.

Peering through a night lit only by stars, he could see just far enough ahead to guide his horse. Then the lane curved, and his vision was limited further by a thick hedgerow running along the road's edge. The sound of jangling harness and horses' hooves came from the distance, and he slowed his mount. As he rounded the curve, shots rang out.

Chapter Twenty-One

Adrian threw himself over Chloe, pushing her down. By the time a third bullet whistled overhead, they were flat on the floor of the coach. The back of the soft leather seat where they had been sitting seconds before was split from the impact of the first ball. The coachman had whipped the horses into a full gallop, and he could hear the outriders returning fire.

Bracing one hand beside Chloe's head, he reached up to tug the bell rope, then fumbled with the catch of the door opposite the side from which the attack had come.

As the door swung open, cold air whipped in through the opening. The racing horses slowed. Adrian pulled Chloe to her knees and ordered, "Hold tight to me. We're jumping."

Adrian twisted in the air so that he hit the ground first, with Chloe's weight landing on top of him. Unable to curl himself into a tumbling position, he took the full impact of their fall. His last conscious thought was how appropriate it was that they end their lives in the same position as when they met.

Chloe's voice, soft and urgent, penetrated the fog clouding his mind. "Oh, Adrian, breathe. *Please* breathe."

He moved his head restlessly against her silk twill lap as warm tears landed on his ear. After running a mental inventory that assured him nothing was broken, Adrian struggled to sit up, ignoring the dizziness and pain shooting through him. His head struck a thick hawthorne branch. "Bloody hell!"

Chloe cautioned softly, "Quiet. We're beneath the hedge-row. Six riders just raced by after the coach, so we're probably safe, but now I hear someone else coming. If we stay very still, he might not notice us."

Adrian groped for the pistol tucked at the small of his back. He remembered thinking when he put it there that it was a hell of a thing to take on his honeymoon. Besides, he was seeing double and doubted he could hit a target six inches ahead, but willpower had saved him in the past. Pressing a protesting Chloe farther into the thicket, he squinted in the direction of the hoofbeats, which became louder every second.

Adrian turned to cup Chloe's chin in his hand and kissed her lavishly. He was sure that if he died within the next five minutes, he would carry the memory of her to the afterlife and beyond. "If something happens to me, stay quiet, do you hear? There's only one rider, and he won't expect an attack from the hedge. We need that horse."

Dropping to his stomach, he inched across the verge. Each move was excruciating, but at least his eyes were beginning to focus. He sent up a prayer of thanks for starlight.

The rider was approaching at a gallop. Adrian could sense the animal's exhaustion in the careless action of its legs. Then his returning vision focused on the rider. He gasped. He knew only one person who would ride with such abandon along a dark country road at this hour of the night. The rider sat high in the stirrups, his head tucked along the horse's neck like a jockey's.

"That damn Fitz never did have any sense," he muttered. "How does he know there aren't a dozen men lying in wait?" Adrian had no assurance half the attackers hadn't stayed behind, waiting like cats at a mousehole. "Damn and blast!"

Well, at least now there were two of them to protect Chloe. He levered his body from the ground and shouted "Fitz!" as the horse came even. Then he fell flat on his face.

Dried grass tickled his cheeks as the hoofbeats slowed and the rider turned back, stopping in the shadow of the hedgerow. When the sounds ceased, Adrian cautiously raised his head. If he had been wrong . . .

Fitz's mocking voice spoke from above him. "You poor sod. Cheated the gravediggers again, didn't you?"

Adrian allowed Fitz to turn him onto his back with gentle hands before gasping, "I don't think anything's broken, at any rate."

"Where's Chloe?"

"Tucked away safely in the thicket." Adrian smiled weakly. The mere sound of his friend's voice had worked miracles on his aching body.

"No I'm not. I came out as soon as I heard you call Fitz's name." Chloe's husky voice rang with relief.

"Please don't tell me you threw yourselves out the door of the coach while it was traveling full tilt. Are you insane?"

Adrian appreciated the affection beneath the jibe, but they hadn't time to trade insults. "We have to get away from here. Whoever attacked us may have discovered the carriage is empty by now."

"Help is closer than you think." Fitz lifted his head and listened. "In fact, reinforcements are about to round that bend in this godforsaken excuse for a road."

Adrian pulled himself to his knees beside Chloe as the four riders approached. When he saw David among the newcomers, he glanced sharply up at Fitz, who shook his head negatively.

"Look, Adrian," Chloe whispered. "My father has rifles

fastened on both sides of his saddle, and his coat is rucked up over an enormous pistol. Whatever does he think he's doing?"

"Just be grateful they've come after us." He pushed himself to his feet and pressed a quick kiss on her lips, relieved to find the ground wavering only the littlest bit beneath him. "I'm sorry, sweetheart. Our honeymoon is beginning to look like an encore to our courtship."

Chloe hugged him. "Think of the stories we'll have to tell our sons and daughters."

"If we ever have an opportunity to make any," Adrian murmured irritably, dropping his face against her hair.

"Plenty of time for that later, children." Fitz stood not two feet from them. "You were on the right track, Adrian. A survey three years ago discovered the Cumberland property is overflowing with iron ore reserves. And Lady Ogilvie identified Robert Fenton as the man who hired her."

Adrian looked at him over Chloe's head. "I suppose they promised to cut Stubbs in on the profits?"

"What a quick mind you have. Let's get away from here."

"The yacht's out," Adrian said flatly. "The harbor's probably crawling with thugs. We'll turn back to London."

Fitz's companions gathered around. "Not tonight," Lord Warnham announced. "The horses are winded, and now two of them will have to carry double. The innkeeper twenty minutes' ride away is a friend. We'll be safe there."

David stepped forward, his head bowed apologetically. "Adrian, Chloe, I'm so sorry. I had no idea what was being plotted, I promise—"

Adrian clapped him on the shoulder, shutting off his next words. "No apology needed, old man. Why should you suspect the woman you love of plotting murder?"

"You're unbelievably generous. I'll do anything I can to

285

make up for this." David clutched his hand.

Adrian freed himself and squeezed his cousin's shoulder. "None of this is your fault."

Lionel rode up and held out a hand to his sister. "Lord Warnham says you're to ride with me. Kent will take you up, Adrian."

Chloe gripped her twin's fingers but held back. "You won't dump me in the first stream, will you?"

A wide grin split Lionel's face. "Lord, you never forget anything! How many times must I tell you I'd nothing to do with that? That pony's back was so broad, you slid off on your own."

She eyed him suspiciously, then compromised. "Nevertheless, I'll ride in front."

Adrian boosted her up to her brother, wincing at the strain on his shoulder. "You two can argue another time. We must be off the roads before daylight." He turned and mounted behind Fitz. "This better not be far. Between leaping out of a moving carriage and now riding double, I can only pray I'm still *able* to father children."

"I've no idea why I put up with you. First you complain about dying, and then you natter on about comfort," Fitz commented as he guided his mount to the center of the little band, alongside Lionel and Chloe.

Once under way, Adrian spoke softly in Fitz's ear. "Tell me everything."

Chloe rested her head against her brother's solid chest, straining unsuccessfully to hear the murmured conversation between Adrian and Fitz. Soon they lapsed into silence, their expressions grim.

Chloe smiled inwardly. In a very short time she would have Adrian to herself. After they had taken care of the matter foremost in her mind, she would question him about what Fitz had told him.

Half an hour later they clattered into the cobblestone stable yard of the Pig and Whistle. Two stableboys, knuckling sleep from their eyes, emerged from the stable.

Chloe slid down into Adrian's waiting arms. "Is it too much to hope that that pile of brick has real bathrooms?" The warm solidity of his body made her senses sing.

"With deep tubs, I hope," Adrian answered.

"What must I bargain for the first turn?" she asked huskily.

His whispered reply made her sigh. A shiver of anticipation shook her from head to toe.

"Give the horses double rations and a good grooming after you've cooled them down," Lord Warnham instructed the groom who had run out to join the stableboys. "They've earned that and more tonight."

The innkeeper, still buttoning his shirt, stumbled into the courtyard with reassurances that the boiler was working and the cook was already busy in the kitchen. Given a choice between bed and breakfast, Chloe lowered her lids, afraid her eyes might reveal her thoughts. "I'm more tired than hungry, Father. I may sleep for days."

Adrian dropped a casual kiss on top of her head and said, "I'll bring you a tray."

Rising onto her toes, Chloe whispered fiercely into his ear, "No more than half an hour. Our honeymoon begins this morning." She hurried into the building.

The rambling inn had indeed been modernized five years before. Although the bathtub was uppermost in her mind, Chloe gazed with equal longing at the plump comforter on the bed while listening to the innkeeper's wife's friendly chatter.

"Poor thing, attacked on your wedding trip. What's the world coming to?" Mrs. Honeycutt babbled as she handed Chloe one of her own starched linen nightgowns. "The fire's lit, and the room'll warm up soon enough. I'll bring up some coals for the bedwarmer and take your clothes downstairs to freshen them. There should be plenty of hot water. We keep the boiler stoked."

Chloe headed to turn on the taps.

In her eagerness to rid herself of the kindly woman, her fingers fumbled with buttons and laces. Finally successful, she passed the clothing to Mrs. Honeycutt, who looked at her with a knowing twinkle. "If I was you, young lady, I'd be in the tub when your husband arrives. There's somethin' about findin' a woman naked in a bathroom that's right stimulatin' to a man."

The steaming water felt like heaven to Chloe. Three days of danger, tension, and excitement had taken their toll. She couldn't recall when she had last slept dreamlessly, but now her thoughts were focused on the present and she was edgy. She had the right to a wedding night this very morning, no matter what happened afterward.

Closing her eyes and giving her imagination free rein, Chloe braced her feet against the far end of the tub and sank into the water until it lapped at her chin. Deliciously erotic thoughts lulled her into a blissful state somewhere between consciousness and dreaming. So deep was her trance that she never heard the gentle creak of the bathroom door.

"If breakfast in bed is considered decadent, how does one describe breakfast in the bathtub?"

The low, caressing question broke into Chloe's fantasies. She raised her eyelids languidly to discover Adrian's face inches from her own. Lines of exhaustion bracketed his mouth, but his eyes were dark with desire.

"I love you, Chloe."

The tenderness in his voice clutched at her heart. Her lips quivered as she whispered, "I love you more."

She welcomed his kiss with her lips parted, meeting his tongue with her own and moaning softly. When he drew back, she said breathlessly, "That was the most delicious breakfast I ever had."

He sent a decidedly wicked glance down the length of her body before his right hand appeared above the edge of the tub clutching half a jam-covered muffin. "Take a bite of this. You'll need your strength."

Chloe's gaze never left his as she sank her teeth into the fresh, yeasty dough. She felt a dollop of raspberry slide free and lodge on her chin. Before she could close her lips over the morsel she'd bitten off, Adrian licked the dab away.

"I'm not sure which tastes better, the jam or you," he whispered, setting the muffin on a plate and removing his jacket.

Chewing slowly, Chloe watched his movements, wincing at the sight of a jagged tear in the back of the tweed garment. She swallowed hastily, but before she could comment he held a heavy white mug to her lips.

"Drink some tea."

She accepted the hot, sweet liquid obediently, then opened her mouth to speak, only to have the muffin presented once more. The bite she took almost stuck in her throat at the sight of his bare chest when his shirt followed his jacket to the heap beneath the free-standing sink. She swallowed convulsively. Pale, early-morning sunlight, slanting through the window high on the opposite wall, settled onto Adrian's hair, casting a golden nimbus around his head and burnishing his tightly muscled torso. She shivered with delight. This beautiful man belonged to her.

While she chewed her third bite, his scuffed low boots joined the jacket and shirt. During the next, his trousers, torn and snagged down the back, landed on the little pile. Now that he was nude, apprehension filled her.

As if aware of her sudden tension, Adrian offered her a last swallow from the mug, then set it aside and carefully levered himself into the water between her ankles. "Scoot up, love. Give me some room."

Chloe pulled her knees to her chest and pressed against the warm curve of the tub as he situated himself at the opposite end. Suddenly overcome by feelings of inadequacy, she wrapped her arms around her quaking knees to still her trembling hands.

"Adrian, this is never going to work. I'm not sure . . ."

His disarming smile would have reassured a timid two-year-old; the light in his eyes could easily have set off fireworks. When he extended his hand, Chloe laid her fingers in his palm, her heart beating thickly somewhere in the vicinity of her throat.

"Turn around and sit here." He patted the surface of the water just above his veed legs. "I'm going to wash your back, and if that's all you want, that's all I'll do."

Seconds later, his headache a distant memory, Adrian regretted his impulsive offer. Chloe's delectable bottom pressed snugly against his groin. Her legs, their slim perfection and the elegant arches of her feet shimmering in the gently moving water, stretched the length of the tub.

With one last settling motion, Chloe glanced over her shoulder at him; the apprehension in her eyes had vanished. To his relief, a mischievous twinkle lurked instead.

"Adrian, are you sure this will work?"

"If not, there's a good bed in the next room," he said as he reached for the soap.

The slick suds smoothed Adrian's callused fingers as he spread herb-scented lather down her arms, stroking her wrists and fingers with sensuous promise. Every nerve in her body jumped to life. He attended to her back next, from her neck to the slope of her buttocks, giving each subtle hollow meticulous attention.

Earlier fears forgotten, Chloe breathed shallowly. Who would have thought her wrists would be so sensitive? Or her shoulders? Her thoughts scrambled to recall that passionate night in his narrow little bed above her aunt's stables. She had clung to him with the naive belief that she could convince him to stay; neither of them had taken time to explore nuances or discover the joys of delayed satisfaction.

Cupping his fingers beneath the water, Adrian raised his hand and trickled water over her neck, then pressed his lips against her nape. Heat spread from the caress; she shuddered uncontrollably. "Adrian, I can't take much more of this."

"Ah, love, I've scarcely begun," he murmured, his voice a smoky whisper as his soap-slick fingers cupped her breasts, molding them. She looked down, watching with fascination as her nipples puckered at his touch. A tug of sensation traveled to the heart of her, and she clenched her knees together, pressing back against the hardness at the middle of her back. A strange languor—lassitude with eagerness simmering hotly beneath it—spread through her. She wished ardently that this teasing, wondrous feeling could last forever. Paradoxically, she yearned for the fires to come.

By the time he had cleansed her from head to toe, Chloe was aflame, her senses aroused to fever heat. Hazily, she decided Adrian deserved to feel the same.

Moving like a sleepwalker, she pulled away and turned to face him. Glancing down, she confirmed what she already knew. His body was interested in a great deal more than bathing. "After our adventures, you're deserving of a wife's tender attentions."

"No dessert until I've had my bath? You'll make a wonderful mother." His smile was anything but childlike. "Don't take too long. The main course is ready . . ."

Chloe giggled as she snatched the soap from his hand. She wanted to appreciate all of him, to touch him and look at him—and to torture him as he'd tortured her. "Lean forward so I can reach your back. Relax." She pushed his hands away from her breasts, chuckling deep in her throat.

Lathering her hands, she scooted toward him, running her hands over his back with the intention of wrapping her arms around his tapered upper chest. As her fingers smoothed over his left shoulder, she felt him flinch. For a moment she attributed the movement to her closeness. Then her fingers located a wide, swollen ridge.

"Adrian, you're injured."

"I must have landed on a rock when we rolled out of the coach," he answered, his voice strained and tight.

"And then I fell on top of you. You must ache all over." Chloe visualized the fall, remembering her unwavering faith in his decision to leave the coach.

"I'd go through that and worse a dozen times over to keep you safe," he insisted, his lips moving against the thin skin at her temple.

Her heart swelled with love for him. She tenderly cleansed his back, soothing each bruised area, then turned her attention to his feet and lower legs. "I don't want you to chance a chill."

"Not much bloody chance of that."

His strangled voice brought her glance up to his face. "Perhaps I should finish washing you rather more quickly than I'd planned."

"What a wonderful idea. In fact, I'm clean enough, don't you think?"

His gaze was focused on the cluster of dark curls below her stomach, and she shivered at the heat in his eyes. "I don't care if you're filthy. I want you right now," she said, knowing her heart was in her eyes.

Adrian stood quickly, water streaming down his aroused body. He reached for a towel from the shelf above the tub and drew Chloe up to stand in front of him. "This tub is entirely too confining for what I have in mind."

Water surged over the side of the tub as Adrian lifted Chloe from its depths. Heedless of the puddles at their feet, he dried her cursorily, casting the damp towel aside as quickly as he had taken it up. Reaching for a second towel, he skimmed the soft cotton over himself before flinging it in the direction of the hand basin. He kissed her, devouring the lingering tastes of raspberry and sweet tea.

Without breaking contact, he carried her to the bed, where he threw back the covers and set her tenderly on the linen sheet, then followed her down.

A groan escaped his lips as he gazed deeply into her eyes. "You're so very beautiful and brave. When I think what you've endured since we met, all of it because of me, I . . ."

"Don't talk like that," Chloe broke in.

She buried her lips on his damp collarbone, and their warmth sent tendrils of heat directly to his loins. Her breath came warm and soft against him.

"We're finally here, together. We're safe, Adrian."

He rolled to his back, bringing her with him, shuddering at the feel of her breasts against his chest—and hoping desperately that she was right.

Chloe spread a trail of soft kisses across his torso, inflaming his senses until he felt each woven thread of the sheet beneath him. When she reached the tender flesh of his stomach, he pulled her up against his chest and reversed their positions.

Her dark curls spread across the linen-covered pillow; her eyes were wide and slightly unfocused with passion; her lips were soft and curved, swollen from his kisses. Gathering her breasts in his hands, he gazed down at her rosy nipples, tight and eager between his fingers.

He lowered his head and tasted them in turn, licking and nibbling and suckling while her body arched beneath him. Releasing her breasts, Adrian nudged her legs apart with his knees. Dipping his head, he pressed his lips tenderly against hers while he slipped slowly into her. Their bodies met in a mad waltz, moving to the music they heard in their hearts, whirling faster and faster in a swiftly rising crescendo.

With one last thrust that felt as if he reached her heart, her body contracted around him. He soared into his own release and fell against her, his mind and his body sated. They were both asleep, still joined, within minutes.

Chapter Twenty-Two

Chloe snuggled against Adrian's warmth and watched twilight turn the multi-paned windows black against the night outside, transforming the room into a cozy nest lit only by the bright flames curling around the glowing lumps of coal Adrian had thrown on the fireplace earlier. Several times during the day he had risen from sleep to replenish the fire.

Each time he had returned to the cocoon of sheets and quilts to make love to her as if he would never have enough. Chloe nestled closer, curling her arm across his chest and pressing her cheek into his shoulder, afraid to think of what might lie ahead. She preferred to pretend the worst of the danger was behind them—that they could ride away without looking over their shoulders. Sure he was awake, she asked, "Do you speak Portuguese?"

"It's not so hard. I could teach you to get by in no time, if you like," he said. "Why Portuguese?"

Chloe pressed her lips to the supple skin against her cheek, savoring the taut muscle beneath it. "Brazil," she answered. "I once read a fascinating book about the Amazon River. How exciting to sail into the interior! Think of the exotic flowers I could sketch." She closed her eyes, picturing Adrian sprawled nude on a carpet of lush blossoms.

" 'Exciting' might be an understatement," he replied. His voice held a smile. "Brazil isn't England, Chloe."

She sat up, the lavender-scented sheet falling away from her breasts. "Well, of course it's not. If it were like England, there would be no point in going there." She leaned over till their noses touched, and she smiled dreamily. "One very obvious advantage is that the voyage would take a long time." She rubbed her cheek against the two days' worth of blond stubble covering his jaw. "I'm quite sure we could find something to do with our days and nights."

A rap at the door interrupted his enthusiastic reply. "I suppose this had to come sometime," Adrian grumbled. He rolled from the bed reluctantly. "Who is it?"

"I'm delighted to discover you haven't died from overstimulation," Fitz's cheerful voice replied. "I come bearing food to help you both husband your strength."

Adrian uttered a rude word as he stomped into the bathroom and retrieved his trousers. Chloe pulled the comforter up over her face until she was covered except for a small peephole. She giggled at the grumpy way Adrian flung open the door and glared.

Fitz thrust a large, well-laden tray at him. "No need to be unpleasant, old chap. Why don't you set this down over there, then step into the hall a moment. I promise not to keep you."

By the time Adrian returned, Chloe had risen and wrapped herself in an afghan. She knelt before the tray Adrian had hurriedly set before the hearth, investigating the fragrant contents of the covered dishes. Her mouth watered, and at the sound of the door closing, she picked up a plate and filled it with sliced beef, browned potatoes, and Yorkshire pudding. "I was foolish to even consider Brazil. Does your father do any trade with the Sandwich Islands?"

"Not at present," he answered. When she turned to give him the plate, his face was closed, his expression inward. He set down a dark bundle and accepted her offering.

296

Distressed by his withdrawal, Chloe began to fill her own plate, continuing, "I read that the natives there wear very few clothes. Your mother and sisters would love to visit. By the way, I've decided to forgive you for not telling me they hate corsets and bustles as much as I do."

Aware she was babbling, she poured wine into two tumblers. "We could spend months setting up an office and warehouses. Think of the market for coconuts and pineapple." She stood.

Setting their food aside, Adrian wrapped his arms around her, pressing her face against his neck. She quivered beneath his touch. As he moved his hands soothingly over her back, he murmured against her temple, "That bad?"

Chloe nodded, inhaling the familiar, reassuring scent of him. "I've been trying to imagine someplace we wouldn't have to worry about where to hide next. Someone who was at Warnham House had us followed, didn't they."

"Probably Lelia. Her father waylaid the study that reported high-grade iron deposits on the Cumberland property. There's so much, even the British Empire might be tempted to ask for a loan. Nothing would suit the Fentons better than for David to inherit."

"Does he know?"

"My father and Fitz told him last night. The poor beggar must have apologized at least twenty times before I could get up here this morning."

"He must be heartbroken." Chloe leaned back within the circle of his arms. "Think how you would feel to discover your fiancée loved only your prospects."

"I'd be more distressed to learn she and her father wouldn't stop at murder to acquire them." This time it was Adrian who shuddered.

"I don't know about you, but I'm starving," Chloe said

brightly. As they ate, she wondered about the bundle next to the door but refused to look at it directly.

"I've heard that farm workers sometimes make love beneath the hedgerows. Could we try that sometime when the situation isn't quite so desperate?" Chloe closed her eyes and imagined the daring idea.

Adrian cut a piece of Stilton and put it beside the pear he'd just peeled for her. All through their meal she had talked of everything but the danger they were in, avoiding the subject as pointedly as she had done throughout the night. He said lightly, "In the summer, love. When it's warm."

Draining the last of her wine, Chloe thumped the tumbler back onto the bedside table, patted her lips with the checkered napkin, and sat up very straight. "I've done my best not to pry, Adrian. But what happens next?"

"We make love," Adrian said. He deposited his empty plate on the floor beside the bed, then lay back and held out his arms. When she propped her elbows on his chest and stared down at him, he said, "Until midnight or so. Then we'll head for the yacht on horseback. Lelia's thugs have probably given up their vigil at the pier by now. Fitz intends to trail us to be sure no one else follows, and when we arrive, we'll sail away just as we planned."

"Just like that." Chloe shook her head disbelievingly. "And what about—"

Adrian drew her head down and smothered the rest of her sentence with a kiss. "No more questions, and no more worries. We'll leave the rest to Fitz."

"The fit's rather good, don't you think?" Chloe inquired in a low voice. She revolved in the dim glow of a single lamp. The shutters were fastened, with the curtains snugly closed.

Adrian's smile was tight. He ran his hands over her trim

buttocks, outlined by snug-fitting wool twill trousers. "Honey-cutt's son never could have looked this good in them." He drew her close and held her face to his chest. "I promise you, Chloe, our life will be different when this is over."

They had made frenzied love again and again. Chloe knew he was as fearful as she that each time might be their last. Finally, reluctantly, they had risen to don the clothing Fitz had procured from the innkeeper's wife. In an attempt to lighten their mood, Chloe waggled her hips at him before sitting on the edge of the bed to shove her feet into stout boots, grateful for the several pairs of thick wool socks that improved their fit.

When Adrian didn't reply, she said, "Adrian, I feel so . . . so full. Full of feelings I can't begin to describe, and they aren't all physical. They're in my heart." She stood and reached for a heavy fisherman's sweater, then tugged it over her head. As her face emerged, she finished, "Other women must live very boring lives." She ventured a smile.

This time his only response was a cynical snort as he pulled a dark knitted cap over his light hair. He fisted his hands at his sides.

"Adrian . . . all that time you were in hiding was anyone's worst nightmare, but it's behind you now." Not waiting for a response, she wrapped her arms around his waist and buried her face against him. "You're not alone anymore, darling. I never wanted a dull, conventional, husband—or a dull, conventional, life."

He framed her face between his hands. Chloe felt her eyes mist and her lips quiver at the force of his passionate gaze. "I love you with all my heart, Adrian. I always will."

"My guardian angel must have been working overtime when I met you," he murmured. He shook his head as if to clear it.

Rising on her toes, Chloe pressed a gentle kiss on his lips, then stepped back. She patted the side of her hip. "You know, I'm quite beginning to like Fitz. He slipped a pistol into the pocket of these trousers."

"I'll kill him when I see him next."

"Of course you won't. I'll be a big help if we encounter Lelia or her men. I'm quite a good shot."

Ten minutes later, Adrian and Chloe slipped out the back door of the inn and faded into the shadows. Ten minutes after that, the wide stable door eased open noiselessly, and they led two saddled mounts into the waning moonlight.

Neither swung into the saddle until they were several hundred yards from the inn. Dark scraps of fabric muffled the bridles. The only sounds in the cold, dark night were the crunch of the horses' hoofs against the frozen grasses of the verge and a steady, subdued creak of saddle leather.

Adrian refused to look behind him. He wanted only to look ahead. The rush of cold wind stung his cheeks, filling him with exhilaration. Glancing to his right, he saw the same excitement on Chloe's face. This time they would outrun the danger.

They rode to within a half mile of the bluff. Veering off the main road, Adrian led the way to a cluster of tall shrubs, where they stopped, shielded from sight of anyone else who might be about at this early hour. Their sheltered position allowed full view of the twisting path to the coast.

Adrian reached to rest his hand just above her knee. "We'll stop at the keeper's house, just in case any of Fenton's thugs decided to wait for us." He gestured toward the stone cottage beside the last sharp turn of the little road.

"What about the horses?" Chloe breathed.

"We'll leave them here. Fitz will make sure they're taken care of." Adrian discounted any advantages that might have been gained by the surprise of their arrival and Chloe's disguise. Anyone who chanced to observe her from the rear would know she was a woman.

"What do we do when we reach the cottage?"

"Wait until we know if anyone besides Fitz followed us and whether Fenton's men are still about." Adrian guided his horse closer. Before, he had disappeared to preserve her safety. Now he would take her with him forever, to keep her from harm. He brushed his knuckles against Chloe's damask smooth cheek, unable to keep his hands from her.

"What if someone followed us? We'll be trapped in the cottage." Her voice was taut with worry.

Adrian chuckled. "The place has a secret passage to the sea. My grandfather bought this inlet from a cabinet officer whose father used the place for trysts with his married lovers. The husbands of several of the old fellow's paramours were extremely prominent. The son had converted to Methodism and wanted to rid himself of any connection with sin." Like an eager kitten, Chloe rubbed her face against his hand. "No keeper, I take it."

He shook his head, then smiled at her. "You'll find the place amusing. Under other circumstances, we might even consider it an ideal honeymoon retreat." Then he shifted his gaze from the road they had traveled and for what seemed the hundredth time surveyed the open land between them and the cottage.

Turning to her, he whispered, "The yacht is ready to sail, and there should be a ship's boat waiting at the wharf. If anything goes wrong, or anyone's here before us, you're to run for it. Take that path over there." He pointed to the far side of the cottage.

When she shook her head from side to side stubbornly, he grasped her arm and drew her face close. His voice was cold when he said, "I promise that's the only order I'll ever give you. Follow it." Then he released her and said, "Let's go."

They slid silently to the ground and tethered the horses to a sturdy branch. He led Chloe to a twisting path and gestured for her to follow. Moving swiftly between stony out-croppings, he glanced behind only once to make sure she followed.

A cascade of pebbles fell away from beneath Chloe's booted feet, the sound scarcely noticeable against the roaring of the surf.

"Are you all right?" Adrian demanded in a fierce whisper. Her reply was so soft he strained to hear. "I slipped. These boots are too big."

"Stay close. I want to take one last look." He reached into his pocket for the key his father had given him, slipping the warm metal into the palm of his left glove. "Ready?" At her nod, Adrian melded into the surroundings. Throwing himself flat against the weathered wall of the cottage, he edged the key out and fit it into the lock. The hinges, well-maintained as was everything his father owned, made not a sound as the stout portal swung open.

With a sharp movement of his hand, he directed Chloe to remain outside. Adrian stepped in and stood still, emptying his senses of the outdoors, listening for any foreign sound. The quiet was broken only by his own light breathing as he in-haled the tang of lemon oil and beeswax used by the woman who kept the cottage in a state of constant readiness.

Sensing nothing out of the ordinary, Adrian smiled and pulled Chloe in behind him. As soon as the door was secured, he struck a match and reached unerringly for a squat oil lamp on the table next to the door. Chloe stood in its cozy glow, her pistol held ready.

"What in bloody hell are you doing with that thing drawn?" he demanded.

Chloe looked at the gun, then at Adrian. "What if Fenton's henchmen had been lying in wait for us? Was I supposed to let them kill you?" she demanded.

"I told you what to do."

"I could never abandon you, Adrian. Never." She held his gaze until his softened, and then she turned to inspect the furnishings of the room. If he wasn't aware she would never abandon him to save herself, she would have to convince him. Later. And she would enjoy every minute of it.

Chloe lifted a tin of matches. "We can argue another time, when we've been married longer. Are you sure the shutters won't reveal any light?" she asked as she held a match to the wick of a cut-glass lamp that could easily grace her mother's drawing room.

"This was a trysting place, remember?"

Danger forgotten, Chloe watched as the light refracting through the crystal globe cast dancing shadows on the hand-painted silk wall covering. In stark contrast, a large, service-able oak desk flanked by businesslike filing cabinets stood against one wall. A chair upholstered in glowing red silk sat behind it. Next to the door they had just entered was a black lacquer table lavishly decorated with Oriental scenes in gold, flanked by two plain walnut chairs. A divan even more luxurious than the chair behind the desk faced the hearth.

Chloe gasped at the subject matter of the paintings on the far wall. She heard Adrian's laughter behind her. "Are you sure your father doesn't use this place for some trysting of his own?"

"The furnishings came with the building. They amuse

him," he replied. "He's not a good sailor. As soon as his feet strike dry land, he comes here to do paperwork . . . and let his stomach settle. If you've any doubts, ask my mother. She's accompanied him here many times."

Chloe moved toward the paintings for a closer look, tripping over an unnoticed emerald silk-covered ottoman. Pearl-studded silk fringe was stitched around its contours. She dropped onto it, sinking deeply into the luxurious down filling. "Well!" was all she could say.

Adrian braced his arms on either side of her, trapping her against the luxurious brocade. She pulled him close. "Let's just lock the door and pretend nobody's home," she whispered against his lips.

"I won't feel safe till I get you away from here." He shook his head regretfully and peeled her arms from around his neck. His breath misted in the frigid air as he walked to a built-in corner cupboard and pressed the inlaid panel surrounding the door. The doors parted and slid back into the structure. "I want to check to make sure we weren't followed by anyone but Fitz."

He stepped into the cupboard, busying himself with a cylindrical mechanism suspended from a metal tube that disappeared through the ceiling of the alcove. The cylinder twisted within its recess.

Chloe ran to peer over his shoulder. "What on earth is that?"

"It's a periscope, a series of refracting mirrors in a revolving tube. Have I finally introduced you to something you haven't read a about in a book?"

"Why does your father have a periscope here?"

"Because he found one. My father loves gadgets. Last year he invested in a new company run by a pair of American brothers named Duryea. They're working on a horseless carriage powered by a gasoline engine, and he wants their first product."

Half listening, Chloe stepped in front of him. She looked forward to knowing the earl better; his curiosity must be as lively as her own. "Didn't America use something like this during their Civil War?" She peered into the viewfinder. "It's so quiet out there."

Adrian unwrapped her fingers from the apparatus and pressed his eye against the opening. "And I devoutly pray it stays that way. I want to watch for fifteen minutes or so, and then we'll leave."

Since his voice held the intensity Chloe recognized, she decided to explore the interior of the cottage more fully. A narrow, hitherto unnoticed door beside the fireplace led to a small, primitive kitchen. A cabinet identical to the cupboard housing the periscope was built into the opposite corner. Chloe examined it, attempting to remember how Adrian had opened the other one.

Her fingers glided over the inlaid wood. She found no likely projections. Frowning, she studied the design of overlapping acanthus leaves.

"Aha! That one's darker!" she exclaimed. When she pressed her finger firmly where the grain in the wood was most dense, the panel parted, retracting soundlessly.

Light from the two lamps in the opposite corner of the cottage revealed steps leading downward. The interior of the cabinet was dark and smelled of the sea combined with the dank mustiness of a passage beneath the earth.

Turning, she saw that Adrian was still peering intently into the viewing lens, his attention focused on the barren headland outside. Chloe picked up a small lantern from the corner of the desk and shook it lightly. The kerosene within sloshed satisfactorily. "Not that I expected my father-in-law to allow an empty lantern on the premises," she murmured as she struck a match.

The wick caught immediately, and she crossed the room and tapped Adrian on the shoulder.

His absent gaze traveled over the lantern she waved in front of him to the cabinet across the room. After a whispered, cautionary, "Don't go too far," he returned his attention to the view from the periscope.

Chloe crossed the room to the passage. Exploring their only means of escape seemed a sensible pastime. The steps were cut into stone, their surfaces gritty with gravel and sand. Pebbles scattered beneath the soles of her too-large boots, and once she misjudged a step and stumbled. After that she carried the lantern directly ahead of her in her left hand so she could judge the width of the treads more accurately. With her right she clung to small outcroppings on the rough-carved wall.

When she reached the base of the stairs she stopped, sniffing curiously. Was the scent of the sea stronger? She hoped so. The thought of tons of soil and rocks above her head was discomforting. How much farther did the tunnel go before exiting at the shore?

Straightening her shoulders, she set out again, pausing every few steps to sniff, testing for a change in air quality. Her concentration was so complete that she nearly missed the sound of boots scraping against pebbles and sand ahead of her.

Looking around wildly, she realized there was no place to hide. Whoever was coming must already have seen her light. She turned on her heel, intent on racing back the way she had come to warn Adrian when a voice called, "Adrian? Chloe? Who's there? Tell me you're all right."

Chapter Twenty-Three

"David? Is that you?" Chloe turned toward the voice. "What on earth are you doing here? I thought you were still at the inn. You haven't even a lantern."

She heard his reply before the tips of his boots reached the circle of light. He spoke softly, as if he were afraid of being overheard. "Fitz told me your plans. He thought someone else should come along to make sure you're safe. I know this tunnel well, I don't need a light."

Chloe's nerves jumped. "Why didn't Fitz tell Lord Warnham? Or my father?" She peered up at David's face, searching for an explanation for the tension in his voice.

"He didn't want to disturb them. They're neither of them young men anymore, you know."

In the flickering light she noticed that David's rough seaman's garb was similar to what she and Adrian were wearing. Where had he obtained the change of clothing? "Of course. And since you're familiar with the cottage and the tunnel, you came to help us."

"I stopped to check with the fellow stationed at the wharf. The captain can sail at any time." He smiled and held out a hand for the lantern. "Are you running away from Adrian already?"

Without conscious thought, Chloe wrapped her fingers more snugly around the metal handle. She burrowed her right hand into the pocket of her heavy trousers. "Just exploring. Adrian's checking to be sure we weren't followed."

Something was wrong. How had David arrived without Adrian's seeing him?

"I haven't been in this tunnel since Adrian and I played pirates here when we were twelve or so. Several caverns branch off before the passage reaches the shore. Would you like to see them?"

He had withdrawn his hand, apparently accepting Chloe's refusal to relinquish the lantern; now he gestured toward the darkness behind him. "There's no danger. You and I can explore until Adrian comes. You'll find the caverns interesting."

The urgency in his voice reinforced Chloe's doubt. "Another time, perhaps. I'm going back to Adrian." She turned and fled, the light from the swinging lantern she held reflecting grotesque patterns against the roof and walls of the tunnel. David's curses and his pursuit told her that her instincts had been sound.

The stone stairs loomed earlier than she expected, her toe caught on the edge of the first step, and she stumbled, sprawling forward. The lantern slipped from her hand, landed on the fourth step, then rolled to the bottom, kerosene flowing out around the wick. The fuel ignited, sending a trail of fire up the lower stairs. Chloe rolled away from the flames, screaming "Adrian!" as David loomed over her. The river of light flared, then died, leaving them in darkness.

David clamped his hand over her mouth and whispered viciously, "If he comes down here now, I'll kill him."

Chloe felt the hard thrust of a gun against her side as he jerked her upward. She twisted, wrenching violently against his hold. With a muttered oath, David struck her. A darkness greater than that of the tunnel enveloped her.

Adrian stepped back from the periscope. He had lost track

of the time. He'd become obsessed with searching the darkness outside for any movement, and his eyes felt as if half the gravel in Hampshire had taken up residence behind his lids.

"Chloe?"

How long had it been since she had waved the lantern and pointed to the tunnel entrance? He pulled his watch from his trousers pocket and stared at it. "Bloody hell. She's been down there half an hour." His heart contracted with fear.

Hastily lighting a second lantern, he checked the pistol jammed into his waistband and crossed to the opening, calling Chloe's name softly.

In the silence that followed, he heard a scratching sound at the door. He waited, torn between rushing down the stone steps and investigating the sound from outside. The scratching became a distinctive series of taps, the signal Fitz had used to identify his arrival that long-ago night in Brussels. Darting to the door, Adrian rapped out the response. The simple code he hadn't used in over two years was as instinctive as breathing.

At the expected answer, he fumbled with the lock and eased the door open, his foot jammed behind it as a precaution.

"Let me in, you old granny." Fitz's stage whisper came from down low. "The wind's blowing like Greenland out here, and I'm freezing." When the door swung inward, his crouched figure rolled over the sill.

Adrian closed and locked the door before his friend could stand. "Chloe's been in the tunnel for over half an hour. She went to explore while I made sure we were clear." He clutched the lantern and strode to the opening.

Fitz stayed his progress. "I wish Chloe hadn't gone down there. Adrian, David Mountjoy left the inn just after you did. I followed him and watched him cut over and meet a sloop that's anchored just beyond the headland. Minutes later he came to shore in the dinghy. That's why you didn't see him."

Adrian beat his fist against the sturdy panel. "Damn and double damn. David."

"There's more. He entered the tunnel shortly after you arrived."

Even as fear clawed at his heart, disappointment left a bitter taste in Adrian's mouth. "David knows how to get into the cottage from the tunnel, but he didn't need to. Chloe fell into his lap." Adrian eased his gun free. "I'd better hurry." The sick feeling of disappointment in his midsection disappeared. Deep down, he'd questioned the possibility of his cousin's involvement ever since they'd come face to face at the Overton estate. The attempts on his life had begun after his encounter with David. David, who had always been his friend.

Although Josef had kidnapped Chloe, he had also killed the imposter, Moon. The man had unknowingly protected him from his own cousin.

"Close the entrance behind you. I'll slip around outside and summon reinforcements from the ship," Fitz said, squeezing his arm. "Adrian, there's no reason for him to kill her. Not yet. He needs her to entrap you. Be careful and good luck."

Tamping down his terror, Adrian stepped into the narrow entrance. If anything happened to Chloe . . .

When she regained consciousness, Chloe could hear the distant sound of waves beating against the shore. Bone-chilling cold seeped through her sturdy wool trousers and jacket. Peering from beneath heavy eyelids, at first she could see nothing. As her eyes became acclimated to the darkness, she noted a lighter patch to her right.

As she watched, a shadowy figure emerged. The sound of

labored breathing and boots sliding on gravel reached her ears. Seconds later something heavy landed beside her. David's voice came from above. "I know you're awake, Chloe. I saw you move your head. My night vision is excellent. Meet the sailor who was guarding the wharf. He wasn't expecting an attack from behind."

Chloe ran her hands over the rough floor, searching for the wrist of the limp figure resting against her legs. "I can't find a pulse. You've killed him!" she said, frightened by the man's stillness.

"Don't be silly. The man's alive. I merely struck him on the head. If you don't believe me, listen to him breathe."

David sounded bored, as if unconcerned whether the man lived or died. Holding her breath, Chloe lowered her head and heard the welcome sound of shallow respirations.

"He needs help, David. If he lies here in this cold cave for long, he'll catch pneumonia!" Chloe scarcely knew what she was saying, but she had to use every means at hand to delay David until Adrian found her. "Give up your scheme. They know about Lelia and her father, but not that you're in this with them. The earl will give you all the money you could possibly want," she pleaded.

"Indeed he would, if only to gain your return. You should have heard him bragging about Adrian's good fortune in marrying you. I wanted to vomit."

His bitterness sent chills down Chloe's spine. Then his hands, hard and punishing, dragged her to her feet.

"Have you any idea how long I've hated my perfect, brilliant cousin? When I heard about the survey, I disguised myself as a laborer and helped chart the Cumberland deposits. It was a simple matter to come to an agreement with the land agent, who is a credulous fool. I led him to believe he'd receive a third of the profits if he kept the discovery secret."

He dragged her into the passage and nudged her forward. "Not a month later, Fenton approached me with the information about Adrian's work for Fitz's little spy shop. I plotted everything, even going so far as to court Lelia, that scheming bitch. I hated to direct Fenton's attention to the mineral deposits but it was necessary. As distasteful as the connection was, at that time I needed his help. The greedy fool thought the whole plan was his own idea. He fancied himself a master plotter."

He pushed her toward the wharf entrance. Chloe heard the rush of the waves in the distance.

Then he went on, "When I arranged for my cousin's unmasking, the Armenians bungled their instructions, and Fenton began making mistakes, so I took over. I'm surprised Adrian didn't see through that little charade at the British Museum. Instead, he decided it meant I was harmless." His laugh was nearly a giggle.

"All the time I was growing up, no one ever gave me credit for having brains. I was the poor cousin, the one who wasn't nearly so charming or handsome or brilliant as Adrian. It's rather a shame no one will ever know how clever I really am. Now everyone will blame Lelia and her father for Adrian's murder." He giggled again. "And I'll end up with the title *and* a fortune . . . after, of course Adrian's father takes his own life in a fit of sorrow."

He twisted her arm behind her, sending pain up to her shoulder. "Hurry along now. You've an appointment."

Chloe sagged against his hold, resisting. "But, David, if you'd left well enough alone, surely Adrian would have slipped up and been caught spying by *somebody*."

"I suppose my dear, modest cousin has told you how inept he was. The truth of it is, one reason he was never caught is that your precious Adrian has a knack for disappearing like fog. Now stop talking and move. You've a boat to catch."

Wrestling free of his grasp, she struck out blindly at her captor. "You're a monster! Have you any idea how horrible those years were for Adrian?" Her words ended in a sob as David clamped her arms to her sides in an iron hold.

He pushed her forward roughly. "Stop talking and keep walking. What a pity you couldn't resist my charming cousin. I rather like you, don't you know? But I can't risk your producing an heir. You're bloody lucky I have you instead of Lelia. The bloodthirsty slut would kill you without a thought."

His voice assumed a self-righteous tone. "She has no scruples. At least I needn't marry her now. And the fee I'll receive for you will help me hide in America until I can dispose of Adrian. The bloody title never meant anything to me, but I want that land."

"I suspected as much, David."

Lelia's voice startled David into loosening his hold on Chloe, who wasted no time after dropping to the sandy floor in digging into her pocket for the weapon Fitz had given her.

She heard the sound of a match striking. The glow from a small lantern pierced the darkness, revealing Lelia's diminutive figure. The blond woman was dressed in much the same fashion as Chloe, and she held a pistol pointed at David's middle. Chloe shoved her weapon back into hiding.

"I was just trying to frighten Chloe into cooperating, Lelia. She's too strong for me to handle alone," David said placatingly. "Once she's on the sloop, Adrian will attempt to save her. When the boat sinks with both of them on board, it will look like an unfortunate accident."

To Chloe's ears, David couldn't have fooled a three-year-old. Lelia apparently thought the same. Her lips twisted into a sneer. The contempt on her face stunned Chloe, who scrambled out of the circle of light, her knees wincing at each sharp pebble they encountered.

Without looking down, Lelia ordered, "Don't move another inch, Chloe. David's right about one thing: Adrian will come looking for you. As for the rest of David's twaddle, I've been listening longer than he realizes."

Lelia's shot traveled three feet above Chloe's head, striking David's chest. His dead weight landed across her feet. Without thinking, Chloe reached toward his wrist.

"There's no need to check, my dear. He's dead. I'm an excellent shot. Now get up and come along."

Swallowing against the nausea rising in her throat, Chloe challenged, "And if I refuse? You can't possibly carry me." She clutched her pistol behind her back as she freed her feet from the sickening weight.

"I'll shoot Adrian instead. He's right behind you." Lelia's eyes glittered with malice.

Chloe turned her head and looked up. Adrian stood just beyond the light, his arms hanging helplessly at his sides. She desperately wished he hadn't found her.

"Come closer, Adrian. And drop that gun you think you're concealing." Lelia sneered as the weapon fell to the ground, her eyes flicking back and forth between her two prisoners. Adrian stepped closer to her. "Stop right there," she snapped.

She held the lantern high. "What a handsome couple you are. How unfortunate your marriage was so brief, but your troubled past has unsettled your mind, Adrian. You will wash up on some beach, drowned, after shooting your cousin, whose body will be found outside the tunnel. A quarrel over money, wasn't it?"

Adrian replied lightly, "Why should David and I argue

about money, Lelia? My father was the one who kept him in funds."

The light tilted and then settled as Lelia shifted her stance. "I'll put it about that you objected to the funds your father settled on David when he was thought to be the heir. Perhaps after you married you gave more thought to finances."

"As opposed to before, when I didn't give two pins about money," he said agreeably, inching forward.

Lelia aimed the pistol at Adrian's chest. "Stay put. One of my men will be here soon to take you to the sloop on the other side of the headland. I couldn't bring it in any closer because the yacht captain would have asked questions."

With Lelia's attention focused on Adrian, Chloe edged toward him, extending her arm behind her back to call his attention to the pistol. Within seconds her hand shook so badly from strain that she drew it back against her body.

"I thought you loved David." Adrian flicked a careless finger toward the crumpled heap.

"David lied to me. I'm afraid I must sacrifice Chloe to gain some kind of return on this enterprise," she said coldly. "I have some unfortunate gambling debts which must be paid."

Chloe gasped, guessing what was coming next.

"Yes, my dear, the people who were to take you in hand last Sunday still want you."

Her words were Adrian's worst nightmare. Lelia's malice and greed were no longer masked by porcelain prettiness. She spoke of killing David as if she had just kicked a pebble from her path. Her voice as she outlined her plans for Chloe was chilling. The woman had no sense of wrongdoing.

She was also a practical tactician. Her lightning change of plan at discovering David's defection showed an amazing ability to shift course in midstride. Greed seemed her only weakness. Pretending indifference, he asked, "I don't suppose two hundred thousand pounds would make you disappear without harming me or my wife?"

Lelia's smile was that of a crafty child. "I'm not a simpleton, Adrian. The moment I freed you, you'd have me arrested for murdering your cousin. Chloe witnessed that, remember?" Her lips curved bitterly. "David was never anything but a means to an end. I nearly injured myself laughing at his delusion that he was the mastermind of this enterprise. I certainly never considered falling in love with him. Love is for brainless fools."

"You can't know!" Chloe cried dramatically, scrambling to her feet. She threw herself at Adrian, pressed her face against his chest, and wrapped her arms around him. "Our love for each other was written in the stars. If you kill Adrian, you'll have to kill me, too."

Adrian felt her hands grope beneath his sweater, then the pistol's cold steel against the skin of his back as she lodged it in his waistband. He wondered if she was aware that the rapid heartbeat against her cheek was caused by unadulterated terror for her safety.

"How touching," Lelia sneered. "However, I'm not a complete monster. Say your sentimental little good-byes. I hear my men coming into the tunnel." The gun in her hand never wavered.

Adrian's passion as he drew Chloe into a fierce embrace wasn't feigned. He knew what he had to do as soon as his lips left hers, but the odds were against him. Either way, his body reacted quite normally to her desperate kiss. He nudged his hardening loins against her softness, unhampered by draperies or petticoats. As her tongue touched his lower lip, he wrapped her even more tightly into his embrace.

"How amusing. My men would be thrilled to find you so

. . . involved with each other. They might even demand a turn with dear, sweet Chloe. However, I'm afraid we've run out of time." Lelia narrowed the distance between them.

Hoping her arrogance would cause her to be careless, Adrian pleaded, "A minute more or less can't make any difference. This is all we'll ever have."

"Sentimental fool! Her new keepers are waiting."

Adrian reached behind his back as if to forcibly remove Chloe's hands at the same moment Lelia turned her head to call over her shoulder, "Get in here, Ryder."

Chloe dropped to her knees and threw herself sideways. Adrian's shot struck Lelia's wrist, sending her pistol hurtling across the cave. The lantern fell to the ground, extinguishing as it landed. Her shrieks of rage and pain echoed in the enclosed space, the volume doubling when Fitz burst into the cave, followed by two seamen carrying lanterns and weapons.

"Are you two all right?" Fitz demanded.

Adrian dodged Lelia's fingernails as she leaped at his face. Her other hand, bent at an unnatural angle, battered his ear, and her boot struck his shin a glancing blow. Just as he reached to fend off her hysterical attack, she crumpled to her knees, arms flailing wildly. He looked down. Chloe tugged at Lelia's legs, and stretched them out straight before sitting on them.

"Leave off, you bitch," his gently-bred beloved snarled as she delivered a resounding slap to Lelia's left cheek. "Bloody murderess!"

Held close to Adrian's side, her trembling fingers wiping blindly at her tears, Chloe stepped into the early-morning sunlight dissipating the fog on the little knoll beside the wharf. Seabirds searching for breakfast shrieked a greeting, and welcoming wavelets slapped the dock. Viewing the normalcy of the scene, after the horrors of the last half hour, Chloe suppressed an urge to bury her face against Adrian and weep. Because she knew how tightly he was holding on to his own emotions, she forced back her sorrow.

Silent, stern-faced men ushered two prisoners toward the graveled path leading up to the lane. A launch from the yacht rounded the headland in search of Lelia's sloop.

Chloe's knees were wobbly with relief. The nightmare was over.

As if sensing her weakness, Adrian grasped her more firmly about her waist. She threw her arms around him protectively. He was real. He was whole. And he was safe beside her.

Two men sidled awkwardly out of the opening carrying David's canvas-wrapped body, and Chloe blinked away more tears. "Poor David."

A muscle tightened beneath the blond stubble covering Adrian's lean jaw.

"I'm so sorry, Adrian. He told me how much he resented being beholden to your family. I'm sure none of you suspected how he felt."

"My father never knew. He just didn't want David's family to do without."

"David coveted things that weren't his," Chloe pointed out.

Adrian's gaze followed the dismal little procession wending its way up the path. "He never even really had Lelia," he said sadly. "Not as I have you." His fingers clutched her waist.

Perversely, Chloe discovered she wanted to remind him she didn't appreciate being mentioned in the same sentence with Lelia. Instead, she mumbled beneath her breath.

"Was it really necessary to stomp on her stomach after you slapped her?" Adrian asked seriously.

"I'd do it again," Chloe asserted, drinking in the sight of him. The thin sunlight tangled in his tousled hair, creating a soft golden glow. Dirt smudged his left cheek, and lines of exhaustion bracketed his mouth. He was beautiful. And he was hers. "Lelia was responsible for the two miserable years you spent in hiding. *And* she threatened to kill you," she responded fiercely.

She reached up to pull his face down to hers, moving her lips against his while reveling in the feel of his hard body pressed to hers. She whispered, "She shouldn't have done that. You belong to me."

She kissed him again, then nestled close as he murmured, "I felt the same way when I found the lantern lying in the tunnel and saw no sign of you. I could have taken on an army."

Chloe wrapped her arms more tightly around him.

"I died a thousand deaths until you were safe." Adrian's voice was tight.

"I can't believe you only shot her wrist. I would have killed her." She burrowed into his masculine heat.

There was a smile in Adrian's voice as he murmured, "Please promise me something, sweetheart."

In spite of her exhaustion, her reply was wary. "Anything—within reason. As long as it has nothing to do with corsets. Or soirées or other unreasonable social obligations."

"Agreed." He cradled her chin and raised her face till their eyes met. "Don't ever change. I love you exactly the way you are." The kiss he gave her was just short of reverent. Then, drawing back, he smiled broadly and took her hand to pull her toward the wharf.

"Come on, sweetheart. I promised you the world, and we're off to see it together."